Praise For Mark Teppo and *Lightbreaker*

"Grim and refined, Teppo's aggressive near-noir is rich and strange—heavily and deftly textured. It's got a punch that'll leave you rattled, intrigued, and tasting blood."

— Cherie Priest, author of *Fathom* and
Four and Twenty Blackbirds

"Lightbreaker is a damn good book. It throws some new curves into the Urban Fantasy ride. I think you've got a big, fat hit in your hands."

— Kat Richardson, author of *Underground*
and *Greywalker*

"...good story with a nice twist."

— *Post-Weird Thoughts*

"With Lightbreaker, Mark Teppo has built something out of shadow and starlight that grabs the reader and simply won't let go. The story is dark and dense and beautifully written. It is also eerie and morally complex and yet ultimately hopeful. Perhaps more to the point, it's simply a damn good read and I'm very much looking forward to seeing what Teppo does next."

— Kelly McCullough, author of *WebMage*
and *Cybermancy*

"...awash in unpredictable emotions."

— *The Green Man Review*

LIGHTBREAKER

THE FIRST BOOK OF THE CODEX OF SOULS

Ζωῆς
οὐδὲν
ὑπῆρχ'
ὅ τι μὴ
φῶς

To Jennifer —

The Codex of Souls by Mark Teppo:

Lightbreaker
Heartland (Forthcoming)
Angel Tongue (Forthcoming)

LIGHTBREAKER

THE FIRST BOOK OF THE CODEX OF SOULS

MARK TEPPO

NIGHT SHADE BOOKS
SAN FRANCISCO

First Edition
ISBN   978-1-59780-138-6

Night Shade Books
Please visit us on the web at
http://www.nightshadebooks.com

This one is for Cooper.

Is it the face we know?
Or something beyond the soul?

– Fields of the Nephilim

THE FIRST WORK

"Whom thou flyest, of him thou art,
His flesh, his bone; to give thee being I lent
Out of my side to thee, nearest my heart,
Substantial life, to have thee by my side
Henceforth an individual solace dear;
Part of my soul I seek thee, and thee claim
My other half."

– John Milton, *Paradise Lost*

I

The deer lurched out of the forest on a dark curve of the narrow highway, staggering onto the pavement like a maritime drunk. Silver light radiated from its mouth and eyes, a spectral luminescence that made the animal visible against the dark brush.

I stopped the car and the deer shied away from the vehicle with an unorganized accordion movement of its legs. It was a young buck, a pair of knobby buttons adorning its head. Bloody foam flecked its muzzle.

The light leaking from the animal was spiritual overflow, a profusion of energy not meant to be contained in the deer's simple meat sack. The possession of an other. A human spirit.

As it wobbled across the road, the car's headlights bleached the shadows on its flanks. Not all the shadows disappeared, and what I had first thought were streaks of dirt or soot were revealed to be burns. With some difficulty, it traversed the shallow ditch running beside the road. At the top of the short embankment, the animal paused, chest heaving, and a tiny cloud of silver motes danced at its mouth.

I powered down the window, and the smell rolled into the car, an acrid sweetness of seared meat.

The human soul is too intense for the animal kingdom. The mythologies say Man was created as a reflection of the Creator.

Crafted in His image and composed of the four elements, the human shell was built specifically to carry the fire of the soul. The Word written in flame and flesh. The lesser creatures of the world are too fragile, the fables tell us, they are vessels unable to sustain the intense presence of the Divine Spark.

Why then was a soul possessing the body of this deer? How had it become separated from its proper vessel?

The Chorus were a whispering echo beneath these questions, and—*exquire!*—responding to my curiosity, they arced across the road. Phantasmal snakes wiggling through ethereal space, they kissed the smoldering flesh of the deer, and the contact returned a taste of the hot human presence within.

The deer jerked as if it had just been shocked, the invasive soul reacting to my spectral inquisition. The animal snorted, hot blood spattering from its nose, and bolted. The sound of its movement through the heavy brush was pure panic—that unidirectional flight of instinct-driven terror.

My throat and nose tingled as the Chorus returned, flush with stolen memories. They brought me spoil like worker ants returning to their hive queen. Sensory data belonging to the traveling spirit coursed into my awareness, and for a few moments, I was overwhelmed by this rush of images and scents and textures.

There. A flicker of memory caught my attention. The Chorus wrapped it tightly, and when I squeezed, all of its secrets gushed out. Memory is nothing more than ego impressions imprinted onto raw sense data, consciousness lattices laid over the chemical cages of the brain. It is the psychological bindings—the way these structures become our identities—that anchors the spirit to the flesh. These secrets linger with the soul. The Chorus stretched this illicit memory so I could clearly dissect it. *Yes, there.* The touch of another spirit. More than flesh, more than spit or blood. Spirit touch. And with that touch, came other details. The ones *I* remembered. As I inhabited the foreign memory, my tongue unconsciously touched my lips and tasted her skin again; I inhaled deeply as if I could actually smell her on the night air.

Lilacs.

He knew Katarina. Shortly before this man had become a rogue spirit, he had been in close physical contact with her.

The Chorus, indelibly bound up in the cosmological memory of my past, sang in their eagerness to find her. Their collective voices, usually a persistent chatter of ancient skulls, became an undulating wind of wordless need. In the dark pit beneath them, I felt the twist of a long-buried root, as if its movement was giving birth to a breath of air that the Chorus magnified into a wind.

I left the car by the side of the road, and went into the forest after the possessed animal. The deer could move faster than I, and I couldn't hope to catch it during its terrified flight. But it wouldn't run for long.

The presence of the human soul was devouring the beast from the inside. Soon, he would be forced to find another host. He could use other animals, but they would suffer the same fate as the deer. He needed to find a human host if his soul was going to survive. This stretch of Washington state road wasn't more than a few miles from Winslow and the Bainbridge Island ferry terminal. He was heading for Seattle, and if he found a host and made it across the water, I would never find him in the glittering city.

He was a direct link. His contact with her was fresh, a few hours old. This was the closest I had been in ten years. A gravid tension lay in my testicles, a near sexual response to being in such proximity. The Chorus sang, a lyric resonating deep in my joints, and like a tuning fork, I vibrated with this need.

I had to catch him.

Unconsciously, he followed a faint ley line, and this gravitation made it easier to track him through a succession of animal hosts. The deer lasted about a mile; I found it at the bottom of a narrow ravine, its eyes burst and its tongue bloated and black in its mouth. An owl carried him over a copse of dense evergreens before falling into the sparse fringe of new construction outside of Winslow. A domestic feline, left outside overnight, carried him a few blocks closer to the ferry terminal. I found its twisted and blackened body in the gutter at the edge of an alley. Its stomach had exploded, and he had forced the animal's body another twenty yards before its heart gave out.

The next body was stronger, and it was a half mile or so before I found it. The corpse of the dog was curled up next to a pair of scraggly pine trees, on the corner of a convenience store parking lot. A large husky, the dog's muzzle was streaked with ash and its body was still warm, radiant heat fading slowly from the burned corpse.

A police car—its red and blue lights flashing—drove up the street behind me, and turned into the parking lot. The officer glanced around the lot briefly as he got out of his car, but the bubble lights on the roof of the car made him squint. Spoiled night vision and the fact that I was wrapped by shadows and the Chorus meant he missed me and the body of the dog. He strode into the store and, through the narrow gaps between the advertising plastered all over the glass, I watched his conversation with the clerk.

Yes. The clerk had seen something and dialed 9-1-1. I stroked the dead dog's fur as I sent the Chorus to find out. They scattered across the parking lot, tasting the silver stains left by the passage of souls. Smears of energy, flickers of memory, hints of personality: days and years of transient visitors. Nothing definite. Nothing—

The Chorus boiled near a brown Buick, a late '90s sedan that carried the nostalgia of the Baby Boomer generation in its lines. A stain on the roof, near the driver's side door, was what had caught their attention. Impact spatter. Someone had hit their head hard enough to split the skin.

The wind rubbed against the branches of the pine trees behind me like the wire brushes of a jazz drummer against his snare drum—that persistent whisper of rhythm. The air was filled with the damp scent of pine. Dawn was going to be wet, another rainy day in the Pacific Northwest. Bad weather would make it harder to track this traveler: wind and rain scatter the energy lines, the traces that aren't firmly imprinted on the world. The natural dissolution of ambient spirit noise—ashes to ashes, dust to dust.

The soul had found his host. That's what had happened here. He'd jumped someone in the parking lot, assaulted them as they were returning to their car. The clerk had seen it happen: the convulsion of the victim as he was attacked; the body suddenly whiplashing against the car, head bouncing off the roof; a moment of conflict, and then control. Then, the spirit had run off, leaving the car behind.

The clerk and the policeman exited the store, and the clerk pointed toward the Buick. The young man's finger verified my assessment. The traveler was no longer trafficking in animal flesh; he had moved up to human meat.

The Chorus swirled out along the ground and found the ley running beneath the nearby road. This current was stronger than the one in the woods, enriched by the increased traffic along its vector. The ferry terminal was close. I could feel the tug of its gravity well on the aroused spirits within me. That nexus where all roads meet.

A thin line of orange light creased the eastern horizon as I reached the ferry dock, but the slate clouds storming out of the west kept dawn from cracking the sky. The wind, thrashing at my back, blew rain at a sharp angle, lashing the upper deck and sides of the boat like a bloodthirsty Inquisitor. The ferry shuddered as it started to pull away from the dock at Bainbridge Island. I crossed the exposed upper deck, rain like a cat-o'-nine-tails across my back, the last pedestrian to board the old ferry.

Warm, humid air like the breath of a floral hothouse struck my cold skin as I entered the aft common room. Standing at the back of the long room, I let the Chorus read the spirit layer.

Forty-minute ferry ride, probably less with the wind behind us. During that time, the boat was a floating coffin, cut off from all the aberrant noise and light of the city and the dock. This was my last chance to find the traveler before we reached Seattle.

He had two choices: ride the host body like an unwanted hitchhiker or take control of the shell. The human body is a stronger container than the four-legged ones, but even two souls will eventually cause immolation. One of the reasons for self-combustion, really—that presence of a possessing spirit. However, the flesh responds to the Will of a single spirit, and if this spirit was going to assume control, it had to force the other soul out.

Neither solution was good for the owner of the body. If the rogue soul remained too long, burnout. If the possessor won control, the other—the innocent—would be expelled, and without any training, any awareness of what had happened, they would dissolve into ambient etheric energy. Absorbed by the streams and leys as part of the cyclical reclamation of life. Spiritual death, in other words.

Having read the room, the Chorus ghosted a spectral overlay onto my vision, showing me a different spectrum than the visual one. Streamers of pale florescence ran through the stateroom, the phantom trails of recently passed bodies; a pulsating knot of light winked at me, souls sparking with effervescent eagerness; other clusters of sparks were like planetary bodies and their satellites, celestial bodies in tight orbit around each other.

I bled the Chorus down into faint opacity so as to map this data to the physical arrangement of the stateroom. The knot of souls was the crowd at the espresso cart near the center of the room, and that concentration made it easier to individually sweep the remainder of the passengers scattered in the orange vinyl seats. Most appeared to be long-time commuters with established routines. Some dozed, heads resting against tiny neck pillows; some propped up thick paperback novels or flicked through web pages on tiny hand-held devices with a somnambulant boredom. Inwardly attuned, their ambient energies barely wisped, strands wrapped tight around their bodies like an extra blanket against the cold wind and rain hammering the boat.

There were no unusual sparks, no sign of spiritual contest. All the lights looked normal—the everyday glow which I had long ago learned to filter out. As I walked the length of the stateroom, the Chorus teased and touched the lights for some memory that might help me find the traveler. The flickering touch of these other lives made the back of my tongue numb. I swallowed the wash of sensory data, letting it all decay in my gut. None of it was worth the trouble to keep, not worth the effort of leveraging it against my existent memories.

Outside, between the aft and forward common rooms, I passed a stairwell that led down to the under deck. The car hold. That echo chamber where several hundred tons of inert metal waited to arrive in Seattle. Certain metals obscured spirit light and, while most modern vehicles had too much synthetics and plastics to be useful barriers against detection, there were older models which could be effective shields. I hoped the naiveté I had sensed in the traveler meant he didn't know the best hiding place would be in one of these older cars; I hoped he thought it would be easier to hide among the spiritual noise of the crowds.

Unlike the passengers in the back half of the boat, the commuters in the forward room were eager for work, eager to reach their desks. Monday was always spent lamenting the death of the weekend and now that it was Tuesday, they had begun to consciously focus on the future—on what needed to be done *this* week. The chatter of their voices was a cicadaean buzz that roared over me the moment I entered the forward common area.

Conversations darted like the motion of busy bees pollinating a ripe field. On the spirit level, the room was a sea of swirling and boiling spirit light.

The air was turgid, thick and hot from the overworked heaters beneath the windows. The fogged glass hid the white-capped waves, and the florescent lights made abstract reflections in the condensation on the windows.

Steam drifted off the wet leather of my coat as I walked the aisle between the vinyl booths. I scanned the faces of the passengers, seeking the bubbling radiance of the traveler and his assumed host. Most of them ignored me, their eyes like static recorders logging the world around them, and then immediately pushing the sensory details to the waste bins of their minds. A few met my gaze and quickly glanced away, brief contact broken.

No one stared, no one was paying enough attention to be a decent Witness. But peripherally, some of them would remember me. *Too bright.* I was bound to attract the wrong sort of attention sooner than later.

Through the miasma of espresso roast (another espresso cart doing equally bang-up business in the center of the room), the stink of wet synthetic fabrics, and a jumble of juxtaposed perfumes, I caught the scent of burned meat. Above a stairwell at the back of the room, a sign pointed down. Restroom, lower level. At the top of the stairs, the smell was definitely stronger.

The short flight of stairs doubled back, down to a narrow landing and a narrower hallway, before winding further down into the belly of the ferry. There were two doors—a potted plant between them—off the hallway. Universally recognized signs on the doors: men on the left, women on the right. Tendrils of cold air crawled up the steps from the open car storage below.

I found the body in the first stall of the restroom. The thin door was locked, but the corpse had fallen off the toilet seat, and an arm stuck out under the aluminum partition. Olive coat sleeve, white shirt cuffs, cheap silver-faced watch with a black leather band. The dead man's hand was curled into a ragged claw, fingers curved back toward the palm in a manner suggestive of a tightening of the skin and not a conscious effort to make a fist. He had been an older man: extra wrinkles on his knuckles, age spots on the back of his hand.

A greasy pungency of burned fat drifted off the corpse, a reek that cut through the lemon deodorizer used by the cleaning crew during their nightly routine. The host had been elderly and out of shape—in comparison to the natural leanness of the animal kingdom—and the odor of his burned meat was a dirtier scent than that of the animals. Beneath the stench of the meat was the faint iron taint of blood, still wet.

I sighed and exhaled the sensitive tendrils of the Chorus, letting them taste the ethereal record of the room. Wisps of glimmering light clung to the handles of the faucets and the knob of the paper towel dispenser, and the steam drifting from the bowl of the nearest urinal told me the last guy in the room hadn't flushed. The Chorus glided through the partition between the corpse and me, brushing over the spatter of blood on the inner wall of the stall. They circled the dead man's head and dove into his slack mouth. The flesh was hot but it was an empty shell. They could taste the lingering imprint of two souls: one a faint shadow, the other a deeper discoloration.

The traveler was gone. He had influenced the old man down into the bathroom where he could force the other's spirit out in private. Their fight for dominance had been too much stress, and something had broken inside the old man. The traveler had fled, and the innocent had recovered the use of his body in time for it to expire from the heat damage.

I left the bathroom. There was nothing I could do for the old man. As I reached the landing, the Chorus snapped to the approach of a quartet of lights from the upper deck. Three diffuse, one hard. I drifted downstairs, slipping away from the mid-deck toward the car hold below.

Four men came down from the common room: two in the business armor of expensive suits and precise haircuts, one in the blue jersey of the Washington Department of Transportation, and one with a gold star hanging around his neck on a chain-link lanyard. Seattle Police.

The detective—a wide-shouldered bull wearing an out-of-season jacket beneath an open overcoat—spotted me on the stairs. His eyes were quick, the flitting movement of hummingbirds, and they rapidly digested my physical appearance. I fought an instinctual reaction to hide behind an obscuration, and let him look at me. In a minute, I wouldn't be the focus of his gaze and I could disappear; but for an instant, I just had to stand my ground and appear to be as innocuous as the plant in the hallway. *I am decoration. The unremarkable sort.*

They were heading for the men's room. One of the two suits was babbling, strings of words that were making the state employee nervous and the cop curious. They clattered off the stairs and disappeared down the hall toward the dead man in the restroom. I glided down the stairs, leaving them to their grisly discovery.

The astral traveler was still on the boat. He had ravaged one body already. I had to find him before he attacked another soul, before he wreaked havoc on someone else.

II

The cold air was a hard kiss on my face as I emerged into the open bay. Eight rows of cars waited under the exposed vault of the ferry, and I felt like I was inside a gargantuan whale. Steel spans colored green and orange by rust and weather framed the ferry's open throat. The wind wailed through this gullet, its outrage channeled by the curve of steel over the flat teeth of the cars ordered in precise rows along the bottom. The stink of brine mingled with the pervasive odor of oil and wet machinery, the decaying halitosis of this metal whale.

He was down here, searching for another host. Some ferry passengers stayed with their cars, comfortable and oblivious in their metal and plastic cocoons—their favorite morning talk radio on the dial, their personalized Starbucks beverage in the drink holder, the climate inside their isolated biospheres mimicking the weather at their dream vacation destination. They would be drowsy, distracted, half-awake: easy targets for an aggressive spirit.

DOT maximized the use of space down here, packing the cars tightly together. While the bumpers of many cars touched, rubber kisses between strangers, others kept a discrete eight inches or so apart, just enough room to sidle between. I wove a random pattern through these gaps as I checked passengers.

Through the silver filigree of the overlay supplied by the

Chorus, I searched for conflicts on the spirit level. Hot spots glowed like fallen meteors within rectangular shapes, while thin ribbons of mist streamed between cars. The wide ribbon of a man-laid ley throbbed beneath my feet.

There. A strange flicker of light. One row over and two cars forward. A white Acura.

In the driver's seat, sitting still as a stone, was a middle-aged businesswoman. Her head vibrated nearly imperceptibly, a rhythmic tic like a worn second hand on an old watch, and her hands were clenched about the steering wheel. A wide wedding band with a myriad of tiny diamonds was the only jewelry on her fingers. A thin thread of blood dripped over the curve of her lower lip, the result of an involuntary collision between tooth and skin. Silver light sparked in her eyes.

He didn't have control yet. He was a foreign element in her body; he could be extracted without damaging her, without rupturing the integrity of her shell. Physical damage would heal itself—in time—but a tearing of the sheath would be... *Yes*, she could be spared *that* choice.

I lashed the Chorus into my knuckles, and drove my hardened fist through the window. Glass exploded into the car, ice crystals raining into the woman's hair. She flinched, but not enough to avoid my hand. I wrapped my fingers around the side of her head.

She screamed, a harsh cry of a soprano imitating a tenor, as the Chorus sparked through the physical contact. The invading spirit felt me coming, and dove deeper into her flesh.

She released her death grip on the steering wheel, and started to beat the covered leather in a frenzied rhythm. She could feel the biting hunger of the Chorus, and knowing what they wanted, she instinctively fought to give up the invader. He just burrowed deeper into her psyche.

I let go. She was aware enough now to fight her own battle. By right of ownership, she had the advantage. One soul, one body—the spiritual anchors gravitated to the relationship they knew.

The bawling note of the boat's horn reverberated through the hold. We were in Elliott Bay, the jagged skyline of Seattle visible in front of the ferry. Through the rain, the buildings were limned with the faint orange and pink glow of dawn. We weren't more than five minutes from the pier. I had a little time yet—five, maybe ten minutes—but, judging from the flickering of red, orange, and blue lights coming from the edge of the pier, the situation was about to get very complicated as we arrived.

The dead body in the bathroom stall. The detective had called his friends. Police and fire waited for the ferry's arrival. I had to be done wrestling with the spirit when the boat docked.

In the Acura, the woman's hands went to the steering wheel again, knuckles bone white on the leather. Her head snapped back, smacking the headrest hard enough to rock the entire seat, and then forward as she vomited a stream of silver light.

The amorphous cloud of silver light was lit in the center by the quivering spark of a soul. The diaphanous cloud drifted through the windshield of the car, and the Chorus tightened around my neck as they touched the trailing edge. The woman's soul. He had forced her out of her own body.

The ferry horn blew again. As the subsonic echo rattled the loose metal of the cars around me, the traveler forced a bloody smile onto the woman's lips. I reached for her head again, and he lurched against the side of the car. His hand found the interior handle and he shoved the door open

The metal frame rammed into my legs. A smear of pain wiped across my thighs, and I fell against the car behind me. He shoved the door open again, trying to catch my kneecaps with the edge of the frame. I pivoted away, rolling along the panel of the car beneath me, and the tip of the Acura's door cut into the rear passenger door of the other car. I dimly heard a voice shouting at me incoherently from within the damaged car.

He tried to pull the door free, and finding it stuck, tried to get out of the car instead. He got one foot down and slipped, unaccustomed to the heel of the woman's shoes. As he struggled to walk—forget running—I scrambled onto the hood of the Acura and leaped over the open door. My fingers caught at the fabric of her jacket, and the Chorus lunged through the wool like bloodhounds through thin underbrush.

There was only one soul inside the woman's flesh this time, and the Chorus' hunger nipped at the alien spirit. Kaleidoscopic splinters spewed into my head—a riotous burst of the soul's memories. Buried within the chaotic ghosts was an imprint of his identity. Douglas, son of Frederick and Amber, family name of Rassmussen.

"Hello, Doug." I got a hand on an elbow and pulled her to me, so that I could touch her head again. The full flood of the Chorus roared into her body. Doug screamed, his spirit malforming her vocal cords.

"Let her go." It took a second to find the source of the voice. Two cars back, standing in the aisle, legs apart. The detective, his gun held steady on me.

"This isn't your affair," I hissed through the haze of spirit noise. The woman, kneeling on the ground before me, shook uncontrollably as the Chorus thrashed after Doug's soul. "There's nothing to See, nothing at all. It'll be over in a minute. No one is going to be hurt."

Like stones grinding together, the sound of the engines changed as the propellers reversed their spin. The floor swayed abruptly, and the woman and I leaned with it.

"That's right," the cop said, unmoved by the ferry's shift. "No one is going to be hurt if you let her go." His eyes were chips of mica in his face.

I still had to extract Doug. Once his grip was broken on her flesh, she could return to her body. The cloudy mass of her soul still hovered over the roof of her car. If I pulled Doug out quickly—if I could separate him before he thought to shut her organs down—the body would manage for a little while without a spirit in charge. She would naturally slide back into place. She might even survive the shock of separation and reintegration. But, Doug had to come out first.

The Chorus hissed and spat as they dug down for the anchors laid out by his spirit. Sensing my intent, as if he realized what the Chorus would do to him if they managed to pull him out, Doug opted to flee. In a silver flash, he poured out through the woman's eyes. As Doug ran, the body dropped to the floor like a marionette with severed strings. It twitched on the metal plates of the deck, still alive. As the Chorus retreated from the vacuum, I felt the warm brush of her spirit as it sucked back into place.

The whirling cloud of Doug's spirit left a contrail of sparkling dust as he ran. I hesitated, caught off-guard by Doug's direction. He was running straight for the cop.

The bull stiffened as Doug rammed himself through the man's eyes. The pistol didn't twitch. A moment of control was all Doug wanted, just enough influence to pull the trigger. The cop's arms were frozen; he could only watch himself as he fired the gun.

In illo tempore. The words were a violet sigil swimming in my vision—thought made real and superimposed over my retinas—as the Chorus bent the world around me. According to my Will. The physical objects in the hold became vibratory patterns—everything became more distant and more magnified. The spit of fire blossoming from the barrel of the pistol was overlaid with a tracery of violet lines. The bullet trailed neon curlicues as it spun through the air. Even though the magick field collapsed instantly, the bubble of distorted time lasted long enough for me to move. I twisted away from the path of the bullet.

The bubble popped, and Time lunged forward. The angry bark of the pistol became a growling roar, and the implosion of the bubble howled in my ears. The bullet punched through the leather of my coat, and I felt a razor crease of superheated air along my rib cage. My distortion field had been a weak effort, a desperate spell that had bought me time. Just enough. *Skin heals.*

Doug's surprise attack on the cop was a short-term assault. He just wanted an instant of control, enough to pull the trigger; he didn't want to confront the detective's spirit. However, the bullish tendencies of the cop weren't as easily bullied.

The detective's face was the color of old wax, and veins pulsed in his neck as he fought against Doug's invasion. Doug—seeing little alternative—dug deeper, trying to assert more control, trying to move the pistol. The gun went off again but the bullet went wild, wild enough that it wasn't clear who was the target.

A growling cacophony of engine noises rattled the plates of the deck. Drivers started their engines in anticipation of the ferry's imminent landing as if arrival at the pier was the gate dropping at a horse track, as if the sound of the cop's gun was just the pop of a starter's pistol. Shadows in the hold capered with red and blue light from the police vehicles at the approaching dock.

The cop let go of the pistol. In a moment of lucidity he realized the best course was to lose the weapon entirely. The gun clattered on the metal plating, and in that fraction of time when Doug was still wired into the man's lower brain, I lunged forward.

My outstretched palm struck the cop squarely on the breastbone, and slammed him against a car. The Chorus' touch was electric, and Doug's writhing shape lit up beneath the detective's skin. Doug dropped all pretense of control and ran again. The cop gasped. The combination of my touch and the sudden expulsion of Doug from his flesh left him slumped against the car.

The Chorus raked through Doug's contrail, and more hints of his life force rippled up my arm. Black motes swirled in my vision as the Chorus quivered with the possibility of feeding. They pulled at their restraints. I exerted my Will over them, and silver static glazed through the black light in my retinas. *No, I need answers. I need to know where she is.*

I needed Doug in his real body. I wanted access to his full history, his complete memories. What he carried in his astral shape wasn't enough.

I scrambled after him, over the hood of a nearby car as he churned across the open bay. The Chorus wrapped themselves around the trailing tentacles of his spirit form. I shaped a psychic harpoon, and drove it through the center of his soul cloud. The barbed spike, laced with the fury of the Chorus and my Will, anchored him. Silver strands extruded like kudzu vines from my hands as I began to weave a cage around him. The coppery taste of his panic filled my mouth.

Doug fought with the desperation of a snared mountain lion—twisting and sliding under my attempts to restrain his spirit. He wasn't a neophyte. He knew magick, and had been touched by the Will of another before. Even more, he felt the hunger of the Chorus, felt the need and violence that filled their bite. My legs grew cold and numb as all my energies went to holding them back and building the prison around Doug's spirit.

The car in front of me lurched suddenly. In the windshield, I caught a glimpse of my haloed reflection, a Kali headdress of shining energy riding above a plume of static-charged hair. Doug was a thrashing smear of light in my hands. The driver, a young blonde woman, tried to get around me as the lanes emptied from the ferry. Her car struck my leg, and my focus faltered.

Doug melted in my hands, dissolving into a liquid rush that splashed onto the deck. His insubstantial shape squirted between my legs, and passed through the frame of the car. Much like he had done with the cop, he forced himself upon the innocent shell. The Chorus was close behind, tearing at his phantasmal shape. My connection to his spirit was solid enough that I felt the violence of his strike. He went into her brain and vaporized her fear centers.

Her foot smashed the accelerator pedal and the car leaped forward. The impact with my legs was hard and fast, knocking me aside. The car thundered across the lowered metal plank and crunched onto the concrete of the pier.

Doug stayed with her, clinging to the energized flight reflex he had activated in her mind. In a second, her car plowed past the line of police cars and was gone, nothing left but a spatter of rainwater on concrete to mark her passage.

I had nothing. My hands were empty.

A uniformed officer rushed down the gangplank with his pistol raised. "Stay down!" he shouted at me, waving the gun toward the deck. "Get on your stomach and put your hands behind your head."

I ignored him, staring past the line of police cars. Doug was gone. He could have told me. The Chorus was a furious wall of snakes in my head, a hydra movement of engorged desires. A cold darkness tightened in the pit of my stomach. *Had I lost my connection to her?*

I felt the ragged edges of my soul tear, felt like it was all happening again.

The officer was persistent. "Get your hands behind your head, motherfucker! Move 'em or I'll fire." He wasn't a fool: standing close enough to be sure he wouldn't miss me, far enough away that I couldn't grab his weapon. His jaw was firm. He was trying his best to be sinister.

I touched the ache in my gut and gave him sinister. *Elide.* The Chorus wailed as I came off the deck and closed the distance between us. The barrel of his gun groaned and creased like wet paper under my grip. I didn't stop when I got to his fingers.

III

That stunt got me a free ride in a police cruiser, wrists cuffed savagely behind my back. The back seat stank of stale bodies, but the scent of fear pooling in the car came from the pair of officers in the front. Rumors were already spreading, fantasy informing gossip. These two weren't sure what had happened and, as a result, their imaginations were feeding all the wild stories.

All it takes is a seed.

We entered police headquarters in downtown Seattle through an unmarked entrance in the back, spiraling down fluorescently lit passages of white stone into the sub-levels beneath the street. I was hustled through equally unadorned hallways to a tiny room with two plastic chairs and a cheap metal table. A steel ring was welded to the top of the table.

My jacket and the contents of my pockets had been taken from me at the ferry terminal and, after we entered the interrogation room, they took my belt and shoelaces. A young officer tried for the thin braid of hair about my throat, and the Chorus nipped at him. Trying to keep his cool, he pulled back and made a half-hearted dismissive gesture. Something to hide the tremor in his hands. No one offered to take a look at the bloody nick along my side. The fact that it had stopped bleeding was apparently good enough for them. After that, they locked one of the handcuffs to the metal ring and left me alone.

A history of desperate chain-smokers was an old stink permeating every surface—nearly a tactile crust on the room. The paint on the wall opposite the door was less dull than the other walls. An observation window once, perhaps, sheet-rocked over some time ago. The floor was a cheap parquet, an ugly color stained even uglier. The table and chairs were utilitarian: the table legs were welded to the pitted top, the chairs were the molded plastic sort found around the pool at two-star motels. The room didn't bother to obscure its purpose. Out of sight, out of mind. No one wanted to know what happened here.

I tried to get comfortable. The handcuffs and the ring meant I had to lean forward as if I were considering a session of earnest supplication but hadn't quite committed myself to the act. Easier to lie on the table with my hands resting above my head, wrists next to the metal ring.

I was tired. It had been nearly 3:00 a.m. when I had spotted Doug, and the resulting chase had been unexpected and draining. Prior to that, I had been out on the peninsula visiting an old friend.

Father Lenbier was a retired Naval Chaplain with a house outside of Lofall—an hour from the ferry terminal at Winslow. He had been stationed in the Far East for thirty years before being tossed back across the ocean for his final tour at the Naval Yard at Bremerton. I had been to both China and Japan, and I had wanted to catch up.

I had met the priest in Olso years ago—just two wanderers washed into a back-alley bar, looking to offset the permafrost of the dark winter. His faith provided an interesting counterpoint to the... melancholy that had driven me north. A bottle of Laphroaig consecrated our friendship. It hadn't been my choice—he was the single malt fan—but, by the end of the night, I had learned a measure of respect.

We had spent the evening telling polite lies about our secret histories, and trying to deconstruct the nature of faith via the magic of a bottle of Dalwhinnie 15. The antique market in the Pacific Northwest looked to the East for its history (unlike the New England market which was perversely fixated on Louis XIV's bedroom furniture), and Father Lenbier's stories about the Far East station were filled with useful details. Grist for the small talk which invariably crept up in my business. One must keep up appearances on one's public persona.

Then, on the way home, there had been the deer, with Doug squatting on its spine. Like a guiding star half-glimpsed through a barrier of thick trees or a glimmer of bewitched swamp gas intended to lure the unwary, the animal with its spiritual possessor had drawn me away from the road and into the wilderness.

Chance plays a very small part in the Weave of the Universe. There are currents and eddies in the natural world that influence the mind, but very little of the Universe is driven by random luck. It is a matter of synchronicities, the seeming coincidences have a hidden connectivity. The Weave is the fabric of the World, and its threads are the convoluted tracks of every personal history.

For the last two weeks, I had been tracking Katarina. It had been ten years since we had seen each other—a decade that had done nothing to dull the ache in my chest. On the few previous occasions when her trail crossed mine, the threads had always been stiff and brittle—too old to follow without breaking them. This time, I knew she was still in Seattle. The trouble had been finding something more substantial than the persistent itch caused by her proximity.

The Chorus crystallized in my head, spinning memory. Doug's history. Hazy, but still of some use. *Close enough.* That scent, that familiar taste.

Kat had touched his soul. Last night, she had participated in a ritual of disengagement. I could taste her presence on him. She had directed the wedge used to drive apart flesh and spirit.

In my travels, I had learned many names for the same objects, the same rituals, the same beliefs. All the names carried with them a different history, a different mnemonic resonance. Kabbalist mystics would label her the unclean child of that harlot Lilith, a foul child who sucked energy from a vessel, allowing the *Qliphoth* to invade the empty shell. The modern Hungarian Gypsies—who split their time between modern apartments in Budapest and hand-built cabins in the mountains—named her *"szüz ordog"*: demon maid, a succubus whose ill touch separated the light from the dark.

They taught me other names too. Names meant, not for her, but for me. *Lélek rabló. Fény romboló.* Spirit thief. Light-breaker.

Doug's contact with her hadn't been like mine. There was no fear on him—none of that panic that had overwhelmed me. Their interaction had been a ritual affair, a ceremonial act knowingly consecrated. In the last decade, Kat had learned new tricks and found new friends. They were using psychoanimist techniques: direct manipulation of the soul, spirit possession, and astral travel. New tricks, indeed.

In the last few weeks, I had discovered five groups who operated in the Greater Puget Sound area. One was a weekend wiccan gathering—housewives who sought to influence neighborhood politics and local weather patterns. Another was based out of an underground club in the Capitol Hill district, though it was more of a social organization held together by a mutual affection for rhythmic noise and power electronic music. The others were more rigidly structured—more of the sort that I was seeking, but they appeared to be traditional. Old rituals, older laws. Transgressive and experimental, they weren't. Kat's group, on the other hand, was probably a splinter, a secret cabal bored with the old rituals, who had gone off on their own. Very quietly, and very under the radar. Best to stay hidden in the sexually and morally repressed West, when you were practicing psychoanimism.

The muscles in my arms were jumpy, and the awkward position required by the handcuff ring wasn't making it any easier to relax. A *pranayama* breathing ritual would help oxygenate my blood and alleviate some of the exhaustion. Though, even with the tension release of the technique, my right knee was going to be stiff for some time.

An interrogator hadn't shown yet, leading me to believe they were going to let me sit awhile. I wasn't even sure if they were watching me. If a camera was hidden behind the ceiling tiles, it had escaped my notice. But there was no point in trying to ascertain if they were watching—there were things I could be doing with the downtime—internal things the camera couldn't see. I fell into the *pranayama* mantra, and my breathing found the rhythm quickly. The rest would come—the unwinding of my spine, the unlocking of my hips, the bleed-off of energy through my relaxed fingers…

My mind drifted into the hazy realm of memory and premonition. I dozed, and the Chorus sighed, their voices fading to a tiny buzz of static. The physical world stretched into a transparent film over the surging grid of the urban energy flow. I stretched for the nearest conduit, and slipped into the vibrant ocean of etheric energy pulsating throughout the city.

A Hopi shaman had taught me how to read the geomantic grid of the world. We had spent a week exposed on a knob of bare rock high in the Arizona desert, drinking rainwater and eating peyote buttons. His body, black with pitch, was invisible to the moon, and he had drawn a pattern of stars on his face with orange and yellow paint. He wore a crown of eagle feathers and a necklace of mountain lion claws, and across his broad back he draped a ragged wolf pelt. After three days, when he stopped being a man, he showed me how to taste the earth, how to interpret the scents of the wind, and how to hear the sighing motion of the stars.

In return, I showed him the skein of energy that lay within.

As within, as without, he said, they are mirror patterns. The currents of spiritual power flowed all over the world; they were the rivers of creation from which we came and to which we would return. The shaman, he said—the magus, the mystic—is a fish that breathes both air and water. He can traverse the spiritual currents like a ghost, and still walk the earth like a man.

Since then, I had stumbled across as many schools of magick as flavors at Baskin-Robbins, and the metaphysical rationale for each was as subjective and fleeting as the decision made when choosing a flavor of ice cream. The underlying Truths were like the secrets whispered by the cooks in the back room: there is always sugar and milk, everything else is just preservatives and chemical dyes.

Regional geographies, cultural mores, social histories, divine providences, and local soothsayers all play a part in how the energies of the world are understood. Some schools were filled with shallow spirituality; some were fiercely physical, filled with blood totems and sacrificial rites; some were tangled schemas of mental peregrinations reflected in word games played in dusty parlors. I found schools where simple rhymes sung by children while collecting water contained vibrations of the Word of God; others bound themselves to sequences of arcane gestures and complex physical gyrations like the inexplicable dances of back mountain Baptists and Moroccan fakirs.

In the end, they all reflected the same thing: the world was energy—humanity was energy—and the Universe was a self-perpetuating system. Magick was how we tried to comprehend the chaotic possibilities of creative energy.

I floated on the surface, an idle leaf in the flow, as the Chorus dipped silver ladles in the stream. The warm trickle of absorbed energy further eased the knot in my knee. The twitch in my wrists faded to a dull itch.

Nearby, a disturbance broke the surface of the flow like a fish jumping for a mayfly. A vibrating ball of light, the energy signal moved against the currents, approaching my point of perception. The police were sending someone to talk to me, someone who burned brighter than his surroundings. My interrogator was a magus.

I came out of my trance as the lock on the door clicked. The Chorus took a final sip from the stream, and I wound them down into the dark hole in my chest, hiding them beneath the layers of my meat. The door opened, and I rattled the handcuffs slightly as if the sound had startled me, but made no other effort to get up.

As anticipated, a single man entered the room. He wore a dark green suit with a tiny pattern woven in the fabric, little goldenrod points like seedpods bursting apart in the early summer. His shirt was crisp, and his tie was a mélange of reds and violets—too random to suggest anything concrete, but regular enough to suggest machine generation. The Art Deco design of modern business accessories. Clean-shaven, manicured nails, expensive haircut that gave each follicle individual attention (as well as a tint like summer wheat), cuff links that glittered even in the decrepit light of the interrogation room: the package said "Upper Management."

He closed the door quietly, and examined me. Tiny violet pinholes in his pupils twinkled as if he had pricked himself with a straight pin. He was Seeing me, looking beyond the gross physicality of my shell. He was looking for mystical radiances, spirit glimmers, sigil echoes, and other signifiers of a magickal aptitude. His gaze lingered on the white braid about my throat; under close magickal examination, it would glitter, but just enough to seem like a weak bit of flash and not as a magus' focus.

Completing his initial assessment, my interrogator approached the table. He opened the thin manila folder he was carrying and glanced inside. "I'm glad you find this so amusing, Mr. Markham," he said in response to the ghost of a smile on my lips.

"Awkward and tedious, actually," I replied. I rattled the handcuffs a second time.

His eyes flickered toward the sound. "Well," he said, "I apologize for the inconvenience. Bureaucracy, you know. It's the paperwork that needs to be filled out when a *veneficus* publicly stamps his Will on the world. Fewer lies to fabricate when they keep to themselves."

"*Veneficus?* Is that the popular term now?" *Poisonous,* and a *sorcerer.* How quaint.

He closed the folder and tapped it against my outstretched legs. "You want to tell me what happened?"

"Not really."

A thin crease quirked the edges of his lips. The violet spark in his eyes flashed, and I felt the temperature of the room change. "Too much of a tough guy to talk to me?"

I shrugged, dismissing the shift in energy density. "It's not a question of talking; it's a question of trust."

"I am Lieutenant Pender of the Metropolitan Division, Seattle Police Department," he said, still maintaining the measured façade of Polite Cop, though sarcasm was beginning to creep around the edges. "We can go about this situation two ways: I can make this little nuisance disappear; or, I can drown you in a shitstorm of paperwork. It'll be a year before you can take a piss without filling out a form in triplicate. Your call."

This was our dance then: good cop versus malingering *veneficus,* how schooled was each of us, and how long would we try to hide our knowledge from the other? I assumed his folder contained the results of a database crawl. The mundane information known about me: my ancient and puerile police record, what financial holdings I had in US-controlled banks, my recent spending patterns, my out-of-date political party affiliation, and a scattered list of entry and exit dates at international airports.

What would make him more inclined to consider me as one of his "poisonous sorcerers" was the dearth of real estate holdings or vehicle ownership, a lack of rental history, and a seeming indifference to cell phone technology: the signs of transience, the lack of hooks that tied one to a single location. How he interpreted these two classes of data would reveal what he thought about rogues—adepts who had no clear affiliation with organized temples—and that outlook would temper his amenability.

"You've been in town two weeks, Mr. Markham." He returned to his notes. "Your room at the Monaco—let's see, room 605, is it?—is booked through the weekend, though the folio has been tagged as open-ended. The rental policy on your car is good through the end of the month. You seem to be in a state of flux, caught in some indecision about your plans. Are you planning on staying in Seattle long?"

"It depends."

"On?"

"How long you plan on keeping me cuffed to this table."

He sighed, and traced a long finger across his forehead as if to alleviate some pressure building in his skull. His lips twitched again—downward this time—and he gestured toward the bands circling my wrists. The pulse of his spell was precise and focused. The cuffs clicked open and fell off, clattering on the table like cheap jewelry. It was a simple physical manipulation spell, one we were both very capable of executing. It had simply been a matter of who would show their Will first.

Small victory. It meant nothing really, but it told me we were past the stage of sparring about the existence of magick.

I sat up and swung my legs to my right and hopped off the table. I stood with my back to him, making a show of rubbing my wrists.

"What happened to Gerald Summers?" he asked.

The old man on the ferry.

"Who?" I feigned ignorance as I turned back to the table and my interrogator.

Pender took out a crime scene photograph from the folder. "Mr. Summers," he said, sliding the photo across the table so I could examine it more closely. If I actually needed to, that is. It had been taken from the front of the stall on the ferry, a tightly framed shot of Mr. Summers' head and shoulders.

Summers' wide eyes stared up toward the top of the photo; his mouth gaped in a crooked cry of incomprehension and panic. Doug had only relinquished his grip after Summers' heart had started to collapse. He left the old man with a second of life, just a single tick to feel the shuddering collapse of the failed heart muscle.

"Psychoanimist possession," I said. "Burned him from the inside out." I looked at Pender. "But you knew that, didn't you?"

The skin around his eyes tightened.

"Did you find any of my prints at the scene?" I asked. The single item on my police record was from college. I had made a poor decision at a University of Washington frat party one night. While I had never regretted my actions, the resolution of the evening had involved the police. A full set of fingerprints had been taken. Once in the system, they never came out.

Pender lifted his shoulders. "The forensic investigation hasn't been completed."

"I'll save you the trouble. You won't find any other prints on him. Not mine. Not anyone's. His body walked into that stall, and that was the last thing it ever did. Summers' heart gave out shortly after he sat down. *He* only had control of his body for a few seconds."

Pender was still holding up the picture. "Possession," he mused. "Mr. Summers was possessed by another human spirit? Is that the psychobabble you expect me to believe?" Testing me: *Was he unaware of such techniques or was he probing the integrity of my story, trying to catch me in an inconsistency?*

"Ask your detective how much nonsense it is."

His mouth worked a minute, finding the right sequence of words. "Detective Nicols says he has no recollection of the events."

"Does he? He's probably still trying to figure out what happened." If the detective had any recollection of Doug being in his body, it would be vague—fleeting memories detached from his own personal history. They would fade, dissolving into a general unease, touched off by these ghostly fragments. This disorientation would persist at the edge of his consciousness for a few weeks, then it would vanish like wisps of a bad dream.

Though, he *could* try to hang on to them. Try to attach them to his own storage schemas. He might. He seemed like the persistent type.

"What are you going to do if he keeps thinking about this morning?"

"That's not your problem."

"No, I suppose not. I have a different problem, don't I? What do you want to accomplish here, Lieutenant?" I gestured around the room, indicating the lack of standard interrogation room accoutrements. No two-way mirror. No cameras. No digital audio recorders.

Just two magi, talking.

"I want to understand what happened on the boat."

"I told you: psychoanimist possession. I was following an astral traveler. He started jacking bodies."

"But how did you two get on the ferry? Why were you tracking him?"

I didn't answer.

Pender sighed. He retrieved the picture from the table, and slipped it back into his folder. His attention went to the other pages. "Landis M. Markham," he read. "What does the 'M' stand for?"

"Michael," I told him. "My mother's Catholic heritage. Not my father's favorite." While I preferred it to my given name, that preference was only known to a handful of people. I had been through too many places that believed in the power of names to not protect myself.

"Born and raised in Idaho," he continued. "Moved to Seattle in the early 1990s where you attended the University of Washington. Studied archaeology, though you didn't stay long enough to get a degree."

"There was a scandal," I offered. "Involving hominid skulls."

He ignored my flippancy. "Where did you go, Mr. Markham? You quit your job at REI that same year. Struck by a bit of wanderlust, were you? You've been to a lot of places since then." His finger ran down a list on the page. "TSA provided an interesting list: France, Hungary, Italy, Morocco, China, Indonesia, Ethiopia, Kenya, Brazil, Argentina, Jamaica. Quite the intrepid *traveler,* aren't you?"

"It's the nature of my business," I said. "It requires me to, uh, travel." My voice stumbled on the word. I realized the question underlying his emphasis on the word.

Traveler.

It was a code word, not just a descriptive noun but a title. *A rank.* He was asking me to identify myself: to recognize his word and reply with some acknowledgement, some secret passphrase known to initiates like himself. He was asking me for confirmation that I, too, was a Watcher.

Shit.

This explained our private conversation. Why he dangled the carrot about cleaning up this mess. Pender's offer to make the situation evaporate was honest, if I was one of his brothers. If I flashed him the secret hand signal, he would do exactly what he was here to do: keep the secrets hidden, and make sure the interests of the Watchers were maintained.

The trouble was I hadn't kept up my membership. They thought I was dead. It was the only way to leave the organization.

IV

The members of *La Société Lumineuse* were Witnesses, True Seeing observers whose focus was the preservation of magickal knowledge. A worldwide network of subversive agents and dedicated spies, they were positioned in auspicious locations and key jobs so as to manipulate events and individuals. Secret movers and shakers, acting to keep the occult hidden. They were based in Paris, and their original name has been purposefully forgotten. They had learned from the lesson so brutally put to their original incarnation when thirteen of them were burned at the stake in the fourteenth century. They acted in secrecy because the rest of the world preferred ignorance, preferred not to be reminded of the necessity for guardians of the occult lore.

I had been in Paris once upon a time. Like a fairy tale. Self-cast as the hero of that fable, I studied for several years, even reached Journeyman—a neophyte grade in the art of Watching. Journeymen who demonstrate aptitude and ambition become Travelers and go forth to earn their place in the world, always watching and reporting back to their masters. My fairy tale collapsed before I could be graded for Traveler. Every story has a hero, a heroine, and a villain. In the end, the tale got rewritten; I became the villain.

"And what is your business?" Pender sat in one of the two

chairs at the table. He indicated the other chair. While his body language projected indifference, his eyes watched me closely. *Witnessing.* At the very least, Pender had to be a Traveler.

"Antiques." I swallowed the obstruction in my throat that had been raised by the shadow of my past. I had carefully avoided the Watchers since I had left Paris, preferring the anonymity of death to the… headache of being alive. If he reported me to his masters, they would be curious as to why I was running around without a leash. *One of them would be more than curious.* "My clients have very specific tastes. I have to go where the markets are hot if I want to stay in business."

"How do your clients find you?" he asked. He gave no hint he had even offered a recognition signal, no sense he was waiting for me to acknowledge his code word.

Was I imagining a connection which didn't exist? "Personal references." I sat down.

"Ah, that sort of antique market," he said. "Were you working for a client last night?"

"Visiting a friend."

"The *traveler* on the boat?"

I shook my head. He had just asked me to acknowledge myself again. When he decided I was unaware of his connection to the Watchers—when he decided I wasn't one of *them*—the opportunity to dismiss this situation would vanish. What would my options be? To ask for a lawyer and try to get bail posted? To demand to know the charges being levied against me and protest my innocence?

A pall of silence hung in the room while we both considered which direction to take the conversation. "You pose an interesting problem, Mr. Markham," he said. I didn't intrude into his thought, and he let that statement hang for a minute. He examined the pages in his folder. "Your father taught at Western Washington University, didn't he?" he asked, momentarily setting aside the quandary of my presence.

"Yeah, he taught Washington State history."

"Used to be a farmer. Potatoes, was it?"

I nodded.

"Fairly successful transformation for a man who never finished high school."

"He was good at applying himself," I said. "He worked hard for the degree and was proud of it." Proud, and always a little nervous the rest of the administration would discover he was a high school dropout from southern Idaho. His father had died unexpectedly one summer. He had suffered a mild heart attack while working the field, and lost control of the tractor. By the time they found him and the vehicle in the ditch that ran along the southern edge of the property, the sun had taken him away from the family. My father took over and, even with his youthful will and energetic body, the local potato conglomerate still managed to gut the family for the land. It just took a few years longer than their projections. *Small victories.* My father's mother died in her sleep two days after the paperwork for the sale was signed.

My mother had always been a frail phantom, a child of New England more suited to central heating and sturdy brownstones than windswept winters and arid summers. She died the winter after the dissolution of the family farm. My father brought what was left of the family—me and my sister—west to Seattle, where he tried to bury the past. For the rest of his life, my father, no matter how hard he tried, felt that he could never fully get the Idaho dirt out from beneath his fingernails.

He would come home from teaching and obsessively wash his hands. Before he left in the morning, he would repeat the same ritual—soap and water, soap and water—until they were pink and shining. Innocent. Purified.

I glanced down at my hands, resting on the table. My knuckles, broken more than once; the scars on the back of my right hand, ugly kisses left by steel and bone; the twisted piece of flesh at the base of my left thumb. The things we learn from our fathers: our hands betray what we have done.

"And yet," Pender noted, "you never finished school."

I shrugged, putting my hands in my lap. "My sister was always better at applying herself."

"Chelsea married an investment banker from Barcelona, didn't she?" The question was rhetorical; I knew he had the specifics on the page. "Migel Guastera. She hasn't been back to the States since your father's funeral in '02."

"That seems about right."

"You don't talk much?"

"Differences of opinion make casual talk sort of pointless."

"You don't like her husband?"

"I've never met him."

"Does your sister work?"

"She does art restoration. Local galleries in Barcelona, mainly."

He raised an eyebrow. "With your line of work, there's no overlap? No reason for regular contact?"

"There's a lot of people doing art restoration out there; and I don't have a lot of reasons to visit Barcelona."

"And your business on the peninsula last night had nothing to do with art or antiques?"

I shook my head. "Visiting an old friend."

"He'll confirm this?"

"Why wouldn't he?"

Pender gave me a toothsome smile that didn't extend to his eyes. The dart and feint of our conversation was entertaining him. It was a game he thought he could win. I was starting to tire of it. What would he do if I slapped him with the fact that I knew he was a Watcher? *Testis sum. I am a Witness.* It was a passphrase used in the Witnessing rituals of the Journeymen. It would definitely abort our little conversation, but would it get me out of this room without creating further complications?

He's going to call Paris anyway; you're running out of time.

"Douglas Rassmussen," I said, opting for a different distraction. *Stay away from Paris.*

"Pardon?" He closed the file.

"That's his name. The *traveler*. That's the guy you should be talking to." I leaned toward him. "He left the boat in another body, which means there's another charred corpse waiting for you to find. Not to mention how he gets back into his original body."

"Back to his body? What do you mean?"

"He wasn't acting alone." The flickering colors, the sensory impressions stolen from Doug, danced in my head. "It was some sort of ritual. He wasn't bodiless by accident. He had help transcending his natural state."

"I thought you said there was only one spirit?"

I sighed and looked away. Was he being intentionally dense, or did he just not have any idea what psychoanimism was?

Be sure.

"He and his friends are doing rituals of separation. They've learned how to split the light from the meat. Completely. This isn't astral projection; they are separating *soul* from *body*. I think he was trying to get back to his body; I think that was the whole point of their ritual."

"Why? What was the point?"

"To prove his worthiness, to prove that he was ready to join their inner circle." *To prove he could survive the experience.*

Some of the sly amusement dropped away from Pender's face. "They're organized?"

"It didn't happen spontaneously."

"You seem to know a lot about this sort of ritual."

"He possessed the old man, bent him to his Will."

Violet dots swam in his irises as he waited for me to give him more information. "And?"

"It's an abomination. It kills the body and the spirit. Our

journey to enlightenment isn't a path that requires innocents to suffer. That's not knowledge." He was Watching me now, gauging my unconscious reaction. I gave him little to read, just verbal propaganda drawn from a few thousand years of Roman Catholic history and an expression full of shock and horror.

A corner of his mouth twitched. "Is that part of your religious upbringing, Mr. Markham, or are you trying to impress upon me the depth of your compassion?"

"My compassion."

"Ah," he nodded, and I managed to keep a straight face. "Yes, of course." He touched the corner of his mouth as if to stop the twitch. "And, when you had your talk with this transgressor, were you going to ask him to vacate the old man's body?"

"It was too late for Mr. Summers. I was trying to stop him from possessing another body. The woman in the Acura. Your detective. The driver of the car that…"

Pender's gaze fell toward the closed folder. One of the pages inside had to be the field report from the police on the scene. His fingers moved idly on the cover, tracing some mental pattern in his head. "A Cadillac," he offered. "The car that hit you was a Cadillac SRX. He was controlling the driver's body?"

"Yes."

"And you think his possession has killed this person as well?" His interest seemed piqued, as if I had finally offered enough information that he couldn't dismiss the possibility that I was the smaller problem here. Now there was something larger to deal with than just an adept performing an Act of Will in public.

"Even if he just possessed her long enough to return to his real body—wherever it had been taken—she'll be severely touched. And she'll know who they are." I nodded. "Yeah, if Doug doesn't burn her out, they'll kill her."

"Do you know who they are?"

"No, just the one guy. Douglas Rassmussen. Son of Frederick and Amber." I spelled the last name for him. "I don't know who his friends are."

Something passed through his eyes, something he hid almost as instantly as it flared. I was left with a momentary spasm in my gut as if the ground had unexpectedly rippled beneath me. *The name meant something to him.*

"Well," he said, standing up. "I'll look into it." He held up the folder. "I'll check the databases."

"What about me?"

"I haven't decided, Mr. Markham. You're a wild card and I'm not sure I should let you run free in this city."

"My business is almost finished," I said. "There would be no reason for me to stay here after I was done."

"You never did tell me what your business here was."

"Looking for an old friend," I said. "A woman."

His tongue touched the edge of his lip, almost mocking me. "She break your heart?"

"Sort of."

"Financial dispute?"

"No."

"Pity. Financial disagreements rarely end in bloodshed. Just lawyers." He shook his head as he walked to the door. "Matters involving heartbreak…?" He punched in a code on the door's security lock. As he opened the door, he left me with a parting observation. "They always seem to produce collateral damage."

V

It was hard to say what Pender believed and what he already knew. A Watcher trait: you could never really be sure they didn't know more than you, even when they seemed to be clueless. Some of the lieutenant's reactions seemed too forced, too naive, to be true; while at other times he appeared genuinely puzzled.

I couldn't decide which was better.

After he left, I considered my dearth of options. Regardless of what Pender did with the information about Doug, he knew who I was and, eventually, a report containing my name would be filed with the head office in Paris. After that, it was just a matter of time before the wrong person realized the record of my death was a premature one.

He'll come. It wasn't like Antoine to leave matters unresolved. He'd want to finish our business. The wound had long been healed but, for a second, the skin on my stomach tightened. The invasive memory of cold steel. *He'll need to finish it, and not just for Watcher honor.*

Was there enough time to find Kat? Doug's trail was about to become a clusterfuck of police interest. I wouldn't be able to get anywhere near him without Pender's knowledge. I needed another approach.

I was still rolling that conundrum over in my mind when the

door clicked. A pair of uniforms looked in. "Mr. Markham," one of them said. "Please come with us."

I did so dutifully—up two elevators, and through a number of long windowless hallways. A pair of thick doors disgorged me into a receiving area, and I discovered we were above ground. At a caged window, I signed for my personal effects; then, plastic bag and coat in hand, I was led through a security station, and found myself in the lobby of Seattle Police Headquarters. My uniformed guide nodded at my uncertainty, and pointed toward the door. "Have a nice day," he said.

Through the tall windows fronting the building, I saw Pender waiting on the front steps, wearing a full-length wool coat against the wind and Seattle damp. Hands clasped behind his back, head tilted up as if he had just stepped outside to check the weather.

I sorted through the plastic bag for my belt and shoelaces. After threading them through their respective places, I slipped on my coat and dumped the remaining items into my jacket pockets. The wind teased at me as I exited the building, like a coy lover blowing through the hole in my shirt. I tugged at the lapels—the coat fell awkwardly across my shoulders and back. It had seen better days. *I* had seen better days.

"*Patientia beneficium qui exspecto,*" Pender said to me by way of greeting.

I hesitated, and then inclined my head a fraction. "So I've heard." It was an old society saying: those who watch reap the rewards of patience.

"I should leave you in custody, Mr. Markham." His eyes tracked the cars on the road, registering and cataloguing. "Drop you in a hole; forget about you for a few days." The echo in his voice said it all. *A few days.* He finally looked at me. A grim smile flattened his lips. "But what would I learn from watching you in a small box?"

"My sleeping habits," I said.

"Exactly, and I don't really care much about them. I'm more interested in what you do when you're awake, when you are on the prowl." He looked at the street again. "Besides, how far do you think you can run?"

"Far enough," I said.

He nodded at that. "Probably. But that wouldn't solve your local problem now, would it?"

"No."

His voice dropped to a feigned stage whisper. "So what's to be gained by running?"

He had a point. One that had been nagging at me while I was in the room. If I bolted and went to ground, I could probably disappear. I had done it once before.

But she's here, the Chorus reminded me, tugging at my groin, lighting up my lower vertebrae. *I was close.* Close enough that I could find her in a day or two. If I got lucky. If Pender watched, and didn't act. If he waited to call Paris. If...

A feral smile tugged at my lips, as the series of possibilities became untenably convoluted. Loops within loops, cycles cutting across each other. And, in that confusion, the simple clarity of all of our actions: I sought to seal the circle of my history; Antoine would come, seeking to do the same for his. We all want resolution, in the end.

You two will always mirror each other.

I pushed aside the memory of that voice from Paris, focusing instead on something the Old Man drilled into us. "*Sapienta est aspicio ut sapiens.*" Wisdom has its way, but only for those who are wise enough to receive it.

Pender smiled at the words. "*Vidui.*"

I'll be watching.

"Wouldn't want it any other way." I walked down the steps to the street. My car was back on the peninsula, parked by the side of the road. It was a long walk, even with the ferry ride across the bay. I didn't need the car so much as I wanted to chase my trail.

The ritual where Doug had been separated from his body had taken place across the bay, out in the woods somewhere. While Pender and his monkeys chewed up Doug's trail in Seattle, I could still find his friends.

I only wanted one of them anyway.

I paused at the sidewalk and looked back. Pender, true to his word, was still Watching. I glanced across the street before I turned toward downtown and the waterfront.

Pender wasn't the only observer. The detective, the man whom Doug had invaded and used to shoot me, was watching too. He was sitting in the car parked across the street.

Most of the rain had blown over the Puget Sound and the city during my incarceration. As I stood on the upper deck of the west-bound ferry, the wind pushing the storm east was a persistent pressure on my face. It smelled clean; the pollution in the air had been dampened down by the rain. I could smell wood smoke and pine trees—rural civilization on the edge of the wild.

The ferry staterooms were too small for me right now, a claustrophobic reaction to the time spent in the tiny room at the police station. I needed to smell the forest and the fresh air; I needed to have my face scoured by the wind. Like soap and water, water and soap. While my father had wanted to cleanse the natural world from his skin, I sought its touch. I needed its blessing.

I had only been in custody for six hours. A sign in itself of Pender's position within the SPD. The man could get things done. Of course, I didn't expect any less of a Watcher in the field.

Eventually, the detective joined me on the upper deck. On my walk down to the ferry terminal, I had tried to make it easy for him to follow me. I didn't want to get all the way out to Bainbridge Island, and discover he hadn't been able to follow my trail.

He was several inches taller than me and a good decade older, with a face permanently creased from exposure to the Seattle weather. His hair was short, and there were patches of gray at his temples, streaks that descended into his wide sideburns. While he still seemed like nothing more than an aged bull awkwardly stuffed into a suit, up close I could read a deep weariness—an infection that ran down into the marrow of his bones.

His overcoat was thick and warm, clearly the one piece of clothing he had put some thought into. Underneath, his suit coat was too light for the season, and his tie was too garish to be anything but a designer knockoff. Solid shoes though. A working man who kept track of the days and weeks. Checkmarks on a calendar, months blacked out as they vanished into history. The steady march toward retirement.

In complete disregard of the ban against smoking in public places, he slipped a cigarette into his mouth and cupped one large hand around the end. I looked at his knuckles as he worked the lighter—an angrier and more misshapen tale told in their knotted surfaces than the story pounded into my hands. Boxer, maybe; football, probably. Given his size, my guess was defensive lineman. Just during college and then he gave it up to chase felons and murderers.

He sucked deeply on the cigarette, making sure the tobacco caught. A blur of smoke flickered out of his mouth and vanished, whisked past his collar by the wind. "Detective John Nicols," he said, offering me his hard hand.

I took it. "Markham."

He smiled. "Yeah, with a first name like yours, I'd stick with just the family name too."

"It's a perfectly good given name," I said. "I even let my friends use it."

"Let's not get ahead of ourselves." He sucked in his cheeks, highlighting the shape of his skull. There were dark circles under his eyes, which had been bright green once but the job—*no, something else*—had dulled the color. Now, though, they twitched and moved like he was tracking shadows and ghosts. Like he was Seeing. "I want to ask you some questions."

"Didn't Pender tell you?"

"Pender…" He made a face like he had just swallowed a bony piece of fish. "The lieutenant is… efficient. He knows the right people, and he knows how to get them to move quickly." His cigarette found his mouth, and his words slipped out around the obstruction. "I'm on administrative leave—with pay—for two weeks. My therapist has already been instructed to double my sessions, and she's already offered to write me a prescription for anti-depressants.

"Patrolman Murphy—the kid you jumped—is off the streets. Got himself a promotion."

"Really?"

"No one is talking about what happened to his fingers. Including Murphy." Nicols removed his cigarette, but didn't look at me. "Way I remember it, you did more than crush his gun, but you wouldn't know it looking at the kid.

"He's smart. This is his lucky break, regardless of what really happened. He's not going to rock the boat. He's going to just forget it, along with everyone else, just like Pender wants. The lieutenant has…" He weighed how much more he wanted to say, how much more he wanted to confide in me. An uncomfortable position for a man like him. He grimaced, deciding I probably already knew more than he did, even though I was the outsider. "Murphy's been hooked. He doesn't realize it yet, does he? Pender isn't one to waste any opportunity that can be leveraged. I've never had any reason to run into the guy—I knew his name, his reputation for being a hard-ass—but it didn't take him long to twist everything to…"

"His advantage," I finished.

"Yeah."

"It's a carefully cultivated skill," I said.

I had broken bones in Murphy's hand. The patrolman had, whether Pender allowed him to remember it or not, accepted a gift from a Watcher by letting Pender heal his hand—that was most certainly what had been done to sanitize the scene. Such gifts were never free—these were the sorts of favors that would be called due in the receiver's lifetime. Having been exposed to magick, the young officer would be primed to deal with it again. Such agents were useful. But he didn't know what awaited him in this new world, and I doubted Pender planned on telling him. Murphy had been asked to take on a little faith.

"You're apparently too old to be useful," I said. *Or too obstinate.* "You get the 'let's medicate the lunatic' option."

"Yeah, lucky me."

"Are you seeing things, John?" I asked. Not Detective. *John.* Two men sharing things they have in common, sharing *secrets.* Building a bond.

Some of the techniques the Watchers taught their young were worth remembering. Hell, Nicols probably knew a few of them himself. Probably had been shown them by his mentor when he came on the force. Thus was ever the way secret knowledge passed from generation to generation.

He looked at me, and then his gaze skipped away as if I were too shiny to look at for very long. "At first," he said, "it was just a weird glitter, like being outside on a sunny day without sunglasses. Everything seemed shinier than it should be. But it's getting worse. Now people are starting to glow. From their eyes."

The windows to the soul. Trite, but true: the eyes were the most light-sensitive route to the soul. You could hide beneath the flesh, but it was more difficult to hood the eyes. "What else?" I asked. *Could he see the flow?*

He gestured toward the front of the boat. "I see a big stripe in the water. It runs right beneath the boat. Like we're following it."

Doug's possession had been brutal enough that Nicols' vision had been torn wide open, a huge rift in the protective layer over his psyche. He was Seeing too much and he couldn't turn it off. "It's called a ley line. Spelled L-E-Y. There are natural ones—geomantic lines formed by the magnetic fields of the planet—and there are the ones we make by traveling over the same route again and again."

"So I'm seeing some sort of energy pattern?"

"More of a grid. A framework of flow. We're all part of it. Our first roads followed the natural lines. As we became more forceful with our own desires, we strayed from the leys, and started creating our own tracks. Over time, the constant passage of human energy along a new path causes a shift in the Earth's geomantic fields. The ley moves to correspond to the new route. You can't escape entropy, Detective. All systems move to a state of least resistance."

"And I'm seeing all of this because of what happened on the boat."

"What do you think happened on the boat?"

He looked at me, squinting as the Chorus lit up the narrow choker about my throat, as I let him See the coiled energy in me. He needed an anchor, some place he could ground himself so he could start to understand his altered sight, and I showed him mine—the strands of hair twisted and woven into a tight braid permanently bound to my skin. "Who's Doug?" he asked. "And why do I know him?"

"Because you two were sharing the same space for a little while. Doug was the guy who assaulted your body and tried to push out your spirit."

"My spirit?"

"Your soul."

He laughed, a guttural cough that trailed off as he put his cigarette in his mouth. "My soul," he said as he exhaled, smoke dribbling from his mouth. "Are you shitting me?"

"I have better things to do, Detective." Formal now. Cold. The door to my secrets closed. Make him reach for it, make him try to pry it open again. Make him realize he wants to know what secrets I have to offer.

He chewed on the end of his cigarette awhile, struggling to decide what he could believe, what he thought possible, and what would help him to understand the streams of light he was Seeing. I let him work to his own conclusion, to his own understanding. I never forgot my first night—how my sight had been ablaze with light and color, everything had been richer and fuller than it had any right to be. How the woods had been so *alive*. And yet, beneath all that glitter, how dark the belly of the world.

"This is what happens when a soul is attacked." Give him a glimpse now. A little flash of what he wanted. "You become more aware of your surroundings; you become sensitive to the energies of the world."

"Everyone can see like this?"

"Sure. But not everyone wants to. Nor do they need to."

"If I try hard enough, it'll go away? Sort of like selective blindness?"

" 'It' won't go anywhere. You'll just stop Seeing the lines. Just because you don't understand or believe in something doesn't negate its existence. Your brain records a great deal of sensory data which *you*—the part you think of as 'yourself'—don't bother processing. You've decided—consciously or unconsciously—that you don't need to See. Therefore, you don't."

"If it doesn't go away?"

I shrugged. Choices: some we make for ourselves, some are made for us; what defines us is how we react. Opportunities or obstacles. Ten years ago, I could have tried to blind myself; I could have ignored the cold hole in my chest, and maybe it would have gone away. Maybe. More likely, I would have just stopped feeling it, but that didn't mean it wasn't still there. That it wouldn't have killed me.

"What if I fight it?"

"What is there to fight? You going to dig out your eyes with a spoon?"

He snorted smoke out of his nose. "This is such bullshit."

"Sure it is, which is why you came crying to me."

His eyes narrowed and, for an instant, I saw the bull that had terrorized the offensive line and, later, was used to a similar effect on criminals. "I should throw your ass back into that holding room."

"For what? Because I haven't said, 'Oh boo hoo, Mr. Police Man. I'm so sorry you got something in your eye. Let me get some holy water and just wash that nasty gunk right out.'" I tapped the pockets of my coat. "Gee, I must have lost my supply when those cops were dog-piling on me this morning. One of the other officers must have picked it up and neglected to log it in with my personal effects."

His face reddened as he thought about wrapping those big hands of his around my neck. He considered tossing me off the heaving ferry. I knew the tension that pulled at the corners of his eyes. A similar insanity moved in the darkness beneath the Chorus, a pernicious tendency toward violence.

The darkness had been quiet for a long time, but it had bubbled up this morning with Murphy and the gun. I had been frustrated at being denied the chance to find Kat, and I had listened to *them*. The Chorus had influenced me. It had happened before when I had stumbled upon Kat's trail, but it had been stronger this morning. As if her proximity gave them more strength over me.

As if a secret part of me agreed with their whispers and insinuations; as if, in the end, I was no different from any of them that I had taken. Blood stains everything. Maybe we can hide the visible marks—scour our hands clean—but a secret taint remains.

"Look," I said, swallowing the shiver rising in my throat. "I am sorry this happened to you. Really. It wasn't my choice. But I can't turn back time, and I can't make you blind again. You either deal or you don't. But, either way, it's not my problem, okay?"

He needed just a push, really, to put him on the right path. I wasn't interested in coddling him during this awkward time of lost innocence; nor was his temperament suited to being sheltered from the hard truths. I figured Detective Nicols for a man of action. All he really wanted was knowledge, useful information that would help him make informed decisions. He wanted to trust his senses, wanted to comprehend what they were telling him. He didn't have to understand why the world worked as it did; he just wanted to understand the rules.

He fumed a little longer, suffering the bite of my words until he, too, realized my intent. His jaw worked, muscles flexing in his cheeks, as he swallowed the bitter words half-formed in his mouth. "All right," he said. "I'll deal with it. It would help if I had a name for IT."

"There are a lot of names. Call it 'magick.' That's easy enough."

"Magic?"

"With a 'k.'"

"The 'too cool for school' spelling?"

"Because it isn't card tricks and rabbits in hats. It's not about pulling coins from the ears of eight-year-olds or stringing fifty scarves out of your sleeve. There are a hundred schools of the 'Arts' that are known, and another hundred that are lost, hidden, or otherwise obscured. But they're all part of the same Universe, part of the same system. We are the agents who effect Change. It is our Wills that alter the elements. Magick is a generic term that covers the whole spectrum whether you believe in the Power of God as defined by the Catholic Church, the strength of Allah as envisioned by the Muslims, the Kabbalistic God or the Hermetic God, the God in the Machine or the God in the Wood. Whether your holy text is the Koran, the Torah, the Bible, the *Necronomicon, Liber Null,* or *The Book of the Law.* It doesn't matter. They're all the same."

"They're all right?"

"They're all wrong. 'Nothing is true, everything is possible.'"

"What the hell does that mean?"

I laughed. "It's an old saying that we magi like to toss at one another in that chin-stroking way of saying, 'Ah, yes, I understand the secrets.' It's nearly as ubiquitous as 'As above, so below.'"

He angrily jabbed his cigarette in my direction. "Now you are just fucking with me."

"No, I'm trying to tell you that what *you* believe is equally as important as anything I might tell you. 'Magick' is just a word. Like 'belief,' or 'science.' It only has the meaning you give it. If I can demonstrate and re-create a phenomenon through reasoned and quantifiable steps, you would say that I have 'scientifically' verified the existence of this phenomenon. If you required faith to understand the phenomenon, it would be an act of magick. The terms are subjective to the viewer."

I pointed toward the water, at the silver track only he and I could see running in front of the ferry. "If you told someone about the lines—someone who couldn't See them like you do now—for them to believe you, they would have to accept the validity of your statement on faith. But we See them. It is sensory data that we independently observe and agree upon. Why isn't this 'science'? It's data we measure, it is a phenomenon, evidence based on verifiable data. Why do you think of it as 'magick'? And does that lessen its 'truth' in any way?"

"We could be imagining these lines. Some sort of shared hallucination."

I laughed again. "All existence is a hallucination, Detective, brought about by our persistent state of suffering. It's the first thing young Buddhists are taught."

He didn't share my amusement. "What about the guy on the boat? The guy who got into me." He hid his discomfort by a heavy drag on his shortened cigarette.

"We are filled with Divine Light," I said. "An old occultist once said that every man and woman is a star, a singular point of light set in the infinite night sky. Our light—our spark—is contained by a shell of flesh. This is our vessel. The French philosopher Descartes called our bodies 'bête machines,' autonomous constructs that run without conscious thought."

"Wait a second. Wasn't Descartes the one who said, 'I think, therefore I am'?"

"He did. Is affirmation of 'Mind' somehow contradictory to the idea of a shell of flesh that we inhabit?"

"But he was affirming the nature of doubt, Markham. He said that he existed because he could doubt the existence of his perceptions. You're telling me to accept what I'm seeing on faith." He poked his cigarette stub at me. "Why should I accept that? Why shouldn't I demand a rational explanation for magick?"

"Okay, go ahead. Demand it. Force me to tell you the Universal Truth."

His cigarette paused.

"The trouble with Descartes," I explained, "is that he, while being the daddy of modern philosophy, killed the concept of faith which had informed alchemical thinking for the last eight hundred years. His 'I' is the presence of the thinker. It grounds you in space. His *Meditations* were full of such rot. The realization of existence within the self grounds the self as an object. It is the first point around which the rest of the Universe is defined. Self-knowledge implies position because you now have a spot from which to look beyond self. This egocentric ideology denies us the opportunity to be *not-self*.

"Magick is simply the action of your Will on what is not-self. Until you understand that concept, yes, you must have faith. Until, if you want to cling to Descartes, you have no doubt about what I am telling you."

"Christ." He rubbed at his forehead. "Okay. So, faith. I believe in the Divine Spark. Yes, I do. Yes, it fills my vessel. What's the catch?"

"You can remove the light from a vessel, and the shell—for a brief period of time—will continue to function."

"If you can take a soul out of a shell, then you can put another one in." It was a minor step, but something just clicked for Nicols. A couple of pieces fit together in his head, and he took several steps closer to being free.

"It's just flesh," I said. "Too, too mutable flesh. 'Possession' is simply the act of inhabiting a shell when the true resident has not abandoned that flesh. The spiritual intruder attempts to wrest control from the ingrained control mechanism."

Nicols nodded. "He fired the gun. I had no control over my hands. As much as I wanted otherwise, my finger just squeezed that trigger."

"It was a smart move to drop the gun. Even though you didn't understand what was happening, you could still fight it. The urge to survive is coded pretty deep. Doug got enough control to fire the gun, but as long as you fought back, he didn't have full access." The detective's physique and sports history had helped him. He knew how to bind his flesh to his Will and keep functioning when he had sustained an injury on the field. Doug's possession had been a lucky stab through a small crack, an opening Nicols was starting to realize how to close.

"Why do it?" Nicols asked. "Why would someone want to do this?"

"It's a simple reason: flesh doesn't last. Bones break, skin tears, your organs turn into cancer farms; after sixty years or so, everything starts to wear out. Hell, your physical peak was, what? Your mid-twenties? After that, it's all downhill—a rate of decay you can slow but you can't stop. What if a new body—a fresh sack of meat—just meant moving your soul from one shell to another?"

Nicols thought about immortality; he gave some thought to the idea of living forever, of being indestructible. Who hadn't? It was the Philosopher's Stone of alchemical research, the Holy Grail sought by treasure hunters and students of the material occult mysteries. Immortality didn't just mean a lifetime without end, it also meant having the purest freedom in which to contemplate the Word of God. Alpha and Omega, and everything in between. Immortality opened up your mind on a scale that could—potentially—comprehend God.

But it was an illusory pursuit, really. "Immortality" was nagged by questions that refused to be easily dismissed: entropy happens; everything has an end as well as a beginning; and God, by whatever definition chosen, was the equivalent of Infinity, and no metaphysicist had ever adequately wrapped their mind around that concept.

Still, that didn't stop generations of occultists from trying to find answers to the question posed by Immortality. Sometimes having the goal was as good as reaching it; the quest gave the aspirant something to fixate on, a direction for their lives. There was a sort of immortality in that, a persistence of existence that came from such an endless search.

"Are you looking for Immortality?" he asked.

"Me?" I shook my head.

"Why not?"

"When the novelty of being able to See wears off and you start paying attention, you'll start to understand that everything is energy. All of it. 'Immortality' implies a persistence of vision, a permanence of Ego. That runs somewhat counter to the Universe's insistence on change."

He chewed on the inside of his cheek. "What's your interest in this guy who possessed me?"

"I saw him in the woods, when he was possessing a deer. Surprised us both, and he took off before we could talk."

"Talk about what?"

"He has some information I need."

"That's it? All that on the boat just because you wanted to talk?"

"He didn't understand what I wanted. He didn't stop to listen."

"Why was he running?"

I didn't answer that question, and Nicols stared at me for a long time. He wasn't looking at the flicker of the Chorus in my eyes or the sheen of light on my skin. He was watching me with his cop eyes, studying my human frailties, my unconscious tells and ticks, which would tell him a story that would make sense to his profane knowledge of the Universe.

"Is that why you're heading out here? I thought he went into the city?"

"He did."

He took a final pull on his cigarette. "You told Pender about him, didn't you?" When I didn't answer, he dropped the cigarette on the deck and ground it out. "Yeah, you gave him up. That was the deal you cut. And now Pender's chasing him." He smiled at me. "But it isn't him you're interested in. You want his friends."

"One of them." The Chorus hissed, a black fog in my belly rising up toward my throat, toward my head.

His eyes went to the approaching shoreline. "It happened in a barn," he said. "I have memories that aren't mine. They're like weak Polaroids, snapshots from a trip I didn't take. There's a red barn out there. It's old, hasn't been used to store anything for some time. That's where they did it."

I nodded. I had the same memories, the same trail had been left in my head by Doug's passage. Nicols didn't understand the images in his head, but I did. I knew what they had done in that barn. I knew what rituals had been conducted.

Not so different from another ceremony performed a long time ago. Unlike Doug, there had been no path for me to follow. No one to take my hand and guide me. Just an innocent child, abandoned to the darkness.

VI

A tow truck had absconded with my rental car—a reminder from Pender of his omnipresence—so we stayed with Nicols' car, tracing out routes with the *Thomas Guide* he had in the vehicle. He lived on the Olympic peninsula, and had a fairly detailed knowledge of the roads that were just thin lines on the pages. It still took several hours and a few false starts before we established a better sense of what we were looking for. "Police work," Nicols said after the third barn, "is all about checking every possibility. It's the drudgery that no one expects us to have the tenacity to do, but it is why we get things done. Ultimately you run out of options. You just have to be patient."

Patientia beneficium. I had never been good at waiting.

Nicols shared some of my restlessness. It was at odds with the terminal weariness soaked into the shape of his face but, as I watched the way his eyes flicked away whenever he looked at me, I realized the source of his unease. I was his occult anchor; at the same time, I was alien—bright and shiny in a way nothing ever had been before.

Shortly after sunset, we finally spotted a match for the barn we carried in our heads. A row of ragged evergreens hid the building from the highway, a natural barrier obscuring the property from casual view. We only spotted it because we were on an access road, looking for a way back to the main highway.

The barn had been red once, like all barns built as historical symbols of an anachronistic American cultural heritage. Time and the insistent Pacific Northwest weather had turned this one dull and scarred, like it was covered in old blood. It was fronted by a decrepit farmhouse, squatting like a sullen toad at the end of a woefully uneven gravel driveway.

Nicols pulled the car up to the farmhouse, headlights transmuting the cracked paint into a wrinkled layer of old skin. As he looked in the glove box for a flashlight, I got out and listened. Night was spreading fast, purple to blue-black like a bruise stretching across the skin of Heaven, and the nocturnal world was waking up.

The hiss of the highway was a distant sizzle beyond the row of evergreens. Energy flow along the ley beneath the road was a thin trickle, fading to near nothingness in the distance between cars. An owl hooted at us from the tall trees behind the barn, a solitary call that was more a querulous inquiry than a territorial warning.

Having found his flashlight, Nicols swung its beam across the front of the farmhouse. The windows were boarded over, and the front door was sealed by several clumsily nailed two-by-fours. A "No Trespassing!" sign was attached to the siding beside the door but the faded condition of the letters detracted from the bluster of the message.

The Chorus touched the ley, orienting me on the magnetic poles. The front of the house looked due north, and we walked around the left—the eastern side—of the house to the back. Just as inviting as the front. Nicols examined the slabs of wood nailed over the windows and the back door with his flashlight. I opted for a magickal examination, and let the Chorus read the dilapidated building. Nothing. It was just an abandoned farmhouse, a dead spot on the landscape.

Nicols turned his flashlight toward the nearby barn. He

played his beam across the worn surface of the building for a few seconds, and then clicked off the light. In the darkness of the developing evening, a thin gleam of magick leaked through the warped walls.

Definitely the right barn.

The door was on the west side of the building, and a heavy combination lock held the rickety portal shut. Nicols tugged on the lock once, a half-hearted pull in case it hadn't been closed properly. He stepped back, and glanced at the upper floor of the barn. He was trying to think of some acceptable excuse to kick in the door.

I grabbed the lock while he was rationalizing. *Elide.* The movement of the Chorus in my arm made my skin tingle. The lock held; it was the screws holding the hasp to the door that came out. I tossed the whole assembly aside.

"A little breaking and entering going to bother you?" I asked as I opened the door.

Nicols looked at the lock lying on the scrub grass. "Not as much as how you just did that."

"Just a crowbar of my Will," I said. "Crude, but effective."

"Is that all?" I heard him mutter as he trailed me into the barn.

The barn had no windows on the ground floor, but the interior was illuminated by the phantasmal glow of magickal seals. The barn had been gutted to make room for a ritual platform. It was a large slab of concrete, about three inches thick. It wasn't a single piece, rather blocks about three feet wide—three by three, making it a grid of nine. The platform contained three magickal circles—the central one dominated the space, and the secondaries were laid in opposite corners. The inscriptions along the inner rims were still glowing, the phantom light of residual magick. Drifting in the center of the big circle, coiling upward like a small dust devil, was a wispy column of spirit smoke. More residual energies left behind by the attendees of the ceremony. Left behind by Doug and Katarina.

My chest ached, a chill filling my lungs like atmospheric tension caused by a pressure change. The Chorus slithered along my spine, rising into my head. They wanted that column of smoke, wanted to taste the vibrant lights that had touched each other here.

I swallowed heavily, feeling like a recovering alcoholic who had just found a forgotten bottle of vodka in the freezer. The pressure in my chest didn't lessen as I tried to breathe normally. My lungs were frozen by the resurrection of old memory. I could feel her hand *in* my chest again. The whispers of the Chorus slithered like poison dripped into my ear.

Nicols swung his flashlight toward my face. "Are you all right?" he asked.

I shook my head, stumbling away from the concrete platform. The Chorus erupted as I retreated from the spirit echoes of Katarina and Doug, as I fled from *her*. This was what they wanted. What *I* wanted. Why would I deny them—*myself*—this? Their voices, a shadow conspiracy carried so long. *The taste of her soul,* they hissed, *after all this time. Is this not the cure? Is this not what you need?*

I could taste her on my lips. I could smell her again. *So close.* The tear in my world was so close to being fixed. Like a chain that didn't quite reach. Just a little more, just a little closer, and I could fit the hook into the ready link. Just one more tug.

This need was mine—had always been mine—and yet, was also not-mine. A Buddhist riddle, an existential conundrum bound into my psyche. The Chorus held the memory of that night in the woods. Her hand, in my chest. They reminded me how she had torn my soul. She had ripped out a piece of me; she had let the darkness find a way in.

This memory predated them. This memory was mine, not theirs, and they had taken it into their core. Why? Deep down in the dark where their roots lie, there was something else, a seed—

The vertebrae in my lower back exploded with psychic pain. The Chorus howled in my head, threatening to detonate another psychic payload in my spinal column if I fought them anymore. *Let us—!* They dragged at my leg, trying to make me walk toward the circle.

Magick and mysticism are reflections of the expression of Will. The world is mutable, shaped by the imagination of the magus. His transformation—his ascension—is shaped by the focus of his Will. He acts instead of being reactive. The only prisons that can hold him are the ones he makes himself.

I held my ground, and raised a psychic cage—a black iron prison—around the Chorus. I had taken them all—one by one—and lashed them to each other. I had preserved them, saving them from spiritual dissolution. I was their master; my Will was stronger. They tried a final thrust, but I broke it apart with a needle of force. *My Will.*

I slowly relaxed my fists, the shakes fading. My fingers ached from having been clenched so tightly against my palm. The tension in my chest broke, and my exhalation was a vomit of frost, a gust of cold air spawned by the *Qliphotic* surge within me.

Nicols cleared his throat uneasily. "Ah, yeah, I think maybe I should wait outside." He waved his flashlight toward the ceremonial platform. "You can explain all this to me later."

"I'm okay," I rasped.

He turned the flashlight on my chest. "I dunno," he said. "I know I'm new at this and all, but from over here, it certainly looks like you're not okay. For one thing, you're doing some weird shit to my flashlight beam."

I coughed up a last bit of cold darkness—a wracking hack of sound that was filled with the fury of the Abyss—and the flashlight was knocked from Nicols' hand. "I'm okay," I said, the last touch of the *Qliphoth* fading from my voice.

My eyes were drawn to the spirals of spirit smoke in the center of the circle of power. *It's just a taste. It won't be enough to as-*

suage the hunger. It won't be enough. It will just make you want her more. It'll just feed the need.

But isn't that why you are here? The Chorus retreated, sulking and yet still defiant.

I wasn't sure. For an instant, I had glimpsed something that lay behind them. It was as if I had peeled back the edge of the world, and seen an infinite vastness beneath. In that darkness, I had felt the presence of something watching me.

"Drawing on my extensive knowledge of cheap Showtime thrillers, I'm guessing these are magick circles," Nicols said, a freshly lit cigarette dangling from his lips. The acrid scent of his tobacco disturbed the memory scent of lilacs the Chorus kept looping in my head. I inhaled his secondhand smoke through my nose, welcoming the distraction. "Summoning Balefour, Demon King of the Perpetual Abyss, or some shit?"

"He's a prince, actually. Holds dominion over gnats and stinging bugs. Responsible for plagues, mainly." I smiled slightly at his expression. "I'm kidding."

The Chorus locked down, I carefully approached the platform again. "They help focus the energy of the participants. There are specific types of circles for specific rites. It can get very complicated."

"I'm sure it does," Nicols nodded. He wasn't too sure he liked the idea of me having a sense of humor.

"Doug had his soul pulled out of his body in the big one," I said, ignoring his tone. "He wasn't alone. He had help, and she was assisting him. The other circles are protective, keeping the adepts safe. In case, something goes wrong."

Nicols got close enough to peer at one of the corner circles. Following my lead, he hadn't made any attempt to step onto the platform. "What happens if something does go wrong? What happens to the pair in the middle?"

I flinched, reacting to a poke from the Chorus. A shard of

memory. One of mine. That instant of shock, blisters rising on my skin. Her fingers sliding inside me, like she was putting her hand in JELL-O. My spirit, frantic and desperate to get away from her. I had tried to run—that same instinct-driven response, like Doug in the woods, had been wild and terrified in my body. When she pulled her hand free, all the light began to spill out. Five stars shining on my chest.

"Sometimes people die," I said, pushing the Chorus back, burning the memory away.

"Sometimes?"

"Yeah," I said. "And sometimes that's the kindest thing."

He exhaled a stream of smoke, and watched as it was sucked toward the center of the circle, drawn in by the tiny mystic stain. Nicols had been smoking a long time, and there was enough of him present in that dusty exhalation to be drawn toward the mystical nexus in the circle. His smoke curled upward, winding about the existing spirit spiral like a sycophant eager to please.

"It's a primal attraction," I said as he looked at me with a raised eyebrow. "Systems gravitate to each other. Very little attraction is chemical. Behavioral psychologists would like you to think that we're driven by pheromonal attraction and a promise of hot sex, but actually it's a lot more... alchemical."

I crouched near his feet, and looked intently at the inscribed circle. One of Solomon's—the fourth medal of the Moon, in fact, devoted to protection. There wasn't any additional magick woven into its hollow spaces. There should be something, a protective trigger that kept random strangers like us from intruding. One padlock on a cheap door wasn't a security solution. There had to be something else, especially the way these circles were lit up. They were still holding energy, even if they weren't active. This wasn't a casual installation. They had been using it awhile. *So, where was the booby trap?*

"What's that?" Nicols asked suddenly.

I drew back from the circle. "Where?"

"There. Along the edge." He knelt beside me and pointed to the rim of the platform. "It was just a faint glimmer." Nothing happened as he lowered his finger toward the edge, but when I brought my hand close, the inscription running along the edge glowed, a faint purple luminescence. The esoteric scrip grew bright enough to read as I kept my hand near.

"What does it say?" he asked.

"It's a ward of protection," I said. *There it is.* I wrapped the Chorus in my arm, and touched the surface of the platform. A bright spark cracked when I made contact with the stone, a chain of light and energy shooting up my arm. The Chorus flexed around the current, absorbing and transforming the force, and all I felt was a tingling sensation up to my elbow. "I don't have the key so it rejects me."

Not the most complicated charm to weave. It would take a little while, but a decent adept would be able to put this together. The trick here was how it reacted to magick. Someone like Nicols would be unharmed if he walked on the platform while I would set the stone afire. Which meant it was unstable—volatile, waiting to do damage. I might be able to unravel it, but if I failed, the whole platform would immolate. Probably try to take me too.

The Chorus whined. *No, this is as close as we get.*

Nicols flicked his flashlight beam around the room. "Okay, if we can't get to the circle, then what else is there?" His roving spot illuminated the dry walls of the barn, the empty brackets where horse stalls had once been installed. A broken ladder reached only a few feet down from an upper floor.

A distant crunch of gravel interrupted our examination. Nicols clicked off his flashlight, and I hurried to the door to better hear the sounds coming from outside.

The crunching was slow and regular, a rolling sound that had echoes. "More than one vehicle," I told Nicols as he joined me.

We had visitors.

VII

"Let's go find out who they are," Nicols said.

I grabbed his arm as he squeezed past me. "We have to assume they're the guys who put this here."

Nicols looked at my hand. "I know that," he said. He pulled out of my grip, and reached in his jacket for his gold shield, which he hung around his neck so it was visible on his chest. "I'm not about to go charging around the building with my gun out. I have to assume they're going to respect the shield."

But what if these guys weren't the sort to care about the sanctity of the shield? I kept the question to myself. The thought probably ran through his head every time he pulled the shield out. Still, getting out of the barn before we got pinned inside was an excellent idea. We had more options outside.

As he walked across the yard, Nicols unsnapped the flap on his holster, and his fingers toyed with the butt of his gun. I followed, the Chorus swelling into a plume of aggression. Headlights outlined the front corner of the house, and illuminated the empty field to the west. As Nicols reached the edge of the light, I hung back, clinging to the shadows still wrapped around the side of the house.

Two cars in the drive. It was hard to tell exactly what they were with their lights—brights on, naturally—but it looked like one SUV and one sedan. They formed a right angle—bumper to tailgate—across the driveway, like an open compass bracketing Nicols' vehicle. In the light reflected from the farmhouse, I spotted five men. A mishmash of clothing styles—leather jackets, jeans, long coats. Nothing uniform. Civilians, then, not law enforcement.

Nicols stepped into the light. He raised his flashlight, and caught one of the men in its beam. "Can I help you?" His voice projected a calm and reasoned authority. He was supposed to be here; they were the trespassers.

The guy picked out by Nicols' light swung his right arm behind his back, and it stayed there. Nicols lowered the light to the man's waist, highlighting the fact that he had seen the motion. Nicols' other hand was on the butt of his pistol. He had seen the guy's motion, and rejected it as a casual gesture. The gold shield hanging over his heart flashed in the pale headlights, a wan star that seemed on the verge of going out.

None of the other men moved. Waiting for some signal, whether it came from the man caught in the flashlight beam or from one of the others. It was hard to tell. Nicols appeared to have more patience than any of them, which didn't help the tension of the standoff.

One of them moved finally. A guy in a long dark coat stepped closer to the spray of light from the sedan. His hair seemed like a cap of snow in the reflected light. "We're inspecting our property," he said. I couldn't see his eyes—sunglasses at night, that pointless affectation that did more to signal carelessness than menace—but some of the glow leaked around the edges of the frames as he summoned power. "What brings you out here, Detective?" he asked, referencing the gold shield hanging around Nicols' neck.

"Your barn isn't secure," Nicols said. The Chorus and I smiled at the audacious gambit of his conversation. "You should keep it locked. Vagrants and animals might get inside and disturb your… things." From his pause, it was clear to everyone that

Nicols knew what was inside.

The other man laughed. "Well, you are probably right, Detective." Three of the men inadvertently turned their heads toward their white-headed leader, an unconscious twitch toward a sound that no one heard but the three of them.

Whispering.

It was an arcane bit of magickal ventriloquism, used for centuries when adepts wanted to communicate to each other in situations where vocalization could be dangerous. Whispering was like a point-to-point radio transmission: only the sender and the receiver were party to the words. The tic displayed by the three guys showed their naiveté.

Neophytes.

However, such inexperience with magick wasn't the immediate problem. Though Nicols and I didn't know what he had told them, the gist was clear. The man closest to us swung his arm around, revealing the black shape of a handgun.

I leaped forward, and grabbed the collar of Nicols' jacket. He dropped his flashlight as I hauled him out of the headlight glare. The gun coughed like an angry seal, and chips of wood split from the edge of the house.

"Son of a bitch," Nicols spat in disgust, as he got his back against the wall. His drew his own gun. "A semi-automatic. Whatever happened to cheap revolvers?"

"Couldn't get the job done, I guess." I kept my voice low. The Chorus flushed my surroundings, and generated an overlay of information. "One guy coming," I said to Nicols as I moved in front of him. "Mr. Semi-automatic." My fingers lightly brushed the cracked paint of the wall, the dead frame grounding me, giving me a point about which to swing my army of snakes. "He's got a friend. I can't sense the rest."

"Think they're going around?"

I nodded. "I would."

"Yeah," Nicols muttered. "So would I." He started to sidle

toward the back of the house. I crept in the other direction.

The Chorus sibilated in my throat as I exhaled. I bound them in my hands, pushing them out through my knuckles as glittering spikes of force. As the man crept up on the corner of the house, I held my breath.

He led with the pistol, a quick dart of his arm and head to check our position. He didn't expect to find me just a few inches beyond the barrel of his gun, and he flinched instead of pulling the trigger. I shoved his gun hand through the wall, the wood splintering with a brittle groan as the magick in my fist gave the blow added impetus. He fired the gun once, a quick burst that made a dull spattering noise against the plaster of the inner wall, and then he stopped with the trigger action as I shattered his elbow with my other fist.

The Chorus chased red veins of pain up his arm. They lit his central cortex, amplifying the nerve impulses into an overwhelming rush. He passed out with just a tiny squeak of agony, the plaintive noise a mouse makes as an owl drops on it from a moonless sky and breaks its back.

One down.

The Chorus reacted to a pulse of magick, a night bloom of Will from the front yard. In the back of my mouth, I tasted the acrid hint of old fruit, and I quit trying to extricate the unconscious man's gun from the wall. Nicols was pressed against the house at the back, gun clasped in both hands as he considered a quick glance around the corner. I tried to reach him in time, tried to get my hand on his arm before the spell from the driveway collapsed on us.

An effluvium of dead citrus soured my mouth, and the Chorus flexed in response. I pushed them out, raising a mystical shield against the invisible assault.

The spell actualized with a pop of dead air, and I felt it through my protective ring, felt a tightening in my neck and at the base of my skull as the mystic attack squeezed my lizard brain. I got close to Nicols, but not close enough. The fear spell pulsed over us in the space between two heartbeats, racing through our bodies like an erupting solar flare.

He went stiff, unprotected from such attacks, and panic made his eyes and nostrils widen. The spell wasn't much different than what I had done to the gunman—a psychic assault on the central core of the primeval mind, a blast of inchoate energy targeted for the reptile brain. Even through the protective noise of the Chorus, I felt the wash of bright panic caused by the spell. A threat of fire. Every creature feared fire.

Nicols bolted, a perpendicular course away from the house, straight across the empty field and into the wilderness of the night. His lizard mind had triggered his flight response. He wasn't even aware of why he was running. He just had to get away from the house. He sprinted through the solitary beam of his discarded flashlight, a blur of pant leg and shoe leather, and then he was gone.

I pressed my thumbs into the soft flesh under my jaw, digging toward the bone. The Chorus sparked through my thumbnails. *Colligate. Hic. Nunc.* The invasive strands of panic shattered.

Spark. The Chorus reminded me of the approaching gunman, marking him on my spectral map. The others were beyond the Chorus' touch; at best guess, still circling around the far side of the house. A pincer of gunmen, front and side, closing in on the corner where I stood.

I swallowed a briny mouthful of spit, and made a mad dash across the back yard. I avoided the obvious error of hiding in the barn, and circled around to the far side of the building—the southern side looking at the spindly trees and the distant trickle of headlights.

The Chorus couldn't find Nicols. His trail pointed off across the empty scrub of the surrounding acreage. He hadn't let go of his gun. Even whacked out on phantasmal terror. If I couldn't find him, odds were neither could they. They'd focus on me.

Two, on the left. Glittering stars in my peripheral vision as light-rich bodies came around the eastern edge of the farmhouse. *You like those odds, don't you?* The Chorus slithered through my spine.

As the Chorus tasted the two approaching—adrenaline spikes, elevated heart rates—I did a quick recount in my head. Five, originally, now four: this pair, the guy backing up the one I downed already, and the Whisperer. *Where was he? Where's the magus?*

He could be a real problem. Unmolested, he could be building a spell, something more lethal than the fear bomb he had dropped previously. I didn't have a fix on him.

I moved along the length of the southern wall. The Chorus updated my spectral map, fixing the two glowing dots along the eastern wall of the house. I peeked around the end of the barn, some visual data to flesh out the Chorus' phantasmal map. Chorus-sight made their skin translucent.

The two men cleared the edge of the farmhouse, and carefully picked their way along the back of the house. They were heading for the open door of the barn. I slid out of sight and waited, letting the Chorus keep track of their location while I considered my next move.

The two gunmen were going to check the barn while the third man, the one who had forced me away from the house, kept their rear safe. That was the smart play. Unless I wanted to sneak off behind the trees and hide in the scattered brush, I needed a way to get past these guys.

Nicols was right. Single shot pistols were always easier to deal with. Three guys with semi-automatics was problematic. It would be easier to isolate them, deal with them individually. Pick them off, one by one. But the situation was complicated by the magus. Based on the insistence of his fear spell and the mental acuity it took to Whisper multiple targets, he wasn't a chump. Staying alert for him was going to split my focus.

I crept along the wall of the barn toward the corner nearest the barn door. The Chorus told me all three were in the yard, close to the western face of the barn. As I got close to the end of the wall, they split. A pair of lights getting brighter, one fading.

I faltered, holding my breath. Why the retreat? What did they know?

As the two reached the barn, the Chorus recoiled, flaring into a protective halo. One of the two was a kaleidoscopic flicker. *Layered.* He went into the barn while the other man approached the corner. I didn't have time to figure out what the first man was doing; the second man was going to walk right into me.

I quickly sketched a sigil on my left palm, my finger leaving a faint track on my flesh. I curled my fingers inward, protecting the glowing symbol as the Chorus bled into the inscription, imbuing it with meaning.

The gunman approached the corner cautiously, and before he could take a peek, I stepped out and surprised him. I shoved my left hand toward his face, the fingers of my other hand locked around that wrist. I squeezed my arm, flushing the Chorus down into my palm; he jerked back as the sigil blotted itself over his eyes.

The sigil would only last as long as the retinal afterburn. A few seconds. *Time enough.* I dropped my hands, knocking the barrel of his gun down, and cracked him in the nose with the hard part of my forehead. I felt cartilage snap. The Chorus took advantage of the flesh-to-flesh contact and touched him hard, lighting up the outer edge of his soul. His hands twitched, fingers loosening about the grip of his pistol, and I took the gun from him.

He staggered, blood flowing from his nose. I hit him in the temple with the butt of the gun, and he collapsed like all of his joints had come undone.

The Chorus felt power bloom from within the barn. They

whined in my head, their hunger flexing against my Will, as I went to the door of the barn. There was a near palpable hum in the air.

The other gunman floated over the stone pedestal, his body covered with a thin film of violet light. His feet dangled several inches off the stone surface. The edge of the platform was bright with runes, the protection spell activated but not triggered. The man faced the door, waiting for me. When I saw his eyes, I understood the layering the Chorus had registered. There was more than one soul in there.

"*Salve.*" Guttural bark, each word punctuated with a wisp of black smoke. The air was heavy with the stench of burning meat. "Your. Attention. Is. Unwelcome."

"It's not you that I'm interested in finding," I said.

A rictus grin stretched his mouth out of shape. "Yes. We. Know." He jerked once, a spasm running the length of his body. His mouth and eyes opened wide as if some internal pressure was forcing itself out. A glittering spiral of light erupted from the holes in his skull, a rising cascade of soul fire. The Chorus, ravenous and violent with need, lunged for the soul as it departed the gunman's body.

I tried to pull them back, realizing what was about to happen. By suddenly withdrawing from the body, the possessor—*the magus!*—had relinquished control. The spell holding him up died as well. The gunman fell on the platform. His skin was still polished with a purple light—the film of magick that had held him aloft.

The protection ward ignited. The white letters split the darkness of the barn, and the Chorus shrieked as the erupting light seared the air. I tried to shape them into something resembling a coherent defense as the ceremonial platform exploded.

The concussion shattered the flimsy walls of the barn. The shock wave tossed me across the yard with the rest of the shattered wood.

The glittering spike of the magus' soul shot up into the night sky like a rocket launch. As I fell, my eyes followed the course of the soul as if it were an angel returning to the bosom of Heaven.

THE SECOND WORK

"Men, weary of the light, took refuge in the shadow of bodily substance; the dream of that void which is filled by God seemed in their eyes to be greater than God Himself, and thus hell was created."

– Eliphas Lévi, *Transcendental Magic*

VIII

I woke face-down on a leather couch. The retinal image of the barn explosion and the soul rising into the sky were slowly replaced with the cracked microcosm of a piece of dyed leather. My ears still rang, a tintinnabulation that reminded me of Tibetan prayer bells. All the aches in my lower body rose to a bottleneck at the base of my skull, a sickening knot that felt like a bag of needles being squeezed when I moved. I reluctantly peeled my face off the sofa, and examined my surroundings.

An oil painting of boats at a fishing terminal hung over a gas fireplace, and the tall windows were covered by floor-length jacquard blinds. A pair of torchiere lamps flanked the leather sofa. One of the lamps was dialed up slightly, and its gentle illumination was the only light in the room. Spartan. No TV, no magazines, no newspaper; no one spent much time in this room.

I sat up slowly, and the knot in my neck loosened. I felt like I was filled with a thin layer of mercury and, as I changed my position, the heavy metal shifted. It rolled down, adding weight to my chest, to my torso, pooling in my hips until they ached even more; then it descended to the bowl of my testicles where it settled like the weight of an anvil on my groin. Nothing like a concussive blast to tenderize the whole body like the heavy bag at a boxing gym.

My coat lay on the floor in a heap. Someone must have thrown it across me like a blanket, and I had knocked it off as I crawled back to consciousness. I bent over to pick the garment up, and winced as my bruised kidneys complained.

The leather of the coat was blistered across the shoulders and back, and it reeked of smoke. The zipper's teeth were melted in several places, and flakes of ash floated off as I inspected the coat. It wasn't much of a coat anymore, and barely qualified as a blanket either.

I left its remains on the couch, and attempted to stand. The mercury sensation rolled down my legs, inflaming my right knee. My feet ballooned as the liquid sensation drained into my heels. I took a few steps, staggering like a drunk clown on stilts, and steadied myself on the mantel. I looked at the brushwork on the oil painting for a while, long enough for my legs to finally admit they would move without drifting.

I went looking for a bathroom, and some clue as to where I was.

In the foyer of the house, a black coat clothed the naked skeleton of a hall tree. I knew that coat. Coupled with the pair of shoes casually discarded on the floor nearby, I figured out whose house this was.

I found the bathroom and, while trying to ignore the stain of blood in my urine, I gave some thought to how I had wound up in Nicols' house. My reflection in the unglamorous mirror looked like a bruised piece of meat.

The front edge of my hair had been singed off, giving me that heroin chic punk-rocker look. Blood on my forehead and cheek lent texture to the layer of soot and dirt caking my face. The only thing still pristine was the cord of braided hair about my throat.

No matter what I did, the cord remained unblemished, unmarked. Reija's perpetual reminder. *What you do is who you are, but your actions are not your prison.*

Finishing at the toilet, I washed off some of the grit, and looked over my clothes. My evening with Father Lenbier had been casual; I hadn't planned on a run in the woods or tussling with the local magi. Levi's, evidently, could withstand a concussion wave and a fireball. My shirt, while a decent cotton blend, hadn't faired as well. Scorched and riddled with holes, it belonged in the same dumpster as my coat. SPD would mistake me for one of Seattle's ubiquitous homeless if I wandered through downtown wearing it.

Having dirtied the only towel in the bathroom and, opting to ditch the shirt, I went searching for a replacement. I found Nicols, also face-down, on the large bed in the master bedroom, which, like the living room, was minimalist to the point of being uninhabited. Most of the clothes I had seen him in were thrown in a pile near the door. Judging by the acrid odor coming off the pile, Nicols had lost control of his bladder during his flight from the farmhouse.

No shame there. At least he had come back. Most never stop running.

A haphazard jumble of men's clothing barely filled a quarter of the walk-in closet. A few dresses, shoved in a corner, huddled awkwardly on wooden hangers as if they had been left by a previous occupant. I pawed through his clothes for a shirt and settled on a hunter-green polo. It was a little long on me, but I shoved it into my pants and called it good.

Nicols' breathing was shallow and quick—on the upswing from some deep REM sleep. I had been quiet while ransacking his closet, and it may have simply been my presence which had disturbed him, but he was starting to wake up. I left the room, and went looking for the kitchen.

Maslow's hierarchy: food, shelter, security. The essentials. Start at the bottom, work on up.

The kitchen was surprisingly upscale: maple cabinets, stainless steel appliances, marble countertops, central island with a vegetable sink. The pale green paint on the walls helped offset the austerity of the cabinets and appliances.

There wasn't much in the refrigerator and pantry. Bagels and cream cheese, if I wanted something moderately close to fresh. Coffee, though, local beans. I puttered around for all the necessary appliances, and got everything toasting and brewing.

While I waited, I read the ferry schedule attached to the fridge with a magnetized advert for gutter cleaning. The digital clock on the microwave read 12:23 a.m. According to the schedule—Bainbridge Island to Seattle—there was one more run tonight. After that, nothing until the early morning.

Along with his car keys and wallet, Nicols' cell phone had been carelessly thrown on the central island. As I was slathering cream cheese on a toasted bagel, the phone started vibrating and glowing.

I checked the readout. Local number, but no Caller ID information. Which meant, among other things, that Nicols didn't have the number in his phone's address book. I watched it wiggle and glow, quivering on the counter like a pinned lightning bug, and eventually, it stopped. As I finished covering the other half of the bagel, the phone buzzed one last time—a petulant hum signaling the arrival of voice mail.

"Who was it?" Nicols asked. He was standing in the doorway to the hall, wearing an FBI t-shirt and a worn pair of dark jeans. He had wandered toward the kitchen with a stealth belied by his size, though the Chorus had felt his approach and had given me advance warning of his arrival.

"Didn't say." I nodded toward the phone. "Left a message though."

He picked up the phone and navigated through the menus to the call log. "SPD," he said as he pressed a button to retrieve his voice mail.

He eyed the shirt I was wearing. A large bruise stained his forehead purple and black like he had been smacked with an eggplant. The circles under his eyes were worse than mine, smudges like thick ash. "My wife—Sarah—liked that color." His eyelids fluttered, a visual tic betraying his effort to bury a memory that was trying to surface. "Thought it looked good on me."

The phone offered him a verbal menu of options and he punched a series of buttons on his phone. More firmly than I thought necessary. I busied myself with finding cups for the freshly brewed coffee.

"Three messages," he said. "Any guesses as to who they're from?"

"Pender."

He nodded, a distracted look on his face as he listened to the first message. I sighed. Pender: Lieutenant in the Metropolitan Division, a Traveler among Watchers. Both of which translated to "pain in the ass." I poured coffee for both of us, and meted out the bagel halves onto two plates. Nicols nodded absently as I slipped a plate and cup onto the counter near his hand.

"First call was a reminder that I was on administrative leave, and that I shouldn't be engaging in any activity that might be construed as official SPD business." He pushed a button to delete the message. "Five hours ago." He listened to the tiny voice captured in his voice mail. "Second one," he said, holding the phone away from his ear. "Not as genial. Sounds a bit pissed, actually."

He deleted the second message, shaking his head. "That one came in, oh, about the time I was pissing myself and trying to break my neck by running across a dark field in the middle of nowhere." He listened to the final message. "Now, he's definitely wound up."

"Any specifics?"

"He's had a call from the Kitsap County Sheriff's office. They're at the farmhouse along with the Rural Fire Department. They've got a burned body and, well, it sounds like parts of another."

I saw again the soul rising out of the third gunman, the abrupt departure leaving the owner disoriented and confused. I wondered if that was what happened to Summers on the boat. When control was ceded back to him, the flesh refused his Will. Their bodies simply immolated in the aftermath of the possessor's exit. Though in the case of the man in the barn, the exploding ward had done much more than simply burn the meat.

"He say anything else?" I asked.

"Wants to know if I'm with you. Says you are now considered a fugitive."

"And?"

He shrugged and closed his phone. Putting it on the counter, he picked up the bagel. "I'm on administrative leave, remember? Pender can't really say shit about how I spend my free time."

"Doesn't that qualify as aiding and abetting?"

"Aiding and abetting what? I wasn't there, remember?" he said around a mouthful of food. "What am I supposed to do about this magick thing? It's not just about me seeing things that—shit—may or may not be there. Something happened to me at the farmhouse—something was done *to me*. What do you a call it? An 'incantation'? A 'spell'?"

"It was a fear spell," I said. "Meant to trigger your flight instinct."

"Sure as hell accomplished that. Why didn't you run?"

I smiled at him. "I'm harder to scare."

"Christ." He took a large sip from the coffee mug. "Okay, so it's like my rookie year in college all over again. Everyone's got more experience; they're bigger, faster, stronger. I'm just fresh meat, in on a scholarship and I barely know how to shave. I've got to take these fuckers down when they come at me. Over and over, until they understand that I'm not leaving the field."

Adapt or die. The simple choice all organisms face when evolution sneaks up on them. Adapt along with the world or be discarded. Nicols was starting to figure it out.

He worked through another bite of bagel. "So what value do I have to you? What do you gain by standing around in my kitchen, eating my food?"

"I don't have a car," I pointed out. "And I'm not entirely sure where I am."

"I doubt either issue is really holding you here."

"Well, there is the fact that you came back to the farmhouse, and picked me up before the sheriff's deputies arrived."

"There is that."

"Of course, those gunman probably would have shot you if I hadn't intervened."

He shrugged. "So we're even."

"Okay."

He stared at my face for a long minute, trying to read my expression, trying to ascertain some secrets that would help him gauge his next step. "When's the last ferry?" he asked finally, pointing his cup at the ferry schedule clipped to the refrigerator door.

"Twelve fifty-five," I said.

"The ferry terminal is a five-minute drive," he said. "And we should be earlier than later to be sure that we get on. My goodwill lasts until that ferry hits Seattle. At which point, either you'll have explained to me exactly what I gain by helping you or I'll be turning you over to Pender."

It was simple, really: magick could do many things, but they all took time. Having access to a police officer, and all the databases that came with the badge, made people-hunting much easier. Much quicker.

But it only worked if I had a willing subject. Nicols' price was an explanation. I could afford to give him one. The question raised by his cooperation niggled at me though: What was *he* getting out of our relationship?

* * *

I sprang for hot chocolate at the convenience store on the way to the ferry terminal. We didn't stick around Nicols' empty house to finish our coffee, and the night had gotten cold. I didn't mention to Nicols that the store had been the place where Doug had jumped Gerald Summers. On the ferry, we stayed in the car, drinking our hot chocolate and fogging up the windows with our conversation.

"So Doug knows this woman Kat?" Nicols was trying to make sense of the cursory history lesson I offered, about why I had been charging through the woods and assaulting people on the ferry.

"She performed the ritual with him. You remember that smoke you saw in the center ring? That was a spirit memory of their incantation together. She was both the fulcrum and the wedge that was used to separate Doug's spirit from his meat shell. To make it happen, she had to bring him to a heightened state of awareness, something closer to no-mind where she could get between his gross body and his spirit form."

"No-mind, eh? Some sort of sex ritual?"

I grimaced, and swallowed the sound in my throat. "Yes."

"This the same thing she did to you?"

I hesitated before answering. My head pounded as the memory came on again, as if there was something pushing behind the tattered images. The ritual circle in the woods, the trees with their dark branches and whitened leaves, the other attendants at the ceremony, the light in her eyes and the light shining from holes in my chest as she removed her hand. The sequence was there—like it always was—but something felt off-kilter. Like I was watching a home movie in slow motion, and had finally started to notice the gaps between the frames.

Nicols took my hesitation as disinterest in answering his question. "That's the basis of the bone you've got to pick with her, isn't it? After ten years, I'm not buying that you're still carrying a torch for this woman. I saw you on the boat, saw how you came after Doug. It's not about being scorned or dumped. It's something deeper."

All the way to my core.

The roots of the Chorus were lost in the dark soil. What gave them sustenance? What fed their need? Was it something other than the soul energy they took?

"Yeah, you don't have to say anything. No one operates in a vacuum, Markham. Especially those who insist that they do. Give me some credit. I've been tracking loners for a long time." His eyes were bright and piercing like a hawk fixed on a lone rabbit out in the middle of a field. He was watching me in his own way, reading me as he read all those who came under his eye as a detective. I had to be careful not to give him reason to pounce on me. I had to be as *honest* as I could.

Why did that word seem so awkward? I looked at my hands as if there was some answer to be found in the patterns on my knuckles.

"My initiation into the world of magick was much like yours," I said. The words came slowly as if I was telling a story I didn't quite know, as if it were someone else's tale. "Sudden and unexpected. Your example earlier about fresh-faced football players is apropos. You're not equipped to play but you've got no choice. If you were just the rookie—the new guy with a couple of years high school experience—then I was… the water boy who got drafted into the game because all the other players were injured. I had no clue, and the whole experience probably should have killed me.

"Kat—Katarina Nouranois, her grandfather emigrated from Greece shortly after World War II—Kat was still a neophyte. She had no business attempting the ritual that night. She was overzealous, and things… got out of control. Before she could effect damage control—if she even knew how—the situation deteriorated, and I was abandoned. I had to figure out how to survive on my own."

He nodded and said nothing, just let the words spill out of me. It's an old saw of his profession: everyone wants to talk; everyone wants to confess their guilty secrets. Self-absolution in a private trinity of sinner, penitent, and priest.

"Every light casts a shadow," I continued. "All routes to enlightenment pass through an inversion of darkness. You have to travel both forward and backward, and some people get lost when they reach that border. They can't let go of their hearts and their minds. They can't destroy their egos. They still have fear. They reach the Abyss, take one look at the Guardian and the path beyond, and they're done. They give up."

"What happened to you?"

"I was left at the edge, completely naked and unprepared. I... fell, I guess, and someone caught me."

"Who?"

The Chorus hissed, uncoiling in my head. Blackness crawled up my spine, and I shivered involuntarily as the frayed edges of my memories filled in. "I won't say his name."

"Why not?"

"Names are powerful, *John Nicols*. They make objects real. They give strength to the imaginary."

"So if you say this name, this... Whatever... will be real?"

"I've seen far less be summoned and bound by the power of its name. I'm not about to give this being any more reason to find me. Remember what I said to you on the boat? Belief is a very big part of magick, John."

"It sounds like a very big pile of horseshit to me." He waved his hand. "Yeah, okay, I know. It's all a matter of subjectivity and perception. Bla bla bla. Whatever. Okay, so you met some mysterious stranger in the wood. What happened next?"

"Afterward, I wandered for a year, trying to figure out what had happened. I came back to Seattle, intent on finding Kat. But she had vanished; I couldn't find any trace of her. So I went east and tried to—" I swallowed the bile raised by the Chorus.

"—educate myself. Survive the best I could."

"It looks like you did pretty well. Must have found the right teachers."

The Chorus flexed in my throat, heat on the back of my tongue. "I have an… unusual learning style. Very immersive."

He grunted. "I suppose that's to be expected. It's probably not much of a stretch to fit you with an obsessive personality profile."

There was no way he would understand what the Chorus was, and how they came to be in my head. Their knowledge became mine. It wasn't a matter of an obsessive focus at all; it was simply an act of absorption. I hadn't spent the last decade learning how to do magick but rather had spent it becoming magick. Each voice of the Chorus brought with it a wealth of arcane knowledge and occult instruction.

Nothing is ever lost; it is simply transformed.

"Occasionally I would find hints of Katarina. I would be in places where she had been recently, but I never got close enough to find a warm trail."

"So what changed?"

"I met someone who knew her." A random intersection of threads. I shook my head. The funny way the world was woven. "I broker antiquities for a living. It's a means to an end. I get to travel regularly, and I get to poke about in old libraries and the dusty corners of forgotten collections. My clients like to be anonymous. They appreciate someone who understands the nature of the transaction, who will grease the pipe from one end to the other. I have an office in Los Angeles, but I'm never there. An agency answers the phone, and takes care of my correspondence. I spend a lot of my time on the road, making deals and moving pieces.

"Most have esoteric or magickal histories, and some are black market items. Usually the buyer wants the acquisition to remain off the radar. I don't ask about provenance, nor do I care how the artifact comes available. I am an unaffiliated third party who can be trusted to move the object from point A to point B, who will never reveal the identity of the seller to the buyer, and vice versa. I have a reputation for good, clean work. I don't advertise; all my business is through personal references.

"What brought me to Seattle was an Assyrian statue. It used to be in the National Museum in Baghdad. But with the chaos in Iraq during the last decade, a number of pieces have been secretly removed in an effort to preserve them."

He raised his eyebrows, a number of questions half-formed on his lips.

"I'm under no illusions as to what I do, John. I know all the arguments about the preservation of cultural heritages, but do you just let these objects be destroyed because you can't protect them from chaos and barbarianism?"

He nodded curtly. "For the sake of argument, we'll pretend that I agree with you on this point."

"The statue was large enough that it couldn't be quietly smuggled into the US. Rather a certain amount of hands-on attention was necessary to ensure all the hurdles were properly cleared. It came on a boat from India, and there was a week's delay while the paperwork was processed by the Port of Seattle—this is all very standard, you realize—and I had a lot of free time on my hands. The buyer invited me out to his house one night to see his collection. It was almost an accident, really, but during the course of the evening's conversation it came up that we both knew Katarina."

"Really? Small world."

"It isn't, actually."

He gave me a thin smile. "I know. Rarely do people run into each other by accident. There's always something in their histories that brings about these happy collisions. An old detective I knew when I was younger used to say: 'There are no coincidences, only convergences.'" He sighed and looked out the window. "Now that I can see these energy lines, it seems even more true."

I acknowledged his point. "According to my buyer, there was a good chance Kat was still in Seattle. I decided to stick around for a while and see if I could find her."

"And when you find her?" His eyes, watching my expression now.

"I don't know," I said. The Chorus twitched behind my eyes, a motion contrary to the innocence of my statement. They had a plan. They had been waiting a long time to taste her. *Take back what was stolen. That was the only way.*

Nicols' extrasensory sight may have seen the flicker of light in my eyes. His face was unreadable—a mask of sagging flesh that gave nothing away except a long-suffering weariness with human frailties and self-deceptions. "This isn't about revenge?"

"Maybe," I admitted. Something moved in my gut like a giant sea creature rising toward the surface of the water. An untoward surge of stomach acid for such a noncommittal word.

Honesty.

"Okay, I appreciate that." He swirled the liquid in his cup and drained the last of the chocolate, his throat working.

My hands knotted themselves in my lap as the Chorus hissed at me. *Do you really need his help? Is it worth the complications?* His contacts with the police department could help me track Doug. His badge could grant me immediate access to places that I would have to otherwise force with magick and the force of my Will. Speed was an issue. Pender had begun to regret letting me go and, if he caught me a second time, he wouldn't make that same mistake again. I needed a shortcut, and Nicols was the closest thing I had.

No other reason? The Chorus tightened in my throat. I swallowed heavily, feeling their knot.

Nicols' hands moved toward his coat pockets, reaching for a cigarette, and then stopped. Someone walked past the front of our car and glanced at us, their eyes like phantasmal fire through the mottled condensation on the windshield.

The soul is a guttering flame sunk within our shells. Its light permeates the flesh, driving away the shadows that live in the heart, liver, and lungs. As the spirit is nourished by Knowledge and Reason—the reoccurring mythological symbols of enlightenment's sacred mysteries—the spark grows stronger, coughing and sputtering into a real flame.

The passage of Doug through Nicols' body had been like a burst of oxygen to a starved flame. A channel had been opened, and fuel had been given to his spirit. But he hadn't been damaged, not like Kat's hand on me. His initiation could be temporary. The pipe could be closed. He could return to the life of a guttering candle, burning so faintly that the back of his head would be forever in shadows.

He deserved a chance to make his own choice.

For a long time, I had lamented the loss of my innocence. Like the children in Blake's poetry, I wanted to be purified and left clean. But that could never happen. Not after what happened in the woods. Even if I stopped using magick, even if I sealed myself off and denied the mystical world, there was still a hole. Things could get out; *things could get in.*

In the end, I had adapted. It was as simple as that. I embraced the darkness as my path toward the light. It was the only way I knew.

One direction, one life. One purpose.

I needed to bury the past. In time, all things must be returned to the earth, planted deep so they can be forgotten. The natural cycle will transform them into something new. Ashes to ashes, dust to dust: the cycle repeats over and again. I was cut off from myself, having been transformed that night into something different than I had ever expected to be. A part of me was taken, and wasn't it right that I got that piece back?

Kat was the link. She was the cosmological demiurge who had

created me. She had ripped open the world, and shown me the darkness that lay behind the stars. I was going to be caught in this unfinished loop until I found her, haunted by what could have been until I closed the cycle and moved on. *Take it back. End the exile. Complete your self.*

The Chorus, always happy to remind me in the simplest language possible.

We all deserve the chance for something new, don't we? An opportunity to save ourselves. Sometimes we have to bury the past—bury our old selves—in order to be reborn.

Le roi est mort. Vive le roi. Such is the cyclical nature of all things. *Such is the way the wheel turns.* Kat had killed me, and I had to return the favor.

Two becoming one. I would remake my own world, once I was whole again.

IX

ack-tracking to Kat died as an option when the barn blew up, obliterating any viable trail. The only remaining option was to find Doug again. While dodging Pender and his surrogate eyes.

Doug would have run back to his real body. Without me on his trail, there was no reason not to return to the flesh he knew. If I was right, then Doug wanted access to his group's inner circle, and completing his rite of separation was the sort of act that came with a promotion. He had to make it back in order to show he was ready for advancement.

The magus at the farmhouse—the white-haired man—was one of Doug's masters, one of the elevated adepts of that group. He had possessed the gunman in the barn just as easily as I could put my hand in a sock. He knew the secrets that Doug so desperately sought.

Your attention is unwelcome. He had known who I was—maybe not my name, but he knew of me—and that meant someone had told him. Best guess was Doug. Just as soon as he had been grounded in his meat again. Who else knew? Had Doug told everyone in the group? *Had he told Kat?*

Would she know it was me? Doug might have plucked some of my identity from when I was binding him. He certainly could offer a physical description. But was it enough to warn her?

I had to find her before she made a decision about that knowledge, before she decided to run.

After getting off the ferry, Nicols made one call while we were waiting in the traffic. By the time we crawled one block along the waterfront—a deluge of vehicles from Pioneer Square was snarling all lanes along the water—he had Doug's essentials.

Traffic thinned out at Pier 70, and Nicols pointed at one of the tall buildings visible on the slope above the bay. "Washburne Tower," he said. "Upscale Belltown condominiums. Doug lives in number 1712. One bedroom condo."

"Drive past" I said. "Let's see who is watching."

"Pender, probably. Or someone who will report to him if we show."

"That won't be a problem."

"No violence."

I smiled at Nicols, a feral grin tainted by the black root of the Chorus. "Of course not."

Nicols merged into traffic flowing up the hill, and turned left onto Second Avenue at the top of the rise. The Washburne Tower was part of the urban modernization of Seattle's Belltown district—towering residential condominiums replacing the squat brownstones from a half-century ago. The building was a mass of dark angles and a thousand glass eyes staring sightlessly into the night. Sporadic squares of light suggested residents were either still awake or slept with their lights on, afraid of being suspended in darkness.

Nicols drove by the building. The ground floor was retail: a coffee shop, a wine bar, a dry cleaner, and a small deli barely big enough for its three coolers of wine and beer. The shops were all closed, lit by neon and recessed security lighting. A quartet of silver-edged doors sat beyond a tiny courtyard of heavily manicured shrubbery. A wide staircase led down to the street. The residential entrance.

Nicols angled his chin toward a cream-colored sedan parked

across the street from the courtyard. Pender's eyes. A pale man with a thin face had his head back against the seat rest. The only thing he was keeping an eye on was the inside of his eyelids.

We circled the block, and Nicols parked on the opposite side of the building. A service alley cut into the geometric symmetry of the building, a narrow slit leading back to a loading area. We crossed the street like phantoms, and melted into the wan shadows of the alley. Sodium lights lit up a short loading dock and wire gate that led into the building's underground parking. Overhead, a pair of security cameras. A trio of green dumpsters and two recycling bins huddled tightly together like they were homeless seeking warmth in numbers, their rubber tops still wet from the recent rain. A card reader rose out of the ground next to the security gate, and a single unmarked door stood between the gate and the short tongue of the loading dock.

Nicols nodded toward the door, drawing my attention to the single keyed lock. "Can you magick it?" he asked.

I nodded, and the Chorus flowed into my palm. Hand against the lock, I felt them glide into the tight fit of the keyhole. I worked the muscles at the base of my fingers, undulating my palm and the Chorus went rigid, filling the empty space around the tumblers. A twist of my wrist to the right and the lock clicked open. We walked in like we owned the place, and Nicols shut the door gently behind us.

Nobody seemed to care. The dimly lit hallway was quiet; the only sound, other than our breathing, was the hum of distant HVAC. Nicols brushed past me, heading for the lobby. We found another unmarked door that put us at the back of the grand foyer, behind the bank of elevators. An open car gaped invitingly, and we slipped onboard like a pair of soft-shoed dancers.

The ride to the seventeenth floor was smooth, and both of us watched the news scrawl on the tiny TV monitor mounted on the inner wall of the elevator cage. Flooding in New Orleans,

Hollywood starlet in rehab, Congressional back-biting: *plus ça change.*

I did the lock trick on the 1712's pair, and we slipped inside Doug's condo to check out his view and the 800 square feet that came with it. Seventeen-twelve was on the northern side of the building, affording us a view of Queen Anne and the Seattle Center. Not much in the way of water or mountain, which meant this condo had been slightly cheaper than the western- or eastern-facing units. Maybe. These days, it was hard to say if that sort of aesthetic detail depressed real estate pricing anymore.

The architecture adhered to the modern minimalist trend still hot in the celebrity gossip magazines—off-white walls with white cabinetry and steel appliances. Personality-bare living waiting for its owner to imprint it. Doug, however, appeared to have very little aptitude for interior design. His only contribution to the décor was a pair of generic Indonesian landscape prints on the living room walls, a flat screen TV hung on the wall between the prints, a couple of glazed vases in the insert over the gas fireplace, and a wildflower calendar in the kitchen. The furniture was Swedish Geometric, straight from the nearest IKEA warehouse, and the contents of the kitchen drawers and cupboards had been bought on the same shopping trip.

Nicols looked in the refrigerator, counted the bottles of spring water and glanced in the crisper to see if anything was still fresh. Two bottles of champagne lay on the top rack. A lonely box of baking soda sat in the back.

Half of the top rack of the dishwasher was filled with teacups, and the bottom rack had two small plates and a handful of silverware. The sink was empty, and the garbage can underneath contained a profusion of Styrofoam and paper to-go cartons. Nicols poked at a few of the containers. "Thai," he said. "A lot of Thai."

"So our boy isn't big on hanging out at home," I said. An old rotary phone—molded plastic that qualified more as a piece of shit from Goodwill than a retro artifact from The Sharper Image catalog—was plugged into the phone jack beneath the wall calendar. He didn't seem to have an answering machine. "It's hooked up to the internal switchboard," Nicols explained, seeing my confusion. "Like every other kid these days, he's completely dependent on his cell phone. This is for the intercom in the lobby." He played with the twisted cord. "The fifty-cent solution."

The vases were molded assembly-line artifacts meant to look hand-made but the "Made in Taiwan" sticker on the bottom ruined that mood. Against the wall opposite the TV, there was a table between two tall bookcases. I did a quick scan of the books in both cases as Nicols went through the two-drawer file cabinet shoved under the desk. Crowley, Mathers, Plotinus' *Enneads,* an abridged version of Frazer's *Golden Bough,* a recent translation of *The Corpus Hermeticum,* Eliade's *Shamanism,* and *The Nag Hammadi* caught my eye. The rest of the "esoteric" titles were the sort of pabulum sold by the case to the local New Age shops. The other case was filled with thrillers, *New York Times* bestsellers, and Oprah's Book Club selections that made one look well-read, and a scattered handful on fly fishing.

"Investment banker," Nicols announced as he found a stash of financial statements. "Looks like he works for a brokerage downtown." He flipped through the pages in a file folder. "Five years now." He glanced at the bookcases. "Anything?"

I shook my head. "Nothing you couldn't buy at Borders. It's mostly stuff the big publishers flooded the market with a few years ago when everyone was talking about New Age Magick, trying to address Pre- and Post-Millennial fears. That sort of bullshit." I swept my hands to include both cases. "Little of it is really useful. It's the sort of collection you'd find in the room of a fourteen-year-old girl who thinks being a wiccan pagan and a lesbian are the same thing. Doug's well beyond the 'let's make a love potion!' crap most of these books offer."

"What about the useful stuff?"

"It's the wrong sort of details. Eliade's *Shamanism* is a good magico-religious overview of the old techniques, but the rituals Doug and the others are doing aren't part of the archaic practices. The couple of Crowley books are better, but they're still filled with distractions and practices which have no bearing on what we saw in the barn.

"Admittedly, these skills aren't going to be publicly available—most of the practical manuscripts were hand-copied, passed from magus to magus. They aren't the sort of thing that you're going to leave haphazardly on a shelf. The last time I had the opportunity to examine a real alchemical text was a year ago in Singapore. A fourteenth-century copy of *Speculum Alchemiae*. The buyer paid more than five hundred thousand dollars for it."

"So if he's really experimenting in radical stuff, why is there so much junk on his shelf?" Nicols asked.

"Exactly. He seems to lead a pretty Spartan existence. Why waste the space on populist crap written for dilettantes?"

Nicols put the folder back in the file cabinet. "He's never here," he sighed. "The DMV records put him at twenty-eight years old. According to his pay stubs, he's making six figures a year. But there's no sign that he's even paying attention to anything. There's not a shred of personality in this place. Might as well hang a 'Vacancy' sign over the door."

"I figured you'd appreciate the décor."

"Why is that?"

"It's not much different than your place."

Nicols sucked at a tooth as he looked around again as if to see the room from a different perspective. "No," he said with some care. "He's never lost anything. This is just a shell that hasn't been filled."

An involuntary shiver ran up my spine. *A shell.* A husk emptied of light and life, one that didn't recognize its lack of humanity.

It just kept breathing and functioning, waiting for something to make it feel less empty. Something to fill it.

"You okay?" Nicols asked, watching me.

"Fine," I replied. "Goose on my grave. That's all."

"Is that something we should worry about?"

"No. Just an old memory."

"Sneaking up on you?"

"Something like that," I muttered, walking toward the bedroom.

A flicker of energy caught my attention, and I stopped in the hallway. A sparkle—glitter on glass—coming from the bathroom. I set the Chorus in a defensive array, and pushed open the half-closed door with one finger. Light flickered from the bathroom mirror, a dancing knot of magick like a captive butterfly under glass.

I felt Nicols at my back. "What is it?"

"Not sure."

The magickal form in the glass didn't have an edge to it, nor was there any sort of signature attached to the flickering charge. It was just a small bundle of energy transfixed beneath the glass, free to twist and shine in its reflective prison. It was a static spell, an incantation caught inside the mirror. Without a regular infusion of energy, it would fade in a few days.

I walked toward the mirror, hand outstretched. Nicols sucked in his breath noisily behind me. The light spun faster as my finger, kissed with the focused fire of the Chorus, approached the glass. When I touched the glass, the mirror cracked. Nicols made even more noise, and I heard the safety-snap on his holster pop open.

"It's all right." I stepped back to the hallway. On the end of my finger, stuck as if it were glued, was an oversized playing card. The back of the deck was stamped with a multicolored Rose Cross, a rainbow pattern of petals arranged at the center. I plucked the card free, and turned it over so Nicols could see its face. Through a veil of geometric patterns, a soldier in green armor struggled with his golden chariot. Tiny cherubs, lashed to the ornate frame with wire and ribbon, were too slight, too ineffectual, to pull the heavy wagon.

"What is it?"

"It's a tarot card. From a deck designed by Aleister Crowley," I said. "It's the Prince of Swords."

He glanced at the broken mirror, trying to process what he had seen: a spark of light drawn through a piece of glass, transformed into a playing card by my touch. How were such things possible?

"It's a message," I said, ignoring the question on his face. "Left for me."

"From Doug?"

"No. From Pender."

He scratched the side of his nose. "Okay, I'm not up on the secret codes. Nor—" His eyes strayed to the broken mirror again. "—the ways you guys leave notes for each other."

"It means Pender knows who I am."

As if the words were a trigger, darkness striped across the face of the card. The corners curled inward, and I let go of the card. It didn't fall; it just vanished into a cloud of dirty vapor. Poof. Leaving nothing but a tiny rain of ash.

X

We would have been happy to find any hint of Doug's extracurricular hobbies: printed emails left carelessly in the trash, a desk calendar with circled dates and cryptic references, notes scribbled in the margins of his esoterica, secret society-style robes and objects of office hidden in a valise shoved in the back of the closet. What we found instead was the not-so-subtle suspicion that the place had been cleaned. The condo had been sanitized by Pender so as to remove any occult impropriety. Now, it was just the empty apartment of an energetic investment banker who spent most of his time chasing clients, spending money, and reading pop magic books. Nothing more.

After the dismal return on breaking the law at Doug's, Nicols insisted on getting something to eat. We repaired to the nearest 24-hour restaurant—Minnie's on the corner of First and Denny. Caffeine and starch. Post-midnight brain food.

I was having trouble sitting still as Nicols looked over the menu. My lower intestine was busy knotting itself over the fact that the hunt for Kat was going to have to be abandoned. My small window of opportunity had closed. The back trail was gone, and not only was Pender waiting for me, he was already removing what scant clues I had to go on. Doug's group had gone to ground. I didn't have the time to look under every rock.

No way to them. No way to her.

Seattle wasn't safe anymore. The psychic card in Doug's condo meant Pender had made contact with Paris. The Prince of Swords was the sign that he knew my history, knew what had happened between Antoine and me. *He is coming.* That was the message of the card.

My stomach took on some of the tension in my lower intestine, the Chorus clawing its way up through my torso. *So close. She's so close.*

"All right," Nicols said, jarring my internal confusion. "Let's hear it."

"Which?" Why was the Chorus nipping at me like this? They could be persistent, but never as overt as this. It had first started at the barn, and I tried to recall the sensation I had felt there. Hidden layers. The false reality of the surface, like the glassy mirror of a still lake. The sense of awareness underneath.

Could they hide something from me?

"Why you're running from Pender. What that card means. The whole story."

"Why?" *Why were they pushing me?*

"Because you're getting ready to bail on me. I step away to use the restroom, and you'll be gone when I get back. Just like that card. You keep looking out the window like you're expecting someone, like you're waiting for a signal to run."

"What if I am?"

"Where does that leave me?"

I exhaled, trying to remember the *pranayama* technique from yesterday morning. "Did I ever give you the impression that I needed a side-kick?"

"No, goddamnit," Nicols growled, "that's not what I'm talking about. Pender. What am I going to do about him?"

"Ignore him," I sighed painfully. "He's only interested in me."

His response was aborted by the arrival of the waitress with a pot of coffee. She managed to pour coffee and take our order with one eye closed as if she had woken up moments ago.

"I can't ignore him," Nicols said after she left. "He works for someone else. It took me a while, but it finally dawned on me that a guy like him—a guy in charge of making problems disappear—wouldn't do it because he's a generous spirit. He does magickal clean-up because that's *his job,* which means he's got a different chain of command." Nicols smacked the table with his thumb. "His interests aren't mine, aren't SPD's. He'd fuck us all in order to serve his real boss, wouldn't he?"

I shrugged, a "Wouldn't we all?" dismissal of his question.

"You can run and hide. I don't give a shit really. But I don't think it's Pender you're worried about. He's not the one who has the hooks in you. There's something else going on. But hey—" he spread his hands "—not *my* problem. I'll be quiet. Just sit here until my eyesight clears up, and everything goes back to normal."

I stared at him until he put his hands back on the table. "It's Pender's boss that has you spooked," he said. "And he's coming here, isn't he?"

I tried to repeat my earlier shrug of dismissal, but couldn't pull it off. The gesture turned into an involuntary shiver.

"Pender is a member of an organization known as the *La Société Lumineuse,*" I started. "They're based in Paris, and their job is to watch. Watch and protect. Magick is supposed to remain… hidden. Outside of Paris, we call them 'Watchers,' and they've got agents everywhere. Their allegiances are to the organization, regardless of their local affiliations. Yeah, Pender would drive a car over you if it served his larger purpose. The Watchers are… both myopic and zealous." *To put it generously.*

"What about you? What are your allegiances?"

"Pender called me a *veneficus* during my interrogation. Latin, and it means both 'poisonous' and 'sorcerer,' depending on your need. Though, in my case, I think he meant both meanings.

I'm… without a master."

"What does that mean? You're a rogue?"

I nodded. "I belong to no one—no coven, no order, no society. I've never met one of the Secret Chiefs, and I don't know the special handshake of the Mormon Church. I am a wild card—a child of chaos—and the Watchers don't like the unpredictability of adepts like me… especially when they used to belong to the family."

"They're after you just because you haven't paid your dues?"

"It's more complicated than that."

"I'm sure it is completely byzantine," he said, raising an eyebrow as he sipped from his cup. "So boil it down for me into something resembling a simple explanation."

I looked out the window. It had started raining again. A thin mist streaked the window, and the pools of water in the street were filled with yellow and green reflections. Minnie's was warm, and the smell of grease and burned meat was neatly hidden under an effluvium of gardenia and peppermint. Other than a quartet of young students on the other side of the triangular-shaped room, we were the only customers.

It was nearly 3:00 a.m. on a weeknight. If Antoine was on a flight from Paris already—even if he had gone straight to de Gaulle after hearing from Pender and caught the very next flight to Seattle—it would be midmorning before he arrived. At least.

Getting out of town was easy. One Suggestion to anyone driving north, and I could be across the Canadian border by the time Antoine arrived. Vancouver was large enough to confuse my trail. I could extend my head start there.

That wouldn't deter Antoine though. Not now, not when he knew my death had been faked. Hiding in Vancouver—or anywhere, for that matter—would just delay the inevitable. He'd never stop looking for me. Did I want to run for the rest of my life?

What other choices did I have?

Kill him, the Chorus insisted. Finish what he started. Cut a deal with the Watchers. Face them instead of showing your back. They twitched, sending a ripple of energy up my spine. *Stop running.*

And behind that suggestion lay the ever present lure of finding Kat, of returning the favor done to me a decade ago.

This isn't about revenge?

I tried to shake off Nicols' question from the car, but it was stuck in my head. Revenge? Was that all that drove me?

And Antoine? What do you think drives him? *Is it any different?*

It was like a whole section of the past had been overwritten. We had been seekers of knowledge, students of the arts who only sought to comprehend the luminous divinity of creation. Instead, we had become creatures driven by something as primitive as revenge. Had we drifted so far?

"A few years ago, I was in Paris. Studying to be a Watcher," I told Nicols, choking down these questions as if they were a glob of poisonous bile. "I had made the second rank—Journeyman—and fell in with one of the 'rising stars'—one of the golden children who was slated to ascend far in the ranks. Antoine Briande. He's from a long line of occultists—his father's father and that man's grandfather were both Watchers. Heresy and alchemy are an inextricable part of his heritage, the sort of pedigree that opens all manner of doors to an eager student. Me? I was just a mutt from the streets who showed promise and passion. We had nothing in common but, well, we discovered a common fascination."

"A woman," Nicols offered.

"No," I started, thinking of the philosophical curiosity we had both shared. But that wasn't the truth. Not entirely. "Yes," I corrected. "A woman. Her name was—is—Marielle."

Summoned by my confession, the memory of that last morning in Paris flooded my brain. An act of re-creation brought about by the power of her name. The magick of names, and the power they hold. Over their owners, and over those who believe in them.

Marielle. Standing on the apartment balcony—the stolen hideaway we had tumbled into the night before—blowing soap bubbles toward the morning sun. The dawn of my last day in Paris, the last hour before my relationship with Paris had been severed. All ties cut, with one stroke. Her. My friendship with Antoine. My future with the Watchers. Everything.

I struggled to find my voice, lost as I was in the past. "Antoine invoked an old Law of the organization, and challenged my right to membership. *Ritus concursus*. Trial by combat; I had to prove my worth. He went old school, and demanded a duel with swords. No magick."

"Since you're here, I guess you won. What's the problem? He challenged you."

"Nobody won." I toyed with my silverware, seeing the table knife as a longer, deadlier weapon. "Well, they thought I was dead."

"Ah, I see."

That morning, beside the Seine, on the walkway beneath the Pont Alexandre, Antoine had delivered a decisive stroke, piercing me front to back. The pain had been intense, a febrile fire that had devoured my insides. Somehow I had managed to stay conscious; I had managed to continue fighting. Antoine had been caught off-guard, his sword still stuck in me.

"I took his hand," I told Nicols. "I cut it off before I fell into the Seine. They never found my body."

I could still remember the impact of the river, how it had hungrily filled my mouth and throat in an effort to drag me down to the bottom of its channel. But the Chorus hadn't been willing to die. They had filled my lungs with hard shadows, forcing the water out. The mixture of gore and water in my wound had been transmuted into tender flesh, sealing the hole. Making me whole. *Again.* I had been carried away from the bridges and cathedrals of Paris by the river, a tiny submersible filled with secrets and regrets.

"Antoine couldn't reattach what he couldn't find." I smiled. "My permanent reminder of what he had lost." I had lost both the sword and his hand in the river. *Buried in the mud and muck.*

The waitress approached with our food: eggs, bacon, toast, and home fries for Nicols; eggs and a strawberry waffle for me. She came back with more coffee, and we let the conversation hang for a minute while we ate. Like my existence for the last five years, frozen in place, waiting for resolution to matters interrupted.

There were a lot of other memories of my time there: the endless nights exploring Montmartre; the week I took him climbing in the Pyrenees and showed him how to jump off cliffs; the trip to Chartres with Marielle, where we three finally acknowledged the tension binding us together; or the night spent in the catacombs beneath Paris where Antoine and I faced the ancestral spirits. We had been friends. Until the end. Until our blades had touched. Our bond was dissolved by blood and water, washed away like so much history beneath the bridges of Paris.

I had taken his hand, an irreplaceable part of him. Just like Kat had taken something from me. I knew what he faced every day, what each dawn reminded him: he was not whole. I had created his imperfection. He wouldn't forget.

And maybe in our imperfections was where our innocence died, where we gave up wanting to know the truth of the world. Where we decided, instead, that we would be defined by fear and anger.

"So he wants his pound of flesh?" Nicols asked. "Just like you with Kat. But neither of you will call it what it is. It's just old-school vengeance."

The forkful of strawberry-covered waffle turned to cloying ash in my mouth as the Chorus swarmed up my throat and bled darkness on the back of my tongue. I spit the food out on the side dish where I had scraped the excess whipped cream. The damp mass sizzled through the fluffy mound like a hot rock melting through snow.

Like a magma dome growing in the cone of an ancient volcano, something was rising inside me. Something that fed the Chorus. It had lain in darkness a long time and now, with Kat near—with Antoine coming—it was growing.

Vengeance. Wipe away the hurt by hurting those who wounded you.

I wiped my mouth. "I'm a fallen—" I was going to say "Watcher," but I got caught by the previous word. *Fallen.*

It was Milton who made Lucifer human in *Paradise Lost,* who gave a name to that which consumed the fallen angel. I had read the book in high school, loved it for some reason, and had come back to it several times since. Milton said that Lucifer was consumed by revenge. He wanted to pull down the gates of Heaven because they were closed to him. Not privy to the complete scope of the Father's plan, Lucifer had dared to ask. All those children who dared to question the plan, to peek behind the curtain, to look inside the box, or to eat from the tree: all of them fell from grace.

"Fallen—?" Nicols prodded me to finish the thought.

"Revenge," I said. "It is like Pride, or the sin of Ignorance. It is a failing of the flesh."

He shrugged. "The Catholic Church has been saying that for centuries. I can't believe this is a new concept for you."

"No, that's not it. The Church can't claim to have invented these sins. One of the antecedents of Catholicism was an Egyptian writer named Hermes Trismegistus. His discussion of the soul and the flesh wasn't marred by all the histrionics of organized religion. He argued that demonic influences held sway over the flesh by means of the baser appetites, and that the soul was held back from its reasoned ascension by these influences."

When the Chorus had rescued me in Paris, they had revealed a venomous intent of their own. I hadn't consciously realized how or why they would act in such a way. I had been... distracted, and as quickly as their secret had risen, it had vanished again. Hiding inside me until such time as it could poison me again. This was the source of my desire for revenge, what railed at me now to continue my search for Katarina.

Qliphotic. That old familiar darkness, so comfortable with the idea of vengeance.

Nicols still didn't see my point, and I realized I wasn't articulating it very well because the more I tried to concentrate on the source of my dis-ease, the more it squirmed away from me. Like a shadow trying to avoid a flashlight beam. "The Prince of Swords," I said. "On one level it's a reference to our duel. But on another, a purely symbolic level, it represents Mind without Purpose. The Prince acts, but may not understand why. Revenge, John. We are driven by it, but what is the root of it?"

"Ah, maybe the hand you took?"

I sighed. "Not Antoine. Me." He couldn't see inside my head, couldn't see the way my memory was fraying. "You're right, John. Part of me wants to run and hide from Antoine. But it's an endless cycle. I'll always be running. But another part of me wants to stay, is arguing quite strenuously to stay and fight. Face Antoine because he stands between me and Kat."

"You can't let go of her, can you?"

I shook my head. "And why can't I? Is it just revenge that I want?"

"We all have our demons," he shrugged. "If that's what you're trying to tell me. I get it. I'm not going to absolve you of any action you might take, but I understand it."

"No, I'm not sure this action—this need—is mine." The Chorus tugged at my spine, unease drifting through their rank like dank smoke. "There's something else." I shook my head, trying to shake something that clung. "Uh, maybe. Yes."

"Yes what?"

"Another perspective. I need a second opinion."

"Now?"

"Why not? I don't like the idea of running, but I suddenly don't trust my own motives for staying. I need another opinion. From someone who can more objectively see through me. I need someone who can read the Weave. I need a fortune teller."

XI

Cities, when you can see the ley energies, are generally structured the same: grids oriented to the north-south meridians; flow patterns that move east to east; hot spots surrounding the popular nightclubs; and one or two hubs of concentrated power, bubbling over like artesian wells. Each metropolis, however, has its own character—its own idiosyncrasies and quirks—and the trick to navigating the urban flow was knowing how to acquire a decent map. It's just a matter of commodities trading. As in any modern civilization, the most natural rhythm of all is the ebb and flow of capitalism.

Cab drivers instinctively navigate the flow patterns of the ley whether they are adepts or not; bus drivers sense the knots and whirlpools of radiant energy, their network shifting and adapting to the changing influences. The seemingly random spray of graffiti is actually the hidden key to understanding how the city is carved up, and the midnight taggers are always hungry, eager to share in return for a secret or two. Fortune tellers—the real ones, at any rate—know the local illuminati. They know the covens, the packs, the temples, and the societies; they know which shape and affect the local flow, and which are full of noise and flash.

My local contact was a Georgian fortune teller named Piotr Grieavik. I had met him on my third night in Seattle, and my ability to provide proper remuneration was matched by Piotr's knowledge of the city.

Piotr's shop was a twenty-two-foot Airstream trailer. After nightfall, it would appear in the corner of a parking lot near one of the white energy rivers. Its silver shell would pick up an unnatural gleam under the sodium lights of the parking lot, while the curved front windows would be lit by a warm glow as if the inside of the trailer was coated with amber. In the back window, there would be a curled piece of neon. An intricately woven pair of rings, the red and blue neon light was Piotr's calling card. Lit, he was receiving visitors; dark, he was occupied with a client.

In the early hours of this Wednesday morning, we found Piotr's trailer down near the Fisherman's Terminal in Interbay. The trailer smelled of incense, a bouquet of jasmine and pine that lay heavily on the tongue and helped to mask the smell of the nearby fishing boats. Ornately carved dragons sat in the corners of the central room, their bellies filled with incense cones. Thin strands of smoke drifted lazily from their flared nostrils.

A plush half-moon of a booth took up most of the room. Comfortable seats arced out from the curved walls like a welcoming matronly embrace. Piotr sat on one side of the dark table, playing solitaire with a normal deck of cards.

He was bald and his remaining hair—eyebrows and forearms—was white, stark contrast to the burnished copper of his skin. His teeth were smooth and even, and when he smiled, the wealth of lines creasing his face and hairless head melted away. He talked of a history that went back eighty years—stories of life at sea on a succession of Merchant Marine assignments—but the buoyant lilt of his affected English left you with an impression of youthful naiveté.

"Hello, wolf," he smiled as Nicols and I entered his warm salon. He was wearing dark pants and a crimson shirt beneath a fringed vest adorned with patches and decals of astrological symbols. Fish splashed down the left side of his chest, and a bull wrapped

itself across his right shoulder. His smile broadened as he spotted the bag of candy in my hand. We had stopped at a QFC on
Queen Anne to buy sweets. "What do you have there?"

The basic rule when seeking information from an oracle,
I had told Nicols when I had asked him to stop at the store:
bring a gift.

I put the bag on the table near his half-finished card game.
"Caramels," I said. "A couple of different flavors."

On the top of his discard pile, the card he had turned over as
we had entered: the jack of spades.

He caught my glance, and tapped the card several times with
a blunted forefinger. The top knuckle was missing, as was the
knuckle on the middle finger next to it. Both of them, supposedly lost in a fishing accident, and I hadn't bothered to call him
on his white lie. It was enough that we both knew, just as he
didn't talk about some of my secrets. The cards have a way of
revealing a man.

"The Prince of Swords," he said, giving it its tarot name.

I nodded, not surprised to see the jack. Energy patterns were
coalescing. Coincidences were simply a manifestation of system-
ic orientation. "This is Detective John Nicols," I said, introducing
my companion. "Seattle PD. We're working together."

"Ah," Piotr said. He turned his attention to the sack of
caramels. "There are neophytes in the ranks of SPD now, are
there?"

"Inadvertently. And he's not the first."

Piotr selected a candy and unwrapped it delicately. "No," he
noted, glancing up at Nicols. "Not the first…"

"Have you seen Lt. Pender recently?" Nichols asked.

"Not recently." Piotr smiled at Nicols as he popped the chewy
candy in his mouth. "The lieutenant has a tendency to neglect
my sweet tooth," he explained. "Unlike Markham, who always
brings something."

Nicols nodded, a gracious inclination of his head. The sort

of salute usually reserved for visiting royalty. He was good at reading situations and swallowing his own ego in order to make people comfortable. One of those traits of invisibility so useful to a homicide investigator. "It would appear the lieutenant believes his position exempts him from certain obligations," he said. "And you aren't influenced by his shiny badge now, are you?"

Piotr's smile widened. "Influence is the butterfly which flaps its wings and changes the weather a thousand miles away. Pender is not a butterfly."

"Nor am I," said Nicols. "But I'm starting to wrap my head around the basic concepts of your special style of chaos theory."

Piotr turned his eyes toward me. "When the calf is born, accidental or otherwise, the farmer cannot put it back. The animal must learn how to stand, how to suck from its mother's teat. The farmer may assist the calf when it first learns, but if it is to survive, it must find its own strength. Wouldn't you agree?"

"My dad owned a potato farm," I said. "They didn't need much coddling. You just put them in the ground, and they grew all on their own."

"Ah, the life of the vegetable farmer. So dependent upon the cycles. So trapped by the wheel." Piotr pushed a hand through his game, dissolving them into a haphazard mix of red and black.

The trouble with fortune tellers was their constant exposure to the vicissitudes of chaos, which gave them an unconscious ability to know the course of a thread throughout the Weave. They were oracles, unconscious soothsayers who spoke in enigmas and mysteries. Most of them weren't even aware of the esoteric precognition that underscored their words.

I hadn't told Piotr anything about my past, neither stories of the farm nor anything about my initiation into magick. And yet, he always seemed to be readily aware of my mood and my intentions, as if they were warning labels printed across my chest. *This one is hunting, and has become lost in the woods. Devoured by darkness.*

Piotr's hands, like the brush of palm fronds back and forth, moved across the cards, and they became a deck. He shuffled them twice, and all the cards, regardless of their previous orientation in his motley deck, flipped themselves face-down. The backs of the cards were green with yellow and red lettering—a garish logo for one of the Indian casinos that haunted the curve of I-5 through the tulip fields up north. With a deft motion of his hands, he cut the deck, and turned over the top card of the bottom half of the stack. The jack of spades.

"The jacks are but mere princes," he said. "Swords to spades; the work in the field remains." He put the deck back together and set it aside. "Do you come under the influence of a sword?"

"It's the sword hanging over his head," Nicols offered.

Piotr smiled again. "And you wish to know why your hand isn't on the hilt?"

I nodded. "Yes, I do."

Fortune tellers. I could see a vague shimmer of the Weave when I tried, but real precognition always made my skin itch. A Deterministic Universe was not a model I found very comfortable. I, like Pandora, hoped that Free Will was what was left in the box.

"Please," Piotr said as he stood. "Sit." He crossed to the miniscule kitchenette where he put the deck of playing cards in a drawer. As Nicols and I squeezed ourselves around the other side of the table, Piotr opened a cabinet and got out a wooden box. Inside was a large deck of tarot cards.

The deck was his own design, hand-painted and enchanted over a period of four years. On one of my previous visits, he had told me its history. This was the third deck he had done since coming to the United States. For many years, he had worked menial jobs—washing dishes, picking fruit, detailing cars—and the casting of fortunes was done on the tailgate of pickups, in cramped storage closets, and over upended crates behind gas stations. When he had saved up enough money to open his own shop, he burned the set that had given him life, and made a second, one meant to give him security. The third was meant to show him the way to freedom.

Dark with color, they were based on the original Visconti-Sforza designs that Bonifacio Bembo had painted in the mid-fifteenth century. Piotr's flourishes came from personal knowledge of Persian and Oriental motifs as well as Aleister Crowley's unavoidable influence upon twentieth-century magickal thought. *My efforts to read the world,* Piotr had told me when I had asked about the designs.

He took the deck out of the box and offered it to me. I took the cards, and started to shuffle them. Cold and slick, they stole heat from my fingers as I made them dance cheek to cheek.

"Tea," he asked, and Nicols nodded for both of us, more out of politeness than need. In the cupboards, Piotr found a small teapot and matching china cups—frosty white with tiny inlays of blue fish. He set the kettle to boil, and after putting several spoonfuls of loose tea into the pot, he returned to the table. I laid the shuffled deck between us.

"Do you wish the Prince of Swords to stand for you?" When I declined, he nodded toward the stack of cards. "Usually, I do an arrangement called the Celtic Cross," he said to Nicols as I cut the deck. "It's a ten-card layout that speaks of where the significator—" he inclined his head toward me "—has been and where he is going, and what forces are available—as adversaries and as allies—to him or her. The person requesting the reading has the option to pick a card to represent themselves in the reading, a self-designated avatar, before we start. This will help ground the reading, in that it gives the etheric energy a place to gather."

"So why didn't you use the Prince?" Nicols asked.

"It's not one I would choose for myself," I said. "It's someone else's symbol."

"But it has significance. What did you call it? 'Mind without purpose.'" When I didn't answer, Nicols turned his question to

Piotr. "What does that mean?"

The teakettle started to whistle, and Piotr went to the stove to turn off the heat. "The Prince of Swords represents Unfettered Mind," he said as he filled the teapot with hot water.

A redolence of ginger and mint filled the small room, a fresh scent that reminded me of the crisp Himalayan spring. Using a narrow lacquered tray, he brought the teapot and cups to the table. "The airy part of Air," he continued, "is where the Mind is released from the prison of the body and allowed to act without restriction. The actions of the Mind are based purely on its desires, and it is guided solely by its internal supra-religious logic."

"That's much clearer," Nicols said dryly.

Piotr gave him a tight-lipped smile, a slender movement of his face that was both melancholic and tragic. "These actions are not tempered by Spirit or Body. It isn't Lust; nor is it any of the baser emotions. Mind is simply Intellect. It is Force without Reason."

Nicols looked at me. "The whole reading is going to be like this, isn't it?"

"Most of what I've learned has been like this."

"And here I thought you were being obtuse with me on the ferry just to yank my chain."

I shook my head. "I tried to keep it simple."

"Apparently," he sighed. "Okay, let's pretend I understood what you just said." He pointed at the deck. "Markham opted to pass. So what happens next?"

"His unconscious mind chooses the first card." Piotr's fingers brushed the deck and the top card seemed to turn over on its own accord. A man and a woman stood face to face, and their hands touched cheek and chest of the other. "The Lovers," Piotr said.

Nicols raised an eyebrow. "Now why doesn't that surprise me?"

I wasn't surprised either. I had never drawn the Lovers before, not even when I had specifically been charting a path toward Kat. But now, here, *close enough to touch,* my history with her was overpowering. A burning sensation melted through the lining of my stomach, acid released into my body cavity. I didn't want to face the wrath of Antoine and the Watchers, but the Chorus wanted Kat. *They wanted me to want Kat.*

Piotr placed the card on the table, and picked up the rest of the deck. With a smooth motion like wiping water off a mirror, he laid out five more cards. The first one went down across the Lovers, forming a stubby cross. Then one to the left, one above, one below, and one to the right. He paused, as this was the first part of the Cross. These six cards represented the current situation, and I needed to reflect upon them before looking to the future.

He set the rest of the deck aside, and poured three cups of tea while I considered the cards. Even with his shortened fingers, his grip was firm on the kettle.

Our hands betray us. You can never really escape your past, can you? Ignore it, certainly, but it still haunts you. Always informing the etheric world around you.

The card to the left of the Lovers was the Nine of Swords, beneath was the Eight of Swords, above was the World—the last Major Arcana card. To the right was the Prince of Swords—still caught in my threads, though now it lay in front of me—and laid across the Lovers like a prudish loincloth was the Queen of Cups.

"That's a lot of swords," Nicols noted. He blew on his tea to cool it. "The Eight, the Nine, *and* the Prince again."

Eight was interference, chaos strewn across the path. So many directions, so many currents of flow. They divided the magus' focus, kept him from realizing his Will. *Distractions,* the Chorus whispered. As it lay beneath the Lovers, the Eight was the root of my question. The entanglements of the recent past that had ensnared me. The history from which I sought to extricate myself.

These eight swords were the confusion of *Malkuth*. The black iron prison that prevented us from leveraging Reason to effect our escape from the persistent cupidity of the flesh.

The Nine of Swords, by virtue of being on the left, was my past, that empirical truth that I couldn't escape. This was the realm of the Chorus, that anarchy of cruelty trailing behind me, all the way back to the night in the woods. This card was the world as I remembered it, as I was born into magick on that night of violence and pandemonium. These nine blades, blood-tinged points piercing the earth, were symbolic of my ruptured body.

Kat had broken me and left me in the woods. As my soul bled, leaking light like oil draining from a punctured pan, something had come to me from the shadows. Yes, that was what it was. The *Qliphoth*. Always hiding in the shadows—of the trees, of my thoughts, of my spirit. He had whispered to me, that voice so like the sibilant echo of the Chorus. *There is no hope. You are going to die. Unless…* How cruel the guttering spark of life; how cruel that instinctual craving for light. How tragically *human* was the desire for a second chance. Any path is better than no path at all.… *Let me show you how to live.*

"So many swords," I whispered. I touched the Lovers, my finger drifting across the woman's head and settling on the man's. *Why did you do it?* The card shivered under my touch, slippery and moist.

The Chorus retreated, folding in on themselves as they realized how transparent they had become. So engorged with the desire to find Kat, they had also allowed me to more fully see that part of the past which they had been obscuring. This proximity to Kat, this opportunity afforded me by the brush with Doug and the psychic touch of her presence, was kicking many things loose.

Too many things.

I had let him in. The *Qliphoth* entered through the rupture in my soul, and had shown me how to maintain the illusion of life. The way to retain light, the way to fuel the flesh: these were the secrets of the Chorus.

Piotr tapped the edge of the tray, drawing my attention away from the cards. "The tea," he said, his finger tap-tapping against the lacquer, "is good for the spirit. It calms divergent energies."

The Chorus burned in my throat, bringing tears to my eyes. He didn't flinch from what he saw in my eyes. "It only has the Will you give it," he said gently. "It only has what you feed it."

I blinked, and all the fierce heat was shuttered as if I had shut a furnace door. Lashing my Will to my arm and hand, I—very carefully—reached for the delicate teacup. As I raised it to my lips, Piotr dealt the remaining four cards.

And, like that, the past was gone. Hidden again, beneath the burr of Chorus noise. Beneath the black water in my soul. Like the Loch Ness Monster, all that remained was a nagging impression that *something* had shown its face. Some apparition had surfaced, albeit briefly.

The last four cards of the Cross were a vertical line just to the right of the Prince of Swords—the future as a wall to be surmounted in contrast to the cross of the past and present. From top to bottom: the Five of Wands, the Priestess, the Star, and the Prince of Cups.

"These cards are various aspects of the future," Piotr said to Nicols. "What Markham brings with him to this reading; what affect others will have; what he fears about this possible future; and, ultimately, what this future will be."

"This one is upside down," Nicols said, putting his finger on the Star.

"Please don't turn it," Piotr said. "A reversed card has an equally significant meaning. In this case, it indicates that Markham believes he has no hope of attaining the state represented by the Star."

"'Every man and woman is a star,'" Nicols quoted. "Markham told me that. Yesterday, when I first met him. He said that we were all stars."

"Did he now?"

Crackling ice ran up my spine, and white-light explosions blew off against the nerve clusters in each vertebrae. The Chorus, burning an image with frigid clarity in my brain: a downward-pointing, five-pointed star. A sigil. One without a protective circle. The Chorus strained against their psychic restraints, sensing my confusion. My fingertips were cold, as they assaulted my nervous system.

The Star, reversed. *Refused.* A black hole in the heavens, a break through which the *Qliphoth* slipped into Eden and spat his poisons into the shadows at the base of the Tree. My roots, deep down in *Malkuth*, drank from a lake of venom—killing my legs, deadening my trunk, leaching toxins into my brain.

My hand couldn't hold the teacup, my fingers numb. The tea spilled, and the infused water looked like it was darkened by blood. *Blood in the water.* I tried to breathe, and felt like I was in the Seine again.

I had seen it, and now it couldn't trust me not to dig it out. That shadow of my past erupting through the agency of the Chorus. Blood, black in the water. Black, in the sky.

Then, suggested as an afterimage of the stars exploding along my spine, I saw through the illusion. Through the possibility of illusion. This past that had shaped me, this history I had been bound to—Kat's hand in my chest, the icy stars on my skin, my soul leaking out, the voice in the woods telling me how to live—who had built it? Was it my memory—was I its Creator—or was I just a fool following a path of least resistance? Trismegistus sought to teach his sons how to free themselves from the tyranny of the demonically touched flesh. Reason, in one hand; Insight, in the other.

Had I forsaken both?

I staggered from the table, fleeing the accusatory shape of the cards. My hand fumbled with the handle, and I forced the door open. I fell to my knees on the pavement outside. Cold air on my face, but my throat and lungs were already numb.

Overhead, the sky was black, blank of stars. The world wiped clean. Lost again within that dome of darkness.

I heard the wind, blowing through the rigging of the boats at the dock, and it sounded like the rasp of the leaves against branches. Voices in trees, whispering. *It is done. It is done.*

Close enough to touch.

Our hands, betraying us.

XII

"This looks suspiciously like vagrancy." A voice forced itself into my head. "Or public drunkenness."

I came back to the world of the flesh, struggling to find myself. On my back, face turned toward a star-dappled sky, arms crooked like the wings of a dead albatross. Prickly heat filled my legs, making my ankles and feet ache.

Pender, on my right, wrapped in his long coat. His hands were in his pockets, and his jaw moved precisely around a piece of gum. He looked fresh—pressed and steamed. When he saw that I recognized him, he nudged me with a foot. "Lying about like this," he said. "It's more than a little sloppy. How much have you had to drink tonight, Markham?"

My mouth didn't work; all I could manage was a series of blinks and twitches. He bent down, examining the awkward movement of my face. "Having a seizure?" he asked. "Some ancient LSD payload finally detonating, or has some old curse foisted on you by a weekend witch finally taken root?"

I twisted my head to the side, and spat out a glob of black pitch. Pender wrinkled his nose at the bubble-flecked material from my lungs. "Hate," I croaked. "I'm full up."

"For whom? Your little renegade spirit Doug?" He shook his head. "You aren't interested in him. You want someone else. Doug's just a means to an end, isn't he?"

I swallowed more of the blackness, sending it back into the pit of my unruly stomach. "He's my link."

"I could be your link," he said. "Maybe you're asking the wrong questions of the wrong people. Maybe you're trying too hard to find something that isn't lost."

"Maybe you don't know what you're talking about." Pender stepped back as I levered myself to a sitting position.

He pulled a Polaroid out of his pocket and tossed it in my lap. "Maybe I do." It was a picture of Kat.

Her face had become thinner over the last decade and her hair was shorter, though still streaked with red highlights. It wasn't a face that would launch a thousand ships, but it had filled my dreams—filled my head and consumed everything. Seeing a fresh image of her face, I realized how easy it had been for Paris of Troy to descend into obsessive madness, to fixate on abducting Helen from Sparta as the solution to his brain fever. *Yes, yes, this is the best solution. The simple path is the correct path.* Covering the picture with a cold hand, I tried to put Kat out of my mind; I tried so very hard to quit the past.

"Settle it," he said. "This is a one-time offer."

An involuntary whimper escaped my lips. My insides streaked with black lightning, a volcano erupting in that pit from where the Chorus grew. *Yes. Take back what is yours. Close enough.*

Pender watched me for a few seconds, a smirk pulling at his lips, before he walked away. His car was parked on the far side of the empty lot, and as he opened the door, the interior light flicked on. Before the door shut, I caught a flash of movement in the receding shadows of the back seat. The Chorus still raged within me, still thrust themselves against my Will, but I squeezed them into a knot. Squeezed hard, and focused. As the vehicle left the lot, I strained to part the shadows in the back seat.

He wasn't alone. There was someone else in the car.

"Who was that?" Nicols stood in the doorway of the trailer. "Pender?"

I slumped, barely able to shake my head.

"He just left you here?" He walked toward me.

Shivering, I offered him the Polaroid. I still couldn't speak.

I didn't have to. He looked at the picture for a long time. "This her?" he asked finally. He flipped the picture over. "There's something on the back. 'Scarlet Woman plus Hidden Light equals Beast.' And there are some numbers underneath: 393 + 273 = 605." He paused, doing the math. "That's not right, 393 and 273 add up to 666."

"Six-six-six is the number of the beast," I groaned, the Chorus finally letting go of my voice. "Six-oh-five is the number of my hotel room at the Monaco." The difference was 61. Another message: 61 was *Ain*—the Abyss, the cold darkness where the *Qliphoth* thrived.

"The picture was taken in my hotel room."

Nicols flipped the Polaroid over again to re-examine the portrait. "She's there?"

"She's waiting for me."

Settle it, the Chorus oozed, dripping poison in my ear. I was caught between terror and desire, shivering with the promise of their commingling. *Take it back.* My lost soul, my lost heart. The Lovers, hands on hearts and heads, energy flowing back and forth in an endless loop, mixing themselves together. *This is the way to heal yourself. Make you whole again.*

One path, one direction. Through darkness into light. This was the way promised me.

Were the *Qliphoth* capable of keeping promises? Was the flesh capable of not betraying itself? Was the Word still true if it came from a false Godhead?

God created the Demiurge who, in turn, created the World. God was the Word, and He gave it to the Creator to speak it. And, having made the World, the Demiurge forgot who gave him the power to Create.

Was my world a lie? The history I remembered—so fractured

with dark light—was it a fabrication? Made solely to provide framework for the insistent noise of the Chorus? As I had gotten closer to Kat, they had become more frenzied, more inflamed by... what? A desire for revenge?

But was it deserved? Was it true? There were cracks in their rationale, joints that didn't quite fit. As if the history they purported to be true was actually bolted together—some Frankensteinian construct that wasn't entirely... me. Beneath them, providing direction and intent, was something else. Some other version of reality undimmed by these false memories.

There was only one way to find out. I held out my hand and Nicols, thinking I wanted the picture back, put it into my hand. I shook my head. "I need your car keys."

"I don't think this is a good idea," he replied.

"I don't care what you think."

"You're not rational, Markham. Your obsession with this woman is screwing with your judgment." He gestured toward Piotr's trailer. "I saw you in there. Hell, I saw what happened when you got close to a memory of her at the barn. Your head is all fucked up about this woman, about what you think happened, and it is going to get someone killed."

I got to my feet. "Her?"

"You," he said.

The Chorus churned, finding cause for violence in Nicols' inference. I made to bind them, and they responded by compressing into a lodestone in my chest. A magnetic attraction pulled at me, tugging me south and east. I looked along that axis—straight across the Interbay, right through the whirling globe atop the Seattle Post-Intelligencer building, through Belltown and the curve of the Performance Center—and I could see the phantom shape of my hotel. The Chorus pulsed, and this magnetic line of desire stretched tight between Kat and me. They wanted release. From this conversation, from this damp parking lot. They wanted to run like dogs who had found the scent of their prey.

"Why would Pender give you what you want?" Nicols asked. "What does he gain by doing that?"

"What are you talking about?" The humming sound of the magnetic connection was making it hard to think.

"You said it yourself: they're schemers. The Watchers shape events by influence and manipulation. Do you think this situation is any different?"

I fought the pull in my chest, clinging like a drowning man to Nicols' words. Yes, and the reading Piotr had just thrown. The Eight of Swords had been my foundation. They were the roots entangling me. *Interference.* Obstructions raised by other forces and other agents who would attempt to distract me from my goal. *Perhaps the detective himself is such a distraction,* the Chorus whispered. *You have her. You've been given permission.*

Take it.

I shook my head, shaking off their voices more than denying the truth to Nicols' question. "You think I'm going to kill her."

"Yeah, the thought crossed my mind. Has more than once. I don't think you're stable, Markham; I think there is some serious damage in your brain. But here's the thing—and you should listen to this because I know what the fuck I'm talking about—killing Kat isn't going to fix what's wrong in you."

I held out a hand for the keys. "You don't know anything about me." A black bubble rose in my throat.

"Christ!" he exploded. "You think you're the only one who's had his heart broken?"

"It's not like that."

"No? Because you're certainly acting the part. I've been cleaning up after people for twenty years. When lovers get jealous or angry, when families self-destruct, when people just get stupid: I'm there. I'm the guy who has to see the aftermath; I have to tell parents that someone—a lover, a friend, a sibling—someone just took their baby away from them. You don't think a day doesn't go by when I hear some pathetic fuck whining about how this bitch just broke his heart and so he gave her what she deserved? 'She sucked off the mailman and so I put a gun in her mouth and blew her head off.'"

I flinched, and Nicols jabbed a thick finger at me. "Yeah, last week. That was some gang-banger's entire rationale: *she deserved it*. Three days later, the guy is screaming in his cell, yelling for his dead girlfriend because he's finally realized what an enormous mistake he's made. I can't help him. He's confessed, the evidence has been processed, and the DA has already cut a deal with the nickel-rate public defender assigned to the case. Guy's going to Walla Walla for ten to fifteen. You think that's going to fix the hole in his heart? You think that's going to bring her back?"

The Chorus whined, and I moaned aloud in concert. My legs twitched like a dog's who could see the open fields but knew there was an invisible fence, a radio frequency barrier that would trigger his electric collar if he strayed too far.

"Pender's got nothing on you," Nicols said. "Nothing that will hold up in court. You kill Kat, and he'll have you for murder one. Don't think he's not going to be watching. He'll let you do it—there's no doubt in my mind about that. But as soon as her heart stops beating, he's going to climb so far up your ass that he'll know what you're having for lunch the moment you swallow."

The Chorus slavered, and with an immense effort, I bent them back, driving them away from the febrile edge of my consciousness. My teeth chattered as I tried to speak, my words coming out in fragmented chunks. I closed my outstretched hand, digging fingernails into my palm, and tried again. "I'm lost," I croaked. "Ever since she touched me. I fell onto the *Qliphotic* path and I don't know how to return, John."

"Which path?" He didn't know the word; he was a child, after all, a wide-eyed innocent snatched from the Garden and abandoned in the shifting magickal reality. He didn't know about the Tree and the pathways, about the dark hole through *Daäth* and the nightside of the *Sephiroth*. He didn't know what happens to those who fall.

"I need to find her. She's the key, John; she's my way back."

"How?" he asked. "How is she going to help you?"

The Chorus smiled behind my teeth, black daggers hidden by white enamel. "I need to ask her what really happened. I need to know, John. I need closure."

He looked toward the ambient glow of downtown Seattle. "Yeah," he said quietly. "Don't we all?" He put his hand in his coat pocket. "Okay, this is wrong. I just want that to be clear. I think this is a bad idea." I could hear his hand opening and closing around his keys. "I'll drive."

"Thank you."

He shook his head as if to dislodge my words from his shoulders, like leaves brushed off. "Don't thank me yet," he said. "If you raise a hand at her, I *will* pistol whip you myself."

The foyer around the elevator bay was extended by a niche cut out of the wall opposite. A large mirror and a mahogany George III sofa table, round across the front and topped with a tiny swatch of fabric and a vase of silk flowers, filled the space. The hallway ran both left and right, making right angle turns just beyond the pair of unmarked doors that flanked the foyer niche. Laid out like a square, the halls ran the length of the hotel and then right-angled again to meet on the far side of the floor. My room was halfway down the left hallway. Opposite the turn was the emergency exit, tucked back next to the elevator shaft.

I made it to the right angle, Nicols trailing behind me, when I felt a burn of magick. I turned, rotating the Chorus off my left wrist—a peacock fan of iridescent defense. I tried to shove past Nicols, pushing him toward the indentation of the stairwell door.

The spell pounded me against the wall, the shockwave billowing along the sheetrock, making the sconces flicker and the paint blister. Sound became watery—blood in the ear canal. Gritty steam obscured the hall, and my teeth ached with the taste of tinfoil.

Nicols was on his knees, leaning against the emergency exit door. He rolled over, a grimace of pain knotting his face, as he got his back to the door. He fumbled for his gun and got one shot off, before the twin darts of a Taser gun struck him. I heard—distantly, like the chatter of a flywheel—the Taser discharge, and all the fight went out of Nicols.

There were three of them, outlined in the fog by the Chorus. The bright one in the back was the magus from the farmhouse. I recognized the glittering cascade of his spirit.

I crawled down the hallway. Another Taser coughed, and the plastic darts rattled thinly against the wall behind me. I graduated to scrambling like a dog as the three men breached the forward edge of the fog.

My room—605—was two doors down, and I didn't even bother with the electronic key. I just smashed my hand through the plate assembly with a wedge of the Chorus and shoved the door open. As I ducked into the room, I saw three more men round the far corner of the hallway in front of me.

Surrounded. No way out but through my room. Past Kat.

Who wasn't there.

The lights were off and, even when the Chorus amplified the ambient light leaking around the curtains, it didn't make any difference. I was alone in the hotel room.

I could smell her. *Lilacs.* She had been here. Recently. The Chorus exploded in my heart, daggering into the nerve clusters of my spine, blowing themselves into the chambers of my brain. My bones felt like they were cracking as the Chorus convulsed within me, reacting to her proximity. My vision went blank, *Qliphotic* darkness eating through my brain. I was erupting, detonating the psychic payload I had been carrying these last ten years.

Katarina. Her hand in my chest, squeezing my heart, breaking my light. *Katarina,* a tiny part of me wept, *this is all I have. This is all I am.*

Who am I if it is all untrue?

At my back, the magus hurled a javelin of soul fire. The Chorus—raging and exploding through me—caught the missile, chewed it up, and spat it back at him. What had been a single thrust of soul-charged energy was returned as a hailstorm of black needles. My *Qliphotic* Chorus drove him across the hallway, and I pinned his soul to the wall in a thousand places.

His panic was a wet spray in my head, screaming on multiple layers of perception. "Shoot him! Shoot the son of a bitch already!" Luminescent tears bled from his eyes.

I didn't even feel the first Taser, didn't even react to the discharge of the weapon's voltage. The second pair of darts managed to break the Chorus' concentration. The third pierced the armor of darkness wrapped around my chest and lit my lungs on fire. The fourth turned the world white—*fiat lux*—and I shattered, fragmenting into minute shards of glittering glass, like a disintegrating prism.

This is all I am.

All I ever was, falling.

THE THIRD WORK

"I am the flame that burns in every heart of man, and in the core of every star. I am Life, and the giver of Life, yet therefore is the knowledge of me the knowledge of death."

– Aleister Crowley, *Liber AL vel Legis*

XIII

Somewhere between death and dream, somewhere deep in the twilight of the nightside tree, I rediscovered myself. *Eye within Ain*. With that knowledge came a vision of how to find my way back. Separating light from dark—*quod esset bonum*—I dreamed how to fall and—*it is done*—did so, end over end. A skein of lights hung beneath the gray fingers of a layer of clouds arrested my descent. This net held me, floating. *Like a leaf in the flow.*

As I remembered how to breathe—as the mundane necessities of the meat came back to me—the sea of lights flexed and dipped in concert with the pulsation of my imagination. Was I breathing in time with them, or were they synching to me? Which came first: breathe or desire? With this synchronization came a dimensionality to the sea: valleys began to grow, peaks started to rise, and the lights began to enfold me.

Below me, coursing like arterial flow, was a torrential deluge of spirit lights. Feeding this massive tributary were small streams and rivulets of glowing light, tiny magma tracks that cut jagged paths through weighty darkness.

Distinct from the yellow-white glow of the streams were the peaks, detailed with red and pink and purple lights like stalagmites wrapped with strands of luminescent flowers.

To one side was a rotating light, a red eye that swept across the jeweled landscape. In a plain between two hillocks, the spotlight revealed a flat darkness, a negative space that held no lights.

I turned, and freeing myself from the tangle of lights, moved through the flow until I reached the black stain. The world became more real around me as I glided across the lights. Distantly, I realized this landscape was the spirit map of Seattle. The dark spot was the kinked bean-shape of Lake Union.

As I hovered over the transparent surface, the lambent cyclopean gaze—the light of the Space Needle—glided over the motionless water. Beneath the water, I could see the dim outline of bones—the tangled skeletons of giants.

A pair of bodies, locked in a perpetual embrace, turning slowly in the water. In their right hands were enormous cups, and their left arms were woven through the rib cage of the other, fingers wrapped around the spine of their bony lover. Their skulls were nestled together as if they whispered secrets.

The Needle's eye looked away as my outstretched hand brushed the surface of the water. I felt a cold kiss—phantom memory, ice in my chest—and my fingers were pulled into the lake. As I split the surface of the water, the spirit grid of Seattle vanished. Snuffed out as if they were candles drowned by a wave.

I sank toward the bone lovers. Their cups were identical—flat bases, hexagonal stems, rounded bowls with fluted edges caked with black rust. One held the corpse of a tiny lobster while the other held the coiled husk of a serpent. A lotus flower—petals sumptuously full—was caught in the chest cavity of each body and, as they turned, the flowers remained fixed in place. They were the axis points upon which the corpses spun. A universe founded by two positions in space.

Tiny rubies suddenly dappled the black dome behind me. The jewels blossomed, elongating into stalactites of fire. Hardened and cooled by the elemental touch of water, the fire became long swords, stained with blood.

Nine swords. Not behind the lovers, but above. The swords descended into the water until they touched the rotating bones of the skeletons. Their points cut shallow grooves as the bodies continued to turn.

Beneath the twisted lovers—the layers of the dream extending deeper and deeper into the wet twilight of the psyche—a churning froth bubbled. I fell further into the water, my way lit by the bleeding blades.

I came upon a flat five-spoked wheel. Along its edge were unfinished porcelain faces frozen with stoic expressions. A shrouded corpse wearing a death-mask of hammered steel was lashed to the surface of the slowly rotating wheel. It held a soft and vibrant globe of glowing seas and limned continents.

A rainbow-colored fish floated beside the wheel. A naked cherub, sitting awkwardly astride the fish due to its enormously engorged phallus, was goading the fish toward the corpse. He beat the fish on the head with the rounded knob of his heavy cock. The fish, stunned with every blow, swam erratically, veering to the left every time it was bludgeoned. The cherub, unaware of how his abuse was keeping him from his goal, only beat the fish harder.

As I floated closer, the fish faltered. Its fins fluttered more slowly; a thin ribbon of white ooze drifted from its gasping mouth. It looked in my direction, seeing me in my dream-state, and expired. The cherub furiously beat the fish harder, but this wasn't the way to bring back the dead.

In death, though, the fish drifted closer to the wheel. The cherub leaped from its back, straining to reach the rim of the wheel. Dancing along the thin width of one of the spokes, he minced toward the body strapped to the wheel. He clambered up the shrouded body, and threw himself upon the tiny earth, wrapping his short arms around the luminescent planet. Rearing back like a wild insect, he thrust his fat stinger into the curved side of the planet. Having pierced the earth, he started pumping away at the hole he had made. A priapic demiurge seeding his creation.

The wheel stopped its rotation, and the hands of the corpse came free of the globe. They spread outward until they rested against the curve of the wheel. The palms rotated up. As the cherub raped the glowing planet, a white fluid began to stream from the corpse's hands, like smoke drifting up from an extinguished fire.

I rose with the white ink of the smoke. The underside of the lake's surface was disturbed, the flickering distortion of a bent mirror. On the other side, these twin lines of smoke became substantial. The marbled stone of alabaster flesh. The pillars leaned together, vanishing beneath a diaphanous drapery.

She was a giant, equal in size to the corpses interred in the lake, standing in the water. As I reached for the surface—a reflection of my touch from a few moments earlier when I had been drawn down into the water—she raised her skirt and showed me where the pillars of her legs met. A single eye—a reflection of the lighthouse that watched over the city—gazed down. An inflamed eye—black fire in its iris, blood leaking from its ducts.

As my fingers breached the threshold, below reaching above, nine drops of blood fell. Nine tears splashed into the lake and floated, whole and round, down on the cherub raping the world. The child laughed, reaching with one hand to smear the blood onto his buttocks and thighs. He reached between his legs to slather the blood of the virgin eye—*Nia,* the inversion of *Ain*—onto his hard cock.

I came back, and found myself bound. My hands were numb and locked behind my back. Something covered my eyes, and a hard object was firmly lodged in my mouth. Breathing was difficult as my nose was clogged with dried blood. As the dream vanished, this was what remained: sore, tied, gagged, drugged, and deposited somewhere cold and dark.

I ached all over, as if every muscle had been pulled in the wrong direction. Prickly nettles ground in my joints as I tried to move. My back and feet were cold. Eight points of fire still danced on my skin.

Four Tasers, in the end. The memory came back with more than a little reluctance. Like an archeologist reconstructing the past, I followed the secret history mapped out on my body: four on my chest, two sets of sparking pairs radiating across my upper rib cage like a half-realized constellation; a pair on my right arm like freckles gone bad and cancerous; and a final set on the outward side of my left hip, aching like an old war wound that got stiff when the weather changed.

There was a ninth spot—unlike the others, but still part of this history. On the inside of my right arm, a weeping vacuum nestled in the fleshy valley of the joint. A needle, containing some pharmaceutical cocktail intended to keep me docile and pliable. *How docile?* I reached for the Chorus and it was like clawing through layers of muslin. But they were there, and I could feel them reaching back. The cocktail was wearing off.

I rolled onto my side, and pressed my face against the floor. I had been stripped down to my pants—no shirt, no shoes, no socks—but my face was the only naked flesh not completely numb. The steel was ridged, and in the valleys I could dimly smell the old taint of blood and oil.

I rocked back and forth, dragging my cheek across the ridge. It wasn't sharp, but it was rough enough to catch the edge of the blindfold. Nausea rolled through me, and I stopped. But it was enough. The blindfold had slipped.

The change in illumination was negligible but I had accomplished something. I had changed the situation in my favor. *My Will be Done.* A first step. The rest were easier. I scraped my cheek some more, and the cloth slipped off my eyes entirely. Yes, too dark to see anything, but I didn't need the light.

The object in my mouth was held in place by a heavy strap.

The same method wasn't going to get that off. *Wrists*. I bent my fingers toward my bound wrists until they made contact with the bindings. So little feeling. Was that metal or plastic? I strained further, feeling like I was bending hardwood, and one finger managed to pluck at the edge of whatever was binding my hands. It flexed. *Plastic, just an industrial-grade zip tie.*

Fire. I tried to focus my distorted thoughts on the flame—that incendiary element of change, that alchemical burn. Fire strips away the old, turning the dead into ash and dust—grist for the eventual rebirth of everything. Washed away by fire. *Mahapralaya*. At the end of the Hindu Kali Yuga—this current Age of Iron—the world would be dissolved in fire. The Greeks called it *ekpyrosis,* and as it was translated into the Latin by the heretics, it became *conflagratio*. The World-Fire. When it burned itself out, God would start anew. Yes, *fire,* come to me.

A lick of orange flame guttered in my mind's eye, a spark catching in those dusty memories not yet thrown away. Nineteen, climbing in the North Cascades. Early fall. Nightfall, the temperature dropping quickly. Building a fire. I remembered nursing it to life, coaxing it with tiny branches and dry sticks, and I nursed that memory now in the same way, teasing it out with my Will. From spark to mental vibration to etheric manifestation. My hands grew warm as I directed the fire through my arms and into the bleak winter of my fingers.

A ghost light bloomed in front of me, an external reaction to my spell. Surprised, my focus broke and the tiny flame died. The ghostly lettering vanished almost immediately like a hibernating serpent returning to its winter slumber. But I had read the words. I had recognized them.

Protection sigil, keyed to the presence of magick. Just like the barn. Any strenuous magickal activity and it would explode. Immolation. *Conflagration*. It would have been funnier if I wasn't tied up.

The same spell as the one in the barn, though in this case it was meant to keep things in instead of out.

The ghost light hadn't been much, but in its brief glow, I had been able to pick out a few more details about my prison. The letters had been written on a metal plate attached to a wall that was as corrugated as the floor. A shipping container. I had been in enough of them over the years to recognize that ribbed construction. Just never so up close and personal. From the lack of ambient light, this one must be fairly well sealed. A firestorm would last just a few seconds before all the oxygen was consumed. The threat of such an explosion was a pretty effective deterrent: nowhere to hide, and not enough ambient force to raise a shield against the explosion. A cheap and efficient solution for those who wanted to hold a magus, or kill one slowly. Starvation worked as well as a knife, and it had the benefit of being indirect action. Like the way foreign diplomats in ancient Mongolia were wrapped in furs and rugs before being trampled, so that their sacred blood wouldn't touch the earth and allow their curses to take root.

I flexed my shoulders, pulling at the straps around my wrists. My fire had been hot, although brief, and it might have weakened the restraints. I strained, and the ties parted grudgingly like a string of taffy stretched to its elastic limit. As I kneaded cold skin with equally cold fingers, my hands came alive with the prickly resumption of unobstructed blood flow.

When the nerve endings in my fingertips were warm enough to feel something, I investigated the mechanics of the gag. As my finger slid off the rounded rubber hump protruding from my mouth, I realized it was nothing more than a ball gag. Available in any sex shop. I found the buckle in back, and wincing as I had to pull the belt tighter around my head, I undid the restraint and spit the rubber ball out.

I tossed the whole contraption aside. Not a souvenir I wanted to keep. The metal buckle clattered against the ridged floor.

In the death of that echo, I heard other sounds. A body moved and someone inhaled sharply. And then, a human voice. "Is someone there?"

It had been ten years, but I knew that voice.

Kat.

XIV

The thin film over the magma pool in my heart broke at the sound. The poisonous fire filling me in the hotel was just a minor burp compared to the volcanic upheaval brought about by that voice. The Chorus, shredding the chemical barriers in my head, rode the cresting edge of a venomous *Qliphotic* exultation. Their soul-sense radiated from my skull, seeking Kat's light.

She heard me coming and scrambled against the door panels, trying to find some way to push them open. Instinctively, she started to pull energy from the ether.

The wall behind her lit up, a white line of words glaring beneath her hips. A whining chatter of metal against stone forced its way through the Chorus' noise. As the illuminated letters revealed my approach, she began to shout over the pitched shriek of the protection ward, frantically constructing a magickal defense. The shrieking sound rattled my back molars as a firestorm began to coalesce, the floor starting to steam.

The explosion would kill us both. Didn't she know what it was, what her spell was doing? She couldn't draw enough energy to protect herself from the ward's explosion.

The Chorus giggled, a chuckle of black humor magnified by the roaring echo of the erupting darkness. *Fire*, they giggled, *she's not trying to protect herself.*

My fingers closed on her throat. I slammed us both against the wall and she groaned from the impact. "Goddess, no," she gasped, her hands fighting against the pressure of my weight. Her spell fled, dying in the collision, and the warning glow of the ward died as well. Back into darkness. *Back into the wood.*

My face, so close to hers, was filled with her smell: the memory of charred lilacs, the verdant flush coming off her skin now, tinged with an acrid bite of fear. Her hair was in my mouth and against my cheeks as she struggled beneath my hand.

I pressed the length of my body against her, pinning her flush to the wall. She turned her head and our cheeks met, her wet face anointing me. "Please," she whispered, her lips straining for my ear. "Please."

Settle it, the Chorus hissed, their voices issuing from the angry smoke in my lungs. *Kill the bitch,* they implored, writhing with need. *She's asking for it.*

Another echo intruded through the heat haze of the Chorus. A stained memory of Nicols. Standing in the parking lot beside Piotr's trailer. *"Guy's going to Walla Walla for ten to fifteen. You think that's going to fix the hole in his heart?"*

My mouth rubbed against her jaw, my lips twitching against the shiver of pain racing through her skin. I felt it in my groin and stomach as well. Her heart, hammering in her rib cage, was a seductive rhythm. *Just a handbreadth away.* I could reach in and touch it. I didn't even need magick. I could do it the old-fashioned way: by ripping her flesh, by cracking the cage of bone about her precious organ. *So close.*

"Please," she whispered again. Her mouth was so dry the word was barely a husk of its letters. "I don't understand. Who are you?"

The question broke against the black wall of the *Qliphotic* infection. A phantom voice in my head—my own traumatized innocence—echoed the question. *Who?* The Chorus screamed, the interfering noise of knives against knives, attempting to drown the question. Drown the tiny creature trying to dig itself out of the muck in my soul.

The Eight of Swords. The eight blades of interference. My roots, sunk deep in the darkness of *Malkuth*—the physical world, the realm of the weak flesh. The Chorus had been goading me for years. Their need had perverted my desire. Had led me astray. *Take back what was stolen from you,* they cried, *hurt her in the way she hurt you. Dominate her; break her Will.*

Kat's stomach pressed against my hip, her shirt shaking against my naked skin like a banner blowing in the wind. The scent of her skin and her soul burned into my cortex—just as it had been seared there so long ago. Lilacs. A field of smoldering lilac bushes. Was this *my* desire?

I squeezed her throat, the Chorus burning my hands with an urgency of violence. They darted through my skin, tasting her flesh, licking at her fear. She struggled under my hand, twisting in my grip. Her face turned toward me, and I could see the Chorus reflected in her eyes. I could see how she saw me. "Markham?"

Her hand found my face, her fingers questing for my lips. Touching me as if she couldn't believe I was real. "After all this time." Her voice was barely a whisper, such little air as could be forced past my hand. "Why?"

She didn't know. The Chorus was in her, invading her mind, caressing her spark with their eager tongues. She couldn't hide from me; I read her pure. *She didn't know.*

My memory was false. She had never touched me in the way I had remembered. She had never broken my spirit. Her mind was bereft of the history in my head.

What world were they trying to force on me?

The Chorus reacted angrily to my hesitation, flailing against my doubt. Their eruption was a volcanic attempt to take control. *Just a little tighter. Just a little more pressure.* These scintilla of captive souls fought to drive me to the final resolution of *their* desires, struggled to make me close my hand. Complete this cycle of fiction.

Was I just a creature of their illicit design?

I let go, much like Nicols had dropped the gun instead of fighting for control. *I just let go.* As I retreated, the loss of her touch—of her presence—sent the souls in my head into full revolt. I fell, unable to stand, and my legs and arms spasmed uncontrollably. My fingers, unable to choke Kat, tried for my own throat instead.

My lungs were clogged with wet soot. Deep in my belly, the orphic egg—laid those years ago in a moment of panic—cracked, and its tainted alchemy spilled out. It was a poison meant to melt the ravaged splinters of my spirit, meant to melt me down so that I could be reformed as a *Qliphotic* child.

If Kat was innocent, then I was not.

The tear in my soul was my transgression, a symptom of my failure. My fear, festering for years. The *Qliphoth,* the demons of the dark side of the Tree, made their children through despair and panic. All roads lead through the Abyss, and it is the fearful who are torn off the path. Those who think they are not worthy fulfill that expectation.

The Star, inverted, was me. I had caused this grief. I laid the seeds of what was exploding now. I was the cause… I was a fallen star.

But… still a star. Still a spark of the Divine Spirit, however gone astray. Even though I was nothing but a vessel filled with betrayal and deceit… even though I was nothing… *no thing…*

I rolled onto my side and threw up. From my tailbone on up, flexing everything in one direction, I threw it all out of me in one enormous eructive heave. They wanted violence, blood and gore for their pleasure. Instead, I gave them a violent denial. *Nihil non est.* My throat and mouth strained to expel the vileness in my gut, an explosive decompression of a decade's worth of entrenched darkness. I vomited a second time and then a third, the wave of cancer lessening to a bitter trickle. By the fourth and fifth spasm,

I had nothing left, but my body continued to heave anyway, finding some tortured revelry in this act of expurgation.

The *Qliphoth* extrusion hissed in the lightless room, a simmering puddle of viscous acid. It wanted to return to me, to swim inside the warm sanctuary of my flesh and to bathe in the hot nourishment of my blood. It wanted the delicious sweat of my fear.

But it couldn't have me. Not anymore. I was done with it, done with all that it wanted.

Still, its desire remained. If I was going to reject its tainted kiss, it would find someone else. The blood on my lips told me as much, the violent desire of the *Qliphoth* still lingering. It existed to consume. That was its only nature. It had festered in my gut and fueled my flesh's basal desires for that sole reason. *These are my roots, sunk deep within the material world of Malkuth.*

I raised my fist, lashed with lightning—the walls going white with shock, screaming and keening with near eruptive force—and brought my hand down in the center of the midnight puddle. I struck its core, touched it where it wanted me to touch Kat. I grabbed the vile heart of the *Qliphotic* essence—revenge, in its core—and blasted it with light.

The room hazed with steam, crackling with burning ozone. For an instant, I feared I had gone too far and had triggered the wards but, as the fractured droplets of the *Qliphotic* essence absorbed and contained my spell, the ward exhaled, losing light and sound. In a few heartbeats, we were in darkness again.

But it wasn't as black as it had been.

"Have you hated me that long?" she asked finally, her voice raw and tentative. "Ever since…?"

I wiped my chin and spat, clearing my mouth of the nasty taste. Clearing out the last vestiges of that bilious venom. "Part of me," I said. "Yeah, a part of me."

"I'm sorry," she said. "I never meant for anything to happen.

I never meant for…"

This? I thought. *Never meant for me to become what I am?* The Chorus was silent and submissive after the explosive purge of their secret taint. Their strength had lain in the hidden egg of the *Qliphoth*, the psychic child planted in me by the darkness in the woods. They had been influencing me, their continual seduction ensuring that I provided nourishment for the offspring, for the demonic payload I had been tasked to bring to term.

This was why they had been driving me to find Katarina, why they filled my head with thoughts of her death. They wanted her blood on my hands, wanted me flush with the exquisite rapture of having taken her. That was the trigger they had sought, the act which would have breached the metaphysical wall that had hidden the black Tree.

They would have welcomed me then, taken me down into those roots where the egg had been hiding. *This,* they would have revealed to me, *this is the secret of the flesh.* They would have let me See what I had done, Willfully, with intent.

This is the *Qliphotic* promise of the body—the darkness' hidden, dreadful secret—this is the inheritance of the material passions. This psychic mind-bomb of violence and rage. This is the real promise of mankind, the only true enlightenment our species can ever hope to attain.

"Yeah," I whispered, responding to Kat's plea for communication. She reached out to me in the dark, reached out to touch someone else, to know she wasn't alone. "It's part of what makes us human, isn't it? The shame and the regret."

"I tried to find you. I did. But it all fell apart so quickly. We were separated. All of us. I wanted to go after you and bring you back—" She faltered, realizing how empty an excuse her words were. "We were supposed to show you the Way. You should have seen the Tree, seen the Ten and the Path."

She moved in the dark, slow steps along the wall. I could hear the sound of her palms rubbing against the steel. "Ah, Markham, we opened your eyes to the spirit world, and I am sorry that you had to find out about it in that way. I'm sorry I didn't tell you." She crouched down to find me. "But you survived. You've learned the Arts."

A hard laugh coughed its way out of me. "Kat, I saw the Tree." Now that the *Qliphotic* veil was gone, new images were surfacing in my head. The Chorus tried to hide them, but they were buoyed by a forceful insistence. A need to remember, suppressed too long. *Yes, the Tree.* I had seen the Tree of the Sephiroth.

But the ceremony had been interrupted at this moment of revelation, and we had been scattered. There, among the shadows of the pines, I had Seen a different Tree, a black reflection. "I touched the nightside. I Saw the *Qliphoth*."

"How? That's impossible. We just opened your eyes. We didn't have a chance to guide you. You barely saw the Tree. How could you find the back pathways? I don't understand what happened."

"I fell through *Daäth*, Kat. I met one of them in the woods. I met a serpent who walked like a man, and he stuck his tongue through the hole in my spirit. He told me shadows could get into my soul, and there was only one way to keep them out."

"Keep them out? How?"

I let her see the Chorus. I raised them up and lit them with fiery incandescence. The walls responded in kind and, for a second, the room was filled with a kaleidoscopic orgasm of moving light. The color bleached out of Kat's skin, her skull visible. Her hair was a black cloud about her head and her eyes glittered like diamonds trapped in ragged stone. She Saw me. I had no doubt. "Dear Goddess," she whispered, her voice echoing in the sudden extinction of light.

She was quiet a long time. "You've been lost ever since that night, haven't you?" Her hand touched my foot, and her fingers were so warm I almost cried out from the shock. "He touched you, and you listened to him. I am so sorry. You've been carrying this poison all that time."

Her warmth spread through my ankle and heel, melting the permafrost in my toes. The heat spread to my calf like sunlight warming the core of a rock. On the wall, the white line of letters began to glow, a faint luminescence that outlined the shape of her head and body. "Was it all his voice that you heard? Was there any of your own desire in your heart?"

"I don't know. I can't remember." My body began to shake, deep sobs rising up from some long-covered wellspring.

"Has this violence been the only thing you've wanted, Markham? Has there been anything else? Try to remember. There is still a void in you. Just because you've expelled him doesn't mean he can't come back. You have to fill the void yourself. You have to remember something that has always been yours. What have you been seeking all this time? It hasn't been me. What have *you* wanted?"

Peace, I tried to tell her, but my teeth were chattering too hard. As her hand climbed to my knee, I reached down and grabbed her wrist, pulling her into my embrace like a drowning man grabbing a scrap of flotsam. My mouth found its way, my lips tasting her skin. Her fragrance—oh, memory is such a shabby thing when confronted with the aroma of a living scent—flooded through the crust of blood in my nose. The inhaled aphrodisiac went straight to the cold part of my brain and started wildfires.

We had fucked a lot when we were dating, animal movements in the light and night of our lives. We fucked because we were young, bodies so easily inflamed by the desire to touch and taste. We weren't the type whose sexual encounters lasted for hours and broke furniture and annoyed the neighbors and left us dehydrated husks on the floor. We were just enthusiastic about putting our parts together in various rhythmic combinations.

The sex was the intersection of our lives, the common denominator linking us. Her friends were prone to discussions about mysticism and meditative states reached through pharmaceutical psychology. They tended to be nocturnal—lovers of libraries and dark coffee houses, wan and wide-eyed in daylight. Mine were outdoor enthusiasts: climbers, BASE jumpers, skiers. We loved the rain and the weather, the play of light on snow, the crisp emptiness found far from concrete.

There was some overlap in the pharmaceutical area but, for the most part, our relationship fed the aspects of our psyches unfulfilled by our choices in friends and companions. I was the philosopher among the climbers, the one most prone to wonder why we wanted to climb up to Heaven and touch the stars in the night sky. She was unafraid of rocks and trees and air untainted by the heavy pressure of burned fossil fuels.

We met at REI; I was working a summer job there, helping out with the climbing wall. She approached me, on a lark she said, and asked how the whole climbing thing worked. I had put her in one of the harnesses and let her try the first few handholds. She had caught me looking at her ass.

Later, lying in bed, she confessed she had only come into the store to meet me. "The Hermit at the base of the mountain," she had said, explaining in her way what sight had lured her into the store. It was years later, when I learned about the tarot from a scarred astrologer in Budapest, that I understood what she had been telling me.

Katarina and I had always made love like we were trying to bridge some gap, like we were struggling to complete a puzzle we didn't even realize we were trying to solve. We were frenetic in our movement: grasping, pulling, pushing, tugging—always moving in opposition. In the brief fusion brought about by orgasm, we experienced a momentary glimpse of the solution—the top of the puzzle box where the picture was complete—and the sight always left us on the verge of understanding. Always close; never realized. Our quest of the flesh eternally incomplete.

Both of us had been with other people in the interim. Now, in the steel prison, our histories showed in the tiny hesitations that interrupted our motion, in the instinctual manner in which we found and forgot our rhythms, in the familiar way we drank from the hollows of our throats and shallow pools of our collarbones as we became thirsty. She bit me on the shoulder, breaking the skin, and I dented the flesh beneath the high point of her pelvic arch with my thumb. She sighed when she came and I held on, greedily wanting to bring her to that point again. She laughed and gripped me tight, flexing her hips and back until I cried out.

When all the hate was gone, what was left wasn't love, but just the memory of presence. What was left was an imprint of connectivity. We had sought to be one once, and the failure of that quest held no negative connotation. It was simply part of what moved us. We fucked like old friends who finally figured out that physical touch was as intimate as we were ever going to be. With that realization came a certain amount of grace.

XV

"Where did you go?" she asked later, curled up next to me. We were a tiny island on a steel sea, a bare bump of bone and flesh. We lay together because two were warmer than one and because there was no distance between us anymore. Until the container was opened, we existed outside of time and the world. We both knew it wouldn't last.

"A lot of places. Canada, the Southwest, back East. I saw a lot of Europe. China. Indonesia. Africa. I spent a year in Finland and two years in Paris."

Her fingers moved across my collarbone and touched the braid of hair around my throat. "And this?"

"Finland."

She tried to hook her finger under the braid and discovered that it wasn't separate from my skin. "What is it?"

"It's a gift from someone I— She helped me through the first year, showed me magick." Reija had named them; more than just a label, her binding had given them definition, and in doing so, had made them controllable. She had tried to teach me strength. "It's her hair."

"A forget-me-not?" Nearly a teasing note in Kat's voice.

"Yes, but not like that."

She quietly traced the course of the braid. The Chorus boiled at her touch. While their *Qliphotic* source had been expelled, the soil down there was still tainted, still ripe with their desire. She shivered slightly as she felt the skin of my chest and neck twitch.

"I quit all the magick stuff for three or four years after the ceremony that night," she said eventually. As the Chorus stopped raising goose bumps on my skin, her finger idly drifted along the slope of my body, charting the twists and knots of the last decade. "The group dissolved after the raid and we all lost touch. Adrift…"

Her memories of the ceremonial initiation had flowed into me when I had attacked her earlier, filling the holes that had been torn in my history. Now, I could remember the chaos of the Forest Service raid, the uniformed men with flashlights who had interrupted the nocturnal rite. Kat's group at that time had been pagan Gaia worshippers, attempting to link their Western Druidic heritage with the animist spirits of the natural world, and they had returned one too many times to the same spot outside of Rockport. The solemn ceremony had been splintered by the sudden presence of Forest Service rangers and Sheriff's deputies. The acolytes panicked, abandoning all pretense of ceremonial unity, and the torch-lit glade had dissolved into a scene of medieval chaos. Myself and the two other neophytes had been left behind, wide-eyed babes abandoned in the woods. Left to face our panic on our own.

I shifted my leg, sliding my foot between her calves. She parted easily, effortlessly, and unconsciously, and then closed again around me. "But you came back to the Work."

She nodded. "I did." She seemed on the cusp of telling me more and I said nothing, letting the silence draw it out of her. "I traveled too. I did the Grand Tour of Italy: Rome, Venice, Florence, a few other places." I felt her cheek move against my skin—a brush of warm flesh—and I knew why the memories caused such a flush in her. Venice was a haunted city. Its fili- greed buildings, its burnished glass, and its emerald canals still inflamed the romantic idealist. I hadn't been immune myself, and gotten involved in an affair that had taught me some different things than I had come to find.

"When I came back, I found some of the old group. They had become Hollow Men, though they used another name back then. 'Technomancers,' I think. Or 'Argent Lords of the Dawn.'" She shook her head, her hair brushing against my chin. "They went through quite a few names before 'Hollow Men.' They had become city-bound, neo-industrialists, and they were scattered along the coast in Portland and Seattle. Urban chaos magicians without any real focus."

Doug and his friends. The white-haired magus. "But they found a focus in psychoanimism, didn't they?"

She nodded. "Yes, manipulating the soul, independent of the flesh. Shortly after I came back, they became involved with a couple of magi who had recently completed pilgrimages to India and were heavily into Vedic meditation. They had a handful of prayers they claimed were from the *Artharva Veda*. Ritual chants to cleanse and purify the spirit, to de-foul the materialistic flesh."

"Your friends found gurus."

"Yes," she admitted. "I was still on the fringe, not completely privy to the thoughts of the inner circle. I wasn't part of the decision to bind the group to these men."

"What was the lure? It had to be more than scraps from the *Artharva Veda*." There were a lot of rituals claiming that lineage; I had never seen one that could actually hold up to any scrutiny.

"They claimed to have found a synthesis between these rituals and the Work described in an eighth-century Persian alchemical text. They were working from the Latin translation—fourteenth or fifteenth century, I think—and they had made a purification rite. A unified expression of being and not-being. It was complicated: two days of fasting and meditation before another twelve hours of ceremonial magick. Lots of sigils, lots of mantras."

Her finger traced the pitted circle of one of two bullet scars. I had taken a couple of small caliber rounds in the chest—high on the right side—a few years ago. An art negotiation gone wrong in a no-name Bangkok bar had left me with holes, one clean through and one puncturing the upper portion of my right lung. The wound in my lung had threatened to be a problem but the shooter, having had an instant to regret his aim, was taken by the Chorus and used to repair the damage. The enduring legacy of my *Qliphotic* infection.

"I had been tracing the history of pagan Goddess worship in Italy," she said, her fingers wandering between the scars on my chest. "I found some old ceremonies belonging to Demeter, one of which was the practice of tuning spirit fields." Her hand paused and her head moved, her breath touching my skin. "A harmonic resonance between souls."

I touched her shoulder, felt her hair under my fingers. "Synching energy vibrations," I said. My knowledge of the matter was vague, and based on what I gleaned from Doug's head, I could hazard a few guesses.

"The Hollow Men ritual culminates in a spiritual readiness—a sartorial condition where the initiate is etherically disengaged. The body is alive, but in a state of suspension, and the soul should be able to release itself freely from its anchors.

"But when they tried to put it into practice, they couldn't do it. They couldn't complete the process of separation. They knew what they needed—some sort of final release that would silence the self—but they couldn't do it. They couldn't do it for themselves."

I made the connection. "And this is where you came in."

"The ceremony of Demeter gave me the tools to become a co-participant in their ritual. I could tune their vibrations. I could focus their bodies and dissolve their active minds."

"Sex Magick," I said. "The old-fashioned way."

"There's nothing old-fashioned about it." She sounded slightly defensive, even though my tone had been light. "You know how oblivious we are to ourselves in that moment of rapture. Sex Magick is just as viable as any other style of theurgy."

"I know," I told her. "There are aged generations of Thelemites who are still trying to live up to Crowley's interpretations. *Love under Will* as long as you are bowing to My Will and all that." Crowley's interpretation was decidedly English and male, which subsumed a great deal of the more ancient fertility rituals. The kind that Kat had apparently found.

"Crowley gets it all wrong because he never Saw beyond the end of his dick." She shook her head, her hair moving through my fingers. "It isn't just about reaching orgasm and seeing that white light of nothingness. When I give them that release, they are submissive to me. I am their Whore-Goddess; I am the fertile earth in which they bury themselves so that their spirits may be freed. We re-create the burial of the vegetable god. It is this symbolic harmony that allows them to pass into simultaneous Being and Nothingness."

The vegetable ritual, the oldest example of the Hermetic truism. *As above, so below.* The natural cycle reflected in the world mythologies. Goddesses take suitors from the mortal world and give them divine providence by allowing them to plow the sacred field with their profane cocks. Inanna and Tammuz. Aphrodite and Adonis. Cybele and Attis. This is the way Kings were made. This is the way Kings were buried.

I had been bound by this cycle as well. The Chorus had tapped that proto-historical model, that ingrained psychic belief structure, and had bent me around it. We seek death and rebirth as often as the sun rises. We seek to create and re-create, covering our mistakes, burying our errors, hoping—*next time*—we would get it right. What had my quest for Kat been but a distorted attempt at the same thing? In our aborted chemical romance, I had been a Black King—charred and improperly cast—to her

Red Queen.

Her hand moved down, and she found the ridged scar where Antoine's blade had gone through me. It had slipped under my rib cage and pierced my back, just missing my spine. A clean thrust that would have been fatal had it been a half-inch either way. But it hadn't, and Antoine had been as surprised as I. It was his one mistake. And it only cost him a hand.

"Why do you keep the scars?" she asked. "Do you not know how to repair your flesh?"

"I do," I said. "But they help me remember."

"Remember what? The pain?"

"My mortality."

She was quiet for a moment. "They think pscyhoanimism can be used to extend life," she said, idly rubbing the sword scar as if it were just an appliqué that could be removed. "They've done things I thought impossible. And the texts they have hint at many more possibilities: group minds, cosmic consciousnesses—"

"Body-jacking," I interrupted.

Her finger stopped. "Yes," she said. She said it quietly, as if verbal recognition of my words would be heard as an admission of guilt. "They can move between bodies. It wasn't something I taught them. It was Julian's—"

"Who?"

She ignored the question and, for the moment, I let it go. I had a sense—a taste—of which one was Julian. I had pinned his spirit in the hotel when he had tried his psychic assault. The white-haired one. *I know your name.*

Her hand drifted back up my chest and stopped over my heart. Her wrist turned as if she were trying to put her fingers in the dial of an old rotary telephone. "Here," she said. "This is where I touched you. I can feel it in your aura."

She moved her hand away, leaving five glowing rings on my skin like stars writ across the heavens. Coupled with the pale scars of the bullet wounds, the pattern looked like the constellation of Orion. The Hunter drawn at a downward angle as if the sky were tilting.

"*Ex lux et vita,*" she whispered.

From light and life. The world unmade and made anew in a flash of light. A sudden pain pierced my throat like an arrow from Eros' bow gone terribly astray. For the last ten years, my persistent memory loop had been a false precognition, a bogus prediction wrapped around an imperfect imprint of the ceremony in the woods.

Archaic cultures would regularly gather at their sacred spots—their places of epiphany—and re-create their symbolic worlds. These magico-religious spots were where Now and Then collapsed into a singular point—*in illo tempore.* They would compress the world and make it anew. *Ex lux et vita.* Those at the center—at the axis of their world—got to make the future.

Even as I had tried to consciously forget Katarina in the subsequent decade since my aborted magickal initiation, I couldn't escape the cyclical nature of the world. Unconsciously, I wanted to return to the beginning. I wanted to restart my world.

This was the divine secret whispered to me in the woods. This was the First Lie I told myself. There was no *Qliphoth* monster, no serpent, no dark demiurge in the woods. Just my own frightened spirit staring up at the sky and seeing only darkness. I hadn't been able to see the pinpricks of Heaven. There had been no reflection, no way for me to remember that I, too, was a star.

The fire is going out, I whispered to myself in the woods, and there is only one way to preserve it. Take more fuel. Gather more sparks. *Light begats light.*

Thus the seed was planted, buried deep by my own hand. By my own ignorance.

Kat's hand moved to my lips, and then to my cheeks where she felt my tears. "I'm sorry," she whispered, pressing her lips to the five circles over my heart.

I wrapped my hands in her dark hair as if I was burying them;

as if by hiding the evidence, I could make the blood vanish. *Our hands, they betray what we have done.*

We murder; we create. The dark is but a shadow of the light. A reaction is simply a response to action. Our cycles are but mirrors, degenerate reflections of the primal effort that split the Limitless Universe.

Ex mortis et tenebris. From death and darkness.

"So am I," I replied.

XVI

We heard the lock first, a clangorous beat that rang up and down the length of the container. More discordant percussion followed—metal shifting and clattering against metal. A broad beam of stark light swept into the chamber as the portal opened.

Four men entered, dark silhouettes against the wash of light. The door closed, and three of them stood in a line along the back wall. The other man held two objects: a folding chair and a storm lantern. The thin flame of the lantern made short shadow puppets along the base of the wall and, while its weak light reached the man's face, it left the three guards cloaked in shadow.

The guards were armed, the subtle glint of metal visible in the gloom, and I wasn't inclined to test their eagerness to shoot me. Based on the chair and lantern, the visit seemed casually interrogative and, since I had a few questions for my captors, I thought I'd see where the conversation went.

Kat and I were sitting side by side in the center of the container, about ten feet away from the door. The clacking and clanging had given us sufficient time to make ourselves presentable. We were sitting like eager students when the foursome arrived, little learners ready for the start of the lesson.

"I realize the accommodations are somewhat less than comfortable." The man sat in the chair, crossed his legs, and idly plucked at something on the leg of his trousers. Nice clothes, neat beard, rings on his fingers. A European gentleman, my first guess. German, or Swiss.

"Well, once I got the ball gag out, it did seem a trifle chilly," I said.

"Ah," he said, resting his hand flat on his leg. "A sense of humor. Good. We can talk, then."

"Can I pick the topic or do you have something specific in mind?"

"Something specific, Mr. Markham."

I glanced at Kat, registered the cold fury in her face. Judging by the way the man wasn't looking at her, I had a feeling he knew the cause of her expression. "Who is this clown, anyway?" I asked her, trying to keep him from running the conversation.

"Bernard du Guyon," she spat.

"She's not very happy with you," I offered.

Bernard raised an eyebrow. "Ms. Nouranois' displeasure has made itself evident to me but—" he raised his shoulders "—there is very little I can do about it right now."

Her body tensed, and we all felt the violence of her desire. Bernard tried to appear oblivious, but his shoulders tightened unconsciously. Interesting. Putting Kat in here with me hadn't been his idea.

"We should probably get off that topic of conversation," I said. "I wouldn't want things to get any more awkward."

Bernard was happy to follow that lead. "Do you know why Initiate Rassmussen was making his exodus?"

"Is that what you're calling it? A rather destructive method of initiation, don't you think? All that collateral damage."

"I believe you are somewhat to blame for that, Mr. Markham."

"What? If I hadn't intercepted him in the deer, he would have ridden it all the way to Seattle? Even if I hadn't been there, he would have realized he needed a human host when he reached the ferry terminal. The animal was burning up. It wouldn't have survived." I shook my head. "He was going to end up in a human host. There was no other way for him to cross the water."

Bernard didn't contradict me, nor did he offer any defense of Doug's actions.

"Look, I've seen other techniques like this. Different cultural contexts. You aren't the first to experiment with the separation of soul and body. You needn't act like I've stolen your magic underpants."

"These underpants, if you will, are old, Mr. Markham. Egyptian."

"Hermetic?" I said, a note of surprise actually sneaking into my voice. "I thought the works of Hermes Trismegistus were more philosophical in nature. More talking about souls and matter than actually separating the two."

"You're familiar with his philosophical works? *The Divine Pymander* and the *Asclepius?*" Bernard leaned forward, betraying his interest in this topic.

"I have a passing familiarity with his work. I was in Cairo for a few months around the hundred-year anniversary of Crowley's reception of *The Book of the Law*. I had an opportunity to study his efforts while I was there." My visit to Cairo had been more about Trismegistus than being party to Crowley's centennial; but, like all children in possession of illicit secrets, we never tell the whole truth when asked to reveal our sources.

"What is your impression of the ideas of Hermes Trismegistus?"

My awareness of the texts seemed to intrigue him. His voice had become more professorially inquisitive. Was there some test hidden in his questions? Some probe to see if I knew the secret phrases or if I was amenable to a certain line of thought? Unlike Pender, Bernard didn't seem to be looking for a canned response; there appeared to be an honesty of interest in his query.

Which didn't stop me from being coy in my response. I still

hadn't made the connection to Doug's ritual of separation. Trismegistus was philosophical. He hadn't left behind any ceremonial works. Though a vague thought nagged at the back of my brain, a fragmented history of Trismegistus' work that wasn't quite coming together for me. "They're vague. They're a school of thought masquerading as a technical journal. Hardly a good guidebook for practical application." I hid behind a first-year's response, further coloring it with a dilettante's dismissal of ceremonial magick. "But, then again, very little of that esoteric stuff is ever really useful."

"You don't think the separation of Douglas' spirit from his body is a practical application?" My answer riled him.

"No, I'm sure it has its uses, but I'm not sure you should be pretending that it originated with the Hellenistic Egyptians. Like I said, I've seen rituals like it in the Caribbean, in Africa, in Tibet. Even in India. Separating the spirit from the flesh is an old pastime, far older than the pyramid builders. It's like any of the primitive magick systems—different words and rituals for the same end result."

"The end result," Bernard said quietly. "You are a practical man, Mr. Markham? Just the ensuing effect is the only thing that interests you? No room for wondering how such speculation came into being?"

"No," I said. "Speculation is my daily discourse. I eat philosophy for breakfast. My interest lies in the interpretation of the Word and the world."

"But both the Word and the world are always subjective, Mr. Markham. The only thing not predicated upon our perception is the Divine Light. Are you so mired in the discussion that you haven't considered the source of All? It shines whether we see it or not. 'Dixitque Deus: "Fiat lux." Et facta est lux.' As if there could be existence prior to light."

And God spoke: "Let there be light." And there was light. All good Sunday School children know this story.

"So Christianity got it all wrong then, did they? Must have been why they burned out the pagans."

"No, *'fiat lux'* is the third verse of the Bible. Do you know what comes before?" The question was rhetorical as he answered before I could formulate a reply. " *'Terra autem erat inanis et vacua, et tenebrae super faciem abyssi, et spiritus Dei ferebatur super aquas.'* "

This interrogation had fully strayed into a discussion of philosophy. But for the steel box in which it was conducted, this conversation might be nothing more than discourse between student and teacher. His quotation was specific: a question as to my knowledge of both the Bible and Latin. "The earth was without form and was void," I said, paraphrasing. "Darkness moved upon the face of the deep; and the spirit of God wandered across the face of the waters." I spread my hands vertically. Darkness below, the Spirit of God above. "Or something like that."

"Yes. 'Something like that' is exactly the problem. Your memory of the verse is hazy because the Church doesn't want you to remember it. They'd prefer that you ignored *Genesis* entirely. Stay in the New Testament only. But it is there, *in exordium,* that the secrets are kept, that the true reality is made clear. Before philosophy, before language."

"My memory is hazy," I said, "because you've drugged me. Not because I don't know my Vulgate."

"Ah, the opiates." He paused, and plucked at his pant leg again. "I am sorry about that. I am told you are… hmm… not 'prone' necessarily, but 'ready,' yes, 'ready' is the word I want. You are ready to do violence, Mr. Markham. Prudence suggested that we might be wise to bind you so that you could not engage in any activity that might cause injury. To yourself or others."

"Prudence, huh? Prudence has a different name, doesn't she? Who are your friends? Are you their academic, their librarian?"

"I did that sort of work for associates of yours. In Paris."

"Associates?" I laughed. "Hardly. I'm *persona non grata* with them."

He nodded. "Yes, I have heard that. It's a good thing they don't know where you are."

My laugh died in the corner of the room. Ah, the crux of the matter. *I owed him.* I was a pawn to be played at his discretion. "What do you want, Bernard?"

"I want to talk," he replied. "I want to see what sort of man you are. If your material passions masquerade as ideological fervor or if rational thought can sway your course. Are you a man of ideas, or a creature of action?"

Hermes Trismegistus told his sons—in more than one sermon—the most important tool given to mankind by the Divinity was Reason. This ability allowed men to shape their minds, to use their Wills to overcome the passions of the flesh. Reason would guide us toward enlightenment.

I had a feeling Bernard wanted to know if I was keen to this idea. All this dancing around the philosophy of souls had a point. Was I a talker or a doer? Did I know something about the topic on the table? All discourse aside, what was my interpretation of the Word? And, could I be swayed by the application of a good argument?

"The only vice of the soul is ignorance," I said, settling on a truism I remembered from the texts.

He smiled. "Indeed. And pursuits of the soul, do they not guide us toward a reconciliation with that Heaven from which we have been separated?"

"Hermes would like to think so." Now, the discussion. The laying out of the argument. What was he leading toward?

"But you're not so sure."

I glanced around the dim room. "I'm still here. Since the whole topic of transmigration and previous incarnations hasn't come up, I'm hesitant to open that can of worms. Let's just say that I'm still seeking some empirical evidence and leave it at that."

"And Initiate Rassmussen. Was he seeking empirical evidence? Did your interruption deny him a precious opportunity?"

"We never crossed the water before," Kat interjected. "We never forced the others to ride souls. This was never about possession."

Bernard looked at her and shook his head fractionally. "My dear, they all crossed over. You weren't invited to the rejoining because it never took place at the remote site. They always came home to this temple. Every one of them."

"Son of a bitch." She leaned forward, raising her fist, and a clatter of hardware behind Bernard preceded a trio of red dots on her upper chest. Laser sights from the guards' hardware. I put a hand on Kat's arm. She shrugged me off, but made no attempt to get to her feet. The dots remained on her chest.

"Okay, Bernard," I said. "We get it. Julian has something else in mind." I was pretty sure Bernard had more than a small hand in whatever they were doing, but by carelessly suborning him to Julian, I was hoping to push him toward actually talking about it instead of dancing around the edges. Besides, I wanted to see the reaction I got from name-dropping.

Bernard pursed his lips and pressed a finger against his slim mouth. As he considered his response, something microscopic on his pant leg finally caught his attention and he flicked the speck away with a sigh. "Your semantic barbs will not prick me, Mr. Markham. I will not be drawn into a tawdry shouting match."

"No? How about some straight-forward discussion then? You still haven't told me what you want. My blessing?"

He shook his head. "No, we have already been blessed."

I looked at Kat. "The Pope's been out?"

"Protector Briande—"

I flinched involuntarily. *Protector?* How had Antoine gotten that far? Five ranks in as many years. How could he—and then I realized the way it could be done. *Ritus concursus.* Antoine was clawing his way to the top, and, apparently, had the skills to pull it off. Losing a hand hadn't apparently done much to slow him down.

Bernard took note of my twitch. "Yes," he laughed. "A real Protector. Here, looking for you. What have you done, Mr. Markham, to anger him so?"

One of the slices of memory in my head rotated into an orientation where it found a natural grouping with a number of disparate elements. This combination of past events triggered a brief flash of illumination. For a second, I could see the Weave surrounding me. I understood the forces pulling the threads.

Antoine was already here. It was Antoine who had been in the back of Pender's car. Pender hadn't left the card mirage in Doug's mirror. That had been Antoine. As was the message on the back of the Polaroid: *61.* A cryptic reference to the Abyss. Antoine hadn't told Pender anything about our history; his directive to Pender had simply been to Watch me.

The hotel had been a ruse, a snare meant to direct me along a path of their choosing. Nicols had been right: there had been ulterior motives beneath Pender's seemingly benevolent act. Pender had probably suggested the plan to Antoine—let's get him where we can keep an eye on him. Let's bait this snare with something that we know he wants.

It's a good thing they don't know where you are.

More pieces fell into place. Pender was the Hollow Men contact within the Seattle infrastructure. He had known about Doug before I told him. And, when I ran like a fool with a hard-on toward the hotel, Pender had called his friends. The Hollow Men had snatched me from Antoine's Watch. Because they had some purpose for me.

No. More tracing of the Weave's intricacy. My disappearance would distract Antoine. I was the flashy coin held in one hand, the object meant to snare the audience's attention while the other hand performed the magic trick. My purpose was simply to be out there, somewhere, a nagging itch Antoine couldn't scratch.

Meanwhile, whatever secret plan Bernard and Julian had been concocting with their secret manuscript was coming to fruition. Whatever they were hoping to achieve with their psychoanimist research. Body-jacking…

"You're going to take control of a Protector," I realized. "You're going to subvert his Watch."

Bernard put a finger to his lips again, but this time he was hiding a smile. "Oh, nothing so mundane as that, I'm afraid. We have a much grander plan in mind."

XVII

More extreme than taking out a Protector? My confusion must have been evident in my inability to articulate a reply. "The Watchers aren't known for their forgiveness," I finally managed.

"Spoken like a man who knows." Bernard chuckled. "We are about to embark upon an ambitious project, Mr. Markham. A project that goes well beyond the discourse of *The Corpus Hermeticum*. One that requires industrious men with extraordinary talents. *I* think you qualify…" He hesitated on the remainder of the sentence.

"Julian doesn't like me," I finished for him.

He hesitated, considering his answer, and then sighed. "Julian doesn't like a number of things."

"So he is in charge?"

"No," Bernard disagreed.

I glanced at Kat and raised an eyebrow. "That's funny. It doesn't seem that way. I mean, call it what you will but he's not the one who locked himself in a crate with me. With you in here…" I raised my shoulders as if to say that I didn't really have an opinion on the matter. All the while making it clear that I thought his presence inside was certainly not the action of a man in charge.

"You're being childish, Mr. Markham. Provoking me won't

achieve anything."

I looked at Bernard again, held his gaze, and slowly raised the Chorus behind my eyes. "Nothing childish about it," I said. "Especially in light of what Julian knows." I let the Chorus pulse around me once, their wave setting alight the inscribed sigil. In the background, the three gunmen raised their pistols in a frantic effort to cover me with their laser sights. But, in the sudden darkness following the ward's illumination, they discovered the lantern had gone out. They couldn't see well enough to find a target for their little red dots.

In the tiny chaos caused by the Chorus' suffocating touch on the lantern's flame, I did exactly what Bernard warned me against. In the dark, I Whispered to him, my voice riding his ear. "Julian let you come in here because you were expendable." Bernard shouted incoherently, and I heard the chair tip over as he leaped to his feet. Boots scuffled as anarchy gathered the four men together, scrambling their efforts.

A flashlight clicked on. It reflected from Bernard's white shirt, momentarily freezing him in a bright spotlight, and then it swept in a flat arc across the floor.

Kat reached out in the darkness and found my hand. When the flashlight discovered us, we hadn't moved from our position. A second flashlight covered us as well, while the third lit up the door panel. The plastic butt of a handgun rang against the metal—three strikes, followed by two more. The heavy lever holding the door was lifted from the outside.

Kat and I raised hands to shield our eyes as the four men retreated through the open door. "An infantile prank, Mr. Markham," Bernard chided me as he left. "It wins you no favors." The portal closed and the bar and lock clanged into place, sealing us inside.

"Well," Kat said after a moment. "He's kind of right."

"Yeah, but it made me feel better," I said.

"Ah," she replied. "I'm glad that's one of those critical personal policies that you're clinging to."

I stood and fumbled across the room to where Bernard had left the storm lantern and sniffed at it carefully. There was still some kerosene in the reservoir. "It also put him off his game," I pointed out. I opened the tiny door of the lantern and snapped my fingers. The Chorus made a spark that leaped onto the oil-soaked wick. I adjusted the flame and lifted the lantern to better expose the container. "You heard him, Kat. They're planning something stupid. I'm the bait to distract Antoine. It wasn't their original plan, but they're certainly taking advantage of the circumstance. And until I know why they opted to make that change in their plan, I'm going to make mischief."

A finger-length in width, the metal plate on which the fire-storm sigil was inscribed made the circuit of the wall. It wasn't a solid piece of metal but the pieces were fit snugly enough it was nigh impossible to find the seams. Even the plates on the end panels made allowances for the doors. The spell could have been written on the bare wall, but dealing with the ridged construction would make the process of crafting an unbroken line of text unbearably time-consuming.

Knowing it was based in Solomon's Lore and that it was similar to the ward used in the barn made it easier to discern the pattern in the script. By the flickering light of the storm lantern, I traced the sigil. It looped around the room four times, and it ended like it began: with the symbol of fire. Arcane punctuation marks.

"This container," I asked Kat after I finished my initial examination. "Do you know where the Hollow Men store it?"

"Julian owns a warehouse down in SoDo. It's a couple of blocks from the old Rainer Brewery—where Tully's roasts their coffee now. He has some connections with the Port of Seattle and a couple of the shipping companies so it's possible this is at the warehouse."

"But you've never seen it?"

"No. But there's a lot of the warehouse I haven't seen."

"Who is Julian?" I asked as I started my second examination of the script. "He's one of those guys with the Hindu background, isn't he?"

"Yes."

"He's also the Master of the Temple?"

"Yes."

Good news, that. It meant there wasn't another magus waiting in the wings. Julian and Antoine were more than enough. I didn't need a third adept to deal with. Doug had some skills, but they weren't anything I needed to worry about. "What about Bernard?"

"He's an alchemist and a craftsman."

"Do you know anything about what he's talking about?"

Kat hugged herself, staring into the darkness beyond the lantern's glow. "No," she said softly.

I believed her. Her function in the Hollow Men ritual gave sense to the memories I had lifted from Doug. Kat was their Anima, the spirit avatar that allowed them to sever their meat ties. She taught them how to attain a pure energy state. But they hadn't told her what they planned to do with this psychoanimist knowledge. And, as she had realized by now with their casual dismissal of her safety, they no longer had any use for her.

"What happens after you teach them to break free?" I asked.

"It's a test for advancement. They are awarded the rank of Ascendant."

"What comes after Ascendant?"

"Anointed. It's the last rank."

"How many have you Ascended?"

"Doug was the seventh."

Seven. Shit. Okay, maybe there were a few I needed to worry about. "What about Julian? You do him too?"

She took the question wrong for a second and, in that glimpse of her naked emotions, I realized something about our relationship, about how the ugly severance that night in the forest had left us both raw. Unfinished. "Yes," she said, hiding herself from me. "I Ascended him. He was the first."

"Okay," I said, moving past what I had seen. "That means there are five guys who can body-jack that I don't know about." Five spirits who could be in anyone, who could surprise me at any time. More reasons to take advantage of Bernard's momentary insecurity and get the hell out of the container. More reasons to figure out a way to undermine the ward and get out of jail. The world, rushing back in now, filling us with the urgency of time.

As I examined a likely spot in the back corner where I might try my idea, the lock on the container clanged and the hinges groaned. I walked away from the section I was inspecting and quietly waited for our captors to return. Fortuna wasn't inclined to give me much of a break today.

This time, there were five gunmen—sporting an assortment of pistols and Tasers—who accompanied Julian and Bernard. Julian wasn't surprised to see me with the lantern while Bernard's mouth screwed itself tight. His mouth got even thinner when Julian leaned toward the bearded man and said something too quiet for me to hear.

"Put the lantern down, Markham," Julian called out after Bernard gave him a terse nod. He put his fingers on the metal plates on either side of him, completing the circuit broken by the open door. The letters along the wall flared white-hot. "Now," Julian said. "I'm not really in the mood."

The base of the lantern clicked on the metal floor when I set it down. I took two steps back, signaling compliance with his wishes. Julian was most likely bluffing with his threat to ignite the ward but I didn't see the return on pressing him now. And, judging by the ease with which he had sacrificed one of his soldiers at the barn, he just might not be bluffing. I wasn't about to wager our lives.

Julian nodded to his men and they approached me carefully. The two with Tasers raised their weapons. "Is this really—" That was all I managed. The first pair of darts hit my bare chest and my body locked up. The current from the second hit went right into my brain and switched everything off.

As a means of sowing discord and spreading propaganda, torture has been co-opted by a number of governmental intelligence organizations, imbedding the images and ideas into the mainstream social consciousness. But, like everything dragged into the shallow end of the pool, the practice has lost a great deal of its magico-religious refinements.

While the obvious intent was to break the flesh and Will, torture could also be used to break the soul. Hermetic thought—and the thread runs through most of the Gnostic literature and philosophy—argued there are two aspects of humanity: the gross mortal aspect of the body and the immortal, immutable aspect of the soul. While both were still part of the Ineffable—by whatever name you like to call it, it was that which resided in everything and which everything resided within—it was the body that was cast as the villain. The body dragged the soul down to the world of matter and decay. Only through purification and prurient separation from the decadent and materialistic nature of the body could the soul remember its divine origin.

The Zen Buddhists encapsulated all of this in the simple koan of asking you to remember the face you had before you were born. That was the high road.

Hermeticism—the fragmented thoughts and writings of Hermes Trismegistus—didn't condone torture. The work didn't even mention it. Very few of the old texts do. It was only the black cancer of the Middle Ages that infected esoteric thought with the concept of scourging the flesh—assisted by the whips and devices invented by the Catholic Church during the heyday of the Inquisition.

Breaking a man was an act of subjugation, of bending his Will to the desires of his interrogator. Those who couldn't create, turned to domination. The shortcut of the diabolists. Mankind was always on the lookout for a good shortcut.

The Iron Maiden was one such subjugation tool. A large cabinet topped with a sculpted head of the Madonna, the device had long iron spikes mounted on the inside of the door panels. When it was closed, the poor bastard inside was strategically pierced to ensure maximum non-lethal agony. The victims of the Maiden's embrace would die slowly, in a great deal of pain. Compounded by persistent needling from their interrogators about the need for repentance. Before the blood loss killed them, damning them to the hell reserved for heretics.

Maidens were unwieldy and a nuisance to transport. Few were made and, other than one found in Iraq a few years ago, they've been out of favor for a long time. Which isn't to say that the concept has lost its appeal.

When I woke up from being Tasered again, I found myself inside an Iron Maiden, the porcupine tickle of its spikes against my skin. I tried to not squirm too much as I tried to make sense of my new surroundings.

At the very least, I wasn't in the shipping container any longer.

My wrists were restrained again, held in place by thick leather straps. My bare feet were resting on a cold piece of metal, and I was in a partially reclined position, leaning against a curved chair back. A large breastplate attached to the frame of the chair held me down at this awkward angle. Studded with metal spikes, the interior of the plate was lowered close enough that the points pressed against my flesh. They weren't penetrating. Not yet. As long as I kept still.

Behind me, I could see an insulated cable descending from the ceiling. It split into thick cords terminating in metal posts attached to the peak of the chair. The chair (what I could see of it) was a massive piece of work: heavy oak pieces, worn smooth from years of attention; pitted iron bands wrapping the arms and legs. There were stains on the wood and dark oxidation scars on the metal.

It was an old electric chair, and the purpose of the thick cable suddenly made sense.

What were the odds of me holding still when they flipped the switch and threw a lot of juice into the chair? Not only would I be quaking and baking, but every heaving twitch of my chest would impale me more and more on the spikes of the Maiden.

My own fear was going to get me killed. And, before I thought about it more than that, I tried to redirect my active mind into a meditative state. *Om vajrapani hum.* One of the bodhisattvas of Mahayana Buddhism was Vajrapani, the angelic Buddha aspect who represented focused action. *Om vajrapani hum.* Breathe in through the nose, out through the mouth.

I felt my chest relax. Some of the pressure from the spikes eased, and I could focus on the area beyond the electric chair and its sadistic breastplate.

The room was long and white, a coat of industrial paint on the walls and ceiling. A trio of floor lamps made round pools on the ceiling, the ambient scatter reflecting off the white walls. Directly in front of me was a tall object covered with a dark red velvet cloth.

On my left was another chair much like mine though without the added chest plate. Kat was strapped to the seat. I tried to see behind me, tried to fully comprehend the size of the room, but when I turned my head too far, my chest naturally rose. Kat and I weren't alone; the Chorus felt soul vibrations in the room, but I couldn't place them without letting the Chorus out. It didn't seem like a good idea to start exploring when I was so precariously poised.

"Ah, Mr. Markham." Bernard wandered into my field of vision, coming around from my right. "You've come back."

Closer now than in the shipping container, I got a good look at him. He was well-groomed, wearing a white silk shirt with loose cuffs, expensive shoes, and sharply creased wool pants. His dark hair was cut close to his head in an unassuming style favored by the recent fashion dictates of glam rock stars and the eternal vigilance of Cistercian monks and penitent ascetics. His neat beard subconsciously aped the shorn point of his widow's peak—as above, so below—making his face look like a long spear blade. He had a pair of platinum rings on his right hand—index and ring finger—and on his left wrist was a diamond-studded watch with a revealed mechanism and the inset cutout of a Maltese Cross. He really did look like a European precious metals broker. The Vacheron Constantin watch helped.

"Thanks for inviting me." My voice was full of dust.

"In our earlier discussion, you said your interest lay in seeing how someone interprets the Word and the world." Bernard waited a half second for me to correct him. "I wanted to share my vision with you. I wanted to show you what is possible."

The flicker of his eyes drew my attention to the draped object. It was taller than Bernard, and the red drapery was depressed in the middle and raised at three points along its outer edge. The edge was traced with fine gold needlepoint, an undulating line of arcane symbols too intricate to read from across the room. The base looked to be about four feet wide. I caught myself trying to catalogue and identity the object against my mental inventory of antiquities, but the covering confounded my professional assessment.

"Do I really have to be strapped down for this?" I asked. "Does she?"

Kat stared at the object, the muscles in her throat working. She didn't know either, but she appeared to have an idea.

Julian, wearing a nimbus of translucent fire, stepped up to the back of her chair and placed his hands on her head. Kat jerked away from his touch and he laughed softly. "We want your undivided attention," he said.

The halo of flames about his head was an etheric shadow of his activated Will. A friend to fire, he had the Idea of flame already formed—an active security measure should Kat or I attempt to liberate ourselves. Before we could summon our own fire, he would burn us both.

"All right, so we're a receptive audience," I said. "Do we have to make cooing noises when you show off your toys or is this open to discussion?"

"By all means," Bernard said as he walked over to the shroud and grasped the cloth. "I'm curious as to your opinion." He pulled the fabric off.

Three statues reached toward a central ring, a wide band of polished silver covered with a crawl of arcane script. The statues—each one standing about four feet tall—had the ibis head of the Egyptian god Thoth and androgynous bodies, nothing but smooth stone at their groins. In the center of the silver circle was an articulated sphere made from joined pieces of glass. The sphere reflected none of the light in the room; instead, each plate seemed to exude darkness, shards of black that killed the ambient glitter.

Lightbreaker.

The three figures stood upon a single platform, a sturdy base of hammered bronze. Their lower legs and knees were made of bronze as well, the joints whorled like conch shells. They had no feet, seeming to rise out of the bronze plate. Above the knee, they became brass, extending up to the curved shape of their torsos. Shoulders and arms were like the silver of the ring which they held, and their throats and skulls were made of gold. Their faces and long beaks were black stone. Onyx or obsidian. They had no eyes, no mouths, no features other than the perfect arc of their beaks.

A triptych of hieroglyphic characters was inscribed on their chests. The writing on the silver band looked vaguely familiar, as if it might be related to the pictograms of the Egyptians, but I couldn't recall where I had seen it before.

All in all, an interesting art piece, but nothing that was going to force academe into a flurry of dodgy speculation. I thought it might fetch mid six figures in a quiet sale—maybe a million in a live auction. The style of the figures was definitely Hellenistic—even the orientation of the legs reflected the *Kore* stance—but due to the strange glyphs and unusual number of the figures—three Thoth figures was an unheard of grouping—dating the piece was out of the question.

The mirrored sphere, though, made all the difference. It floated inside the ring with no visible means of support.

XVIII

"That's it?" I shrugged, hiding my curiosity beneath a layer of Bohemian disinterest. "You've got me strapped down beneath this medieval Maidenform brassiere just to show me a vaguely Egyptian-looking knockoff of Nebuchadnezzar's statue?"

I heard wordless noises like hyenas chattering behind me—more Hollow Men, out of my line of sight. A thin smile crept across Kat's face. Bernard seemed vaguely disappointed. "Your insouciance is tiring, Mr. Markham."

"It's a reaction to being shot with a Taser," I replied. "Makes me giddy in all the wrong ways."

"Just show him," Julian said. "He's not going to be amenable to conversation until he sees a demonstration."

Bernard shook his head. "That's an untenable option."

"Not on him," Julian said. He tapped a finger against the frame of Kat's chair.

"What?" Kat struggled in her chair, trying to look behind her, straining to see what Julian was doing. I tensed my wrists, and the metal buckles on the thick leather straps rattled.

Julian held my focus as he reached his long index finger toward the top of Kat's head. His nimbus darkened, flickering into an orange and red crown.

"You bastard," Kat hissed, pulling at the straps around her

wrists. The Chorus twitched in my head as they felt her gather energy. "Let me go."

Julian pressed his finger into her hair and smoke licked up from the smoldering follicles. "Now why would I want to do that?"

She jerked forward in the chair, trying to evade his burning digit. A tiny orange triangle of fire persisted on her head, eagerly devouring her hair. Julian slapped her head, extinguishing the small flame, and then threaded his fingers in her hair, pulling her against the chair. "Listen," he growled into her ear. "We appreciate what you have done for us. Our Anointed are grateful. But your services are no longer required. There is no place for you here anymore."

She calmed down, still defiant under his hand but no longer reckless. "So I'm to be discarded then," she said. "Tossed out like an old piece of clothing. You think you know all of the ways in which I can be useful?"

Julian looked at me. "Well, baiting the snare was the most useful thing you've done for us. But—" he stroked her hair "—that's all you had left to offer."

Her eyes glittered as she collapsed the energy around her, coalescing her Will. Julian grimaced and stepped back. He signaled to the men standing behind me and I heard the clunk of a heavy switch being thrown.

Current arced across the frame of the chair, coursing through her body in a crackling pop of noise. She screamed, throwing herself against the bindings. Her spell disintegrated into microcosms of personality as the current shook her brain.

The jolt only lasted for a second or two, but it was enough to demolish her resistance. As the current was cut, she collapsed in the chair, smoke drifting from her shoulders and head.

Electrical current was one of the simplest forces to transmute. It was so close to light in many ways—just a stream of charged particles—that converting it through the filter of Will was one of the first elemental transformations a magus learns. The electric chairs would deter us from aggressive action—requiring us to focus our attention on the alchemy of the energy. When our Wills faltered, the current would become an issue.

Bernard stared at the floor, his face flushed. A muscle worked in the hinge of his jaw, flexing again and again. This wasn't his way, yet he hadn't lifted a finger or said a word to stop Julian.

The white-haired magus lifted her chin with a single finger and leaned her head against the back of the chair. Her face was covered with sweat and her eyes were unfocused. Her tongue moved against her lips, seeking moisture but also recoiling from the salty taste of her sweat. "Part of you will be joining us," he said, an uncharacteristic tenderness in his voice. "You brought us this far, and we're going to take the next step with your help. It's not an empty sacrifice."

Bernard moved his head as if he was shaking water off his face. Raising his arms, he turned toward the statue and began to speak a ritual prayer. Hard and sibilant consonants, lots of glossolalia, phrases that went on forever. It wasn't a tongue or a ritual I knew.

Julian knew, and with an expression bordering on animal wariness, he stepped back from Kat's chair.

What did this statue do? Was Bernard summoning something? Letting something loose?

The Chorus gibbered in my head as the energy patterns convulsed in the room. The ley energies twisted from their natural channels. I felt motion against my face, a strong suction toward the strange device, and my stomach recoiled at the distortion of the natural energy flow. It was as if a giant magnetized coil had been switched on and everything ferrous was being pulled toward this energized core. But the attraction wasn't magnetic, it was mystical. The non-reflective mirrors of negative light were pulling at our souls.

Bernard brought his hands together over his head in a single clap, a pop of sound that had no echo in the room. In a sudden rush of motion, the individual panes of glass boiled with white smoke. The direction of the smoke was different in each facet, and the sphere seemed to vibrate in place. With a noticeable gulp, the spectral pull vanished, replaced by an oppressive weight. I found it hard to breathe, difficult to suck in air as if the atmosphere had suddenly become much denser.

Bernard separated his hands and, as he uttered a final guttural word, a pale glow spread between his fingertips. The lettering on the silver band surrounding the sphere fluoresced briefly, reflecting his signal. The swirling smoke within the mirror facets moved faster. Each panel seemed to find some orientation and the whole globe filled with a churning vortex. Red streamers began to fall through the vortex, moving perpendicular to the rotation of the whirlwind. A chaotic smear dripping down.

It didn't stop at the lowest point of the sphere. The mist kept descending, curling out from the base. It widened as it drained, inverting into a mirror image of the tornado spinning within the globe.

Bernard said a few words and the vortex inside the mirror tore itself apart, subsiding into a senseless disturbance. The red mist beneath spun down, threading itself through an invisible point, and turned itself inside out. Like a balloon being inflated, something rubbery and moist unfolded from the inversion of the tornado column.

It was the size of a small dog—a starved animal mostly rib and skull. Its head was a surreal conglomeration. Its skull seemed canine, but it had no ears or eyes and its nose curved outward in a long proboscis. Instead of a mouth, a tiny slit gasped at the end of the hard beak. The creature was furless; its body a taut sack of translucent flesh over a cage of red bones.

The tornado completed its inversion and, with a curving motion of its elongating spine, the creature popped its back legs into place. It shook itself in a sinuous wiggle that started with the head and rippled along the length of its body.

Bernard pointed toward Kat, commanding the creature in the guttural tongue. The beast's long nose quivered as it picked up her scent. Like a hairless insect, it scuttled across the floor and leaped onto her leg.

Kat contorted and twisted in the chair as it clung to her pants like a macabre seed pod. Her feet drummed arrhythmically against the floor. The ibis-hound mounted her lap, crouched against her pelvis for a second as she tried to buck it off. Then, it leaped for her torso.

Like a fat tick, it dug its talons into her shirt and dragged itself onto her chest. It struck at her, its snout spiking through the center of her forehead, and Kat went into epileptic convulsions. The ibis-hound held on. Its thin sides heaving, it began to suck.

The Chorus shouted in my head, an explosion of alarm mirroring what I was already seeing. With each successive pulse of its body, the ibis-hound sucked off a portion of Kat's soul. Its mangy body swelled with glittering sparks.

Julian, anticipating my reaction, gave the signal for the electrical current in my chair to be engaged. Pain exploded across my chest, a thousand points of electric fire burning. My lungs seized as the current ignited my nervous system. My flesh smoldered and burned.

I struggled to protect my brain, to shelter the synaptic currents of my own system from the squirming and sparking fury of the electricity. Shards of white light shredded my vision, daggers piercing my retinas.

I made the current into pain. Pain was tolerable. Pain was transient. Like a violent spring storm that lashed itself against the ground until its strength was broken. Then it faded, subsiding into ambient atmospherics. Particles without focus, energy without purpose. The current became harmless electrons.

The surge stopped and I sagged in the chair. On my chest, the points of the Maiden had pierced and burned me. My limbs felt like ragged stone blocks discarded at the bottom of a quarry, and each breath was physically difficult.

Saturated, the creature returned to the trinity of figures. It scaled the nearest statue, an agile mountain climber who knew all the secret handholds, and danced along the figure's arm to balance on the edge of the silver circle. With a great convulsion, it expelled the soul out its long proboscis. A rain of light fell across the faceted sphere. The extrusion of Kat's soul fell through the mirrored surfaces where it landed, vanishing into the devouring darkness within the glass. The facets grew darker as they drank the offered soul, as if the hunger inside each face increased with the influx of energy.

The creature tight-roped back along the arms and crouched on the golden head nearest Kat, leaning toward her. It had but one purpose, a single desire: to continue its harvest of her soul. It was too small to drain her all at once, and so it would keep returning as long as her light remained.

Bernard bound the ibis-hound in place with a word. "It doesn't require this form to properly function. It mirrors the form of Thrice-blessed Hermes as a matter of symbolic convention—a framework you can visibly comprehend. A full withdrawal of the spirit is far less theatric, but is very much a manifestation of the mystery…"

I wasn't listening. Kat slumped to one side in her chair, held upright by the manacles about her wrists. Her breathing was so shallow as to be nearly unnoticeable. The Chorus dusted her, finding the outline of her spirit beneath the surface of her flesh, and what I feared was easily visible. She had a hole, a rippling darkness that was already burrowing deeper.

"—*Book of Thoth.*"

That caught my attention. "What?"

"*The Book of Thoth,* Mr. Markham." A grim smile touched Bernard's lips. "You haven't been paying attention, have you?" He stepped close to my chair and leaned toward me. "I know its secrets."

The Book of Thoth? I was even more stunned than when he had alluded to doing something to Antoine.

"I did it, Mr. Markham. I built his Key." He indicated the statues and the mirrored ball. "I built the theurgic mirror, and I can gather the souls of the living."

I recoiled at his words, the Chorus rising like enraged snakes in my head. I heard Julian shout at the Hollow Man assigned to the power switches and, before I could act further, the switch was thrown again.

Still off-guard from what Bernard had said, my Will was broken by the surge of electricity. I fled the sparking light and hid in the darkness that had been my friend for so long.

XIX

Like lightning splitting the night sky, consciousness returned in a rush. My body convulsed, and finding no restraints, a series of spasms ran through my arms and legs—sympathetic memories of the electroshock. I cracked an elbow against cold metal. I wasn't in the interrogation room any longer; this was the familiar womb of the shipping container.

I reached out and there wasn't any other presence. I was alone.

Kat.

My chest seized, and the pinpricks of the Maiden's touch burned. Not all of the ache in my joints and muscles was from the chair. Not all of it.

I could run from many things, but not my brain; it resurrected ghost memories: Kat, struggling to avoid the ibis-hound, her face stretching as her soul was sucked from her body; the ibis-hound's fat ticklike body rippling and flexing as it took her energy; the expression on Bernard's face as he watched—he wanted what he saw as much as he hated it.

My hands drummed against the cold floor, knuckles banging against the ridged metal. As if I could beat my way through. As if naked, wanton rage was enough.

You have to fill the void.

Kat. In the core of my heart, in the absence of the black root of *Qliphotic* obsession, there was a twisted knot of responsibility. My fault: her sacrifice, her death. She was inextricably tied to my soul, and the connection didn't blind me to her complicity with the Hollow Men, but I knew what the touch of the ibis-hound meant. I knew that hurt, that sensation of light being sucked away. I knew what flooded into the emptiness.

The floor wasn't going to yield. My knuckles were just being mauled by the metal floor. I curled up on my side, and tucked my sore hands against my bare stomach. It wasn't enough to be filled with rage. There had to be direction. Focus. The Will needed to be focused. Be smarter. See beyond the confines of this box. *Anticipate the motion of the threads in the Weave.*

When a magus understands the flow of forces, when he attenuates himself to the ley energies, he can discern patterns and structure. The Watchers call it the "Weave," the Akashic Record of humanity viewed as interwoven threads and patchwork designs of cultural movements. They see themselves as modern-day Fates, cutters and knitters of the Weave's individual threads.

We are patterns of energy—Ego and Identity—bound into shape by the Divine Spark. The Universe is a closed system that recycles itself, and we are agents that perpetuate that cycle—energy in, energy out. While a magus cannot violate the basic laws of the Universe—nothing is ever destroyed, it is simply transformed—he can direct forces in accordance with his desires. He learns how to read the Weave, and how to anticipate the course of its threads.

The art of prescience—of glimpsing the shape of the Weave and seeing how threads are woven together—is the inner secret of the final ranks of the Watchers. This Fateful Precognition allows Protectors to subtly engage the Weave, but it is the Architects who are expected to shape the world. The lesser ranks could only achieve brief glimpses, random flashes of clarity. Nostradamus was afflicted with persistent glimpses of the Weave, a precognitive fever he tried to articulate through his portentous poetry.

The tarot is a shortcut, a tool that lets us intuit the intersections of threads. Skilled readers are savants of pattern recognition. They don't see the future; their experience gives them the insight to understand how the threads are knotted together. One of the hardest tasks in reading the cards isn't gathering the threads but understanding the twist of the strands.

More often than not, you're asking the wrong question. The trick is to realize what the right question is before the brief glimpse you've been afforded vanishes.

I thought about the shortcomings of my question. I had tried to give it enough specificity that a small patch would have been revealed, but instead, Piotr had shown me a large spread of the canvas. Yes, at the center had been the intersection of mine and Kat's threads, but I hadn't bothered to take in the surrounding threads. I hadn't paid attention to their intersections.

It had been the same way when I had been a Watcher: the lack of being able to see the big picture. *You think too narrowly, Michael, too focused on what you want. It distracts you.*

I had thought it was luck, or a miserable oversight on their part, that the Maiden's electroshock therapy hadn't killed me. But, as I tried to discern the Weave, I realized there was another reason why I hadn't been the test case. Why they hadn't used me to demonstrate the ibis-hound.

Bernard's device harvested souls. In his dementia, he thought he had discovered the lost *Book of Thoth*. He had found the secret of the Egyptian Demiurge: the One Way, the Key of Immortality.

The Book of Thoth, however, was more fiction than fact. One of those legendary books that pervade our occult history, the *Book* is said to have been torn apart, and the pages became the first tarot deck. Its secrets were encoded in the mysteries of the cards. Another legend has it that the knowledge of those pages was too luminous for the unskilled human mind. The Library in Alexandria burned down because an unsuspecting acolyte tried to read the *Book*. He burst into flames and took everything with him.

Regardless of the *Book*'s existence, there was evidence in *The Corpus Hermeticum* that Hermes Trismegistus wasn't interested in mechanical aids. Much less a device that would harvest souls. Hermeticism—and later, Gnosticism—was an individual practice, an internalized revolution that allowed the practitioner access to Heaven.

What, then, was the device for? It was some kind of theurgic mirror. But did it reflect energy or was it meant to absorb energy? If it was a container—if it only took energy in—what was the use of that stolen power?

Though maybe stolen soul energy wasn't the point. It was the act that mattered. In taking part of her soul, the ibis-hound had created a vacuum. The Universe abhorred vacuums, and was wont to give them over to darkness. If Bernard hadn't let the ibis-hound finish its unholy task of breaking her apart, then the *Qliphoth* would poison Kat. They would fill her, and with a chunk of her soul missing, she wouldn't be able to ground herself enough to resist their influence.

I had been torn by the ritual in the woods, a tiny rip in my spirit, but it had been enough to infect me. I had been lost, an ignorant child wandering in the wilderness, and my fear had consumed me. I let it find purchase in my fractured self. I had let it grow. Kat's injury was massive in comparison. What hope did she have against such spiritual decay? Was it possible to be strong enough—to be *aware* enough—to fight back against such an invasion?

Was this the question I should have been asking at my reading? *How do you resist? How do you fight back?* Kat and I were the Lovers—this primary position was the imprint of my subconscious—and the card laid over us was symbolic of the objective world. It had been the Queen of Cups, the watery part of water. She was a reflective card—her own true nature was enigmatic and difficult to ascertain. My *Qliphoth*-spattered nightmares had given birth to the reading, and the Queen an unconscious clue that I had built my own spiritual prison. My cage was my own, and I would need to gain that perspective—that level of self-awareness in order to understand how I could free myself.

In the penultimate spot of the reading, the position of future awareness, was the Star. Inverted, representing my apprehension, my fear of failure. My perception of what had happened a long time ago—the unsheathed blade of the Prince of Swords—was a false history I hadn't let go. If I released this past, if I welcomed the idea of my prison as my own, then was the Prince of Cups—the final card of the reading—the path for me to follow? Was he what I was to become?

But all efforts to comprehend the Weave, via whatever mechanisms a magus employs, are just guesses. Some more educated than others. All precognition was a game of What If? Piotr's tarot reading was just one possibility, and a lot of its interpretation lay in my attitude, in what I brought to bear on the symbols. Was the cup half full? Half empty? Which way was it going to flow? It would be hard to say until it was too late to do anything about it.

But a hint lay there, floating in this amorphous drift of symbols and signifiers, a suggestion that there was a way out. Paths leading into dark woods also led out. A neophyte could find his way again; he could survive being lost.

Without the natural flame of the storm lantern, there wasn't any way to grow a fire without magick, and magick meant setting off Julian's ward. I crawled every inch of the container in the dark, trying to find some flaw in the ward. Some tiny hesitation in the script that could be exploited. Nothing. Julian's work was too precise.

My stomach knotted itself over and over, and the rest of my insides were equally shriveled. Two days, maybe more, since my last meal. Minnie's? What had I eaten? Details were starting to become vague.

Some time later, when I was too weak to move, I hallucinated. Visions of psychedelic butterflies and phantom lizards with rainbow-striped crests. The tarot dream came back and started to loop in my head, the details getting more surreal and psychotic with each iteration.

An ocean of light poured over me, and the rushing wave came with an overwhelming racket of church bells. I floated off the floor, and gasping like a lungfish coming out of the mud, I gulped at the light. It was transformed—*habes aquam vivam*—and I choked, unprepared for such a transformation. The light grew firm, shadows intruding in the blankness, and I began to remember what these shapes were. My hands trembled as they reached to hold the bottle against my mouth.

"Let him finish it," a voice said. "He needs to be coherent." I tried to distinguish this shadow from the others.

The water slowed to a trickle and, under the vacuum suction of my infantile need, stopped. My stomach ached from the sudden influx of fluid even as the rest of me sighed in delight. I lowered the plastic bottle and held it out for more.

The light went out: rough fabric over my head, a rope cinched against my neck. I inhaled instinctively, and my lungs choked on a cloying miasma. The cloth was soaked with an anesthetic and, with each breath, I pulled more of it into my lungs. The butterflies came back—more and more of them—and I drifted away, covered by iridescent wings.

I woke under a rounded roof, a cupola of iron girders rising to a capstone of riveted metal. Long shadows crept along the ribs of the roof. Tainted by the scent of dead fish and seawater, the air was damp and cold. Beneath me, a row of rivets pressed into my shoulder blade instead of the flat ridges of the container. My head was a block of wood, and based on the taste in mouth,

I had been sucking on dirty wool.

I rolled onto my side and sat up. Metal bleachers from an old high school gymnasium lined up along one wall. On either side, oil drums burned with blue flame. Hollow Men, dressed in gray robes with deep hoods, were scattered across the seats. At the base of the bleachers stood two men—one in the same gray, the other in a black hoodless garment. I recognized him, though Doug was taller and thinner in person. They were standing at the edge of the ceremonial circle in which I lay.

At four equidistant points along the circle—the cardinal directions, probably—there were metal sculptures. Scrap iron fused by blowtorch into skeletal frameworks. Lion, bull, eagle, and angel. Each held a different object: rod, sword, cup, and disk. Tarot suits, held by evangelical symbols.

My first guess was that the circle was something out of Solomon's grimoires, but this was more medieval, more late-period European alchemy in its representation. The statues were the beings seen by Ezekiel in his vision. This was the—

"The Wheel speaks the law of the living and of the dead." Doug's companion spoke the words as liturgy. The phrase rolled around in my head, stirring dull roots. The Wheel of Fortune. The tenth card of the tarot's Major Arcana. The cycle of death and rebirth. The Chorus moved sluggishly, old snakes reluctant to rise from their hibernation.

"*Rota taro orat tora ator.*" Doug said his part of the ritual. He was wearing the sort of shift that went over the head and tied around the waist with a length of old rope. Though Doug hadn't bothered with the rope.

Still unsteady with nausea, I managed to stand. A glob of thick spit was rolling on the back of my tongue and I worked it forward until I could spit it out. My input to the ceremonial rhetoric.

"Kings and princes are equal upon the circle of fate." The priest ignored my commentary. "And their fate is determined by the rotation of the Wheel." A mutter of agreement ran through the rank of Hollow Men. In the wan light of the blue flames, they looked like empty statues.

"You have been challenged by Douglas Rassmussen, Initiate Ascendant in the Order of the Hollow Men. While you have no rank within the Order, a temporary conveyance has been established to allow you to fight upon the Wheel. At the resolution of this combat, this conveyance will be terminated. You will have no recourse to membership or recognition by the Order. Is that clear?"

"Yeah," I said, finally getting my words under control. "I get it." I rolled my shoulders and shook out my arms. The turgid Chorus finally moved out of my belly and into the rest of my frame. I was weak from a lack of food—the water hadn't done much beyond whet my appetite—but I was functional. Functional enough for Doug, apparently.

It had been his voice in the container, when I had been given water. *He needs to be coherent.* If he wanted me dead, they would have killed me in the box. They wouldn't have bothered with all this pomp and nonsense. This was a sacrament that met some ritual need of Doug's. I couldn't sense Julian, and I doubted Bernard was one of those watching; this was an unsanctioned event. Those two wouldn't have bothered with showing me how the mirror worked if this was where I was going to end up.

Doug had deviated from the plan. He wanted something of his own. A little piece of me. "In the old days," I said as adrenaline finally started to charge my blood, "they would just rope off a section of floor and let us beat each other bloody. No one gave a shit about recognition or rank."

"We've grown more civilized," the orator said.

"I suppose he's planning on reading my guts if he can?"

Doug nodded.

"So much for civilized," I said. I raised a hand and waved Doug over. "Come on, chump. Quit letting your master bore us with his liturgy. Come and take what you think you deserve."

The orator looked over his shoulder at the assembled host. "Witnesses?" he asked. They all raised their right hands. He nodded at them. "I'm done talking then," he said, sweeping a hand toward the ring and me. "Shut him up," he said, breaking from his stoic character. Raising his hood to cover his face, he stepped back from the circle.

A puff of light followed Doug as he crossed the border of the circle, a mystic ripple that preceded a clatter of metal. Long triangular pieces of steel rose up from the trough at the edge of the circle. Speaking in one sepulchral voice, the Hollow Men incanted an old propulsion spell. They stamped their feet three times to focus, actualize, and initiate the magick. Machinery beneath the floor groaned, and the triangles began to move along a recessed track.

They spun about the circumference of the circle, their rotational rate increasing in time to the beat of the Hollow Men's feet. The blades became a blur, and the Hollow Men stopped. The barrier at the edge of the circle kept moving.

So many blades. I had drawn a lot of them in my reading. The Wheel was where they all came to pass.

Doug stripped off his black robe as he prowled along the edge of the circle. Underneath, he wore a dark track suit. He bunched up the collar of the robe and held the garment in one hand.

Chorus-sight revealed a sphere of violet light around his head. Tiny contrails drifting in his wake like long strands of mist. It wasn't a complex spell, hand-to-hand combat was the worst time to attempt an intricate incantation. While one fighter was busy shaping energies, his opponent would just brain him with a rock. Combat magic was sharp and quick. Not like the fire spell Julian had had floating over his head—that sort of magick took time to nurture and position. The tiny streamers coming off Doug's head were something else…

Doug raised his hand to his mouth, whispering to the robe, and some of the violet light from his halo slipped into the robe.

He let go of the garment and it spread out like a manta ray. Its edges rippled and pulsed as it soared across the ring.

It was just a cotton robe—it couldn't harm me—but it could distract me. If it managed to wrap itself around my arm or leg, I would be encumbered.

I side-stepped its first lunge. As it fluttered past, I charged the desiccated atmosphere in my mouth and spat a drop of fire. The hot spark struck the robe's fluttering wing, melting through the flight aspect of the spell. Fire beats air. Even in alchemy, there are Roshambo rules.

As the robe fluttered to the floor, I heard a screech of metal. Behind me. I had lost Doug. Misdirection, not a distraction. The robe had been a decoy. I glanced over my shoulder.

Doug had gone to the bull statue—the sword-wielding aspect on the Wheel of Fortune—and he had extricated the weapon from the statue's hands. Of course, the statues weren't just for show. They would have a deadly practicality. As Doug raised the sword and charged, the Weave twitched and I Saw the pattern. *The Prince of Swords*. Realized Mind, obsessively focused on a single goal.

Me. Antoine. Doug. We were all the same.

XX

The sword was a heavy two-handed blade, probably not all that sharp, but even a smack with its dull edge was worth avoiding. I back-pedaled and tripped over the flopping robe, which immediately wrapped itself around my left leg. Doug's first swing went over my head, whirring like the wing of a predatory bird.

Doug had no formal blade training, obvious in the way he let the weight of the sword over-extend him. He recovered clumsily, and opted for an easier downward stroke as a follow-up attack. Dragging the cloying robe with me, I rolled away from his swing.

Sparks danced on the riveted floor as the sword stuck. The force of the impact stung Doug's hands, and he struggled with his grip. While he tried to control the blade, I kicked at his knee with my robe-wrapped leg. I missed, but got close enough to confuse the robe.

The spell laid on the cloth was simple and didn't include a decision tree for target resolution. Confronted with choices, the magicked cloth partially unwrapped itself from my leg so as to greedily snare Doug's knee as well. Doug staggered back from the overly friendly robe, dragging the sword across the floor. I flushed the Chorus into my leg, momentarily deadening the liveliness of my flesh. The robe fell off my leg, sensing only

Doug's retreating body as an active target. It rippled across the floor and he swung at it.

I scrambled like a monkey for the nearest statue—the rampant lion, pentacle-shaped shield in its paws. As Doug, having slain his creation, came after me, I pulled the shield free and got it up in time to block his clumsy swing. My left arm, braced along the underside of the shield, went numb. He hit the shield again, and my clumsy stance collapsed.

We were close to the edge of the circle, close to the whirling barrier of steel blades. As he swung the sword like a lunatic golfer, forcing me to lower the shield so its bottom edge touched the floor, I realized he didn't need to actually hit me with the sword. He was keeping me off-balance, forcing me to retreat from his wild swings. Forcing me back into the spinning blades. I could hear their hungry whisper behind me, the keening relentlessness of their sharp edges.

Doug knew this arena. The motif was familiar and he knew how to play to its strengths. I was playing catch-up in a game running in sudden-death overtime. I had to wrap my head around a viable strategy. Now. Another step back and I'd be diced.

Doug danced away, giving himself a little space. The wind-up for the big swing. I could move left and right, but I was running along the edge of the ring. How long could I dodge his attacks? To get some real distance, I'd have to run, dropping all pretense of defense. He would have one clear shot. Sharp blade or not, one would be enough.

He spun, bringing the sword around at his waist. Head height for me. I raised the shield and braced myself for the impact. Doug hit hard, and I held my ground by shifting the blow off to one side of the shield. The rim of the shield crossed the plane of the circle though, and with a chattering bite, the triangular blades sheared off an arm of the pentacle.

Too close. The blades tore the shield from my grip, and it clattered against the floor. Out of easy reach. I stayed low, trying to duck-walk toward it.

Doug minced about in a gangly two-step with the sword, trying to keep me off-balance with his unpredictable movements. I couldn't avoid his next strike. His blade or the blades behind me: he liked those odds. Either was fine. Though he'd prefer that I stood there and took his blade.

The Chorus tightened at the base of my neck, squeezing my spine. Two choices. *Which one?* They rose like a pressure wave, carrying with them a chaotic burst of insight.

Blind Fortune turns the Wheel. Tied to its rim, the vegetable kings are pulled down by its persistent cycle. The cycle of the seasons. Kings are buried by the children; the children become kings. The Wheel, always turning. The alchemical and Hermetic symbol of transformation. Death. Burial. Rebirth.

Thoth guides the newly born. Thoth, who became Hermes in Hellenic Egypt. Hermes Thrice-blessed. Hermes Trismegistus. *The only vice of the soul is ignorance.* Reason guides the soul; the Enlightened Mind breaks free. The body is buried, and we are reborn by digging out of this grave of flesh. Reason allows us to make choices. Not the random circumstances of fate, but informed choices.

Sword raised, Doug trotted forward to deliver the killing blow. He hesitated at the peak of his back swing, the expression on my face giving him pause.

I was smiling.

This is not a death of my choosing.

"What are you laughing at?" The tip of the sword, raised over his head, trembled slightly.

"Something said to me recently," I said. *"Ex lux et vita."*

The Chorus erupted in a flash of visible light. Doug recoiled from the starburst, and the sword wobbled in his hands. I kicked his kneecap, connecting this time, and he went down, the joint of his leg bending at an obtuse angle.

He bellowed like a gored wildebeest, hands going to his shattered kneecap. The etheric strands streaming from his head thickened like fire hoses filling with water.

Energy. Channeled energy.

Doug was connected to lines of force, and these conduits were feeding him power. At the other end of the strands were his buddies, the sorcerers sitting in the bleachers. Doug was getting help from the sidelines.

He snapped his leg forward, and a spurt of violet energy around his kneecap popped the joint back into place. The magick nimbus brightened about his head as he near-levitated to his feet. Blood-stained tears—quivering tracks of pink luminescence—spread from the corners of his eye sockets. He interlaced his fingertips, and a storm brewed in the hollow of his hands.

Lightning. I needed a ground, something elemental to hide behind. I scrambled for the damaged shield. The pentacle was the suit of earth, and even with one arm missing, it was my best protection.

A tempest blossomed like a midnight flower between his palms, and with a ragged noise, the storm spat a jagged cable of lightning. The discharge struck the center of the shield, the pentacle attracting the lightning. The shield grew hot against my arm, but most of the energy was dispersed by the earthly ground of the symbol. A shower of crackling sparks, the bitter smell of scorched ozone in their wake, cascaded from the shield.

Doug coalesced energy for another bolt, the force lines pulsating around his head. I had to break his concentration. The weather flower was a volatile construct, difficult to control. I charged, the hot shield raised, and I plowed into him with all the grace of an out-of-control semi truck. The tempest popped, a pressure wave pounding my ears.

We went down in a confusion of limbs. Beneath me, Doug reached around the edge of the shield. A web of electricity danced between his fingers, weather still storming in his hand. He strained to touch my face.

I tucked in my chin and shoved his hand away with the shield. His arm hit the Wheel, sparks erupting from his fingertips. I smacked his unprotected face with the hot shield, eliciting a cry of surprise. I got both forearms behind the shield, ignoring the searing burn of heated metal—it was hotter on the front—and firmly pressed the star-inscribed disk against Doug's face.

He bucked me off, a violent rodeo-worthy undulation. The shield stayed, stuck to his flesh. With a scream that was more outrage than pain, he pulled the pentacle off his burned flesh. The star's outline was livid on his skin; his left eyelid was melted into the socket, a fused tab of burned meat hiding the ruin of his eye.

"That looks like it hurts." I fed him a smug grin as well.

He had too much accessible energy. I couldn't beat him by magick alone. I had to keep hurting him, keep goading him so he reacted without thinking. A course chosen by my Will, not his. Antagonizing him would keep it physical, down in the brutal animal arena. Down where I knew a few tricks.

Doug threw the shield away and scrambled for his sword. I needed a weapon, so I ran across the arena to the eagle statue. It held a long staff—the symbol of fire. In response to the heated touch of the Chorus, the bird blessed me with the metal stick.

Unlike Doug, I had experience with weapons. As he tried to hit me with the sword, I parried his clumsy attacks and responded with sharp taps: one to the thigh, one to the kidney, one to the back of the head. After the third shot, his enthusiasm for straight weapons combat flagged. As I banged aside his half-hearted swing with the long wand, he let go of the sword. He caught the end of the wand as I tried to jab him in the stomach with it.

Halo glowing, he shattered the staff with an exhalation of power. I had already let go of the wand so instead of losing a hand, I was just peppered with shrapnel. Blood stippled my stomach, and I could feel the acidic bite of metal under my skin.

I tried to steady myself, and my foot slipped off the base of the eagle statue. Doug, seizing the opportunity, came in close and pounded me in the stomach with an energized fist. Something moved unnaturally in my gut and I choked on a wet cough. "How about that?" he snarled. "Does that hurt?" His burned flesh was vivid, and his remaining eye was filled with burst blood vessels. The lines streaming across his cheek were more blood than tears.

I spat in that bloodshot eye, the Chorus igniting the spittle as it left my mouth. His eye collapsed in a gush of hot steam, and he retreated. His pain confused him, and unable to see, he tripped over his own feet.

Grimacing against the molten pain in my stomach, I staggered along the rim of the Arena to the bull statue. *Vis,* I told the Chorus. *Give me strength.* They lit my hands as I reached up and tore off the two-foot-long curved horns of the statue.

By the time I returned to him, Doug had incanted an *udjat* eye—a floating sigil on his forehead giving him rudimentary sight. He turned his head like a mole questing for a scent, and when he turned in my direction, I caught him under the chin with one of the horns. The uppercut knocked him back down and, as he tried to get up, I kicked him in the ribs. He rolled away from the blow, sprawling onto his back.

"*Compunge.*" The Chorus flowed into the curved horn, and I stabbed him high on the left hip with the magicked tip. The horn, sharpened and shaped by the Chorus, slid through bone and flesh until it struck the metal plate beneath his body. I leaned against it, and the horn slid into the floor until it was firmly planted in the plate. He curled forward around the metal spike. A bug protecting its belly.

I clobbered him on the forehead with the other horn, knocking him flat. Before he could curl up again, I put the second spike through his right shoulder. As the metal horn ground through cartilage and bone into the floor, he howled like a tortured animal.

"Do you yield?" I shouted at him, making sure the Hollow Men could hear my question over his agonized cries.

Energy sparked off his head and the *udjat* eye spun madly in the center of his forehead. He moaned around the spikes. All the magickal opiates in the world weren't going to blot out the pain.

I repeated the question, and he found the wherewithal to form a response. "Never!"

The Prince of Swords. Unable to see anything but his singular goal. Unable to realize his forward motion had been arrested. Incapable of knowing when to stop.

I retrieved his discarded sword. As my hand closed around the hilt, I fell back into memory, and was flush again with the fury that had led me to the bridge in Paris, to the duel with Antoine. Tied to that was the black rage that had nearly pushed my hand through Kat's chest. Blind idealism. Slavish devotion. The crippled Prince. The hubris of a mind so precise in its tunnel vision that it was unable to see beyond the pinprick of its immediate goal. No Will. No Reason. Just unrestrained passion.

"We are all your princes," I whispered to the sword. Antoine. Doug. Myself. Slaves to the point, fanatics who walk the edge.

Our hands. What we do. It is all written there.

My choice, now.

Doug screamed as he twisted against the horns. I rolled him forward with my calf and put my foot against his tailbone, elevating his right leg. "You're not afraid to lose your body, are you, Doug?" I asked. "You're on the rise. You can deal with this."

The Chorus sharpened the blade as I brought the sword down on his right leg, just below the knee. The blade went through, slicing off his calf and foot. His leg jerked, showering the deck with blood.

I swept up the piece of twitching meat and hurled it at the audience of Hollow Men. The severed leg hit the barrier of blades and vaporized into a spray of bone, blood, and flesh. The

Hollow Men in the front row recoiled, and those connected to Doug channeled their outrage through the conduits, pumping the pinned man full of energy and adrenaline.

Doug, full of animalistic howls, was still lucid enough to fight back. His right hand scrabbled on the deck, struggling to reach my foot. I swept the blade down on his wrist. He tried to jerk his hand back, but his arm was pinned beneath the edge of the blade. *Almost.*

"This is for Gerald Summers. That old sack of meat you used and threw away." I twisted the blade, feeling it cut through bone and muscle. "Nothing more than a cheap coat, was he? Something to wear once and discard. Nobody cared what happened to it. Right?" The blade sheared through the ligaments at the end of his wrist.

A contorted mask, Doug's face was a riot of uncontrolled expressions. Neural networks overloaded with pain were being blocked off while the Ego retreated to the core of etheric power still flowing into the damaged flesh. Through this opacity of pain, Doug started to use the conduits to heal himself. To fight his way back into control of his body. Pain is transitory. Eventually, the spirit extracts obedience from the flesh. Flesh can be remade.

"Show me your magick trick, then." I raised the gory sword. "Let's see what you can do without your flesh." I drove the steel sword through the center of his skull, burying the point in the floor.

Doug's spirit—a glistening, twisting shape of diaphanous energy—erupted from his corpse. In this pure form, I could See energy pumping along the extruded veins of the conduits, pouring power into the maelstrom of Doug's sparkling spirit.

I knew what he had to be planning. There was only one viable body on the platform. He had reached the rank of Initiate Ascendant within the group. He knew how to body-jack. He was going to try to possess me. His psychoanimist trick of taking over a body.

I laughed at him. "You have no idea how fucking stupid a plan that is," I said, and spiked him with the Chorus.

His spirit convulsed, shrinking to a dense clot of white-tipped will-o'-wisps. The ravenous Chorus tore at this spirit mass, shredding the outer layers. Doug swirled like an emergent galaxy, throwing off spiral arms of gossamer light. I could taste his panic. He knew. *Lightbreaker.* I was going to devour him.

I survived the dark night in the forest because I listened to the *Qliphoth,* because I welcomed the hunger into my heart. I survived because I learned how to break spirits and take their light.

Doug tried to fend off the Chorus, but they were already inside him, nipping through the veils of his soul. He cried out, but I was the only one who heard him. He started to beg, his voice keening in my head; he whimpered for mercy; I ignored all of it.

The Chorus devoured Doug and, in an orgiastic rush, I felt his essence pour into me. Faster and faster, the jumbled collection of Doug's sense data and memory associations gushed into my head. Most of it would vanish quickly, chunks and blocks of memory dissolving into random noise and color; but, *for this instant,* his entire life was mine. All the sensory details of his existence were there: I witnessed what Doug had seen; heard what he heard; tasted the meals he could remember eating; knew the scents that made him think of his mother. I held his doubts, his dreams, and his errors. I knew his dirty little secrets; I knew why he had been left behind. I knew why he had come to my cell and dragged me to this duel. I *was* Doug.

This was the promise given and then taken away: Doug had been grudgingly granted the rank of Initiate Ascendant, but he had not been Anointed. The biting betrayal in Doug's heart was that only the Anointed were allowed to participate in the Great Work sponsored by Bernard and Julian.

Bernard's theurgic mirror had a greater purpose than just storage. The ibis-hounds were *takwin,* artificial creatures made by the device, but they weren't the sole function of the device. The spirit creatures harvested souls for a purpose, a purpose which Doug had been *denied*.

The Chorus rippled and snarled under my skin, rampant chimerae resplendent with fiery halos, in response to the discovery of this knowledge within Doug's fading history. *Settle it,* they growled. In their teeth, they held the conduit threads, those open pathways feeding Doug. Channels straight into the magickal cores of the other sorcerers. *Open fucking doorways.* I could barely hold them in check.

"Gentlemen," I Whispered to the assembled host of Hollow Men, my voice an unavoidable serpentine hiss in their ears. "Doug is gone. His rank was worthless, and I have broken him."

I stepped away from the blood-spattered corpse, my hands held casually at my sides. "I have no quarrel with any of you. But, should you wish to take umbrage at my departure from this Arena, now is the time." I gave the soul threads a slight tug. Several of the Hollow Men jerked at my touch. "See through me if you can. See through me and know that I will do to you what I did to him. Know that I walk out of here. Now."

The Chorus poured themselves down one of the threads, fiery lions burning through the mystic wire. They ignited the organs of the Hollow Man on the other end. Setting fire to his heart, his liver, his lungs, his stomach—all of it, burning with phosphorescent heat. A tongue of flame shot out of his mouth as he screamed, setting his hood on fire.

The others reacted, equal parts panic and incantations. The fire spread; first one, then another soul igniting when touched by the incandescent spark of my Will. The blaze became a conflagration, a pyre of burning flesh and hot metal. The chamber burst finally, unable to hold the light and heat any longer.

Mahapralaya.

This is the way the world ends.

THE FOURTH WORK

"…ye must understand also that this Multiplicity is itself Unity, and without it Unity could not be. And this is a hard saying against Reason; ye shall comprehend, when, rising above Reason, which is but a manipulation of the Mind, ye come to pure Knowledge by direct perception of the Truth."

– Aleister Crowley, *Liber CL: De Lege Libellum*

XXI

From a window seat at Denny's, I watched the firefighters contain the warehouse blaze. Julian's building was an unassuming four-story brick structure with plain windows evenly spaced about the façade. A series of loading docks ran off the southern side, with tall doors of corrugated metal large enough to accommodate easy loading of shipping containers.

I had found the one used for my prison on the first floor. One of the fleeing Hollow Men had thought he would be safe inside.

SFD had three engines on-site, and snakes of white hose were strewn about the red trucks. Lines of steaming water soaked the old bricks of the warehouse, playing a game of tag with the red and orange flame in the shattered windows. Yellow-suited figures ran along the raised concrete dock like ants trying to salvage their queen from the inferno inside.

"Looks like a good-sized fire." The waitress had a double order of sausage and cheese omelets, toast, and home fries. She put the plates down, one of them at the place setting across from me as if someone else was going to join me. I didn't bother to correct her assumption. I was going to wolf down the first plate in short order. The second one wasn't going to have time to cool. "Ketchup?" she asked.

I shook my head, and with a final glance toward the fire, she wandered off. I focused on the omelet in front of me. While I was filled with etheric energy, taken from the Hollow Men, it wasn't the same as real food. The material body needs material fuel—one of the inescapable rules of the Universe—and it had been four days since I had eaten. The waffle at Minnie's, early Wednesday morning.

The newspaper in the rack outside the restaurant said it was Saturday. The fire had cut through the morning fog blanketing the industrial district south of downtown Seattle, an early morning glow that must have confused drivers on I-5 as if the sun was rising in the west instead of the east. A single fire engine had responded initially but, after a rapid assessment, the on-site commander had called for backup. The fire was in the walls and floors.

The Arena had been in a subbasement, several floors below the ground. The conflagration had started there, with the immolation of the first Hollow Man. There were those who had just watched—Witnesses, not participants—and I had let them go. The others, the eight who had given Doug magickal aid, they had been my prey.

Four died in the subbasement; one in the eastern stairwell; one hid in the shipping container, and I had closed the door a moment before I set off Julian's ward; one tried to fight back, thinking he could ambush me on the second floor; and the last one tried to fly away. Filled with energy stolen from the others, I had given him a boost. He turned into ash, a black smear across the damp rooftop.

You have to fill the void.

It had been easy. A bright burning fury encapsulating a decade of pent-up helplessness. Years of fear. All focused through a need for vengeance, to take from them what they had taken from Kat.

The void in my soul. I poured energy into it because that was the way I reacted to a Universe that made me afraid. Its nihilistic enormity. What were we in this vast emptiness? I killed, not because of the *Qliphotic* taint, but because it was the only way I knew how to be a Creator.

"Nice of you to order me something."

Nicols sat down across from me. He turned over the nearby coffee cup and placed it near the edge of the table where the waitress would spot it. "There any ketchup?" he asked, unrolling the silverware from the paper napkin.

"I'm sure she can bring some," I said.

He did a good job of appearing to be noncommittal in looking at me, but I knew there were physical differences from the last time he had seen me. Unlike other scars, I had no desire to keep marks from the last few days. I had wiped away the pattern of burn marks on my chest, fixed the torn ligament in my knee and regrown my burned hair. The body is mutable if the Will is strong. The braid of Reija's hair was a stark white band about my throat. I had also acquired clothing before leaving the warehouse, replacing my blood-stained pants with a nondescript blue track suit I had found in a locker. Nicols noticed the reverse haircut, surely, just as he noticed how rested I looked compared to him.

The jeans and hooded sweatshirt augmented his exhaustion, failing to disguise the slump of his shoulders and the unhealthy tinge of his skin. The disheveled arrangement of his hair suggested he had been sleeping in his car. Smoking there too. His clothes reeked of musty tobacco.

He looked out the window at the fire, not unaware of the view afforded this table. "You're very shiny," he said. "I Saw you from the street." I heard his emphasis. In my absence, he had come to believe in his Sight.

And I *was* very shiny. Filled with the light of the Hollow Men, I knew I'd be hard not to spot from the street. I wasn't ready to flush all that energy; it was a ready reservoir of useful power. The increased visibility was a trade-off I could live with in the short term. Besides, all the wrong sort of people already knew I was here.

"You happen to be in the neighborhood or do you have a fetish for fire?" I asked, nodding toward the excitement down the block.

"Very funny. Thanks for hanging around at the hotel. I appreciate the concern for my well-being. It was just a Taser, after all. I suppose you get shot with that sort of thing every day."

"Not *every* day. I'm sorry about that. You were right. It was a trap. But not one of Pender's design."

"Yeah," he nodded. "I figured that out when he arrived. He was convinced you had orchestrated that mess: shot me, taken the girl, and made a run for the border."

"What did you tell him?"

"Nothing. He was eager to have me corroborate his story." He shrugged. "So I did." He leaned forward. "I met your friend."

"Who?"

"Antoine."

He *was* here. My insight into the Weave had been correct. There was a larger game afoot, and we were being moved about in accordance with a coordinated plan. "So Pender's act was for his benefit."

"Yeah, that's what I figured. He was trying too hard to sell his story."

"Did Antoine buy it?"

Nicols settled back in the seat, exhaling noisily. "He's... ah, 'inscrutable' is a good word. He's *not fucking there* when you try to look at him. And forget trying to read his body language. It's like trying to read patterns in running water. He knew I could See and the fact that I couldn't read him at all may have amused him. Or maybe not. I just don't know."

"Antoine was always good at hiding himself."

"He's more than good." Nicols shook his head. "Pender wanted to hold me for questioning. 'Observation' was the term he used.

But Antoine—Jesus, he barely said anything and Pender was still ready to shit himself—wasn't going to have any of that. He told Pender to leave me alone."

I smiled. *Nicely done.* My abduction had been meant to be a distraction, but Antoine had simply brushed the misdirection aside. He left Nicols in play, knowing the detective would look for me.

"What about Kat?" he asked. "Did you find her?"

I looked at the fire, at the cloud of black smoke rising from the ruined warehouse, before I nodded.

The waitress wandered over with the coffee pot. She poured Nicols a cup, and while she refilled mine, he talked her out of the ketchup bottle in the pocket of her apron. He smothered his omelet and I looked away, my stomach churning. Too much like blood.

"Where is she?" He hacked off the end of his omelet, a clean slice done with an executioner's precision. Like a sword through a limb.

"I don't know." I hadn't found her body: not in the container, not in the interrogation room, not anywhere else in the building. Kat was gone, and a part of my heart told me—over and over—that she was already dead. She had been broken and the invasive darkness would devour her. Even if I had been able to find her immediately, how was I going to save her? I hadn't been able to save my own soul from a tear more imagined than real. What was I going to do for someone who was actually missing part of their soul? And now, three days on, how much could possibly be left? How much of Kat was left, and how much was turned into something else.

A *Qliphotic* echo looped behind those questions, a lingering remnant of the poison. It still sought to influence my Will, to lure me into that immolation of vengeance. That *Mahapralaya* moment. Find those who killed her. Do to them what you did to the nine. They all deserved to die. They all conspired to take her from you. Every one of them. *Break their souls.*

I stabbed my plate so hard the fork stuck into the porcelain. "I don't know." I looked out the window, and my exhalation left ice on the glass. Part of me repeated what the voices were saying; part still liked that empty and cold worldview.

Cancers linger. They never die quickly. Their hearts can be extracted, but their roots are persistent and they don't die overnight. The rot stops, but the decay can still be infectious. Days, weeks, months—years, even—would have to pass before it was truly gone.

"What happened?" Nicols prodded me, a gentle nudge to shake me loose from this cycle of endless recrimination. A simple question, seemingly innocent, but his eyes were hard and he didn't blink.

"I didn't hurt her, John. I found her and… everything… it was all wound around a lie. Some story I told myself so often that… she wasn't responsible, John. She was just… a symbol. Just something that reminded me of what I had lost."

He looked away, and not because of the nakedness of my confession, but because of his own reaction to my words. His own secret. What was it? I grabbed onto this question as a way to escape my own thoughts, and I pieced together the clues he had left me: his empty house, and the clothes still in the closet; his reference to on-going therapy sessions—started before the incident on the ferry; and his mannerisms, deliberate and yet hesitant—a corpus of non-verbal communication that had become a dead language now that the only person who had understood his gestures and affections was no longer here.

Sarah. He had referred to her in the past tense.

"I'm sorry, John," I said. "My issues aren't the same. Not at all."

His jaw paused. "Yeah," he said, putting his fork down. "They aren't."

A burst of cheap music trilled from the pouch of his sweatshirt. Nicols dug out his cell phone, looked at the display, and his eyebrows pulled together. He flipped it open and raised it tentatively to his ear. "Nicols."

The conversation was one-sided; his contribution was several noncommittal grunts. I tried to read something in his expression, some indication of what he was hearing. "Yes, Ma'am," he said. He shut the phone and a reaction to what he had just heard crystallized in his eyes: fear.

"That was my captain. I've been recalled to active duty. I'm supposed to report to a suburb called Ravensdale immediately."

"What's going on?"

He shook his head. "She wouldn't tell me. But she did say that the call is going out to everyone. We're all being sent, every cop the city can spare. Something has happened."

Bernard. The theurgic mirror.

In my heart, there was a spurt of fire. *Break their souls.*

On the *Thomas Guide* map, Ravensdale was a tiny community off Kent-Kangley Road, tucked away on the eastern side of the ridge from the larger suburb of Kent. What the map failed to show was how the cone of Mt. Rainier dominated the horizon this far from the urban center of Seattle, a mottled white and gray peak towering over the surrounding bumps of the Cascade Range. The aftermath of Tuesday's storm had fled the valley, leaving only a thin layer of clouds gliding across the pale sky.

A piebald blanket of pine trees blanketed the foothills of the mountains. The verdant growth of trees was broken in irregular intervals by construction. Persistent urban encroachment. The escalation of property values in Seattle proper continued to push people further and further away. As we drove out Maple Valley Highway, Nicols pointed out the creeping edge of the frontier: first Newcastle and Kent, then Maple Valley and Covington, now Ravensdale.

When we reached the police roadblock, we queued up behind three other cars. King County Sheriff's deputies gathered around each vehicle as it rolled up to their four-car barricade. I rolled down the window as we crept forward, listening to the wind and the sounds from the forest. Both were hushed, as if afraid to be the ones to tell me what had happened here.

One of the three cars in the queue was turned away. Two guys—radiating annoyance and anger—glared at us as they rolled past. As if we were somehow responsible for denying them access. Nicols' casual wave didn't improve their mood. "Erickson and Stenhill. From the *Times*," he explained. "I've never seen them in anything but a foul mood."

When it was our turn, Nicols offered his shield and ID. The young man at his window seemed too young to have been on the force long—first or second year, probably; the Chorus could taste him. He read the details on Nicols' ID carefully, comparing image to face, and then he leaned down further and looked over at me. "Who's this?"

"He's with me," Nicols said.

"I need to log him," the deputy replied.

Two of them spread out on my side of the car, their hands firmly on their pistol butts. The Chorus heard their heartbeats, and showed me silver adrenaline spikes running across their shoulders.

My hands shook as the spectral ghosts moved in my spine. They were so eager, and I realized how unhinged I still was from the expulsion of the poison and the subsequent fight in the Arena. My control was marginal, my own desire for violence too close to the surface. I was too ready to listen to them. Too ready to *burn*.

"Name's Markham," Nicols said, unaware of my mental struggle. He carefully spelled my last name for the cop. "Special attaché to SPD from back east. He's trained for this sort of thing."

A flutter of pale fabric moved in the shadow of the trees along the road. The fourth deputy—the one who remained near their cars—shouted, pointing out the movement. Struggling to pull their guns, the pair on my side spun around. They missed the convulsive shudder that ran through my body as I let the Chorus out, as I let them touch the approaching figure.

An old man scrambled out of the woods, scuttling on all fours like a rabid squirrel. Dressed in flannel pajama bottoms and a t-shirt so old it had turned gray, he was a strange apparition wildly out of place in the context of the woods. Gnarled and distorted, his face was a melted wax mold. His eyes were gone, black holes in his pinched face and his tongue was a shriveled stick in his mouth. Dark motes drifted from his sagging mouth, a haze of ash.

Before the deputies could decide to fire, the old man scrabbled onto the road, and rammed my passenger-side door with his head. His hands clawed for the open window.

I grabbed his head, evading the snapping trap of his mouth, and the Chorus, wreathing my body like a phantasmal film of silver smoke, collapsed into the point of contact between my flesh and the man's dead skin. With an infernal roar like an industrial boiler lighting, the old man's body ignited. Light into darkness, a sacrament that was anathema to the debasement violating the old man. *Qliphotic.* Soul dead. A piece of flash paper, he vanished into a greasy smear of smoke, and in a second, there was nothing left but a tiny stain of soot on the road.

Nicols retrieved his badge and ID from the astonished deputy. "Like I said, a professional." He eased the car forward and gently rolled us through the narrow gap between the police cars. As we picked up speed beyond the barricade, I looked back. The one who had spotted the old man first was talking into his radio while the others stared, dumbfounded, at the smear on the road.

"Drive faster," I told Nicols. "He's calling us in. He's got my name."

"What the hell was that?" Nicols' calm façade cracked.

I noticed what was strewn across the back seat of the car. The blanket covering most of it had slipped down. Two file boxes filled with papers and books, and it looked like more books on the floor. Unlike the collection on Doug's shelves, this assortment was a better primer. Nicols had been busy.

"*Qliphotic* zombie," I explained. "When the soul is gone, all that remains is a hunger. They're drawn to bright lights. Vacuums fill."

He nodded. My examination of his library hadn't gone unnoticed. "Yeah," he said, jerking his head at the books. "It all started with a vacuum. *Ain Soph* collapses into *Ain*. I got that far in one of the Kabbalah books back there. But where did this zombie come from?"

"Ravensdale." I heard Bernard's voice in my head. *We have a much grander plan in mind.* "Yeah," I said, answering his unasked question. "There's going to be more of them." The Chorus quailed at my imagination, sending a line of fear running down my spine. "He's taken them all," I croaked. "Every soul in Ravensdale."

As I said it, as I voiced the terrible enormity of what might have happened, I realized why the old man had charged the car. Wrapped with energy stolen from the nine at the warehouse, I was the brightest light in the valley. A psychic magnet, a lodestone for every empty shell within several miles, and I was heading for ground zero.

XXII

Nicols drove past the single shopping complex on the edge of Ravensdale. Swarming the parking lot were off- and on-duty officers from SPD, in addition to King County deputies, policemen from Kent, Auburn, Bellevue, and other local communities. They were like an unorganized hive, a massive interagency effort that hadn't yet settled on its command structure. All the little workers with no work to do. Nicols passed the confusion—it wasn't a nest we were interested in kicking—and angled down the right-hand split of the road just beyond the swarming police presence. A half-block later we hit a T-intersection.

"Which way?" Nicols asked. The view in either direction offered no hint.

I glanced down at the *Thomas Guide* page in my lap and realized the road we were on was one side of a triangle—three roads that outlined a section of scrub land. "There," I said, looking over my left shoulder. "That's the closest thing this town has to a focal point."

Nicols pulled over, and we left the car to walk up the slope. At the top, we found an area sectioned off with yellow police tape. Five bodies lay on their backs in a circle—feet pointed out—inside the boundary of the yellow tape. Each wore the gray robe of the Hollow Men, hoods pulled up over their faces. Whorls of red paint, spotted with tiny black letters like a trail of ants, ran along the top of each naked foot. I knelt and peeked under one hood. Similarly adorned concentric circles—three of them—had been painted on the corpse's forehead. Sigils.

"The Anointed," I said.

"Excuse me?" Nicols asked.

"They're Hollow Men, friends of Doug. He called them the Anointed. Five who had completed the ritual of Ascension and been judged suitable for 'Anointment.' Doug didn't know what the term meant; he just knew it afforded them access to secret knowledge. The hidden mysteries of the inner sanctum, or something equally as specious. Doug wanted in, and I had gotten in the way."

Nicols didn't ask what had happened to Doug or how I knew these things. He was looking toward the tight cluster of houses on the other side of the main road from this grassy knoll. Shouts, tossed our way by the mercurial breeze, indicated members of the task force were making discoveries. Corpses. Still ambulatory.

"They're coming," Nicols said. "The zombies. They're drawn to you, aren't they?"

I nodded and quickly checked the other bodies, looking for a familiar face. Julian wasn't one of them. Kat had said he was Anointed—the first to be so—and Bernard was probably one of the other seven she said she had assisted. With these five, that accounted for all of them. But what was the purpose of being "Anointed"? Was the title just a misleading appellation, a buzzword that disguised their true purpose as sacrificial lambs in an unholy rite?

The area in the center of the circle of dead men was roughly about the size of the mirror's broad base. I shivered involuntarily as I imagined the *takwin* ibis-hounds assaulting the five as they lay still on the ground. What had they been promised to make them agree to having their souls sucked? Doug's memory was still sharp with outrage. He had wanted that rank; he had sacrificed for the privilege of being one of the special ones. The ones allowed to participate.

The deaths of the Anointed, the deaths in Ravensdale: they were only the beginning.

"Oh shit," Nicols said, his hand suddenly on my shoulder.

There, across the field, a single figure came toward us, walking a straight line from the parking lot and the swarming host. A tall man, dressed in a gray coat that flowed back from his legs like the spread of a heron's wings. Sunlight collected at the end of his right sleeve as if he was holding a mirror, or a star. On the psychic level, he was a shifting apparition, both a hole and not a hole in space.

Antoine.

"Hello, *mon ami*," he said as he reached the outline of police tape. "It's been a long time." He inclined his head toward Nicols. "Detective." The word was ripe with inflection and subtle echoes. An acknowledgment of a tool's usefulness. *You have given your Will to my cause.* The Watcher way of making an individual's efforts seem independent of their manipulation and influence.

"Hello, *Brother*," I said, with a little added gravity of my own. *I know what you are doing.*

Antoine's smile was the result of generations of breeding and training, perfectly pitched to disarm and charm. His hair, like a lion's mane—full of strawberry and blonde highlights—was combed back from his forehead and flowed gracefully on the collar of his silk shirt. The end of his right arm was covered with a smooth knob of silver.

"You seem *well*," he said, and the twinkle in his eyes wasn't entirely a trick of the light.

I nodded. "My tragic case of consumption seems to have cleared up." I filled my lungs. "It's the country air."

He gazed at the tall trees and the distant mountain, so close via a trick of the atmosphere. "It certainly does have restorative powers." He inhaled deeply as well. "None of that stink of the city. It is very nice."

"Too bad we're not vacationing."

He shrugged. "Yes, a pity."

"How many, Antoine? How many in Ravensdale?"

"Nearly nine hundred," he said. Nicols made a choking noise, as if the number was caught in his throat. I was cold, through and through, frozen by the magnitude of what had been done. Unprepared for the casual admission of such destruction.

"They're coming back," he continued, a sardonic grin tugging at his lips. "You, so flush with all that blood and life you have taken, are just too bright a lure for them to resist. You, Shiva's dark child, are summoning them with your presence." He scuffed the dirt. "Right here."

They were coming out of the woods now, staggering slowly and awkwardly. Newborns learning to walk. Their ruined eyes and black mouths were holes deep enough to drown in. *How many, Lightbreaker?* whispered the wind issuing from those holes. *Did you not enjoy it?*

"This was your Watch," I said, focusing on the bigger issue. "You didn't know what was going on. You let this happen."

"Did I?"

"You were too busy fucking around, leaving me notes and hiding in the shadows. You should have been taking the Hollow Men apart, not wasting your time with our little vendetta. You played right into their hand by being distracted."

"Was I?"

"Son of a bitch." Nicols drew his gun and pointed it at the Protector. "He knew they were going to do this." Antoine stared at me, ignoring the weapon. Watching my expression, Watching me untangle the threads.

Nicols' conclusion certainly seemed like the one Antoine was intimating, but I wanted to be sure. I wanted to See the threads, and make sure there wasn't some subtlety I was missing. Why would he condone such an experiment? Antoine wasn't being smug—he was as inscrutable as ever—and that made me consider the possibility there was some strand not yet revealed. "Bernard's an academic; he's not part of the family. He worked *for* you."

"Bernard du Guyon was a professor of Medieval Studies at the Sorbonne," Antoine agreed. "But there was a scandal, disputes about his methodology and awkward questions concerning a rare manuscript in the university's possession. He fled to Bonne, and became an alchemist.

"Well, he always had been an alchemist, really. Teaching gave him access to the university's collection of Renaissance and Medieval manuscripts, and the one in question was purported to be the second part of Ficino's *Theologia Platonica de immortalitate animae*. M. du Guyon believed the text was filled with technical marvels, mechanical ways of realizing Ficino's theories."

"But that was his job, wasn't it?" I said. "To find heretical works and magickal grimoires in the archives. He knew you would pay him well for such artifacts."

Antoine shrugged. "Possibly. But we already had a complete catalog of the Sorbonne's collection. We've had it for sixty years. Anything dangerous had already been purged. The claims of both Bernard and the university as to the identity of this pamphlet couldn't be true. No such text exists. Nor has it ever."

"He thinks he's reconstructed *The Book of Thoth*. The real one. Where did he find the pieces? This second part of Ficino's *Theologia*. Was that part of it?"

Antoine shook his head. "It doesn't exist."

"A lot of things don't exist," I said. "That doesn't mean he hasn't read it."

Antoine smiled at that, his eyes flickering toward Nicols and the gun. "The mysteries of the occult. Seeing things that aren't there. Reading books that weren't ever written. All very confusing, don't you think, Detective?"

Nicols held the gun steady. "You haven't answered his question," he said. "Where did Bernard find the pieces?"

"Ah, you are going to be tenacious about this." Antoine sighed. "Well then, perhaps he had access to a very private collection. One that had all the right pieces. Maybe a complete copy of the *Kitab al-Zuhra*, for example."

"Someone tainted by a manuscript scandal isn't going to get access to any private collection," I pointed out.

"One came up for sale recently."

"Where?" I had three or four clients who would have leapt at a chance for Jabir's *Kitab al-Zuhra*. I should have heard about a copy going on the market.

"Vienna."

"The Van Gröteon library?"

Antoine nodded, a glimmer of amusement on his lips.

"The whole library?"

He continued to nod.

"Who bankrolled him?" I couldn't keep the amazement out of my voice.

"Who indeed?"

"Fuck this verbal tap dance," Nicols said. The pistol shook in his hand. "You bankrolled him. You let him perform this experiment. You let this happen." His voice rose. "What the fuck did he do to these people!"

"He seeks the Key to Immortality," Antoine explained patiently.

"The what?" Nicols steadied his arm. His voice cracked on the word, his nerve dangerously close to breaking.

"The Way that allows access to God." Antoine was unmoved. "Given the opportunity, wouldn't you take it? Don't we all have questions we'd like to ask Him? About Sarah, for example?"

"Mother—" Nicols nearly fired his gun. The tendons in his neck were hard, and his face was wound into the spot between his eyes.

Antoine watched him, and nothing changed on the Protector's

face. He just watched the other man struggle with his demons. *Sarah. Don't we all have questions?*

"Leave him out of this," I said. "He doesn't deserve to be kicked around." Nicols gasped at the sound of my voice, and realizing what he had almost done, he turned away from Antoine. His arm dropped to his side, and he held on to the gun tightly.

With the barest glimmer of disappointment, Antoine surveyed the tightening circle of zombies, the once-living population of Ravensdale, as they lurched and staggered toward the small hill upon which we stood. The members of the task force had stayed back, avoiding the shuffling soul-dead. "He's part of the Weave, Markham. Just like you and me." He raised his shortened right arm, and waved it to encompass the surrounding zombies. "Just like all of them. I can't cut him out of the pattern any more than you can."

"Stop trying to twist him, then. Let him find his own way."

"And you haven't twisted him? Is it not your interference in the Weave that set him on this path?"

"I've tried to guide him—"

"Like you've guided yourself?"

The flush in my cheeks spread to my neck and made my voice shake. "He's an innocent."

"No one is innocent," Antoine countered. "There is just ignorance and enlightenment."

I nodded toward the approaching line of zombies. "Is this enlightenment, then? You gave Bernard what he needed to build the mirror; you let him activate it. As a result, all these people have been collected. They've been *harvested*. For what purpose? Making *Qliphotic* shells? There is no 'Way' here. This is just carnage."

For an instant, Antoine's guard slipped and I saw the abject sorrow hidden beneath. Like a scar on his heart, he would never reveal the true temperament under his impenetrable psychic armor. Not to me. Not now. Even though we shared similar grief about what had happened, we stood on opposite shores, separated by a gulf of our own making. Separated by steel.

"You are summoning them. Like moths to your flame," he said, a grin smoothing over the break in his armor. "I will offer you a deal, *mon ami*. Divest yourself of your stolen energy and we shall talk about the past. And the future. You will not dissuade me from what must be done, but we can at least end it with some civility."

"The alternative?"

He sighed. "I have no time for distractions. Your thread in this part of the Weave is done. You will be removed. Decisively."

A single zombie was already halfway across the field, a staggered row of shambling soul-dead not far behind. They wanted my light and, in the same way I had obliterated the old man by the road with a blessing of that energy, Antoine wanted me to dismiss the dead of Ravensdale. One massive pulse, a coruscating stroke that would drive away all the darkness. A final blessing for the restless dead.

I have no time.

I had thought Bernard and the Anointed Hollow Men had planned to use their newly learned psychoanimist techniques to take over Antoine. But Bernard had hinted at a larger purpose for the theurgic mirror. If Antoine had bankrolled the creation of the mirror and this experiment, then why was he here? Why wasn't he with them?

Because they weren't finished. Ravensdale was just a test run, the first part of something else. But it couldn't be about theft. What was the point in taking all this energy? Unless… there was a way to use it somewhere else. To do something…

He seeks the Key to Immortality.

And not just Bernard, but everyone. Why wouldn't Antoine want it as well? But he had lost control. All of his coy obliqueness aside, his Watch had failed. He was on the defensive, reeling from this sudden reversal. Key pieces he had thought were under his control had disappeared.

I was a thorn, an old wound that refused to heal. He wanted me removed from the Weave. One less thread to follow. One less mischievious child—

They all had a plan. Antoine. Bernard. Pender. They all saw me as the chaotic element that could disrupt the other team, but I was also the *veneficus*, the uncontrolled poison. I didn't belong to any of them.

Certainly not Antoine. Why had I run from him for all these years? Because I was afraid of him, or was it because the Chorus knew how fear worked on me? They knew my secrets, knew which strings to pull.

I hadn't backed down when Antoine had challenged me in Paris. Was I going to start now?

"Okay," I told him. "I'll take your deal."

Before even they could read the lie, I split the Chorus open, tearing them like I was rending roses. Petals falling through my fingers. They keened and whined, fighting the assertion of my Will, but I dug through them and tapped the storehouse of the energy I had stolen.

Antoine narrowed his eyes slightly as he sensed the bloom of power. Nicols raised a hand to shield his eyes from my abrupt brilliance. The nearest zombie increased his speed, his head twitching back and forth. A light-blinded moth, unable to stop its suicide dive at a hot bulb.

I gathered what was left of the Hollow Men, and raised it through my frame, letting it bleed through my lungs and heart and throat. A twisted knot formed over my head, a ball of lightning that thrust angled shadows across the field. I let the outer edge of the ball spit flares like an aroused sun as if I couldn't quite keep the sphere of power in control. As if my Will wasn't completely focused.

I waited for Antoine to tire of Watching my engorged Will, to turn his head and Witness the demolition of the dead. I waited for him to look away. As his attention shifted, I released the ball of coalesced Will.

He knew he had made an error the instant my Will realized itself. Phosphorescent streamers erupted from his frame as the energy wave struck. He held his ground, clothing vaporizing and skin tearing as the annihilating angel of my Will flayed him. His muscles and fat started to sizzle and burn, and then the true weight of the spell hit him and he was hurled from the field.

In the time it took to exhale, Antoine was thrown more than a hundred yards. What was left of his body inscribed a shallow arc across the landscape, a low-flying meteor of burning tissue. The arc of fire that filled his wake dispersed in a crackling rush and the trees bent with the echo of the atmospheric discharge. His body crashed into a parked car in the shopping mall lot.

The nearest zombie was blown into ash. Behind it, others were knocked down, while those still further afield were disoriented. Their magnet was gone, swallowed by a rush of fire and fury. The only bright light remaining was the ambient swirl of energy coming off Antoine's burned shell. It was enough to turn their hunger, and they drifted away from the field, staggering toward the smoking wreckage of the car.

I grabbed Nicols' lapel and dragged him away from the circle. "Let's go. Before he gets up."

"What?" His feet stumbled as he tried to keep up with me. "He's still alive?"

The Chorus read a vibration. I knew it. I knew it well. "Yes," I said. "And I've just made him angry."

XXIII

Nicols drove aimlessly and recklessly for a half hour, speeding down two-lane highways that cut through the forested hillsides, that bisected communities smaller and sleepier than Ravensdale. He fled, inchoate sounds issuing from his mouth, with no destination in mind. His hands: one gripping the wheel like a drowning man clinging to a life preserver, one beating against the molded circle. Finally, on a road that appeared to run straight until it was swallowed by Mt. Rainier, he pulled over to the shoulder and got out.

He paced back and forth in front of the vehicle, shouting and raging. In an unintelligible dialog, he started arguments, screamed denials, spat accusations, and choked on the rebuttals. He smoked two cigarettes: the first, in a short series of violent inhalations; the second, in a reflective frame of mind. As he finished the second, grinding it out on the fractured shale, he summoned me from the car with a rigid index finger, indicating exactly where he wanted me to stand.

"Tell me everything," he said as I got out of the car. "I want to hear it all."

I told him about the shipping container, about Kat, about the poison I had been carrying for the last decade. I told him about Bernard and Julian, and the theurgic mirror they built; I told him what happened in the Arena, and what transpired after.

He started to chew on the end of another cigarette when I finished, staring at the ground between us, not seeing the rock. "This library—Van Groenig's."

"Van Gröteon."

"Right. You think this is where Bernard found what he needed to build this... mirror device?"

"Yes," I said. "A man can be swayed with a single book—it takes only a page to convey a secret. But it takes a bunch of books to synthesize the record of human experimentation. Libraries are dangerous; we ably demonstrate that we have a predilection for destroying them—Alexandria, Dr. John Dee's, le Comte de Saint Germain, the Nazis."

"Where did this library come from?"

"During WWII, Hitler was obsessed with the occult; he wanted magickal tools, objects that would make him invincible. That would win the war for his side. Himmler, who was even more obsessed with the occult, had a group charged with collecting artifacts, relics, books, and the like. The Ahnenerbe-SS.

"After the war, most of the artifacts in Nazi collections disappeared. A lot of relic hunters have been chasing rumors and myths for the last fifty years, trying to track down the grimoires, the black-magic reliquaries, the holy and unholy relics—you name it, people have been looking for it."

"People like you."

"Like me. Like my clients. The Watchers have a lot of them; you can be sure of that. But not all of them. There's money and influence to be made in finding the lost artifacts first."

"So Van Gröteon beat your friends to it?"

"Somewhat. Gustav Albrecht Van Gröteon was an industrialist who made a fortune for himself and his family in the new Austria following WWII. He managed to get his hands on the majority of Himmler's personal library. Van Gröteon wasn't an occultist; his interest in the books was more... protective. He thought that if a non-practitioner had them, then there was less chance of them being used for the wrong purposes."

"But they were."

"Not during his lifetime. The Watchers honored his desire and left the library in his care, though I'm sure they had additional safeguards. Claudia—Van Gröteon's granddaughter—doesn't have the same reverence toward the occult texts as her grandfather. I've done business with her; she had to have some scarab rings done by Elsa Schiaparelli.

"I've been to the family house on Glanzinggasse and I've seen the library. It's a very impressive collection. Bacon, Jabir, Agrippa, Flamel, Beato: a lot of alchemical tracts and heretical treatises on magick. I could have sold a number of those books for six figures each, and I'm sure the same thing has occurred to Claudia. She has very expensive tastes."

"And she sold the lot to Bernard." Nicols lit another cigarette.

"No, I think she sold it to the Watchers. She knows they're the only real buyers. Any other party would have just brought their wrath down on her. As long as the library was in her possession, they knew where the books were, and they could keep a Watch on them. They weren't floating around.

"If she ever tried to sell the books to someone like Bernard— some small-time Swiss alchemist—they would have swooped in and taken everything. She would have gotten nothing. No, they probably paid a pittance of what the library was worth, but she got paid at least. And, in her situation, I'm sure the money was already spent."

"So the Watchers gave the books to Bernard."

I nodded. "Or, at least, gave him access so he could finish his research."

He looked around, staring at the trees as if he hadn't noticed them before, hadn't realized how far we had gone into the woods. "Why here? Why not somewhere in Europe? Why travel all the way to the Pacific Northwest to build this thing?"

"Because the Watchers don't participate in experiments. He's a crackpot alchemist with an unsubstantiated idea, but that doesn't mean they aren't curious. They'd want to be sure he wasn't actually onto something. They know the way the old secrets are hidden. Sometimes it is the insane ones who crack the codes.

"Even if they didn't give a lot of credence to his ideas, they'd be inclined to let him try it out. They'd let him set up some experiments in a controlled environment somewhere—a location far from their back yard. Seattle is a long way from the bright lights of Europe; this is the backwater of the magickal world."

"Lovely. Welcome to the Pacific Northwest, where alchemists and meth-heads think no one will notice what they're doing." Nicols snorted smoke from his nose. "Antoine doesn't know what is going on, right? All that crap about talking to God is just bullshit. Bernard's device just takes people's souls."

"I think that was its intention. That's what Bernard sold them: a means of extracting and holding souls. Not like this, but individually. Everyone is interested in Immortality, John, even if they pretend otherwise. An artificial construct that can preserve a soul? That would be worth fighting for."

The Key. The Stone. The Grail. We gave it many names.

"But I think it does something else too," I continued, shaking off the Chorus' interest in the device. "So does Antoine. They used Antoine's Protection to get it made, and they hid its true purpose from him. He won't admit to it—not to you or me—but he got played. Badly. A thousand people died on his Watch. That's a huge failure."

"You think?" Sarcasm from the detective. *Good. He was controlling his fear.*

"So why did he let them make it?" Nicols asked. "Is this part of the Watcher credo? Watch them build toys that will lay waste to the world? What is that? Some perversion of altruistic occultism that doesn't allow them to take toys away from kids before they hurt each other?"

"They always operate for their own ends."

"That's what I'm saying. We know Bernard's angle, but what did Antoine get out of it? There are only two real causes behind every action: love or power. Everybody wants something; everyone is always thinking: 'What's in it for me?' So what's Antoine's angle? Doesn't it make more sense—God, it's so wrong—but doesn't it make sense that Antoine knew they were going to fuck him? He knew they were going to run off with the device; he knows they want to 'talk to God.'"

I saw the ugly simplicity of his thought process. Like Occam's razor, Nicols cut through the tangle of threads and made the Weave seem simple. Unadorned, yet still a complex pattern of our needs and desires. Love or power: always the validation. Such a simple thing. While the Hollow Men thought they were being clever, Antoine knew what they were planning. And, as I thought about it, I realized how *I* would keep tabs on their activities.

Pender.

Antoine didn't have to track their progress, he just had to know where their final ritual was going to take place. Pender would know. He wouldn't be so stupid as to be a part of their scheme—a plan that violated every precept of the Watcher credo—without being privy to the final experiment.

Unless—the niggling thought intruded—*unless they hadn't told Pender.* Unless they knew Pender was the link that could be compromised, and hadn't included him in their plans.

Nicols was still looking at the trees. Silent, natural watchers. "Sarah was killed a little over a year ago by a drunk driver. A hit-and-run incident on the Aurora Bridge. He lived—the motherfucker walked away with barely a scratch on him—but, even with the air bag, several of her ribs were broken. Her right lung was punctured and it took them too long to cut her out of the car. She died during the transport to Harborview. There wasn't a fucking thing I could do.

"In the months since, I've realized how pointless my job is. I catch murderers—people who have *acted*. I don't do anything to stop them before they take a life. I got the call after she had been killed, even though the driver of the other car was drunk hours before he crossed the center lane and plowed into her car. I only get summoned after the fact. After the deed is done and someone has died. Can you see the futility of that? The pointlessness?"

He realized he had chewed through the filter on his cigarette and threw the whole thing into the road. "Goddamnit, Markham. All I've wanted is to stop something from happening, stop someone before they acted. In the last few days, I thought this—" he waved his hand in front of his eyes "—this magick shit would be the ticket. It would let me See them before they committed their crimes.

"I thought this would help, but it hasn't. I've just been privy to… God, I can't even… nine hundred people, Markham. Nine hundred. That's more than the number of people who have been killed in Seattle in the last ten years. In a single night, Bernard and Julian eclipsed the last decade. Hell, SPD isn't—I'm not—equipped to deal with this scale. They aren't serial killers. They aren't random murderers. They're just—"

"Abberations," I said. "On every scale."

"That doesn't change the fact that it happened." He clenched his fists and raised his hands. "What are you going to do about it?"

"What do you mean?"

"They're not done. You know that. So what are you going to do? Are you just going to let them continue?"

"I'm not sure what you think I can do." I shuddered.

"I Saw what you did to Antoine."

"That was a lucky shot. I caught Antoine off-guard. And I hit him with everything I had. If Bernard has access to all that energy he's stolen—and that's got to be a part of what the device does—he's a hundred times more powerful than I was an hour ago."

"You're just going to walk away?"

"I'm not sure what you want me to say, John. Beyond the fact that I don't know where they are, I don't have the skills—or the resources—to take them on. I used up all the energy I took. What have I got left? Moral outrage? A thirst for revenge? Those aren't enough. He won't even notice me." I glanced over my shoulder, looking back the way we had come. "Besides, I've got—" Antoine. Who, most assuredly, wasn't dead. He had resisted the blast for a second which meant he had been able to deflect energy. Deflection meant focused Will. I had burned him—badly—and it would take him time to recover, but he wasn't done. Not now. It wasn't a question of if he would come after me, it was a question of when.

"Is that all you care about?"

"I'm a *veneficus,* John. The poisonous free agent no one claims, and who won't be counted in any assembly. The only person watching my back is me. Like you said, no one has time for 'altruistic occultism.' We all want to find the secrets of the Universe for ourselves. For power. Not for a thousand-year reign of peace."

All I had was a chance for a head start. I could run and hide somewhere. Try to figure out what I was going to do about this hole in my heart. Vengeance wasn't enough to fill it.

Now that the blush of the Hollow Men's soul energy had worn off, I could see how I needed something that wasn't tainted by the past. I needed a new directive and, as long as I was running from the past, I wouldn't have any chance to find my own way. I would be continually pushed. Never finding my own pace, my own way. I wouldn't submit to Antione, but that only meant our antagonism continued. And would do so until I found a way to break free.

The path out of the dark wood had to be earned; it couldn't

be stumbled upon by accident. I had to find my own way.

He chewed on the inside of his lip, staring at me. Seeing me. *Watching me.* "How many in the warehouse?" he asked finally.

I flinched. "Nine." *He knew.*

He nodded and took out his pistol. "Okay." He raised the gun and pointed it at my head. "Landis Markham, you are under arrest for the premeditated murder of those men. Put your hands on your head, turn around, and get down on your knees."

"John—"

He half-squeezed the trigger, rocking back the hammer. "Do it. Now."

I complied, and my hands were wrenched down to the small of my back where they were cuffed tightly. With a hard shove from his foot, he sent me sprawling on the shale, my cheek grinding against the broken rock. Nicols walked out of my field of vision and I heard a car door open and shut before he returned.

I rolled onto one shoulder to better see what he was doing. His gun held in one hand, he fumbled through a folder of loose pages, scattering paper across the shoulder of the road. Finding the page he sought, he bent down and shoved the paper in my face. "Nine or nine hundred," he said, shaking the page, "It matters. Every one of them matters."

The page was a photocopy of a tarot card—the Tower. A single bolt of jagged lightning split the crown of a tower, spilling the two inhabitants out. In the margin and beneath the picture was the unorganized palimpsest of Nicols' notes. Two words in block letters across the top: "MY FUTURE." Beneath, an underlined sentence. *"Nothing is ever lost; it is simply transformed."*

Nicols had gone back to Piotr and had his own reading. The last card had been the Tower. *Destructive change.* This was the future Piotr had shown him.

"I'm sorry, John—" I started.

"Are you?" he interrupted. He didn't so much as drop the page as throw it at me. "Hasn't this all been about you, about your obsessive quest for this woman? When haven't you been focused on your own fucking redemption?"

I didn't have an answer for him.

He stepped back, raising the pistol and resting the barrel against his head. "Every one of them matters, Markham. So you don't care about nine or even nine hundred. One more shouldn't faze you a bit."

I shook my head. "Don't do this."

"Stop me," he said. "Show me *altruistic occultism*. Show me that I'm wrong. Isn't this how you cross the Abyss, Markham? By being selfless?" The hammer on his pistol was still cocked. It wouldn't take more than a tiny squeeze for him to pull the trigger, and I knew he would do it. He hadn't been able to shoot Antoine. Not then. But now, when all of the last few hours had had a chance to sink in, when he had realized he had Seen too much. Lost too much. He was on the edge of the Abyss, and the Monster there—Choronzon—was coming to tear him apart. He wasn't ready to leap the gap, no more so than I had been a decade ago.

Was I any more ready now? Or was I inured to the pain? Had I become such a hollowed-out shell that I wasn't yet aware of how much I had truly lost? If it were me that Choronzon sought, was I any more prepared?

How long are you willing to run?

I closed my eyes, falling inward to find the boiling storm of the Chorus. They unfolded, arranging themselves into an icy fractal pattern. They came at my bidding, subdued by what I had seen at Ravensdale, but they still came at my command.

"Open 'em, you piece of shit." Nicols' voice quivered. "Look at me or I will—swear to God—put one in your belly before I shoot myself. Look at me, you son of a bitch."

I did, and the frigid snowflake expression of the Chorus froze him in place. Another burst of their magick, guided by my Will—*convertant in fraxina*—and the handcuffs dissolved into white ash. I stood, shaking the metallic dust from my wrists, and took his gun from his stiff fingers.

How long?

I pointed the gun across the road, over the trees, and pulled the trigger. The gun bucked, and the roar of the shot echoed for a long time. I stood there, and listened to it until I couldn't hear it anymore. And, after a little while, the wind came back and the trees started whispering again.

How long would you run?

I sighed, and—*libertas*—released my hold on Nicols. He jerked wildly for a second, and then caught up in time.

"One isn't the same as many," I said, offering him the gun. "It's a far cry from making a true difference."

"It's a start," he conceded. He clicked the safety on with his thumb as he took the gun. He holstered his weapon and offered me a crooked smile, a wan expression filled with both trepidation and relief.

"I don't know what to do," I said, answering the question in his eyes. "I can't save everyone. I'm doing a shit poor job of saving myself." *Fill the void.*

"You and everyone else." His grin straightened out. "Just don't run away on me, Markham. That's all I'm asking."

XXIV

I knelt at the side of the road, and gathered the scattered pages. Numbered in the upper right corner, each page was a photocopy of a single tarot card—Crowley's deck—with extensive notes. Nicols' re-creation of his precognitive visit to Piotr's. I put them in order as I retrieved them, the wind making me chase a few. I saw the Prince of Swords and the Three as well, their blades slicing through a ruby heart; he had drawn cups too, the Nine and the Princess; a single wand (the Two, inverted); the Ace, Four, and Five of Disks; and, in addition to the Tower, he had received the Hanged Man, the only other Major Arcana card in his reading. "What were you trying to figure out?"

He shrugged. "I asked how to find you. Though, the more I read up on this stuff, the more it seemed like I had asked the wrong question."

I nodded. "The reading gave you a glimpse of a broader world-view, something higher level than your simple query."

"Yeah. It's like checking the weather report to see if you're going to need an umbrella today and having the meteorologist tell you the entire coast is preparing for landfall of a Force 5 hurricane. There's a sense of scale that creeps in, makes you feel pretty insignificant. My petty needs are pretty fucking irrelevant when compared to the motion of human existence, aren't they?"

"And yet, here we are." I offered him the folder. "Trying to make sense of it all."

He waved it off. "I've stared at it too much—know it by heart now—it needs a new pair of eyes."

I glanced up and down the empty road. We hadn't seen another car the entire time we had been pulled over. "Know where we are?"

"Somewhere near Enumclaw, I think."

The name meant very little to me. "What do you want, John?" *Peace;* I heard an echo in my head.

"They killed nearly a thousand people, Markham. I want to stop them from killing any more."

"We probably won't be able to."

He shrugged. "I've got to try. I can't take the idea of walking away. It's failure on such an astronomical scale that, if I start to think about it, I'm going to lose my nerve. I've just got to do something."

"Okay. We can't do anything here. We need a destination. An idea of where they have gone."

"What are they going to do?" He corrected me. "If you figure out the why or the what, the where becomes easier."

"Okay. So, the 'what.' Bernard is a Hermeticist, and Antoine said he's an old-school alchemist. Which follows, because a lot of alchemy rose from efforts to decipher Hermes Trismegistus' *Emerald Tablet.* I would have thought he'd be fascinated with the idea of transmuting himself instead of what he's done with this mirror device."

"The Great Work is an attempt to remake your Image." Nicols nodded. "I know about the *Emerald Tablet.*"

I raised an eyebrow. "You've been busy. Getting yourself educated." I glanced at the two boxes in the back seat of the car, my professional curiosity piqued. What library had *he* raided?

He shrugged. "Trying to understand the way you and your nutbag friends think. After the way things went at the hotel, I figured if I was going to find you, I had to stop thinking like an old homicide detective and start thinking like an insane occultist, trapped in his own personal symbolic hell."

"Symbolic?" I said, fighting a tiny smile. The last few days certainly had felt about as "symbolic" as getting hit on the head with a brick.

"It's all symbolism and creative mythology with you guys," he said. "Anyway, I've been skimming, mostly. Not enough time to really absorb anything. Just picking up keywords and wrapping my head around the general landscape. I've had some practice at this sort of thing; we do it all the time when we're prepping for an interview. If you can talk about things that interest the person you're interviewing, in language they understand, they tend to relax. They tend to say things they hadn't planned on saying."

"Like what Antoine said about distractions. He had no time for them."

Nicols nodded. "Because he's on a schedule."

"Yes, but because he's chasing a timetable that's already in motion," I mused. "Say Bernard and Julian are hiding themselves from a Protector. Where are they going to hide? How long do they think they'll be safe?"

"But if they're going to do something else with the mirror, they don't have to hide that long."

"But they do have to remain hidden."

"Okay. That means they're probably not in Seattle."

"How you figure that?"

"Because Pender would know. The other Hollow Men would have an idea. Piotr might even be able to find them. Antoine would have no compunction about tearing the answer out of any of them. Even if they didn't consciously know. Going back there would be a risk I think Bernard and Julian would be idiots to take. They're on their own."

I sucked on a tooth, feeling the Chorus churn in my stomach. Nicols was right: they were unshackled from the eye of the

Watchers, free to conduct whatever final experiment they had in mind. But it was a small window of opportunity. They knew Antoine would be coming, that he would restore his Watch. They had to move fast, and Antoine knew they were on a forced march as well.

They had stolen the souls of nearly a thousand people. They couldn't (or wouldn't) return them, so they had some other plan. Some other use for all that energy. The only one I could think of was the one I knew best: making the energy their own and using it for an Act of magick.

The Anointed. The five Hollow Men who had been sacrificed to the device. They were soul-walkers, men who could leave their bodies. Men whose souls remained inviolate outside their bodies. Could they retain their ego consciousness within the mirror? Were they agents who would direct the force when the time came to utilize it? Much like the Hollow Men in the Arena had channeled power to Doug, could these soul-walkers send energy to Bernard and Julian?

Maybe Antoine's suggestion was right: maybe they were trying to talk to God. If they were going to assault Heaven, try to knock on the Gates of God's House and force an audience, they would need that raw power. But, more importantly, they'd need some sort of access point. They'd need an—

"Axis mundi," I breathed.

"Excuse me?" Nicols asked.

"It's Latin for 'pillar of the world.' The point about which the planet rotates. In a magico-religious sense, it's the point where God has reached down and touched the world, where primitive people think the Divine Spirit has manifested itself in their profane world.

"Cultures that believe in a cyclical rebirth of the world also believe in a point around which the world is reborn. Sacred sites allow the religiously devout the opportunity to not only remake the world, but to influence the next iteration, by standing at the spot around which the world turns.

"Look, in Hinduism, this current age is called the Kali Yuga. It's the Age of Iron and it ends in fire. It's called *'Mahapralaya.'* *Ekpyrosis. Conflagratio.* The World-Fire. "It's the macrocosmic version of individual redemption: everything is forgiven in fire; all sins are burned away and everything is possible again."

"This thing can do that? It can bring about *Mahapralaya?*"

"What other reason is there to steal the souls of a thousand? Think about it in terms of conventional weaponry. Why would you buy guns? Because your enemy had arrows. Why would you buy a cannon? Because your enemy had single-shot rifles."

"Why would you build a nuclear bomb?" Nicols followed the progression. "Because the guy who made one first got to rewrite the rules."

"Thoth was the Demiurge in the Egyptian tradition, the Being who fabricated the World from the Word. Ptah built it, but Thoth imagined it. He was still within the shell of the Divine, but he was closest to God. His Key to Immortality is a means of remaking the World."

"Slow down," Nicols said. "This is exactly what I was talking about. You just go off into your own world with all this myth and symbol crap. I can't keep up."

"They're going to kill more people." I spelled it out. "They're going to gather as much energy as possible and try to force God into re-creating the world."

Nicols snapped his mouth shut, swallowing his objections. "They're going somewhere urban," he ground out. "And, if they're not going back to Seattle, then the closest place is Portland. In Oregon."

Nicols drove south and west, the mountain off his left shoulder. The roads were narrow and twisted, contorted tracks through the wilderness, but each curve, each bend, brought more signs of civilization. I was useless as a navigator as he worked his way back to the main highway, so I studied his chart and his notes. Seeking an understanding of the Weave around him, of how our threads were tangled together. Piotr had done the Celtic Cross for Nicols. Ten cards: six to show where he had been, four to point to the future.

The first was the Ace of Disks, a strong foundation that prepared the initiate for his expulsion from the garden of innocence. Laid across this card were more disks, five of them. Nicols' notes indicated this card had been reversed, inverting the standard definition of sanctuary into a chaotic representation of being cast out of safety. The expulsion from Eden again, the loss of innocence. Naked in the world.

Third—the card placed above the first pair—was the Hanged Man, the agent that sought to guide him. An enlightening inversion, a suspension reversing the magus' worldview. The Fisher King, the mad visionary of the land. The future hanging on the cusp of tomorrow, waiting to be revealed.

I thought about the card that had been my crown—the World. Also known as the Aeon, it was the promised fruition of the enlightened effort, a new world order brought about by philosophers and mystics. In my dream, however, it was a sexually rapacious cherub who was changing the world.

And, just like that, the symbolism became clear. The little fucker's cock was a staff, a pole, an *axis mundi,* and he had been planting his seed—his magickal nature—into the miniature planet. It was a perversion of the old agrarian rituals, but it made sense. The cherub was Bernard, raping the world in order to remake it in his own image.

In an intuitive flash, I knew I was the Fisher King in Nicols' reading. I was the inverted magus in Nicols' worldview—my feet suspended, my head pointed down to the earth. I was the adept who had vanished into the tunnels of despair on the back side of the Tree in order to find enlightenment.

Wait for the light.

I shivered, beginning to understand the collision of our threads. The flash of enlightenment that had come to me in the Arena about the Wheel of Fortune rode heavily in my head. The cycle of death and rebirth, kings buried and born again. It was Crowley, following Waite's lead of adding Christian and Kabbalistic imagery to the Wheel, who connected the cycle of death and rebirth to Thoth. The ibis-headed guide who waited to carry us up from the burial of the flesh.

What about the *takwin*, the ibis-hounds? Were they angelic guides then, and not spirit thieves? Was part of the road to Immortality a vanquishment of the flesh?

Nine hundred sparks. The number made my tongue numb. All those souls, cast upon an unknown path. Was it the road to Dissolution or Immortality?

The fourth card in Nicols' query was the inverted Nine of Cups. The root, *Malkuth*, where the soil is black and our unconscious grows unexpected passions. The inverted Nine was an affirmation of his entry into the world of the Mysteries. The start of his path.

Where does it lead?

Fifth was the Prince of Swords. Across the top of the page, he had written "MARKHAM."

We are all your princes.

I grimaced. My brain was already linking my recollections of Doug on the Wheel—blood-drenched and broken—to his neurological pain memory. I witnessed and experienced his death as the Chorus mapped all the memories into one composite. The Prince of Swords had been in my future and, now, as part of Nicols' future, it was behind us. A bottleneck passed, nothing more than a distorted legacy that I would imperfectly remember. *Part of me. Broken, but still part of me.*

Nicols' immediate future was the Three of Swords, Crowley's "Sorrow," the pain that shouldn't be denied. The hurt subsumed into the magus in order for him to ascend. The betrayal inherent in this sacrifice was tempered by love, but that didn't make the pain go away. It just made it tolerable. That was the failing of Milton's Morningstar. He couldn't understand that God never stopped loving him. Even as he fell.

The last four cards were a precognitive glimpse into the ruddy water of possibilities and permutations, and for the first, I was heartened to see that Nicols had drawn the Four of Disks. These were the Four Watchtowers, the Enochian citadels that held the keys to the elemental magicks, and they were the heart of the magus' empire. The card hinted at an attainable gnosis in spite of Nicols' larval state.

I've tried to guide him...

The next card was the Princess of Cups, and I tried to recall Crowley's interpretation. He deviated with the Cups. Is she like the Prince? No, the earthy part of water, the *grounded* source of inspiration. The artesian spring of Mind. What was the connection?

My eighth card had been the Priestess. An equally obtuse reference; it hadn't been Kat, after all. Was the Princess another thread we couldn't fathom?

I sighed, and moved on to the next card. *Secrets still hidden.* Nicols' penultimate card was the inverted Two of Wands, and I smiled. This one I knew. *Who wasn't afraid of new experiences?*

But those new experiences led to the last page: the Tower. A lightning bolt blows off the crown—this was *Kether,* after all, the pure Wisdom of the Sephirotic Tree—and kings tumble out of the ruined building. Falling into the sea of darkness that surrounds the tower.

Nicols glanced over. "Yeah, I'm fucked, aren't I? That one is never good."

"It's all relative," I admitted. "You've got it written right here. 'Nothing is ever lost; it is simply transformed.'"

"It was moderately entertaining when Piotr tried to make me feel better about pulling it," he said with a tight smile, "but in light of what I've seen today, it's sort of lost its charm."

"The Tower isn't about physical destruction," I explained. "Nor does it mean complete annihilation. It's all relative to the situation you are in. It is a destructive resolution—yes, no bullshit there—but that doesn't equate to your death or my death or the destruction of the Universe as we know it. It just means things are going to be resolved, and the resolution is going to be painful."

"The Three of Swords," he said. "That's a physical hurt, isn't it? I've got that one coming, don't I?"

That looks like it hurts. I shook off the image of Doug's face, his single eye livid against the burned outline of the pentacle. Scarred by the sign of the earth. "Yeah. The road to the Tower is bloody."

"Wonderful," he muttered.

Images from the Arena swam in my head: the ragged edge of the sword severed the ligaments in Doug's wrist; the blood, black in the shadow-spawning firelight, hot on my legs and bare feet; the first Hollow Man to burn, his blood bubbling out from his mouth and ears as it tried to flee the inferno of his combusting organs. And the others, the Hollow Men who had Seen through him and found me staring back at them.

Paved with good intentions, slick with blood: the road to the Tower.

"If we face the Tower with fear, it will be us who fall from its crown," I said. "That's what the Three of Swords is telling you. The Two of Wands—the card right before the Tower—is your fear, John. I'm not an idiot; I've got my own terror to get a hold of before we find Bernard. That's what the Two of Wands represents: you have every reason to be scared shitless. But the Three of Swords says the pain has a limit. The fear can be conquered; the obstacles can be overcome. You just have to be ready for the course to be difficult."

I flipped back through to the page with the Four of Disks on it. "You've got the Watchtowers at your back," I said. "You started with the Ace of Disks, one of the most powerful cards in the deck. These two cards say your walls are strong; you have the means to build a sanctuary from the pain. This is a reading of transformation, John. It's a destruction of the old flesh and a rebirth into the realm of the light.

"As an adept, this would be a very good fortune to get." I was trying to spin this in as positive a light as possible. A focused Will opened many doors for a magus, and such focus required a belief in the possibility of success. "The path to enlightenment is hard and painful. It is supposed to be. It's not for everyone; the obstacles can seem impossible." I tapped the page. "But this reading? You can do it. You can reach the other side."

"Okay, Deepok, enough with the cheerleading. I get the picture." He looked at the open folder in my lap. "Well," he added. "I don't, entirely. But I get the message. I do have one question, though: How? How are we supposed to find Bernard? It's a big fucking city, and you and I don't know it well enough to turn over the right rocks before we run out of time."

"No," I said. "We don't." I realized what the Princess of Cups represented, what my own Priestess meant. "We need to find someone who can tell us. We need to find a local oracle. We need to find someone like Piotr who knows the city well enough to guide us."

"People who know the flow of a city," he said, echoing what I had told him days ago and layering in his own knowledge of city informants. "Cab drivers, bartenders, drug dealers, doormen."

I nodded. "Yeah, someone on the ground. Someone who would hear a whisper as soon as it started." I struggled to find the right concept. "The Princess is a feminine principle. She's not the Goddess figure like the Empress, but she's of the same ilk." I thought of what Kat had said about her relationship with the Hollow Men. *I am their Whore-Goddess; I am the fertile earth in which they bury themselves so that their spirits may be freed.*

"Strip clubs," Nicols said. "We need to hit the strip clubs."

XXV

When we reached Portland, I let Nicols guide us through the mirrored rooms of the clubs. A professional courtesy call to the Portland Police Department let them know he was in town. A low-key canvas of some of the strip clubs in the city. Part of an early intel reconnaissance for an SPD case was the story. Mollified by his contact and always eager to maintain ties with fellow officers, the detective he spoke with gave him a list of hot spots.

After the first few, the clubs became a blur to me: the architecture became variations on an already tired temple floorplan; neon signs became obscure bursts of hieroglyphics; the bored and laconic expressions of the dancers morphed into Grecian masks stamped from rust-stained copper.

And the names. Characters who stoked the imagination with their multi-syllabic exoticism: the Middle Eastern mystique of Saffron and Esmeralda, the Oriental inscrutability of Yukiko and Aniko, the European decadence of Chaumineux and Antoinette, and the Egyptian mystery of Cleopatra and Isis.

Too many of them had brittle shells, their shiny war paint translucent to our mystic eyes. We Saw their submerged personalities, their hidden rage at the dull pawing and heavy breathing. We knew their hidden sadness. While their eyes were brilliant reflections of the mirrors and their mouths rich fruit ripe for plucking, the motion of their hands—toward my thigh, toward a watered down drink which they barely touched, toward a cigarette—betrayed their exhaustion.

Part of me understood Bernard's goal with the mirror, what he and the Anointed wished to do with the souls of the world. How many of these people—dancers and patrons alike—would leap at the chance for a new Aeon? For a *tabula rasa* moment when all their sins were wiped away? How many eager souls were there in this city—in any city—who were waiting for a chance to make a break from their torrid existences?

I started seeing Bernard's mirror in every disco ball; the play of reflected light mocking me with the promise of a new world, a better world built from the darkness of this one.

Our plan was a bust, made worse by the emotional toll it took on us. The few who had an instinctive sense of the city's energy flow weren't self-aware enough of their intuition to focus it to our inquiries. We had our faces stroked, our crotches teased, and our wallets emptied, but found no oracular prescience to guide us.

We stank of arousal, fetid air, and cigarette smoke as we wandered out of a club shoved into the front end of an old warehouse down in the industrial district. The sky was a burial shroud stretched tight.

Nicols started to shake out a cigarette from his nearly empty pack and stopped, his tongue touching the edge of his lips. "I think I'll wait awhile before the next one." He tipped it back into the pack. The color had been leached from his face by the dead sky. "We're not going to find anything."

I agreed. "It's not the right approach. Maybe if we had a few days, we could find one who could articulate her understanding of the city's energy flow, but which one? Which club? There are too many choices and we don't have that kind of time."

"We're going to have the same problem with bartenders and cab drivers." He shrugged. "And getting anything useful out of the local drug dealers is going to be impossible, even if I could find them. They'd never talk to me." He barked out a short laugh. "Especially when I explained what I wanted to know."

"We could try the fortune tellers, but…" I raised my shoulders in an empty shrug. "…how many and how spread out they are is going to be an issue again. It's already too late to start."

He looked toward the blocky line of downtown visible beyond the row of low industrial buildings that surrounded the club. The lighted windows of the skyscrapers were tiny beacons, small dots arrayed in a chaotic pattern against the backdrop of stone and steel. "Which one are they in?" he wondered.

The Chorus had been no help. As we had drifted across Portland—crossing and recrossing the river that split the city in two—they had looked for an abnormal energy signature. The concentration of souls in the device should have been a bright star, should have been obvious to anyone who could read urban flow patterns, but I detected nothing. Portland's grid was tainted, I could read that much, but the source of the disturbance was hidden. I could feel the ripples on the surface of the river but, try as I might, I couldn't locate the stone beneath the surface that was the cause.

"Are you sure about the card?" he asked. "The Princess of Cups. Are you sure of your interpretation?"

"Pretty sure. I don't know them as well as Piotr, but I know them well enough."

"Maybe we should focus on something more concrete. What about Thoth? Didn't I see a *Book of Thoth* at the bookstore? Why aren't we just reading that?"

"Because it's the wrong book. Crowley liked to pretend his book was the formative realization of the secrets of Thoth. It's an in-joke. One of the myths is that the copy in the Library of Alexandria was rescued, and its pages became the first tarot deck. But it's a story."

"A library would help, though. Something like Van Gröteon's collection?"

"Something like. Thoth—and Hermes Trismegistus, his manifestation in the flesh—is credited with writing forty-two books. The whole range of human knowledge. Nearly all of them have been lost. The two that are most complete make up *The Corpus Hermeticum,* and are philosophical discussions about the soul. There are references to the other books, oblique mentions in early alchemy tracts, and even a few extracts, but nothing complete. Not enough to re-create the originals."

"But if you were going to piece one together, it would be *The Book of Thoth.*"

I nodded. "Yes, that'd be the one."

"You can't rule out the possibility that he really did it, can you?"

I shook my head.

Nicols' gaze wandered across the line of warehouses and buildings. "There's a bookstore downtown. Powell's. It's an entire city block of books. I know we're the backwater and all out here, but maybe they've got something in their rare book room that can help us." He shrugged. "Hell, they've probably got a decent tarot section. We can get a second opinion on the Princess of Cups."

"Even if they had the books," I said, "The clues aren't going to be labeled in the table of contents. It'll take me hours to decipher anything of use. You've read the *Emerald Tablet.* On a literal level, there's nothing practical in those eighteen lines. Yet it was the core instruction manual for centuries of alchemical research."

He sighed. "We need a good librarian."

An idea struck me, a sudden blossoming in my head as if a flower had just erupted from rich loam. "A librarian," I said. "That's it. The scholars at the Library of Alexandria were the keepers of secret knowledge; they were the oracles of their age. Booksellers aren't the same, but they are kin to librarians. With the right influence, we might be able to get one to speak for us. To See something that will help us."

* * *

Her name was Devorah and she worked in the Red Room at Powell's, surrounded by tarot cards and metaphysical books. Her mousy brown hair was pulled back from her heart-shaped face by butterfly barrettes, and her eyelids were painted like stylized abalone shells. The logo on her maroon t-shirt was for a local punk band who had downloaded graphics from the Key of Solomon to use as a background texture. I wondered if she knew the source of their symbolism; if she knew they had been so perverted from their actual intent that they were useless as magickal seals.

T-shirts are the unconscious nametags of the psyche. In symbols and shorthand, they identify their wearers to like-minded souls: eye contact in a crowded room, conversation starters at the punch bowl, warning signs by which certain types are told to steer clear. Vestments as personality shortcuts.

Whether she knew it or not, her shirt told me she was going to be our oracle.

"Can I help you?" she asked as we approached her counter. She was reading a worn paperback of Milton's *Paradise Lost.* Up close, I noticed her eyes were green and she had a honeyed smell like her namesake. Just a hint, floating amid the scent of paper and glue that permeated the building. Curled around the arc of her left wrist was a tattoo of flowers and honey bees.

"I'm looking for a copy of Crowley's Thoth deck," I said. Crowley believed in the connection between Thoth and the tarot. Not quite the same thing that Bernard had supposedly found, but the symbolism was close enough.

She nodded, placing a bookmark in her book and setting it on the counter. "Large or small," she asked.

"Large."

Nicols, standing next to me, nodded like he was thinking the same thing. He wasn't. He had no idea what I was about to do and, if I had told him, he would have tried to stop me.

We were out of options. I had to See the Weave; I had to find the threads. My Will would open the Way.

She walked over to the nearby display case, and unlocked the cabinet. From the stock of tarot decks, she plucked out one of the larger boxes—the purple set—and returned to the counter. "There you go." She put it on the counter. "Anything else?"

"Do you know much about the tarot, Devorah?"

Her eyes narrowed for a second as I used her name. It was on her nametag, but I could tell the store policy rankled her. It bred familiarity, a level of personal intimacy that bugged her. It was a chink in her armor, and she didn't like it when people were able to reach inside and touch her so easily.

I'm so sorry, Devorah. I wish there was another way.

"Have you ever had your fortune told?" I slit the plastic on the box with a fingernail, and dumped the sealed deck and the instruction booklet onto the counter.

"Once or twice," she said cautiously, a non-answer that kept the conversation alive yet didn't invite me any closer.

The plastic around the deck was tight and there was no easy flap to get a fingernail under. I snapped a line from the Chorus to the end of my fingertip, starting a tiny spark, and melted the corner of the plastic wrap. The spell was quick and faint, not enough to catch her attention, though I felt Nicols shift at my side.

Devorah was watching me with a mingled light of curiosity and annoyance in her eyes. I was unwrapping the merchandise at her station and, while it wasn't an overt attempt at shoplifting, it was a violation of store policy. The tarot decks were under lock and key for this very reason—patrons would get their grubby fingers all over the cards otherwise—and I was flagrantly ignoring the rule.

However, reading the symbols on her shirt, I knew there was rebellion in her, an anarchistic flutter keeping curiosity alive in her heart. As brutish as I was being about the rules, part of her still wanted to see what I was going to do.

I scattered the deck on the table and the Chorus rippled through my hands. I touched and stroked the cards with Willful fingers. "Do you know this card?" I asked, feeling the psychic imprint of the one I wanted. I showed it to her. "Do you know what it means?"

She looked at it, curiosity beating annoyance. "Princess of Cups." She shrugged. "Sorry, I don't know anything about it. Look—"

"We need an oracle," I interrupted. "We need for you to scry for us."

"Excuse me?"

I leaned across the counter, and the serpents of the Chorus wrapped themselves around her arm. I grabbed her wrist and pulled her toward me. The Chorus licked the edge of the card in my other hand, and I slashed the Princess of Cups across her open palm, cutting a shallow line along the course of her lifeline. Laying the card aside, I grabbed her paperback and fingered it open to a random page. I spread the book out on the scattered backs of the Crowley cards—a sea of rosy crosses floating beneath our hands—and dragged her bleeding palm across the open page.

She struggled in my grip, crying out from the pain I had inflicted. "*Vide*," I said, inflicting a different sort of pain entirely on her. The electric charge of the Chorus lit the word as it left my mouth. Her body spasmed, a live-wire reaction that ran from the crown of her head to the root of her feet. I smeared her now limp hand twice more across the book. "I need you to See for me, Devorah. I need you to Read the page."

The Chorus surged into the quiescent part of her psyche, looking for the door she instinctively advertised that she had. When I found it, I broke the seal and forced awake her precognitive talent.

The justification for the spiritual rape was already being written in my head. History writ by those who survive the cataclysms. If we succeeded in finding the others, in stopping Bernard's Great Work, then my actions were justified—a Machiavellian excuse for the fruit it was to bear. If we failed, then no one would ever know. We would all be dead—Nicols, Devorah, me, most of Portland—and my metaphysical assault on this girl would be a minor transgression in the great scheme of the Universe. My sin was small.

Still, so was Kat's action; so was the promise I made in the woods. Tiny acts which, like the chaotic ripple of the butterfly's wings, caused interference waves in the Universe. It was in this seemingly infinite space that a multitude of incremental errors spawned an immense blot.

Devorah's cheeks quivered as I held up the bloody book, and the pupils of her eyes shrunk to minute dots. Her voice, when she spoke, was lusterless; the bright innocence of her throat marred by a scratchy fever. The Chorus swirled in my belly like sun-warmed snakes at the sound, and I grimaced at the pleasure they found in what I had done to her. "As one great furnace flamed," she intoned. "Yet from those flames no light; but rather darkness visible." Her voice grew more agitated with every word.

"I need to stop the darkness, Devorah," I said, trying to sooth her with the sound of my voice. "I need you to tell me where the light is going. How does it all start?"

She shook her head and her eyes twitched in their sockets as if she were fleeing from a vision, a spectral image fixed in front of her face. "Down they fell," she moaned, "driven headlong from the pitch of Heaven, down into this Deep; and in the general fall I also."

I spread the pages open even further. Her prophecies were finding their voice in the text. A drop of blood fell from the book and spattered on the card beneath, the bright blood staining the jeweled center of one of the multicolored crosses on the back of the card. "I need to know, Devorah. I can't stop it if I don't know where it begins."

"But torture without end still urges," she said, her voice growling. "And a fiery deluge, fed with ever-burning sulphur unconsumed."

Nicols—who, surprisingly, hadn't said anything so far—swore loudly at my side. "What the hell is she saying?"

I was trying to keep up and didn't have time to explain it to him. Milton was as dense as English literature got, and attempting to decipher his verse when it was being couched as a precognitive offering demanded a lot of my attention.

"Where does the fire start?" I asked.

She looked at me, a bloody tear starting in the corner of her left eye. "There stood a hill not far, whose grisly top belched fire and rolling smoke," she said. "The rest entire shone with a glossy scurf—undoubted sign that in his womb was hid metallic ore."

The bloody eye. The shadow woman in my dream who stood as tall as Heaven. Under her skirts, she had shown me her eye and it had rained bloody tears.

I closed the book and put it down. The Tower. Nicols' reading also held a physical component. "A metal hill?" I asked. "Is that where I can find him?"

She closed her eyes and her shoulders started to shake. "Let none henceforth seek needless cause to approve the faith they owe; when earnestly they seek such proof, conclude, they then begin to fail." Her voice cracked on the words, each one more fragmented and broken than the last.

I walked around the counter and helped her sit down on the stool. I took her bloody palm in my hands, sealing her flesh between my own. *Valetude.* The Chorus smoothed away the wound in her hand as if the flesh was as malleable as hot wax. "I'm sorry," I said as I put her hand in her lap. "I ask for your forgiveness, but know that I can never expect it."

Tears tracked down her face. The drop of blood smeared across her cheek. Nine drops. Nine swords. *Cruelty.* My past, severed, but not yet cleansed from my soul.

I didn't look at Nicols as I walked away from the counter, heading for the stairs and the street. "Hey," he said, coming after me, reaching for my arm. "What the fuck are you doing?" He gestured back at the crying woman. "Are you just going to leave her sitting there?"

I glanced down at his hand on my arm. The Chorus boiled under my skin and he held his grip for a few seconds before letting go. "Better here than with us," I said, and continued down the stairs toward the exit. He hesitated at the top of the stairs.

Nicols caught up with me again on the corner of Tenth and Burnside. His face was knotted with anger, his big hands working at his sides as if he couldn't wait to take a swing at me but still very aware of what I might do to him if he tried. "Goddamnit, Markham. Not like this. I don't—"

I pointed across the street, through the thick stalks of the steel forest of downtown Portland. "There," I said, interrupting him. "That's where they are."

He looked, following my arm. Peeking over the flat roof across the street was the tip of a black building—a hill filled with metallic ore. Its triangular peak was topped with a neon circle of red light—the bloody eye within the pyramid, the fire within the mountain.

The Tower. At the peak was Bernard and his unholy mirror.

XXVI

Eglanteria Terrace—named, as so much of the city was, after a species of rose—was the flagship of a new millennial architecture. Forty-plus floors of luxury condominiums were stacked on top of eight floors of restaurants, shops, and essential human services. Every need of the residents could be fulfilled without leaving the sanctuary of their building. Self-contained, climate-controlled arks. The only thing it was missing was a petting zoo on the roof.

Placards and posters on the ground floor advertised condominiums available on all floors—"Occupancy at 75%, buy now!"—and the central atrium, open to the fifth floor, allowed us an upward view of the partially filled mall. There were as many blank walls festooned with "Coming Soon!" signs as there were glass and wood storefronts. The property management was clearly having trouble filling this new ark. Humanity wasn't quite ready to return to the medieval castle lifestyle—hidden behind walls in their own private communities—even if the sanctuary had two massage therapists, an 8-screen movie theater, and an Irish pub.

Glass-edged walkways circled the central courtyard, decorated with strands of white lights that made the walls glittering rings of ice; murals suspended from the distant ceiling were painted in an abstract Impressionistic style with a nod toward Audubon's naturalism. Ducks in flight, their beaks pointed north.

The whole place was deserted, filled with frozen light. Nicols said it, his voice a dull whisper that died as it left his mouth. "Like a tomb."

Beyond the elevators, standing like basalt crypts with marble portals, was the security office. The door was sealed, locked from the inside, and, as we approached the small room, the security officer inside slowly banged his hands against the glass.

His eyes and mouth were black holes in his shriveled face. The body had no soul, filled only with the seeping darkness of the *Qliphoth*.

"Shit," Nicols sighed. "Well, we're in the right place." He looked like he couldn't decide if he should laugh or cry.

"They'll be at the top," I said, pulling him toward the elevators. The building's systems were still fully functional—technology rarely noticed the disappearance of human operators—and all fourteen elevators had power. Four of them serviced the mall levels only. The remaining ten were evenly split between the lower and upper halves of the residential apartments. We called a couple of cars, and they all had magnetic strips for key cards on their inner panels.

Nicols set down the duffel bag he had brought from the trunk of his car, blocking the door open on one elevator, and thumbed several of the buttons for the upper floors. None of them lit up. "We're going to need a card."

He unzipped his bag and started laying out the contents on the floor of the elevator. "The security guard will have one. I think retrieving it is your job." Mossberg shotgun with a combat grip, a pair of Sig Sauer pistols, an extra box of shells for the shotgun. After the guns and ammo came a bulletproof vest, a pitted conquistador's helmet, three plastic soda bottles, and a red-and-white-striped bandana with kamikaze-style rising sun. "What?" he asked when he noticed I hadn't moved.

"No rocket launcher?"

He shook his head as he began to load shells into the shotgun. "Don't be a smart-ass. You know the paperwork involved in getting one?"

I took the hint and went to retrieve the security officer's key card.

As the elevator ascended, Nicols adjusted the helmet, pulling it down over his ears. The bandana wrapped around the dented dome so that the bloody sun was right in the center of his forehead. An engorged third eye. Pistols on either hip, shotgun slung across his back, he got down on one knee and offered me one of the plastic bottles. "St. Mark's," he said. "It's been a long time since I've been to church, but they've always been pretty accommodating to wayward children who come back."

The Chorus quivered as I touched the bottle, reacting to an electric tingle.

"It's holy water," Nicols said matter-of-factly.

"I know what it is," I said. "I'm just wondering what you want me to do with it?"

He looked up at the digital display on the elevator wall. The number was already in the low 30s. "Come on. We don't have a lot of time. Bless me already."

"I'm not recognized by the Catholic Church."

"Doesn't matter. I'll believe anything you tell me."

And I got it finally: why he was still with me, why he sought to keep me from running. Why his wife's death was both the impetus and the curse of his continued life.

Was I any different? How had I found direction? Even now, freed from the *Qliphotic* taint, how was I being driven?

I shook the bottle, flushing the Chorus into the water. They made a cheap theatrical flourish of light as they energized the sanctified water—a visible marking that would further give credence to what Nicols believed I could do for him. I spun off the top of the bottle and shook water on him.

He closed his eyes and raised his face to receive the blessing. I took a mouthful of the holy water, changed it to fire in my mouth and spit it over him. He didn't flinch as the fiery spume changed to steam when it struck his water-dappled face. I leaned over and carefully kissed him on either eyelid, the Chorus leaving glittering imprints that sank into his skin. "See True, my son," I whispered.

Like a punctuation mark to the blessing, a pleasant voice suddenly spoke the number of the top floor: "52." The car slowed.

"Drink the rest." I gave him the half-empty bottle.

He looked at the bottle for an instant, delight shining in his face, and then tipped it in my direction. "Thanks."

I turned away from him so that he couldn't see my expression. The void in my gut was an emptiness with presence and weight. These holes are filled by faith, by the things we choose to believe. I heard Nicols sigh as he finished the water.

We believe our faith makes us strong. But that is the Fallacious Illusion of our existence. What assurance do we have that our faith is correctly given? Is it just the fact that we have given it that makes us think it is right? I believed the whispers of the *Qliphoth*. John believed I would keep him safe.

If the only vice of the soul was ignorance, then the only virtue was faith. Like good and evil, black and white, light and dark: this was the dichotomy of our existence. How close one was to the other. How dependent.

And how much a vacuum was left when one was bereft of ignorance and of faith.

The elevator opened onto a marble-floored foyer. Three panel-back chairs were lined up against the wall on the left like tired sentries. Flanking the middle chair were two narrow stands crowned with peace lilies in fat Grecian-style amphoras. A large pair of white doors was the only other exit.

The psychic vacuum of the mirror was palpable. A heavy static laced the air, a taste of burnt wire at the back of my throat.

The suction was a wave pattern that had an amplitude of a few seconds, a rhythm that throbbed at the base of my skull. The Chorus groaned like an old building settling.

Nicols tapped the conquistador helmet three times with the handle of the shotgun, shoving the metal cap even lower on his head. "You ready?" A vein throbbed in his neck, an unconscious physical echo mirroring the drag of the psychic currents.

I grunted noncommittally in reply as I shoved the two re-maining bottles of holy water in the front pockets of my pants. Julian had a predilection for fire. The holy water in and of itself wouldn't have any more effect on him than using a garden hose to put out a house fire, but its sanctified state made it more mal-leable—more readily changeable.

I couldn't fault Nicols for the desire to weigh himself down with the hardware, but it all failed the primal rule of magickal combat: any physical object brought to battle could be used against you. Guns were too easily turned against their wielder. Water, on the other hand, was just a liquid state of hydrogen and oxygen. Useless without the application of Will. Julian could take the water away from me, but he couldn't abscond with my Will.

The penthouse doors were unlocked. We crossed the thresh-old, the gravity well of the mirror pulling us into the room beyond.

The central living space of the penthouse was a long L-shape, and beyond an *Architectural Digest*-style spread of furniture and accessories, stood the theurgic mirror. The tall windows behind it looked out over the Willamette River and the lit arc of the Hawthorne Bridge, gleaming like a handful of fresh-water pearls. The furniture was Italian Industrial Futurist—straight lines and right angles, chrome edging, dead animal hide dyed in grays and burgundies—and the art on the walls was more of the Impressionist Pacific Northwest school that adorned the mall level of the building. Diamond-shaped wall sconces bled weak illumination as if the light was afraid of the smoky darkness of the mirrored sphere.

Two hallways split off at the midsection of the room like the transept of a church. The leg of the L was the dining room, from which issued the steady sound of chanting, a repetitious litany of that guttural language Bernard used to commune with his artifact.

Julian stepped around the corner of the dining room wall. He was wearing a gray and yellow robe, covered with lines and whorls of black script. Floating over his head was a cascade of bright stars. Silver cobwebs stretched from the stars to his head, a crown of filigreed strands.

"Markham." A brief flash of surprise on his face, quickly subsumed into bored disappointment.

"Expecting someone else?"

"I assume you met him on the path." He shook his head. "Not that it matters. This Aeon is almost finished."

I walked through the contortions of the furniture, intent on the far wall and the statue. Julian made no attempt to stop me, his expression slightly bemused and distracted. He didn't seem terribly concerned about our presence. If the crown of light was what I thought it was, I could certainly understand his lack of apprehension. It was probably akin to the conduits Doug had worn in the Arena. Julian was connected to the mirror's storehouse of souls, as was Bernard, who was seated in a meditative pose on the dining room table. The Anointed, in pure energy states, were channeling energy to the magus and the academic.

An involuntary chill ran up my spine. *All those souls, keening and whispering in their heads.* I remembered the constant buzz of the Chorus when I had first made it a part of me, how that incessant sound had nearly driven me insane. In their case, the noise was magnified a hundred times. *Soul-speak.* The chatter of the bodiless.

"You've brought your friend." Julian snickered at the sight of the shotgun in Nicols' hands. "He's got better weapons this time. Not that silly pop gun."

"The man's adaptable." Walking toward the mirrored sphere was uncomfortably easy, my feet nearly tripping over themselves in delight. The psychic pull of its hunger became more and more difficult to resist. Like the insistent voice of the Chorus, the stroke of its wave was a seductive lure. Feel the collapsed weight of a thousand souls. Right here. *Close enough to touch.*

I dragged myself to a stop just short of an arm's length from the statue. The Chorus, split between hunger and dread, were a whirlwind of chaos in my skull. *Touch/fear it.* I declined both options, and stayed a safe distance.

The facets of the sphere seemed to twist at right angles, a tesseract movement that made the globe appear to be on the verge of implosion. It exerted such a psychic pull that ambient energy was being drawn into the facets of the mirror. I wondered what its gravity would do to magick. If spells would be misdirected due to its influence.

I looked over at Julian standing near the dining room. I was probably going to find out. Sooner or later. In which case, I didn't want to be the one closest to the mirror.

Nicols drifted toward the center of the room, putting the large leather sofa between himself and Julian. It would have been a good defensive position were it not for the gas fireplace behind him. "Julian likes fire," I Whispered to the detective, spiriting my words directly into his ear. Nicols had the presence of mind not to twitch or look; he just kept moving, circling one of the armchairs and gliding toward the right-hand hallway that led to the rest of the penthouse.

Bernard ignored all of us. His litany was an endless loop, each phrase precisely enunciated with no sign of strain or exhaustion. *How long had he been chanting?* His eyes were fixed on the mirrored sphere and his hands were cupped in his lap. Like Julian, a crown of stars floated above his head. A magick circle surrounded him, drawn with white powder. Salt, maybe. Held in place by the activation of the incantation. I wondered what the circle did; certainly not protection because Julian wasn't inside it. *A focus, maybe.*

"Nice little party." With some difficulty, I moved away from the artifact. "Are we the only ones coming?"

"Far from it," Julian said. He tapped the side of his head. "There's room for many more yet."

"What happens next?"

"The world ends."

"I was hoping for something a little less dramatic," I said. "What would happen if I tried to break your toy?"

"Most likely, it would break you." Julian glanced at Nicols, noting the detective's position near the hallway. The magus' left hand twitched, flexing about an invisible shape, and the lights in his crown twinkled. *Reaching for fire.*

Nicols noticed the motion as well, and the barrel of his shotgun dipped to cover the twitching hand. "What's it supposed to do?" he asked, keeping Julian's attention.

I drifted closer to the dining room, a hand resting on the edge of my pocket. My fingers touched plastic.

"You know nothing of alchemy, do you?" Julian asked Nicols. "It's the final step of the Great Work. *Solve et coagula.* First you dissolve, then you recombine."

"Is that what you call what you did to the people in Ravensdale?" Nicols spat. "*Dissolving?*"

"Yes. Their souls were poured out of their bodies. The flesh is just a shell, a mold in which the soul is kept. It wasn't necessary."

"A shell? You left a town full of shells!"

A lascivious smile spread across Julian's lips. I was near enough to him now to see how tiny his pupils were, how a tiny black webbing infected the sclera of his eyes.

"He knows," I said. Goose bumps danced along the underside

of my arms. I had driven psychic spikes through his soul when I had pinned him to the wall in the hotel. The darkness beneath the Chorus, the vile spit that had been rising in me, had infected him through that contact. "*Qliphotic,*" I said, pronouncing the word like the curse that it was.

Julian nodded. "They're filled with appetite. The flesh is always receptive to hunger, always ready to accept a purpose."

"*Solve,*" I said. "How does killing a thousand people bring about the realization of the Work?"

"Killing? We didn't kill anyone. We simply separated them. Purified them for a higher purpose."

"Your purpose."

"Absolutely."

"Not God's purpose."

He raised his hands in a lackadaisical gesture. "We are all God's children. How can any purpose we have not be His?"

"These souls can't be put back. They are dead, regardless of how you define 'killing.' How is that part of God's purpose?"

"Nothing can be destroyed, Markham. This is the truth of alchemy." Julian's distracted expression of bemusement crept back onto his face. He turned halfway in my direction. "You know this is an unassailable truth: transformation is the only freedom available to us. Destruction is beyond our comprehension and ability. God exists throughout us, throughout everything, and everything is Him. We can't strip Him out."

"If you can't remove Him, then how do you hope to perceive Him? Isn't that one of the paradoxes inherent to this whole conversation? I don't recall Hermes Trismegistus having any better answer to that question."

"The Creator is His first shadow, and we are the second. We are a rank removed from the Infinite and All-Encompassing. We are caught within the shadow of the Creator, unable to see beyond."

Julian's left hand was still moving, the fingers crawling in an intricate dance. I pretended to ignore the movement, casually pulling one of the water bottles out of my pocket. I was a few steps from him, standing to his right. Bernard was straight in front of me.

"So you want to get out of that shadow, do you?" I asked, unscrewing the bottle. I took a small sip from the water, positioning my hand around the base of the container.

"How marvelous would it be to look upon God? To be free of the illusions of the shadow?" Julian's fingers stilled their movement and the Chorus felt fire bloom within his body. It raced through his blood and began to collect in his palm.

I shrugged. "What makes you think He wants to be Seen?"

His pupils changed, distending to flat black coins. "We are ready," he said, the levity disappearing from his voice. "When the time comes, we will be deemed suitable."

I nodded toward Bernard. "He will be, sure. He's the one doing all the work. You? You're just standing around congratulating yourself for doing, eh, a whole fuckload of nothing."

The *Qliphotic* influence was in him. It was attached to his flesh and it would be singing to him right now, singing him a song of violence and hatred. I knew how that tune went.

"His hand," I Whispered to Nicols who hadn't moved from his position by the arch. "Watch his hand."

"I mean, you 'separated' those people in Ravensdale," I said to Julian. "What sort of spinelessness is that? Could you even look one of them in the face when you took their soul? Shit, Julian, I killed nine of your boys before breakfast this morning. Sucked and burned every one of them." I took one more sip of water, cool trickle down my throat. "Hell, I even torched your warehouse."

"My warehouse?" The question ground its way out of him, tinged with black anger. His fire quivered.

Focus splitting.

I nodded, a smug grin on my lips as I casually flipped the water bottle at the dining room table. It hit the tabletop, bounced once and rolled against Bernard. Holy water gurgled and flowed out of the open mouth, spilling onto the wood.

Holy water wouldn't do much to Julian, but it would react with the salt on the table, transforming the solid into a liquid. An old alchemist's trick.

XXVII

S plit by the material passion raging inside, Julian was distracted by the flight of the plastic container. His gaze drifted, and the orientation of his body changed as well. I came across the intervening space and hit him with a Chorus-hardened hand. The blow staggered him, and he took several steps back.

Flush with fire, he raised his left hand to hurl a spell at me. Nicols' shotgun roared, a deafening sound that shook the walls, and Julian's hand exploded in a geyser of smoke and flame.

The theurgic mirror inhaled and the rising spray of fire and smoke was sucked across the room, elongated tendrils of magick and flesh streaming from Julian's hand.

Nicols pumped another shell into the gun and shot the magus a second time. The shotgun blast spun him around, and the rain of stars over his head twinkled.

Bernard's crown glittered as well, and he hiccupped in the middle of a word, his head going back like he couldn't breathe. The water was compromising his circle. His body froze, all but the muscles in his neck, which worked and worked like they were trying to move an obstruction.

I ran to the table and smeared my hand through the water and salt mixture. "*Solve* this." I slapped my palm against his throat, leaving salt, holy water, and the hot imprint of my Will on his skin. The flesh bubbled and melted, a chemical reaction from the magicked mixture of hydrogen and chloride. His choking noises became more strident and whatever paralysis holding him vanished. He collapsed on the table, eyes wide and protruding, hands scrabbling at the bubbling mass of his neck.

Behind me, the theurgic mirror inhaled. Its hunger was still immense, but lessening. More diffuse. As if without Bernard's chant, it was directionless.

I distantly heard the boom of Nicols' shotgun, a reverberating echo rather than a local thunder. In its wake came a howl of fire and, through the door on the far side of the dining area, I saw the reflected red glow of flame. A smoke detector went off in the hallway, an alert that passed to the other alarms scattered throughout the penthouse.

I hesitated for a second, torn between going to help Nicols and dealing with Bernard. Julian was going to catch the detective. It was only a matter of time and, at that point, the fight would go badly for Nicols. Bernard was still dealing with his melting trachea. He wouldn't be an issue for a little while yet.

A second later the decision was made for me as Nicols came barreling through the dining room. Flames wreathed the dome of his helmet, chewing at the synthetic material of the bandana. Smoke leaked off the back of his tactical vest and ash darkened his face.

"Shit!" He jerked his gun to the side and dodged toward the living room, avoiding me. He didn't slow down as he reached the leather sofa, tumbling over the back like he was diving for the end zone.

Smoke billowed out of the doorway and flame licked the edges of the arch, darkening the walls. Julian, red fire fluttering along his frame like he was standing in front of an industrial fan, stood in the kitchen like a burning *efreet*. Smoke poured off the wreckage of his left hand, a black plume that was sucked into the dining room by the gravity well of the artifact.

I was between Julian and the device.

He released his flame as I went to the left, diving for the carpet. A phoenix with bright wings and hot talons manifested through his Will and streaked across the living room. It came apart—crackling fingers of fire—as its magick was shredded by the influence of the theurgic mirror. The firebird scorched the atmosphere, leaving an acrid taint of ozone in its wake, and collapsed into a fiery funnel about the three statues. The windows behind them shattered as the fire was explosively decompressed and absorbed by the facets of the mirror. The light of the fire went from ruddy to pink to pale in the span of a heartbeat.

Wind, shrieking like a murder of outraged crows, swept into the room. Naked flames, still caught on the wall in the dining room, flickered and stretched. Nicols peered around the end of the couch, his helmet askew. Down my back, on the right side, I could feel flesh cracking—I had been tagged by the firebird as it had come apart.

Julian stepped around the edge of the dining room table, the smoke from his ruined hand reduced to a tiny strand of black mist. Fire danced on his forehead, mixing with the stars suspended over his head. His eyes were black stones. The right shoulder of his robe was dark with blood, crimson tracked halfway to his waist.

The mirror's suction was strong. I would need to keep the Chorus tightly bound. I shaped them in a line of psychic barbed wire and cracked it at Julian. Poorly anticipating the drag of the artifact's vacuum, my whip missed its mark.

He snarled at the line of sparks and made a grab at the twisting expression of the Chorus with his good hand. It snaked out of his grasp.

Nicols popped up from behind the couch, and fired the shotgun. Time splintered near Julian's ruined hand and the slug from the shotgun slowed, striking his raised forearm. A slow-motion tracery of blood and fire exploded.

In a fast-forward return to normal time, his Will reached into the gas fireplace. Nicols was knocked down by the explosive eruption from the narrow grate. The furniture caught fire and the molded plastic of the occasional pieces steamed and melted.

With my second toss, I managed to wind the psychic wire around Julian's neck. He grabbed my wire, steadying himself, even though the psychic current of the Chorus was shutting down his nervous system. Napalm dripped from his ruined arm and he hurled a spray at me.

Most of it missed, pulled off course by the mystic gravity well, but some of it spattered on my clothes. The napalm seared, lancing my flesh. Burning deep.

He was too strong. Too much power available from the soul crown. His spells were overcharged, a vicious ferocity I couldn't withstand. My Will wasn't enough.

My focus wavered, flickering for just a second, and he acted in that tiny vacuum of intent. He pulled the psychic wire right out of me, and I staggered, feeling the Chorus tear. Down in my core. Again. *Her hand in my chest. That pain. That despair.*

He knocked me to the floor with a burst of fire. I tried to breathe, and sucked in flame. My throat felt like I had just drunk lava.

Before I could recover, he was on me. His good hand touched my throat and fire sang throughout my head. I beat at his hand, but it was like trying to break stone with a peacock feather. Color bleached from my vision and his skin became opaque. I could see his skull as he leaned close to my face.

A pair of pistol shots. Thunder in an enclosed space. Julian jerked forward, grunting from the twin blows in his lower back.

His hands vanished from my throat and I rolled onto my side, coughing up soot. Each breath felt like I was fueling an inferno in my chest.

Julian held Nicols' arm in his hand, the pistol shaking in the detective's persistent grip. The magus beat at Nicols' vest with his stump, smearing burning napalm on the Kevlar material. Nicols strained against the magus, trying to get the barrel of the pistol lined up. Julian shook his head, and bodily threw the detective against the statue.

Nicols groaned from the impact, and he dropped the gun. Flailing his arms, he tried to regain balance against the gravity of the mirrored sphere. His left arm drifted against the silver ring in the middle and, feeling something solid against his wrist, he reached with his hand to steady himself.

He touched the sphere.

A primal howl ripped out of him, a scream echoed by the hidden fear in my heart. The Abyss. The sound one makes when confronted with that nothingness, that complete emptiness. Nicols' cry was filled with both despair and anger—the nihilistic sound of enlightenment of an abandoned Heaven.

A string of soft lights coursed down his arm and vanished into the mirror. Much like the ibis-hound had sucked energy from Kat, the facets of the mirror drank from Nicols' soul, draining his spirit through the contact afforded by his flesh. He tried to break the connection, but his hand was fused to the mirror.

I tried to reach him, but Julian grabbed the collar of my coat. The iron force of his Will wrapped around me, and kept me from reaching John. Nicols swung his free arm out and our fingers just missed.

Julian wrapped his bloody forearm around my chest, tucking his body against my burned back. My raw skin twitched from the hot contact and I felt the napalm of his blood dripping down my chest, scouring tracks as it flowed. "I want you to watch," he whispered in my ear. I struggled, straining to move closer to the mirror and John—almost close enough to touch—but the effort only tightened Julian's cage about me.

Nicols tried to reach me again, but his strength was fading

too quickly. Each pulse of light down his arm lessened his life force. Already he could barely stand, his knees leaning against the statue for support. Tears ran from his eyes, and when he tried to speak, his final words weren't loud enough to be heard.

When his head fell forward and rested against one of the bronze shoulders, Julian released me. I reached Nicols' body as the mirror let go of his fingers, the contact no longer needed. The body was just an empty shell. Detective John Nicols was gone.

I cradled his body across my lap and his face stared sightlessly at the ceiling. His expression was like Gerald Summers' face. The flesh, wondering why its light had failed.

Julian capered nearby, waving his bloody stump over his head. "One more," he shouted over the sound of the fire alarm. "One more for the party." He danced close and bent down toward me, bringing his stump to the side of his head. "I can hear him. Right in here."

My hand touched the leather holster of the unused pistol on Nicols' belt and, in a smooth motion, I pulled the gun out and pressed it into Julian's left eye socket. "Right here?" I pulled the trigger.

The back of his head came off in a spray of pink and gray that contorted in flight as it became subject to the mirror's pull. His legs went rubbery and he fell back on his ass. Mouth working like an out-of-water fish, he struggled to form a thought with half his brain missing.

I unceremoniously dumped Nicols' meat on the floor and put two more rounds in Julian's chest—right through his heart. Just one more thing for him to try to think about. As long as he had the crown of souls, he could still manage to put himself back together.

Grabbing the front of his blood-stained robe, I dragged him over to the window. I thrust my hand into the skein of stars floating above his skull, feeling the crown's electrical surge in my finger joints. The wild lines of the crown fit into the Chorus like bridle bits in the mouths of race horses. "Time to leave the nest, little bird," I said to Julian as I pushed him out the window. His head snapped back, caught for a moment before the crown ripped free, and then he fell.

I raised my star-filled palm to my cheek, pressing the fading rain of lights against my flesh. I could feel them, just as he said, I could feel all of them.

And the Anointed too. Bright lights against the skein of stars. They pulsed, flexing and swelling like gas bubbles. I felt a jolt of energy jerk elsewhere.

To Bernard.

He was standing next to the table, his throat a vein of silver and pink. His voice box was ruined, but he didn't need to actually speak for me to hear him. "It is done," he Whispered. "*Fiat lux.*"

The mirror collapsed. Its implosion was a gravitational well. Deep in the scarred darkness of my gut, something vital tore, something already ripped—not once, but twice. Something I could never replace.

Everything froze, dim shadows against the burst of pure light that came from the artifact. Nothing changed for a split second as the world came apart at an atomic level and then reassembled itself. The same, but fractured, broken, and hurriedly put together without care for a proper fitting of all the microscopic pieces.

Thoth's Key. Bernard had activated it.

The crown of souls clutched in my hand, I jumped out the open window. A desperate attempt to flee the realization of the artifact's purpose. I tumbled from the top of the Tower as lightning split its dome. I fell.

Driven headlong from the pitch of Heaven, down into this Deep.

An incendiary burst bleached the surfaces of the surrounding buildings as if the sun had come to Portland. *Nova stella*, the light atop the tower burned away the night.

* * *

I hadn't jumped from a building for a few years, and never without a chute, but the body remembered. The Chorus streamed behind me, grabbing at the air, and my descent was somewhere between a headlong fall and a clumsy glide.

As I neared the ground, the last glitter of energy from the crown faded, and I Willed it into a whirlwind beneath my feet, a fluffy soup of air that supported me as I reached the grassy lawn. Not far from Julian's shattered body. Face-down on the grass. Not much of a flyer. Not much of a witness either. Facing away from the very cataclysm he had worked to bring about. Missing everything. That seemed fitting.

There were other witnesses, though. Cars in the street, their occupants peering out open windows at the source of the hard illumination that slew every shadow in the street. Couples on the sidewalk, their faces turned upward.

I crossed the landscaped lawn and jumped the low hedge at the property's edge. A middle-aged man with a bushy mustache was half-out of his stopped sedan, twisting his body so he could stare up at the peak of the tower. He neither blinked nor turned his head as I approached his vehicle. His expression rapturous, his eyes were fixed on the star. I blocked his view with my palm and nothing changed; the light still dazzled his eyes.

He was blind to the physical world. Free of the illusion made by shadows. Free to look upon God.

Suddenly, the pure light vanished, and so physically abrupt was the loss that I gasped as if the wind had been knocked out of me. The man in the car winced as if he had been struck in the jaw, but he kept looking. The glittering light in his eyes remained. Even though the star had gone out, his rapture remained.

I looked up. At the top of the building there was a hole in the sky, a swelling ball of emptiness. It was expanding and, floor by floor, the lights went out in Eglanteria Terrace. The darkness was absolute as if the expanding edge was devouring everything it touched. As if it were unmaking the world by degrees.

With the Chorus gibbering like terrified monkeys in my head, I ran. I had no idea how far the dissolution would spread—*Was the whole world coming undone?*—but I fled the vacuum regardless.

It seemed like a futile, animalistic effort. As if I could outrun the disintegration of reality. But, in my heart, I wasn't ready to face this end. Not my choice. I wasn't a willing participant. What drove me wasn't the primitive part of me that wanted to live; what gave me the strength to run was the void left by the *Qliphoth*. I had been swallowed by this sort of emptiness once. *Never again.*

Etched on my palm was the faded imprint of the crown of souls. The conduit had failed as I had fallen; I hadn't the opportunity to integrate my Will to the skein of stars. Bernard's crown had remained strong. I had only broken his incantation. I hadn't taken away his connection. He was still there, at the heart of the vacuum. Most likely, the crown was protecting him. That was why he and Julian were both wearing it. They anticipated surviving this implosion.

I stumbled to a stop. I was more than a block away and, between two tall buildings, I could see the curve of darkness as the vacuum spread. A realization of its purpose cut through the chattering noise of the Chorus. *Solve et coagula.* The dissolution and then the final recombination. *There's room for many more yet.* Thoth's Key wasn't destroying the world; it was harvesting the souls within it.

The eyes of the man in the car had been transfixed by the light. Not because he had seen the face of God but, like a deer in the road, he had been stunned by the illumination. The shockwave following was the rippling gravity wave of the artifact as it sucked in all the light.

How far would it go?

The river. I had seen the Hawthorne Bridge from the penthouse window. Would it cross the river?

The wave of darkness came through the building across the street, a line of nothingness that swallowed the lighted windows and the white stone façade. It wasn't silent. I could hear the sound of the Key's harvest, a chattering echo of a thousand knives being sharpened. The sound of soul-death.

The river was my only chance. I ran, the metallic roar of the gravity wave pursuing me.

I saw the lit arc of the bridge beyond the roof of a low building and I dashed down the nearby alley. A parking lot lay on the other side, adjacent to the Hawthorne Bridge onramp. My heartbeat hammering in the base of my skull, I fled across the empty lot to the bridge.

The sound of knives was too close behind me. A car, weaving erratically as it came off the bridge, swerved to miss me, and I heard it smash into the metal framework of the bridge. If the passengers in the car survived the impact with the railing, they didn't have a chance to scream before the wave swept over them.

The shrieking panic of the Chorus reached a fever pitch, a palpable terror making my teeth ache. This was real death for them. A permanent dissolution they had cheated by remaining in my head. The rising noise of their panic told me that I wasn't safe, that the Key was on the bridge with me. Still harvesting, still sucking up souls.

I wasn't going to make the other side. It was coming too fast. This conscious realization sent the Chorus into a paroxysm of utter desperation. I stumbled, my legs suddenly numb as they tried to usurp control.

Where are you going to go? I looked back. The darkness behind me was total nothingness. *Terra autem erat inanis et vacua.* In a few seconds I would be enveloped by the wave as it swept over me and the rest of the bridge. I could see its leading edge riding the surface of the river below.

Riding the surface. I suddenly remembered the lake from my dream, how the surface of the water defiantly split two worlds. Above was not as below—a state contrary to the alchemical axiom.

What do you See? What do you know? What do you believe?

Questions without answers. Questions of faith. *Let none henceforth seek needless cause to approve the faith they owe.*

I angled for the pedestrian walkway that ran along the edge of the bridge. The railing separating the walkway from the road was only waist-high and I cleared it easily. The river-side railing was a bit higher and I went over it without any thought to form. I cleared it as fast as I could.

White-noise screaming filled my head as the Chorus felt the edge of darkness touch my falling body. They sparked and frayed as the curtain of soul-death swept over me.

I plunged headfirst into the cold water. Behind me, absolute night—bereft of stars, of light—covered the river. But it didn't reach beneath the surface. I dove deep until my strength failed. My strength, but not my faith. Then I closed my eyes, and let the hurt that must be sustained fill me.

John, I'm sorry. It wasn't your fortune you read.

I'm sorry I wasn't stronger.

The river, old lover, cold mother, took me away, her liquid hands trying to soothe my pain.

THE FIFTH WORK

"For no one of the gods in heaven shall come down to the earth, o'er-stepping heaven's limit; whereas man doth mount up to heaven and measure it; he knows what things of it are high, what things are low, and learns precisely all things else besides. And greater thing than all; without e'en quitting earth, he doth ascend above. So vast a sweep doth he possess of ecstasy. For this cause can a man dare say that man on earth is god subject to death, while god in heaven is man from death immune."

– Hermes Trismegistus, *The Corpus Hermeticum*

XXVIII

I dreamt of bees, honey bees circling enormous flowers. The stalks were thick with strange veins, and I could see the rhythmic pulse of these ropy conduits. The heads of the flowers were voluptuous circles of curling white petals with tender pink centers. Pulsating cores of limpid light that blinked a seductive pattern, a Morse signal read by the bees.

I lay on my back, cradled in a bower of thick grass, and I watched a fat bee with yellow sigils inscribed on its thorax fly past. Its face was pink instead of black, a tiny human mask fitted over its insectoid visage. Nicols' face, smooth like a plastic mold, like a cheap mask that captured shape but not personality. The human-faced bee buzzed in tempo with the flickering heart of a nearby flower, and as it approached, the white petals curled, encouraging it closer.

The Nicols bee kissed the pink center and the flower convulsed, its petals whipping inward. A pink creature broke through the dome of the flower's face, and its long pink proboscis struck the bee in the center of its plasticine forehead. Pink tendrils connected the ibis-hound with the flower and, as the tiny soul-sucker drew out the essence of the bee, these tendrils strained and pulsed with the vacuuming rhythm of the ibis-hound.

I fled the dream, fled the field of soul-devouring flowers, but the bee's buzzing panic followed me. The sound increased in volume as I fled through flickering spaces of stereographic visions. The sound became Nicols' death scream, a wordless cry of human frailty. It was the sound of abandonment, of fearful darkness, of failure. It resonated in my head, growing louder, even as I ran further and further from the field of hungry flowers. The echo of his voice grew stronger, becoming not one voice but the sound of a thousand throats shrieking, of flesh sizzling, of knives ringing off metal. Of a city's light dying.

I woke to the sensation of her wet kiss fading from my lips.

The sky overhead was gray and dead, like flesh that had been submerged too long in stagnant water. My back was cold and wet; the tips of my fingers numb. The scream was still in my head, a cry struggling to find voice in my throat.

My lips were warm, though; her breath was caught in my mouth. A hot taste on my tongue, bitter with a leached sourness. Tears.

Devorah.

She held a sharp edge against my neck. Bloody tears dripped from her eyes and her green irises were overwhelmed with swirling patterns of black and gold. "Lest with a whip of scorpions I pursue thy lingering," Devorah said. "Or with one stroke of this dart strange horrors seize thee, and pangs unfelt before." She knelt beside my body, knees pressed against my rib cage, My right arm was flung out straight past her body. Her right hand held the blade against my throat and her left held my head back. Easier to cut my throat. "For proof look up, and read thy lot in yon celestial sign; where thou art weighed, and shown how light, how weak, if thou resist."

I swallowed, feeling the thin edge against my windpipe. The Chorus cowered in the deepness of my core, their rank broken by the wave of soul-death that had touched them. The screaming echo of the city reverberated in their silver strands. "What do you seek from me, Oracle?" My voice bubbled through a film of river water still in my esophagus.

"Be not diffident of Wisdom," she said. Her mouth worked hard on the words. The prescient vision I had brought upon her still burned her blood. "She deserts thee not, if thou dismiss not her, when most thou needest her nigh."

Wisdom. The bounty realized by the soul as it climbed toward its release from the flesh, as it reached for enlightenment. Devorah had been guided by her burning sight to save me from the river, but only to hold my life in her hands. After what I had done to her, was I worthy of being saved? What price was her innocence?

"Ask," I croaked. I could smell the river nearby, the damp of dead water, and, distantly, a scent of burned wood. Not fire, but soot, as if the flames had long gone out. I wanted to turn my head and look at the city, but I knew if I looked away from Devorah's face, she'd cut my throat.

"See, with what heat these dogs of hell advance to waste and havoc yonder world," she said. "Which I so fair and good created; and had still kept in that state, had not the folly of Man let in these wasteful furies." Each drop that welled from the corners of her eyes was an unconscious reaction to her Vision, to the sorrow I had brought upon her. Each drop was a little more of her life leaking away, forced out of her body by the passion of her Sight. Each drop was my responsibility. Who was I to force such sacrifice upon her? "Who art to lead thy offspring, and supposest that bodies bright and greater should not serve the less not bright?"

The rule of the mighty was not to serve their own desires, but to assist in the enlightenment of the rest. Plato's philosopher kings. Alfred the Great who drove the Danes out of England and spent the twilight of his rule attempting to educate his subjects. Solomon, devoting his wisdom so that his people could understand peace.

I remembered Nicols' crown card: the Hanged Man. The suspended magus who waits to have his vision realized, who waits to fulfill himself. The Fisher King who cannot save his kingdom until his wound is recognized.

Kether—the first Sphere of the Sephiroth—was the Crown. The ultimate goal of the seeker of enlightenment. Lights go up; lights go out. It is always to the crown they go. The Wheel grinds the kings down; the Wheel lifts them up.

"Ask," I said again, feeling the open emptiness of my void, that center that I had allowed to be filled with poison and anger, that I had looked inside as I had fallen in the river and found myself hiding there. Nicols had only asked one thing of me. One tiny thing. A decision I had been forced to make in the woods when he had put the gun to his head. A moment of divergence, paths to be chosen. One or the other. Like the dark wood where I had been born into the occult world. A moment of choice. A tiny thing. *This final, fatal choice.*

What do you believe?

"Ask," I said a third time, binding myself to this moment. "Query me your riddle, Oracle. Show me the way to the crown." *Kether*. The eye of God. After everything, the Way was not closed.

Nothing is ever lost.

"Last, with one midnight stroke, all the first-born of Egypt must lie dead," she said. "And shall grace not find means, that finds her way?" I realized it wasn't a knife she held against my throat. Just as I had slit her palm with a symbolic representation of her, she was threatening me with a similar psychic symbol. She held a tarot card to my throat. The answer to her riddle was the identity of that card.

Piotr's reading came back to me, the cards floating in my mind against the churning backdrop of the dream I had had later that night about the reading. Kat and I—the Prince and Queen of water, locked in our embrace—the wheel beneath us with the shrouded and masked body. I understood its mask now, understood it was meant as my death mask. My innocence hidden away beneath a mirror.

Bernard was the satyr cherub with the engorged phallus. The flesh rod was an expression of his priapic quest for knowledge, and his persistent efforts to fuck the world were an attempt to make it climax and give up its secrets. Above us had been the rain of swords, nine blades reaching down from Heaven to prick our flesh. Below, the wheel of five wands surmounted by the empty faces of the unborn. They were opposites, the routes a magus takes in his quest for the top of the Tree—the paths of Severity and Mercy.

Had not the folly of Man let in these wasteful furies? We thought we could Create, that we were wise enough to make changes to the course laid down by God. We thought we could change the world as if that was sufficient apology for failing to change ourselves. Who among us was wise enough to think themselves not beholden to the rest of mankind? Was not murder of another but a murder of self? Was the *Qliphotic* darkness that had claimed me for so long nothing but my own fear of the unknown?

Where was my faith?

And shall grace not find means, that finds her way?

There were two paths: the path of Severity and the path of Mercy. I was on the threshold, caught on the cusp of nightmare and daybreak. At the edge of the wood, there were two paths. I had failed to stop Bernard and Julian from their unholy experiment, but in that failure was there also not an effort to save someone other than myself?

Was the hole of *Daäth*—the entire lost wasteland of the Tree's *Qliphotic* darkness—nothing more than a selfish mistake, a failure of Ego?

For proof look up, and read thy lot in yon celestial sign; where thou art weighed, and shown how light, how weak, if thou resist.

"The Moon," I said. "You're holding the Moon."

Devorah released her hold on my hair and sat back on her heels, lifting the card away from my throat. She held it in front of my face. Two pillars on the shores of a river that cut through the center of the card—separating the world. A pale crab, imperfectly drawn as if it were but a half-dream, crawled in the mud at the bottom of the river. Two jackal creatures—one on either shore—howled at the pregnant moon that hung low in the sky. This was the Moon, the deranged madness that came over the intelligence during the darkness when the sun was dead and rolling beneath the world. It was the card that came after the Star, and it was the gateway to resurrection—the Sun and the new Aeon.

She dropped the card on my chest as she stood. She had been between me and Portland, and her motion was permission to look. I put my hand over the card, holding it to my body, as I turned my head and bore witness to what had been done to the city.

It was a black landscape. I had been pulled from the river near the railway switching yard, a shallow bank bereft of any impediments. From where I lay, I could see the broken arches of three bridges—shattered fingers reaching across the stained river. The destruction—the absolute and empty darkness, *autem erat inanis et vacua*—stretched up the wooden hill to the west of downtown and across the river through the dense suburbs close to the freeway. More than a mile away, and still at the edge of the devastation.

A single spire rose from that bleak ruin, crowned by a flickering ball of pale fire. In the bowl of the metropolis that had been Portland, the only movement was the collapsed light of the thousands of souls that had been taken by Bernard's theurgic mirror.

The harvest was done. All that remained was the fixed point of the souls, the single light in darkness. The tower was the *axis mundi* and the pale light at its tip the signal fire that called out to God. "He isn't finished."

"No." A male voice intruded. Decrepit, it trembled with effort, but it was still a voice I knew. "Not quite."

Standing at the top of the embankment to my left were Pender and another man, a wizened figure wrapped in a brown trench coat.

Antoine.

XXIX

Antoine held tight to Pender's arm as they picked their way down the incline. His skull peeked through patches of still-raw flesh, and most of his lower jawbone was visible as were his teeth. His hair was gone, and his left hand was a claw of bone with scattered flaps of healing skin. The silver stub ending his right arm was a heavy knob. Only his eyes showed any clarity—bright lamps in his scarred face.

Pender wore a smug expression, a grin he couldn't quite suppress. Glee of a nearly realized plan, fruition of a torturous campaign. I wanted nothing more than to beat his teeth out of his head. Tear that fucking smile off his face.

The anger gave me enough clarity to stand, to ignore the vociferous dissent raised by every muscle and tendon in my frame as I moved. "How many?" The words burned in my throat. "How many did he kill?"

Pender sucked a breath through his teeth. "Hard to say. It's been a couple of years since the last census. And," nodding toward the darkness of the city, "it seems to have fallen short of its—"

"*How many?*" I shouted

Pender shrugged. "Fifty thousand, maybe. Give or take a few."

My knees buckled. Behind me, Devorah whimpered like a

small kitten trapped beneath the paws of a large predator. *Give or take a few thousand.*

"Was this the result you sought, Protector?" I spat Antoine's title.

Antoine laughed, a dry sound like twigs breaking.

Pender didn't like the possibility signified by that sound, the possibility that the Hollow Men's clever subterfuge against the Watchers hadn't been as clandestine as they had thought. The players had been played by their own self-inflated cleverness. Uncertainty flickered in his eyes, and he unconsciously took a step away from Antoine.

Devorah spoke from behind me. "Therefore to me their doom he had assigned; that they may have their wish, to try with me in battle which the stronger proves, they all, or I alone against them."

Antoine gave the young woman a hard stare. "Is that Milton?" he rasped. A shudder ran through his frame. "Rhapsodomancy. You forced a librarian to See for you?"

"I needed guidance. You weren't offering anything but semantic games."

"Speak ye who best can tell, ye sons of light," Devorah said. "If better thou belong not to the dawn, sure pledge of day, that crownst the smiling Morn with thy bright circlet, praise him in thy sphere when day arises, that sweet hour of prime."

I nodded, understanding the reason why Antoine and Pender were here at the river's edge. "He's waiting for dawn. You're all waiting for sunrise."

Devorah spoke again, validating my conclusion. "Till morn, waked by the circling hours, with rosy hand unbarred the gates of light."

The world was made anew at dawn. All souls—all light—comes from the sun. A student didn't have to trawl very far in any religion to find that reference. The sun was—like the Creator—the representation of God. This was the light that gave flesh life. It burned the eyes when, as supplicants, we stared at its fiery glow. Every morning as it was reborn in the eastern sky, it reminded us of Immortality, of the eternal cycle of rebirth and resurrection.

Everything is transformed in the presence of the reborn sun. All cycles have an end and a new beginning. The Wheel turns. We fall down; we rise up.

Antoine offered me his own interpretation of Milton. "Evil is done in order to transcend it, Markham. We pay dearly for our knowledge of Good."

"A lot of people *died* tonight." My voice was raw, torn by the memory of who had fallen. Who had died, trying to stop the experiment. "What's the 'Good' in that? Their souls have been harvested for their energy. Their *lives* are over. Milton wasn't talking about mass murder as a means to an end. He was talking about a fucking tree, a fucking symbol. He didn't mean that we had to bloody our hands just to understand humility and humanity."

"They lived lives of fear," Pender said, his ideological viewpoint finally having a chance to express itself. "They would never know ascension. They would never understand the beauty of their light. Why shouldn't they be allowed to give of themselves for a purer purpose?"

"You didn't fucking ask them!"

"Is it just a matter of choice, then?" Pender asked. "Is that the difference? If you had asked them if they wanted to See God and they had all said yes, would we have the right to intercede and stop them? Could we have any care other than to Witness their attempt?"

"What bullshit piece of scripture did you pull that from?"

"Isn't enlightenment our goal?" Pender continued, ignoring my question. "What child doesn't want to be with his Father? What child likes being separated from the embrace of their parent?"

"But we're not separated," I countered, trying to pierce the fervor of his argument. The first principle drilled into the skulls of children is that God is everything and everything is God. It's the basic concept which informs all of Hermeticism and most of Western thought. Just because we aren't consciously aware of Infinity doesn't mean that it doesn't exist. Every child understands the idea of object permanence. Take away a toy and the toy doesn't self-destruct. It is still there, just existent outside the child's perception. The 'toyness' of the toy doesn't change."

"But a toy is an inanimate object. It will never change. It is only a representation of Form." Pender shook his head. "It is a *khabit,* much like we are, of the Real."

"Shadows. Huh," I said, letting go of the argument. He was spouting the same obscene rhetoric that Julian had tried to feed me. Light and shadows. The imperfect Creator that bound our sight so we couldn't see the Truth. Archons and blind idiot Demiurges. Very Gnostic and not unexpected from students of Hermeticism, but still so very broken.

Whispers in a dark wood. All things are broken, all things have holes in them. Man is the only creature that can mend the tears and breaks. Man is the only Creator.

"Man is the true shadow of God."

"Exactly."

"And you and yours needed to remind the rest of this Truth."

Pender nodded.

"They all Saw," I said. "At the end. They all Saw—" I stopped. They all went willingly. I realized I was still holding the tarot card, still holding the Moon with its twin paths. No, they all went. Without Will. The light of the mirror had taken that from them already. "Hermes Trismegistus talked about a schema for one's own soul. Enlightenment is a personal choice. You can't bring a whole society with you. You can't just engage in the wholesale slaughter of innocents just so you can split Heaven and talk to God."

"Maybe an audience isn't what they're seeking," Antoine said.

I stalled for a second, the word caught on my tongue. A horrible flame licked at my heart. "*Mahapralaya*," I whispered. If Ravensdale gave them the power to devastate Portland, what would the collected power of Portland do? What logarithmic scale were they operating on? "He really does want to remake the world."

Antoine remained inscrutable, neither confirming nor denying my accusation. Giving me no sense if this was indeed the goal to which his machinations pointed. Had Antoine intended to step in at this point and take everything away from Bernard? Put himself at the top of the tower instead of his alchemist to face the dawn?

Devorah spoke from behind me. "By thee adulterous Lust was driven from men, among the bestial herds to range."

Lust. There is no room for it in God's pure realm. Lust was what imprisoned the soul in the flesh. Bernard's quest wasn't one of enlightenment, not in the way he approached it. "What happens when God doesn't take lightly to the manner in which Bernard has assumed the mantle of Creator?" I asked. "What happens when dawn arrives and Bernard realizes he's just a psychopath who has murdered an entire city in an effort to prove what may be nothing more than a philosophical distinction?"

"What if he isn't?" Antoine asked. "Murder has been done in the name of God before. What is history but a litany of our efforts to show God our affection by smiting unbelievers? Hasn't Bernard done one better? He's taken those without real faith and made them part of his purpose. He's converted all of them. They are of one faith. One vision. How could God not love that?"

I sighed and rubbed at my face, feeling the scabs and stubble of the last twenty-four hours. Two paths. Was Bernard's way just a twisted variation of Severity?

This time yesterday I had been wreathed in fire, stalking Hollow Men through the shadows of their warehouse. I had been filled with vengeance, flush with the desire to do damage to those who had done harm to me. What had I brought to them? Not enlightenment. I had taken their souls, broken them upon the rack of my mind, and poured their spiritual essence into my vessel. They had been transformed, subjugated to my Will. Could my role be accorded the same distinction, the same rationale as an "act of devotion to God"?

I had justified my actions over the years by warping John Stuart Mills' axiom of the Greater Good: what ultimately served a beneficial purpose was worth the destruction. Love under Will, as long as it was all my Will. Bernard was just applying the same axiom on a larger scale. Thousands died so that he could remake the world in his image, a design that was better simply because he had thought of it. Because he had *faith* in it.

This was the cosmological closure, the bending back of the Universe on itself to a single point. The big magico-religious Bang where the world could be created anew. Here, at the center of the world—at the *axis mundi*—we would be able to perform that Act of Demiurgery that reflected the initial *creatio ex nihilo* effected by God. Bernard would become God by imitating God.

I sighed, and looked at the single star floating above the sea of darkness. "If this is the Apocalypse," I wondered aloud. "Then why did the Watchers send just a Protector? Shit, they would have sent all seven of the Architects. Philippe himself would even be here." The Hierarch's name caused a twitch in Antoine's ruined face, a break in the Protector's death-mask face. *A flinch.* I had struck a nerve.

"He doesn't know you are here, does he?" I said.

Antoine didn't answer, and I knew him well enough to know that he wasn't deigning to not answer the question. He was ignoring me because he was thinking about something else entirely. The Weave had just shown him a new pattern—one he hadn't realized was there. *That had been there all along.*

He had suggested to Nicols and me the existence of a bigger picture, a larger scheme beyond my perception. I had ignored the hints—the presumptive tone had always been part of Antoine's character—but, seeing Antoine's mental peregrinations now, I realized the Weave's complexity may be more than he anticipated. There were threads still hidden, even from him.

"This isn't sanctioned by the Watchers." I tried to chase the same threads. Tried to figure out what he already knew, and what he thought was the truer pattern. "This is a rogue action. There is a revolt happening in the ranks, isn't there?"

It was the corruptive lure of power: that seductive siren that pulled us down into the flesh. I could read it plainly in Pender's face: he was in bed with Julian and Bernard. Siding with the Hollow Men had been his play for power. Just like Antoine, who sought to usurp this action for his own ends. A faction within the Watchers knew; they had sent Antoine, and hadn't realized their toy had his own ideas. Everyone wanted to use Bernard and Julian for their own design. Everyone had their own plan.

"Whoever remakes the world can challenge the Hierarch." I spelled it out carefully, watching their faces for more clues. "That's what this is all about. This is a power play for leadership of *La Société*. Pender and the others thought they could hijack it from you, but you knew they were going to screw you, and you planned on taking it from them in turn. When the time was right. But, not for your brothers in Paris. For yourself. I was just the lucky distraction that everyone thought they could use on the others."

"Perhaps," Antoine said. I stared at his ruined face. Was that a smile on his burned lips? "Perhaps there is another pattern beneath all of our machinations. A deeper Weave than we anticipated."

"What do you mean?" Pender demanded. His hand twitched toward his coat, toward his gun. This conversation had suddenly gone off-script.

"Bernard is there," Antoine said, inclining his head toward the star. "We are here."

"So?"

"There are three of us."

Pender didn't get it. And I wasn't following either.

Antoine was definitely smiling now, a grim death's head. "I was supposed to be here. The lieutenant was supposed to be here. But, you, Markham, dead man lost to us all, how did you manage to get here?"

"Part of my soul I seek thee, and thee claim my other half," Devorah said, providing an answer to Antoine's question.

Answering so many questions. I Saw it too. Beneath the shimmering pattern of our threads, beneath the confusion of the cards and our efforts to interpret them. Under it all, I saw the design.

Tiny steps, seemingly unconnected in their inception—in the infinitesimal realm of their immediate effects. The false memory of Kat's hand on me, the confusion laid upon me in the woods and the poisonous cargo freely taken, the Chorus growing in my head. And then Paris: Marielle, a catalyst for the course prefigured for us; Antoine, an unwitting marionette, acting out his role at the bridge.

The actions of the past cascaded into the present: my arrival in Seattle, the discovery of Doug and Kat again; their connection to the Hollow Men, to Bernard, and to the diabolical plan concocted by Antoine's splinter group within the Watchers. All of it was woven into this knotted nexus. This point, this place. These players. A man, standing on the edge of the Abyss, who hadn't sought to be here. Not the detective.

Me.

The Watchers didn't believe in accidents, nor random chance. There were only machinations deeper than their own influence. Designs which they couldn't twist. And each of them could twist very deep.

And only one of them could twist deeper than the rest.

"I have to go back," I said. My hand strayed to Reija's hair about my throat, fingers tracing the braid of our thread. *What you do is who you are…* "I'm going back."

"What—?" Pender pulled out his gun, violet light rising in his eyes. "You're not going anywhere."

I looked at him sadly for a moment—he didn't understand what lay in the Weave—and then turned my gaze to Antoine. "What say you, Brother?" *This isn't done.*

He nodded, and the metal cap on his hand sizzled into a new shape. Before Pender could realize what was happening—before I could react—Antoine stepped behind the other man and punched through his spine with his freshly formed hand. Silver fingers, wet with blood, erupted from the hollow of Pender's throat.

"It was never meant for me," Antoine said, holding the struggling man upright with the force of his Will. "I am a Watcher, *mon ami.* I had, indeed, forgotten that. I am to be your Witness."

Pender's eyes fluttered, rolling back in his head. Antoine shook his hand, making the lieutenant's arms wiggle. "Time is short," he said. "Take him while you can."

"What?"

"It is a long walk ," Antoine said. "You haven't the strength."

"You have got to be kidding."

"Take it." Antoine's voice was hard, a commanding tone that brooked no more discussion. He flexed his metal fingers, and white fire vaporized Pender's spine. Pender's atlas bone exploded, blowing out the sides of his neck. The back of his coat caught fire.

The Chorus swarmed in my head, ready and willing to take the soul of the man as he died. I was exhausted; I could use the energy. Didn't it feel good? That euphoric rush of strength and clarity. The precision of Will brought about by taking another.

Knowledge of good bought dear by knowing ill. This was the price of our transgression in the Garden; this was the cost of tasting the fruit of the Tree of Knowledge. This was the sacrifice made so that we could understand the difference between night and day, light and dark, dream from reality. We learned to kill when we ate from the Tree. We opened our souls and listened to the passions of the flesh. So that we could know the difference, so that we could chose a path and find our way back to God.

"No," I said, refusing Antoine, refusing the Chorus, refusing everyone but my own Will. I turned away from Antoine as Pender died, his soul leaving his burning body. "His death is your sin. Not mine."

I had enough of my own.

XXX

Devorah stayed with Antoine, the Seer supporting the Witness. She kept her back to the city, always turned away from the carnage that I had forced her to foresee, but in farewell, she turned her head toward the east enough for me to see the dark streaks of dried blood on her face. Her tears had stopped.

I left the tarot card on the river bank. This was one side—one path—and I was going to cross the river to take the other path.

I made the Chorus support me as I walked across the water to the dead city. The river was dark with ash, a turgid inkiness beneath my feet. There were no bodies and very little flotsam, just a continual pall of ash in the water. It got darker and thicker as I reached the western shore.

I stepped onto hard land again between the Freemont and Broadway bridges, just downriver from the Amtrak station. The clock tower at the depot was a crooked black finger in the empty field of steel rails. The cars in the parking lot beyond the station were coated inside and out with grime and soot. They looked like the cracked eggs of giant birds.

The storm of soul-death had blown through every structure, leaving every surface charred and black. The inhalation of Thoth's Key stripped all light, all color, from the world. Windows were empty mouths that revealed blackened throats; walls had been breached and broken like bodies burst in heat, organs exploded and crisped. Older buildings—the northeastern edge of Chinatown—leaned toward the shining tower as if made crooked by the vacuum. Their roofs were torn off, shingles and strips of tar paper littering the street in long patterns.

The skyscrapers were monolithic trees caught in the dead of winter, their external layer of marble and chrome peeled away like cracked bark. They were dead husks, a forest of hollowed-out sycamores. Blighted. Devoured. Empty.

A black forest in a black land. With each step, I stirred up ash and filth; the detritus clung to my clothes and skin, making me a black wraith wandering through a nocturnal landscape.

As I approached the spire, I knew who would be waiting for me. The circle was closed. This wilderness was a hollow vacuum, filled with death and shadow. *He* would come to this place. One last attempt to lure me astray.

I started to hear a whisper, like the rustling of dry leaves, as I crossed Burnside and entered downtown proper. They were nearly invisible against the landscape, covered in ash like the rest of the city, and they gave off no signal the Chorus could find. They were darker holes against a dark backdrop.

Soul-dead. Following me.

I was a beacon after all. Even under the layer of soot and filth, I was the single source of light in the city other than the bright point at the top of the tower. They were denied that light. It was the other side of the Abyss, after all. The soul-dead were trapped in the black crack between worlds. Trapped by the eternal hunger of the *Qliphotic* master of this place.

He crouched in the ruined entrance of Eglanteria Terrace, resting on his haunches. His gray and yellow robe was spattered with dark stains and the back of his head was open like a burst piece of rotten fruit. His single eye was a milky cataract in an otherwise dead mask. A pearl lost in the black reeds.

He had been Julian once. But, after I had infected his soul, something else had taken root in him. And, as his body had lain on the grass outside the building, that root had grown. Had grown into a dark flower that made his shell walk. The flower had many names: Choronzon, called "Coronzom" by Dr. Dee; Asmodeus; Yaldabaoth; Shemal; Yog-Sothoth.

"Samael." I bound him to the name I knew, the name I had learned so long ago in the woods and which I had sworn to never repeat again.

He raised his head and smiled at me, black teeth against black skin. His tongue was red, vibrant and wet like his pearlescent eye. "So bright, little worm. So bright and tasty."

"Your work, Archon. Your hand upon this world."

"Ah, it is. Yes, it is. I Know you. I Made you." He raised his face and sniffed the acrid air—inhaling my living scent. "Lost in her hair, I found you." He made a chattering noise with his teeth. "I came when you called."

I grimaced and looked behind me. The street and the plaza were filling with soul-dead, silent sentinels. Witnesses to this final conversation. They were the still breath of Death, waiting. They crept closer, their rank deepening. Those in back slowly pushed the ones in front forward. They quivered and shook, dead inside but still suffused with a terrible need.

"I no longer carry your lies. Your poison is gone."

"Never gone," he said, waggling a finger. "The flesh never forgets."

This was the fear that tore at our hearts and could never be purged from our brains: the intractability of the flesh, bound by passion. While our brains might lock away the memories and our hearts might burn out the emotions, we were just hiding from our Egos. We made our own personal Pandorian boxes and tried to lose the key.

And thee claim my other half. The lost part of myself that I spent years blaming on Katarina. I had chased her for ten years, thinking there was something she could have given back to me. Something lost which could be found again. It was just an excuse I used to hide the truth from myself; the truth I knew, but had locked away.

Denial and obscuration: that path chosen in the wood, the way that took me further into the dark trees. It had led me to blame Katarina for something that had never happened. I was a victim, a gullible scapegoat who walled off his entire heart to hide the hurt sustained there. The Chorus had become my validation, the voices who kept me from the wall I had built. They gave me reason to not look within. And, with my eyes turned outward, the wound in my heart festered and turned black. By raising those walls, I had given it permission to poison my core, to grow its deadly fruit.

Nicols had drawn the Three of Swords, the pain that must be endured. The trial that must be undertaken. All adepts must cross the Abyss; they must face the demon of darkness—the incarnate foulness of their own Ego—and dissolve it. My devil, born in a moment of fear, had haunted me for a long time.

He haunted me still, standing here on the threshold; he blocked me from my goal, from crossing the Abyss.

Read thy lot in yon celestial sign, Devorah had prophesied for me, *where thou art weighed, and shown how light, how weak, if thou resist.* When the Egyptian souls were taken to the underworld, they were weighed by Anubis at the Gates of the Underworld. Their component parts—the physical organs of the deceased—were placed on a scale and considered against ritual objects. Those incorrectly weighted were thrown to the hounds that slavered and begged beneath the scales. Those who were in balance were allowed access to the Afterlife.

Who we are, in the end when our spirits are being judged and weighed, is a matter of the accreted substance of our choices. We chose the paths and those choices are inscribed in our minds. We may be able to hide our failures and missteps on the outside, but inside, we never forget.

Our hands betray what we have done.

I killed nine men yesterday. They weren't the first. In the last ten years, there had been blood and fire on my hands more than once. And yet, the apex of the Tree had never been closed to me. I was still in the Abyss, but I could yet see the other side. The light from the Tower still called to me.

God never forgets. Nor do we. Is that the pure irony of our existence? We have to kill the Ego in order to touch the other side; we have to lose ourselves in order to ascend. That requires a death of the flesh. Why? Because it can't forget.

Or is it just like Blake says: the "mind-forg'd manacle"? The prison built by the Demiurge and his archons, the black iron cage we trap ourselves with. The mind—thinking too much, thinking too often.

I stepped toward the door, putting aside my racing thoughts, silencing the too-busy mind. Samael shifted his weight and shook his head. Flecks of ash drifted off the back of his open skull. "Not this time, pretty. The light is not for you."

I looked up at the boiling sphere at the top of the building. It was perfectly round, a single furious dot. *Ain Soph* collapses into *Ain*. God expressing Himself in space so as to start creation. Thoth's Key had burned Portland in order to make a vacuum, a realm of darkness in which it would be the only light. *Et tenebrae super faciem abyssi.*

"Nor for you either, Blind One." My hand drifted up to indicate the east. Devorah, on the riverbank, showing me her face as she looked toward that horizon. "What happens when the sun rises? Are you allowed to look upon the face of God?"

He hissed at me, but didn't answer.

"I was a child in the woods. I was afraid. Afraid of everything: what had happened to me, what I felt, what I thought came next. I was scared of dying. I was weak when you crawled out of the darkness, when you whispered in my ear. I wanted succor. I wanted to know that I was going to be okay." I shook my head. "I was too willing to believe your words, to accept what you told me. I should have put aside all those tiny fears and just asked you if I was going to live long enough to see the sun rise."

I looked along the length of my arm, toward the coming sun. "Like now, you would have had no answer, and I would have known you then. I would have Seen you. True."

Just a shadow. My own shadow.

In my soul, I touched the Chorus and gave them a simple directive. They fought me but it was a hollow resistance. They knew I was their master. They knew they had to obey. They collapsed into a point, hidden in my chest. A mirror image of the sphere at the top of the Tower. *Ain* becomes *Nia*—Abyss becomes Eye.

"Every day, I see the sun rise, Samael," I said. "Every day I look upon God and He doesn't burn me, He doesn't condemn me. Because, even as bloodied as I am, I am still His child. I still have His Spark in me."

Samael shrieked, a grinding wail of fury that drowned out the question I had for him. He sprang forward—leaving the threshold—until less than an inch separated us. *So close.* His breath, dry and dead, on my face. His single white eye staring sightlessly through me.

I didn't flinch, nor give ground. My exhalation—filled with the humming power of the engorged Chorus, the children of Samael I had made my own—left dew on his chin and cheeks. Julian's shell was so desiccated by Samael's *Qliphotic* presence it was unable to absorb moisture. Arid dust shaped into form by malevolent Will.

Versus my body. Warm living flesh suffused with my light. Patchwork as it may be, it was still me.

It always had been. It always would be.

"You have no power," I whispered to the shadow heart of my soul. I was the Divine Spark—the Godhead—Samael was my *khabit,* my shadow—the Demiurge who thought the Universe was his. My prison was believing in him. "Not anymore."

He smiled, his red tongue hanging between his burn-black-ened lips. "Maybe not." He nodded past my shoulder. "But I have power over them."

This was the signal the soul-dead had been waiting for. In a wave that was all pressure and no presence, they flooded over me. Their hands pulled at my hair, my flesh. Their cracked fingers tore at my skin, trying to rend my shell and reach the bright light of my soul.

I detonated the Chorus, a localized thermobaric exaltation that cremated an open space around me. Everything became white ash, infused with light. The greedy soul-dead became albinos whose flesh flaked off dry bones which, in turn, became pale motes dancing in the air. The ground, wiped clean of soot; the nearby grass turned to translucent ice. The air snapped, a crackling expression of exothermic change.

Samael staggered away from me, his face and hands rimed with twisted frost. His head tipped back and midnight-colored fluid drained from his open skull. The ichor steamed and sizzled as it splashed on the whitened pavement. He tried to stop me as I shouldered past toward the glowing center of the Tower, but his hands cracked as they touched my hot flesh. His fingers fell off like shards of ice, and the stumps of his arms banged my elbow and back like broken branches.

I was bereft of the Chorus. I had detonated their captive light, emptied myself of their influence and outrage. Their explosive burst had destroyed the mob of *Qliphotic* shells attacking me, but there were still more of them. More empty shells inflamed with hunger.

As the aftermath of the Chorus' immolation faded, another mob rushed across the plaza. But I was beyond their reach. They couldn't enter the wide beam of light within the shell of the Tower. I crossed into the light and gave myself up to its seductive gravity. My purified body ascending. A star, rising.

XXXI

A t the top, the light was a physical presence, a globe wrapped around the peak of the building. I floated against it, the pliable surface dimpling at my touch. As more of my body touched the limpid film, the shell became sticky flypaper. I didn't struggle and the gravity within the membrane pulled me flat against the rounded shape. There was a brief sensation of pain—lightning stroking the plane of my skin—and then the world inverted.

Inside, there was neither color nor tint—polar opposition to the gritty darkness of the dead city. Every surface was bleached white. There were no shadows, only dim lines that delineated edges and borders—variations on the play of light.

The soot of the city no longer covered me. It had not come through the barrier. I could almost see the pale history of an outline beneath me, a fading print of my body done in static-charged ash and detritus. My skin was translucent, my blood a series of pale tributaries running through valleys and vales of colorless flesh. The stark tint of my bones was evident beneath the naked flesh. The blue and gray of my clothes had already lightened to the color of early dawn.

As I walked toward the source of light, I became lighter still, my clothes vanishing into nothingness, my skin becoming rice paper wrapped around a clear gelatinous mass. My bones were hardened crystal, sculpted by an Old Master.

My memory of the penthouse was a historical document of its presence. The obstructions of the furniture were gone. The trinity of Thoth figures no longer stood by the window, their metal frames had vanished. Only the mirrored facets of the sphere remained, a glittering diamond of light that was purer and brighter than all the surrounding white.

Lying beneath the floating sphere as if asleep was a two-dimensional line drawing of Nicols, like an Impressionist caricature dashed off on a coffee house napkin. I bent over and tried to touch him and found he really was nothing more than a collection of a few strokes.

"The memories fade until they are nothing but lines and shadows."

I looked to the source of the voice. Bernard was the only color. His robe crawled with motion. The script—once black, now white—wriggled and squirmed with animate mysticism on a blue and sickly orange background. A silver halo lay low enough upon his head that it bisected the crown of his skull. His face was pale like the visage of a man who has not been aboveground for a year, but it was still the color of flesh. Unlike the bleached translucence of my skin. The ruddy color of his neck looked like a birthmark or an allergic rash.

He inclined his crowned head. "The walker between worlds. I thought you might be the one to return." His voice was quiet and sibilant, his throat still new. "Have you come to take Julian's place?"

He looked through me, so easy to do in my current state. "Yes," Bernard continued, "before I did not understand the nature of the haze that hid you from view. It is gone now, but I think I know why it was there. From his reading of *The Book of Thoth*, Jabir Ibn Hayyan theorized that an alchemist could learn how to actively transform soul energy, that a living harvester was possible. That was his interpretation of Thoth's Master of the

Mysteries—the one who understood how to use the Key. Am I right? That's what you are, isn't it?"

Lightbreaker.

"Oh, this petulant resistance of yours is frustrating. There is so much we could teach each other, Mr. Markham. I want to learn about your technique, about how you take a soul. It was Jabir's theory of soul transformation that pointed me toward the mystery of the mirror."

"You know," I said, breaking my silence, "it probably wasn't an accident that *The Book of Thoth* was destroyed."

"There is a reason for all obscuration, Mr. Markham. Our ignorance must be overcome, we must actively seek to remove the scales from our eyes. The *Book* wasn't destroyed. It was broken and scattered because it was meant to be found again, reassembled by someone worthy."

"You?"

"It is the crowning achievement of my life, putting together *The Book of Thoth*," Bernard admitted. "It began with Ficino—"

"His book from the Sorbonne? The one the Watchers say doesn't exist."

He shook his head. "The second part of *Theologia Platonica de immortalitate animae* doesn't exist. But that's not what I found. A student of Ficino's wrote a tiny tract bridging the *Theologia Platonica* and Jabir's *Kitab al-Zuhra*. The document was a workbook essentially, a paper charting how his master encoded references to Jabir's work, how the Persian hid parts of *The Book of Thoth* within the *Kitab al-Zuhra*." He laughed. "That was the first lie I told them. 'A lost Ficino.' Only Protector Briande saw through my eager bibliomania."

"He sees a lot of things. I just left him on the far bank. With Pender. Who won't be joining us."

"No? I thought not when you arrived. I am surprised the Protector didn't come in your stead."

"Too busy Witnessing."

"Really? So he does believe the Key will work."

"Or not. He might just not want to be standing at ground zero when dawn arrives. He knows what the Key does, doesn't he? You went to him when you realized you needed a copy of the *Kitab*."

"Not just the *Kitab*. There were so many hints strewn across the history of alchemy and Hermetic thought. Roger Bacon laid out the foundation of the mirror in his *Opus Tertium*—oh, how the Catholic Church wanted knowledge of that volume censored, but John Dee managed to find a copy. But it was in Bacon's *Liber de Intellectu et Intelligibili* where the alchemical formulas were hidden. And Llull's *De Quinta Essentia* held hints on how to preserve the energy once it had been extracted. A German writer named Monach wrote an epistle about the pros and cons of conquering nature. Most of it was a retread of Flamel's theories, but his work contained a passage about the conversion of the soul, which proved useful in the fabrication of the ritual that manifests the ibis-hounds. And, from the hounds, came an understanding of scale. How I might collect many."

He sighed like a proud father. "So many pieces to put together, but I did it. I managed to decipher the clues left by our alchemical forefathers and build Thoth's Key." His hands came together, in an old comfortable way that spoke of his familiarity with lecturing. Of being in front of an audience. "Do you know what the hardest part was?"

"Killing?"

"It is a damnation of our souls, isn't it?" His forehead creased slightly, lines forming beneath the stars on his brow. "But it is my moral upbringing that gives me *that* guilt—a hard lesson scored into my flesh. We have to eat the energy of others in order to become closer to God. Isn't that right, Mr. Markham? This feasting means a dissolution of their self, a subjugation of their spirit beneath us. But God is everything, and do we not become everything by devouring others?"

I didn't dignify the question with an answer. What was I going to tell him that he wasn't going to realize was a lie? And what would the truth give him—that I killed in order to make myself whole—wasn't that just the validation he wanted?

"We are such a strange creation," he said when it was clear I wasn't going to say anything, "so fiercely independent—tiny islands, ferociously guarded—and yet we crave company. Is that not one of the funny little circumstances of being human? We are distinct personalities—unique patterns of light—and yet all we really want is to be with someone else. Our lovers, our families, the communities that welcome us, the embrace of the Divine. Do you think we'll ever consciously realize that all of this clinging to one another is just a manifestation of our fear that God doesn't love us, that He has abandoned us?"

"Is that what you offered all of them? Companionship?"

He shook his head. "No, Mr. Markham. I offered them something stronger."

"And what is that?"

"Unity. A purpose."

"What? Death? Not a very grand purpose." I felt a tickle on the back of my neck, and I looked over my shoulder. I wasn't sure if it was an afterimage on my fading eyes from Bernard's robe or if there was indeed a fine line of orange light creasing the purity of this space. "Trismegistus believed that the evolution of the soul was an individual activity," I continued, "a deeply personal quest that required a soul to reason its way out of the cage of the flesh. Yes, sure, we all want to get back to God, but Trismegistus thought we needed to do it on our own. Not in a mass exodus like you've planned."

"The trouble with Trismegistus, in the end," Bernard admitted, "is that his lessons in *The Corpus Hermeticum* were of a solitary path. A solo voyage into the arms of the enlightenment."

"So he made the Key because he got lonely. Being the only

guy who knew the Way. Is that it?"

"No, he realized the world was filled with too much flesh, too many distractions. Did he not argue that the only vice of the soul was ignorance? Did he not argue that the Reasoned Man has every right—no, a duty—to bring those who refuse Reason into the greater consciousness of God? Those whose minds are too weak and shallow, did he not believe they should be guided?" Bernard gestured at the pure light of Key behind me. "If all of those who have been harvested wanted nothing of God, if they were unwilling to partake of Reason and become enlightened on their own, then are they not failing to fulfill the very beauty of their existence? Is what we do evil if we bring them to fruition?"

"I'm not willing to make that call."

"Why not?"

"Because it is playing at being God."

"Exactly." He smiled as if he had just tricked me into a corner from which I could not escape.

I sighed. "I should have put my hand in your brain instead of your throat. Not that you're getting any blood up there anymore."

His cheek twitched. "Your interference—" his hands unconsciously moved toward his mottled throat "—forced me to engage the Key early, before all the energy it held was fully transformed. As a result, it was unable to completely fill itself."

"And I'm real sorry to have fucked up your plans like that."

He laughed, even though the action appeared to hurt his throat. "What do you think your language will gain you here, Mr. Markham? I am at the culmination of a life's work. Do you think your barbed comments will deter me from finishing this? Do you think your weak flesh can stop me?" He waved a hand at my body. "You're already fading. The Key is taking your soul by increments and you don't even know it."

I smiled. "Oh, I'm fully aware of what it is doing."

My body had become a frail phantom, a diaphanous veil barely containing the sparking surge of my spirit. Standing in the presence of Thoth's Key was destroying my flesh. The mirror dissolved my skin so as to free my soul.

That was the reason I was here, after all.

My awareness seemed to shake him slightly, just a small tremor in his tongue as he wet his lips.

A thin crease of orange light drew itself across his face, a widening gleam of warmth. His apprehension vanishing, Bernard looked toward the source of the glow. I didn't look behind me. I knew what he saw. *That sweet hour of prime.* Dawn.

"*Nunc,*" he said. "It is time. I am ready, Mr. Markham. I believe in what I am about to accomplish. What do you have to offer?"

"An observation, I suppose," I said. "For a very long time, I believed in the Devil. I believed that, *in illo tempore,* I met him in the woods. And, actually, I believe I met him again a short while ago."

"And now? This is the final moment of your existence, Mr. Markham. Is that all you believe? That you've seen the face of evil. Have you driven him out then? Is that the basis for your newfound religion?"

"No, I believe he's part of me. Like God."

Bernard smiled. "Ah, the old Hermetic truism. Do you feel His presence, then?" The band of light filled his eyes.

"I don't have to 'feel' Him, Bernard. I am God."

His attention snapped back to me, even though I was almost gone, almost invisible against the burning light.

"Just like you, Bernard. Just like every soul you took last night. We are all God. Separate and distinct."

"No," he said. "God has been hidden from us. We must free ourselves in order to perceive him."

"Free ourselves from what?" I asked. I held up an arm, the orange light of dawn outlining my skin. Such a faint line, such a thin film holding my soul in. "You don't even understand the nature of your prison, Bernard. Because if you did, then you would know that the truest thing that can be done has nothing to do with Will. The greatest change is not external. It is within you. It is the act of giving up being God."

The act of sacrifice.

The penthouse room filled with color, orange and red and yellow and rose, a series of expanding circles of light. Sunflowers bloomed in a dizzying mass of texture and tint, a sea of petals that swept over Bernard and the mirror and my tiny spark of a spirit.

Nunc.

The mirrored sphere in the sculpture broke, the individual facets drifting apart as if released from the adhesive that held them together. The light of the sun danced on the drifting mirrors, splitting into refractions and reflections. The one became ten, round circles of light arranging themselves in a known pattern.

Now.

I released my *self*, embracing the many, and took hold of the Tree.

XXXII

Is this how God dreams?

Katarina, wreathed in red, whispers in my ear. "Your reality is an illusion." Her hand is on my chest. Fingers caress my flesh. World touched by Word.

Behind her, the Tree rises like a plume of white smoke. Its heavy globes split from the trunk and hang like luminous worlds.

Her fingers touch the flickering light of my soul. Her index finger tickles my heart and I arch under her caress, pushing myself against her hand. Though I am bound, chained by my ignorance, I raise myself to meet her touch. *Take me. Free me.*

I cannot see the top of the Tree. A veil hides the last three spheres from my sight. A line is drawn through the neck of the Tree, separating the trunk and limbs from the head. In the center of the line, right in the hollow of the neck, there is a black smudge, a hole to nowhere.

God dreams. *Fiat lux.* The world immolates and is made anew. My heart is on fire, a burning stone within the cage of my chest. She touches me, and I am released from bondage.

Free to climb the Tree. To grasp the center trunk and scale to the edge of the veil. I am free to touch the dark hole at the base of the neck.

The Tree splits, sundering into a vale of darkness, lit by the black fire of negative globes. In the center of the valley, in the depth of the wood that crawls across the black land, cowers the Son of Man. Caught in his throat is the Word that will remake the world.

He has no speech, no gift of tongues. His mouth is a rotten hole through which he feeds the appetites of his body. His hands, instead of writing out the Word and making it real, tug at his flesh. His ears are filled with the sound of the leaves in the trees, almost a voice, almost a whispering promise. "Your reality is an illusion."

A hand emerges from the darkness and the Son of Man does not realize it is his own, wrapped around his emaciated body. The hand holds a seed, dug up from the roots of the black trees, and he hungrily opens his mouth to take the dark Communion.

It sticks in his throat for an instant, caught in the web of the Word, and then it falls into his stomach, wrapped in the beauty of the Word. It falls into fallow ground and yet, sheathed by the Word, takes root.

This is the way the world ends.

I am the architect of my own demise. I am the demiurge of my own ascension. This is the dream of God. This is the seed wrapped in the Word. This is the Tree that takes root and from which springs Creation.

This is the sacrifice called Faith.

We are in a palace of wind and light, buffeted by storms of orange lightning and howling fire. Bernard lies on a table of coiled smoke, his head resting on a strata of cumulonimbus clouds. He is naked, stripped of his civilized vestments. Tears leak from his eyes and water comes out of his mouth as he gasps like a fish drowning on land.

Hush, you need not speak. I know all the words you seek to make; just as I know all the words you have uttered before you came here. He looks at me, pleading with his eyes. He cannot move his arms or legs. He cannot move anything but his mouth and his eyes. I know, I forgive you.

I tear the first piece from his chest, just below his left nipple. It is a morsel of pale flesh, wet with his translucent blood—all the color has left him, all his strength has fled. I offer it to the first supplicant in the long line that stands beside the table.

She is a pale cloud lit by lightning, a swirling nimbus that shapes itself in a memory of her form. Her fabric parts, a hole through which I can see the light behind and beyond her, and I place the piece of Bernard's flesh on what passes for her tongue. The hole seals itself into a ghostly smile and the smoke of her fills with a rainbow explosion of light. She drifts into me, melting through my presence, and my vision blurs with violet and silver light. She passes through me, through the portal of my bones and through the curtain of my flesh.

I offer Communion to all of them: every man, woman, and child of Ravensdale, of Portland. I give them a piece of Bernard in exchange for what he took from them. When his flesh is gone, I rip his organs into tiny strips and break his bones into small wafers.

They are patient, the souls who have passed. Their timeless wait is an incremental span of the Universe's existence. They know, and wait. For there will be enough for all of them. Each one crosses through my gate and becomes part of the wind and light surrounding this palace.

The last one in line is more solid than the rest, and I withhold the final piece of Bernard from him. No, not you.

Please, he whispers, kneeling on the clouds at my feet.

No, I tell him, and his despair is plainly writ on his face. You have not earned this. I crouch and lift his chin. Looking into the mirror of his eyes, I tell him. The path will remain open.

I give him a kiss—*ex lux et vita*—and I accept the sacrifice that brought him here. But it isn't enough. Not yet.

Rede, meus filius.

EPILOGUE

Et vidit Deus lucem quod esset bona
et divisit Deus lucem ac tenebras.
– Genesis 1:4

"She's catatonic. Has been since she was brought in a few days ago." The nurse shook her head. "Found her in an alley near that warehouse fire. She's non-responsive and…" She paused, uncomfortable with continuing this discussion with a complete stranger.

"She's dying," I said. "A little bit more every day. And yet there's nothing wrong with her that you can find.…"

The nurse turned from the ICU window. "Do you know her?"

"Yes."

"Who is she? What is your relationship to her?"

I put an index finger on my lip, my middle finger and thumb touching. The nurse's eyes flickered toward my mouth and her expression loosened as she became transfixed by the spell wrapped in my hand. She lost her train of thought and started to turn away as if I had suddenly vanished. "I—" she began.

I shook my head, finger still on my lip. I could See the wreath of her soul. Its subtle rotation synched with a low pulse in my stomach.

Her head moved as well, a sluggish aping of my motion. "We—" she started, feeling for the right word. "We hope she recovers." I nodded and her head moved in time with mine. Her shoulders and head drooped as if she had been struck by a sudden bout of narcolepsy. She blinked twice and then raised her head. Looking through me, she smiled at nothing—a false memory at best—and marched off, returning to her station down the hall.

I entered the ICU and stood next to the bed. I lifted Kat's arm and stroked the back of her hand. Once. Twice. On the third time, her eyelids fluttered, the tiny wings of hummingbirds caressing her face.

She looked at the ceiling for a few minutes, struggling to remember how she had come to this place and finding nothing in her memory. There were holes in her head, segments of her history now gone. The muscles in her face tightened as she became more aware and the slack simplicity of her comatose expression gave way to a knotted anger. There were holes, but what remained was more than enough to remember what had been done to her.

Kat finally realized she wasn't alone. Her expression went through elation and resignation before settling—like water soaking into a piece of worn cloth—into sadness. "Michael," she said, a whisper of wind in hollow reeds. "I See the sons of morning. Is it time?"

Rede. Go back.

I shook my head.

She carefully touched the spot on her forehead where the ibis-hound had tapped her soul. "I am broken," she whispered. "Is this how the void feels? Such emptiness." Her lips tightened. "Such hunger." Her lips moved around the word but she didn't say it.

Qliphoth.

"I have something for you." I lifted her hand from her forehead and pressed my lips to the center of her palm. She smelled like lilacs. Still.

I unfolded the Chorus, and their voices filled my spine and throat. Like an aria rising from my chest, they swarmed up to my mouth where a single voice—a single note—pushed its way to the front of my mouth. I kissed Kat's palm and breathed out the light that had once belonged to her. I closed her fingers around the star in her palm, sealed her hand tight so that it wouldn't escape.

Wait for the light.

She brought her hand to her mouth and kissed her knuckles, feeling the warmth of her soul radiating through her flesh. Her grip loosened and the starlight escaped through the gaps between her fingers. It raced into her eyes, making the welling tears glitter. Racing through the flesh of her skull, the stolen piece of her soul unknotted the twisted skin of the ibis-hound's kiss.

She sighed, a long breath unraveling from the tension that had been bound and wound in her gut. One of the tears launched itself across the curve of her cheek. "What happened?"

"The Hollow Men are gone, and so is the device."

"Gone? Where?"

"I broke them, Kat."

"Goddess, Michael. Why—?" In her eyes, the rest of the question. Pleading me to tell her otherwise, to tell her that I didn't have their blood on my hands.

"It was the only way I knew."

Another tear started across her cheek. "What price have you paid for me?"

"It was a debt owed." I shook my head. "What I gave away I had kept for too long. It didn't belong to me."

She had Seen the glow of the refreshed Chorus on me—*the sons of morning*—but she didn't know who they were, who they had been. John Nicols was in there, as was the tiny remnant of Bernard du Guyon. The one glittering particle of his spirit that had not been given as sacrament. He would never complete his journey. Not while I lived. There were others as well, voices I did not know. They filled my head with a different song.

Other than Bernard, the new voices were, for a lack of a better word, volunteers.

"Do you remember that phrase attributed to Descartes? Do you remember what he said? 'I think, therefore I am.'"

Her eyebrows pulled together and she sat up, propping her elbows into her pillows. "Yes, I remember it. *Cogito ergo sum.* What does that have to do with anything?"

"Everything," I said. "Nothing."

She laughed. "Are you pulling my leg? 'Everything' and 'Nothing' are the non-answers of the world."

I put a finger to my lip and snared her laughter in a circle of finger and thumb. "Maybe." She stared, lost in the suggestion hidden within the formed circle. "But what if Descartes' phrase was the Word spoken by God that started Creation?"

When she blinked again, I had vanished. Like a dream. Like an illusion.

Maybe this was the way the world began.

Ergo sum.

Acknowledgements

Naturally, a writer's first book can't find its way into the world without agents, editors, and publishers who are willing to take a chance with someone new, and it has been my fortune to have Kristopher O'Higgins and Jesse Vogel (Scribe Agency), Marty Halpern (my editor), and Jason Williams and Jeremy Lassen (the gentlemen at Night Shade Books) all enthusiastic about bringing this project to fruition. I want to especially acknowledge Kristopher O'Higgins for letting this book gnaw at him. If he hadn't tracked me down and asked why the hell this book wasn't on a publisher's desk, the last four years would have been very different. I'm very grateful these years have gone the way they have. Thank you, sir.

Travis Anderson, Jonathan Bond, Tom Dancs, John Klima, and Tom Lindell all responded to strange, off-the-cuff questions at weird times, and Cooper Moo has been unflagging in his enthusiasm for being able to purchase a real copy of this book. Thank you all, and any errors of translation or history or theory are my lack of attention to the details they provided me. Also, I hope those who know Powell's will forgive my dramatic license with the physical arrangement of the store. It used to be like that, you know, but things change.

None of this matters much without Emm, Ess, and Zee. I am only visible because of the light you shine upon me.

My fascination with the work of Ficino, Dr. Dee, Crowley, Hermes Trismegistus, and all the rest is only equaled by my ignorance in the finer details of their philosophical underpinnings. Any gross errors of comprehension are either just that, or me twisting things to meet the needs of the story. I hope that fellow enthusiasts will be gracious in their understanding. In the end, we're all seeking answers.

Salve.

Soundtrack

Julie K. Rose asked for my thoughts about mood music when writing books—for her website that focuses on writers and the music that influences them. This is the soundtrack for *Lightbreaker*:

01. Within Temptation "Our Solemn Hour" (*The Heart of Everything*)
02. Detritus "Collide" (*Fractured*)
03. Curve "Missing Link (Screaming Bird mix)" (*Blackertreethracktwo* EP)
04. Darrin Verhagen "Voiceover" (*D/Classified*)
05. Stone Glass Steel "Acidburn Aesthetic" (*Dismembering Artists*)
06. Darrin Verhagen "." (*Zero-Stung*)
07. Peccatum "Black Star" (*Lost in Reverie*)
08. Detritus "Lethe" (*Fractured*)
09. Shinjuku Thief "Agnus Dei" (*Medea*)
10. 302 Acid "Quest" (*005*)
11. Covenant "Greater Than the Sun" (*Skyshaper*)
12. Shinjuku Thief "Shadow Path" (*The Witch Hunter*)
13. Nine Inch Nails "The Great Destroyer" (*Year Zero*)
14. E.P.A. "With Small Shards of Glass" (*Black Ice*)
15. Sephiroth "Uthul Khulture" (*Draconian Poetry*)
16. Venetian Snares "Colorless" (*My Downfall*)
17. Coil "Heaven's Blade" (*The Ape of Naples*)
18. Shinjuku Thief "Procession of Souls" (*The Witch Haven*)
19. Fields of the Nephilim "Shroud (Exordium)" (*Mourning Sun*)
20. Fields of the Nephilim "Straight to the Light" (*Mourning Sun*)

A track-by-track analysis can be found at: http://writersoundtracks.blogspot.com/search/label/Mark%20Teppo

Carl McCoy and his various incarnations as Fields of the Nephilim was an on-going soundtrack to the creation of this book. *Mourning Sun,* as a symphonic chaos magick ritual, was a daily reminder of what could be accomplished. Writing a book is a solitary journey, but a good soundtrack makes the long miles go by much faster.

FOLLOW MARKHAM as he continues to seek the light in *Heartland: The Second Book of the Codex of Souls,* forthcoming in Fall 2009.

HEARTLAND

[An Excerpt]

The library in Harvey Alleningham's estate ran the length of the north wing, half-buried in the hillside, its eastern wall covered by heavy bookcases. The north and south walls were broken up with paintings and sculptures on marble pedestals. Three matching leather chairs were scattered in an open arrangement about the room, and a gas fireplace nestled in the southwest corner, its halo of blue flame flickering over a central core of reddened fake logs.

Philippe Emonet stood near the fireplace, leaning against a bookcase as he perused a book with a cover more in keeping with an airport book kiosk than a scholastic library. A crooked cane, a twisted stick that looked like a branch torn from an old ash tree and stripped of its bark, was propped against the bookcase nearby. I was dressed in a tailored tuxedo, and I looked shabby next to his Saville Row suit colored like the gray clouds filled with the mournful weight of snow over Seattle. His cerulean tie—the sky lost so long from this region—was dotted with tiny pricks of color, like lemon seeds. On the ring finger of his right hand was the crest of the Watchers: three opals arranged in a triangular pattern in a place setting of platinum. He wore no other jewelry; he had no reason to make any other accessorial statement. He looked good, but he was also older and whiter, an advancement in age that was unexpected.

"*Salve, meus filius,*" he said without looking up.

There was an echo in my head, a reverberation of a time that I could barely remember, of a phantasmal place of wind and light. *Meus filius. My son.*

The Hierarch's words were a ritual greeting—one used for many generations of Watchers—and it had resonances beyond the organization and its history. But it felt wrong to respond—*meus pater*—even as a gesture of politeness. It felt like I was showing respect to something broken and incomplete, as if I were paying homage to an ideal that was anathema to me, a religion incomprehensible in its intolerance.

Philippe closed the book and placed it casually on the shelf. When he looked at me, he dissected my apprehension and found more in it than I could consciously articulate. "Hello, Michael," he said. More familiar. *More equal.*

"Hello, Philippe," I responded awkwardly, the phrasing of… peerage… strange on my tongue. "What brings you to Seattle?"

"What indeed?"

The Watcher method: questions answered by questions, layers of obfuscation and redirection. They were mirrors, invisible spirits who—when they deigned to be substantial—were nothing more than reflections of the space in which they were present. They weren't *here;* they were transient recorders of events surrounding them.

I shook my head. "You summoned me," I said. "You wanted this conversation, and you can actively direct it. Or, I walk out of here, and pretend your messenger didn't find me."

A hint of some emotion quirked the corner of his mouth. Maybe a smile, maybe a frown: it was hard to tell. "You were so young—so innocent of the world—when you came to us in Paris, Michael. You needed a family, a rock to which you could cling in this great river of experience. We were your rock."

"Rocks block the natural—" I stopped. He was doing it already, dragging me into a conversation that was about me and not about him. Twist it back. "Rocks block the channel. They force the flow in unnatural directions."

"True. But hasn't that always been the nature of the stones moved by man?"

"Especially for the Watchers."

He shrugged, and idly pushed the book he had been reading more in line with the texts surrounding it on the shelf. "Sometimes we grow impatient with the journey, Michael. We want to reach the headwaters of the flow upon which we ride; we are unsatisfied with the capricious drift of the natural world. We want to arrive at a destination."

"There is no destination," I said.

"Some of us forget that. Or rather, we neglect to remember that truth."

"Is that what happened? Someone forgot?"

His left leg moved awkwardly, and his hand unconsciously strayed toward his cane. "I did come to talk," he said. "Honest talk, magus, though it is hard for one like me. Among the Watchers, I am the Silent Guardian Who Waits. I am the Hierarch. I do not sit as Judge."

"*Salve… meus pater.*" I found the strength to say those words. *Yes, I could respond to that. Yes, I could give my blessing.* The back of my mouth still hurt, still ached from some words which I could not understand enough to form.

"Ah, Michael. Your blessing is filled with such… You speak to me as if you know what lies in my heart, as if you understand the weight of the burden of my stewardship; and yet I cannot pierce the Weave about you. You are a knot—a convergence of too many threads. More come in than go out, or it may be that more leave than arrive."

"Too many voices," I said. "Too many lives have passed through me."

There was honest sorrow in his eyes. "I am sorry about that."

"But not sorry you planned for it."

"Would you have preferred the alternative?"

"I would have preferred Bernard had never been allowed to gather the manuscripts he did. I would rather you had stopped him before he had even gotten started."

"But what was he starting? And when did we know?"

The subtext, so accessible beneath his question: At what point do we kill all those who might wander astray? At what point do we decide all thought is dangerous?

I felt the Weave—that very tangle the Old Man couldn't read—tighten, and for a second, the room was alight with the tangled web of threads. *Deeper now. Follow the threads between him and me.* Where did his planning start? Where did it go?

He was as tangled in the Weave as I, but his hands were still tugging and threading. It had been his design that had put me in Seattle; his Weaving had put me on a collision course with the Hollow Men and, eventually, Bernard de Guyon and his twisted Hermeticism. While some of those threads had been cut, there were still more, too many strands twisting through the fabric of the Weave. Too many lines touching his fingers.

"What did you want to talk about?" I asked, trying to rise above the recent past and focus on the future.

"I am not here to remind you of the lessons you have missed, of the laws and rules which you have ignored, or of the history and the tradition which you have cast aside," Philippe said, and his words, while they were an admonishment for my betrayal in Paris, were hollow. Like a ritual recitation.

"I have gone astray," I said, trying to follow his lead. "I need to know how I have lost my vision."

He nodded. "Yes, the body has become diseased. It can no longer support life. It must be slain."

"Killed?"

"Yes, Michael, the Watchers must be destroyed."

The Weave churned in the wake of his pronouncement, and

for a second, it was stretched out behind him, limned by the fire, and I saw the entirety of the tapestry it could become, if properly threaded. I saw *everything*.

Nothing is ever lost; it is simply transformed.

The Universe is a closed system. Matter cannot leave, nor can it be added. Everything that ever was, is, or will be, is already here. It is just a question of timing and forms. "Destruction" is a purely human concept, an affection of Man's based on his naiveté about the true nature of God. We "destroy" because we do not understand the concept of transformation.

Philippe waited for me to respond and, when I didn't, he leaned heavily on his cane and limped over to one of the leather chairs. His left leg dragged, stiff and recalcitrant. I wondered if we were talking about the organization or its leader; I wondered how sick he was.

I let the Chorus lick the room, let them taste the air for some drifting hint of Philippe's health. The Chorus colored my vision, and the yellow glow of the fireplace was eclipsed by the halo of intense light around the Old Man's frame—his presence made visible through the filter of magickal sight.

He lowered himself into the chair, fingers digging into the armrest. He brushed away my magickal queries with a wave of his other hand. "The organization has a King," he said as he unbuttoned his suit coat with a gliding movement of his hand, a practiced sleight-of-hand that verged on being a magic trick. "And the King is the organization. You know this mythology?"

"I've heard it once or twice," I said.

He smiled at me. "You have grown cautious since you left us."

"I'm waiting for you to explain yourself. I've been a pawn too long to blindly believe what I am told. I'm waiting for the other shoe to drop."

"Yes," he said. "Information is power. It is the only true power there is."

"Even when you are being direct, you're only telling me a fraction of what I need to know. I was in the organization long enough to realize that our faith was an illusion fabricated by the omissions and lies we were told. We were too young to make our own decisions, to formulate our own understanding of the threads. We had to rely on the Protector-Witnesses and the Architects for our guidance." I shrugged. "I've forsworn that guidance; I am my own Witness now."

"Tell me," he said. "What did you Witness that night when you climbed the pillar of the world?"

"Your *dog* didn't tell you?"

"Antoine's Record is filled with *his* exploits."

I wasn't terribly surprised. Antoine had come to Seattle to shape the Weave to his own end. Though, in the end, he had hesitated. He had seen the hand of the Hierarch in the threads, and had realized we both had been subject to the machinations of the Old Man. Antoine had—"He was the True Record," I realized.

He had killed the only other Watcher present. At the time, I had thought Pender's assassination had been a clumsy effort to manipulate me, to wound my spirit in response to the hand I had taken years ago. But it wasn't. Antoine, by killing Pender, had become the sole Witness.

Philippe raised an eyebrow. "Was it?"

I smiled—feral grin, full of teeth—and said nothing. The Weave split open for me, revealing the reasons for the lack of repercussion from the Watchers. Antoine had returned to Paris, and had taken full credit for stopping Bernard, for silencing the very experiment he had been sent to Witness and Protect. Whatever schism had developed within the rank, Antoine had changed sides with his Record. He had been sent to take part in the attempt to touch the Divine and had, instead, gone back and stood against those who had allowed the attempt to happen. "He's your favored son again, isn't he?"

"None of my sons are ever out of favor, Michael. Even when they are lost, they are still my children."

I looked away.

"What was it like?" he asked quietly. "What did you See?"

I growled at him, an animal sound rising up from my belly, rising through the stiff lines of the Chorus. "Fifty thousand died in an effort to talk to God and remake the world. The experiment failed—"

"Did it?"

"Fifty thousand were taken before their time. They were taken without a choice."

"What were their lives worth in the first place?"

"Who are we to judge the value of a life? Of fifty thousand lives?" I shouted at him, then expelled a wordless howl of inchoate rage that bled fire from my mouth. The leather of his seat darkened from the expressed heat and the wood of his staff glowed as it was touched by the magick of my frustration. Philippe sat through it, untouched and unbowed by the expression, waiting patiently for me to run out of breath.

"You still don't understand anything you've learned, do you?" He didn't raise his voice, but it cut through the echo of my cry as if it were nothing but the breeze left by a hummingbird's wings. "Our knowledge isn't meant for the masses. It never was and never will be. They won't believe you. Their brains aren't configured for such data. They need mystery, unexplained phenomena. They need us to be in the shadows; they need to know we are out there, protectors of the arcane knowledge of the Universe. They need to know that there are men who are carriers of the secret knowledge they aren't meant to have.

"We have struck a very mean balance with the world, Michael. You know this. We have gazed into her dark belly and brought back an understanding of what we have Seen. We have fallen into the caves and crevasses of the earth and have seen the striations and the painted symbols on the walls within. We are the elite, the elect who have been selected to guard and shepherd this knowledge to ensure that the common man doesn't destroy himself in his ignorance."

"Innocent people died for this knowledge." My voice broke on these words, and my cheeks were wet with the memory of the liquid heat of those souls as they passed through me. Each one, taking the offered sacrament and crossing the threshold I had become in the palace of wind and light.

"Innocent people die every day." His voice, hard like iron, beat against me. "Most of them from stupid mistakes and misguided ventures of other mad visionaries whom they had the accident to touch. Most die in darkness and in pain, their minds filled with idle garbage about their bank accounts and whether or not they were loved by their children and respected by their friends. Those people in Portland died in an attempt to bring us knowledge of the Infinite, of the Creative Spirit that made everything. Those people didn't die in vain. They died for a cause. They died so that we could understand why we live, Michael. They died for knowledge.

"In ten years, there will be another million souls born on this planet. In ten years, Portland will be rebuilt and this will all be forgotten. We'll still be destroying the world as we refashion it with our limited bovine imaginations. Time slays us all, Michael, and the vast majority of people that it takes will never make any sort of positive impact on this planet. Why shouldn't they make an actual contribution in the search for knowledge? Why shouldn't they be allowed the opportunity to participate in a transmission to the Other Side? Bernard sought an audience with the Primal Agent of Reality. Those who sponsored him sought to Know the Divine. Can you damn them for the effort they made?"

I stared into his fierce eyes for a long time. The taste of ash was strong in my mouth. "Yes," I said finally. "Yes, I do."

His lips twisted into that hint of a smile again. "I made the right choice then, didn't I?"

"What happened?" I whispered. "I admired you, looked up to you. I was proud to have been a guest in your House."

"You spent fourteen months in my House. You think that was enough time to learn all there was about me? About my family? You think you know me so well as to pass judgment?"

"Judgment is based on words, and your words are placing you in the arms of the enemy."

"Are they? You said it yourself: we only tell you what you need to know. Are you sure these words are mine? Just because they are coming out of my mouth doesn't mean anything, Michael. Words are the weapons of the Watchers; *what we say is not what we mean*. What *you* hear is the only meaning that matters. I am not Witness to my words; you are."

Witnessing. The axiomatic truth of the Watchers. We were all recorders, arrays of sensory inputs that make and remake the world every day with our perceptions. God didn't fashion us because He was curious as to the function of Free Will or Rote Determinism; He made us because He wanted someone to Witness His Creation. He wanted it to be made permanent by our eyes and ears and hearts.

Antoine had maintained my non-existence when he returned to Paris and took credit for Bernard's death. I didn't exist in the Record and, for a time, I was still dead to the Watchers. Was his act one of virtue or personal gain? It certainly wasn't *veritas*.

And Philippe's words now. What did he seek to gain by exciting me to passion? What change—what act—did he seek to bring about by attempting to validate the reasons for the unholy experiment? His words were for me alone. We were on neutral ground—a private place where neither of us had any influence.

"Are we Weavers then?" I asked. "Do we presume to direct the course of threads? Many of those people suffered. Was that our right? To bring them pain?"

"Life is suffering, Michael," he said pointedly. "First principle in the Eight-Fold Path. Didn't the Buddhists teach you anything?"

I swallowed heavily, the Chorus moving with some agitation in my head. I had never told Philippe about my time in Tibet, had never spoken to him—or anyone in Paris—about what had happened at the monastery.

"Do you think their deaths were justified?" He sensed my hesitation. Whether he knew or not, he sensed a hole in my armor, a thin slit through which he could pour more words. "Do you think they died for any reason other than your failure to control the fury in your soul?"

"That was different," I whispered. It was a bad lie, a bad defense which wouldn't deflect him at all.

And he knew it too. "Was it? How many were in that monastery, Michael: Ten? Twenty? Does their small number make your actions any less reprehensible?" He let me reel a moment before he split me open with his next question. "And if they hadn't died, would you have been ready to stop Bernard? If you hadn't learned how to control the darkness in your heart, would you have had the strength to stand up to him in that split second between this world and the next?"

"Speculation," I tried. "Simple, idle speculation. 'What-if?' scenarios have no place in reality, Philippe. You have wandered into the realm of historians and statisticians."

His open hand cracked against the arm of his chair. "History predicts the future. It is the only way we can prepare ourselves for what is yet to come. I expect better of you, Michael. History is our future. You blind yourself if you ignore it. You give your enemies everything they need by failing to look behind you."

He sighed and rested his face upon a hand. "I'm disappointed. You are still such a child, still so lost. You are still frightened by the darkness."

"The *Qliphoth* nearly killed me, nearly forced me to kill someone I cared about."

"No," his voice tightened. "You still don't See, do you? You didn't kill her. You didn't lose control of yourself *because it is your self.* Your Finnish witch knew and this is why she left you, why she wrapped her hair about your neck and abandoned you in the wilderness to face yourself alone. It was *your* shadow you were fleeing. You don't understand the nature of your own light.

"What guilt drove you to take the souls of the spiteful, the evil, the morally bankrupt? Did you think you were doing anyone any favors by taking them into you? They still live; their influence is still felt on the world. You would have been better off simply killing them and letting their souls go free and taking the souls of artists—painters, composers, writers—men with brains who could have made a difference in your intellect, in your understanding of the world.

"When your soul was torn and you fell under the spell of your darker instincts, you chose a dark route to knowledge. You found a path to learning that allowed you to gather more into you than you could have ever hoped to gather in your own lifetime, and you have squandered it. You have selfishly kept it to yourself, to protect *you* from harm, to insulate the weak part of yourself from the strong half of your soul—the half which can make a difference. Who do you think stood before Bernard? Was it those voices in your head?"

"No," I croaked. "It wasn't."

"And what did you discover when you stood at the apex of the tower with all those souls?

My eyes were hot. "Peace," I said.

His light lessened as if the word made him flinch inside, made him see a part of his own heart that understood such a word. "Peace is not for us, Michael," he said quietly. "Responsibility, yes. But not peace."

I could feel the slumbering warmth of the gas fire as I turned to face the fireplace. "All those souls," I whispered, my voice a grating creak of dead wood splintering. "I let them go and they thanked me. They all thanked me for assisting their passage."

"You have been to the zenith of human existence, Michael. You have stood before the gates of Eternity and had their shape imprinted on your brain. I can't decide whether to be jealous or to pity you."

"They were your people, Philippe," I said, facing him again. "They came from your ranks."

"I know." He reached up and brushed a lock of his thick white hair which had gone askew during his outburst. "You are right. When you were in Paris last, this would have never been attempted. Times have changed. There is much that is different now."

Clumsily, he reached down and tugged at the cuff of his left pant leg. Pulling the fabric up to his knee, he showed me the suppurating blackness of his calf. The flesh was rotten and oozing with venom. "The mythology has its hold over me," he said, releasing the cloth and covering his wound. "I suppose I have you to thank that it has only taken my leg and not all of me."

"That's just a malignant cancer," I said, even though I didn't believe it. "That's not Portland."

He brushed away my comment. "Please, Michael. Stop being childish."

If Bernard's plan for the theurgic mirror had been foreseen, then, too, had this contingency plan. If he had killed everyone in the city and failed to harness that power to remake the world, the destruction wouldn't be unmade. The Land would still be wounded. As would its King. Even in failure, Philippe's adversaries were winning.

"What else?" I whispered. "What else have they done?"

Philippe shook his head as if he couldn't bear to speak of such atrocities. "I've Seen too many springs, Michael, too many years come and gone. My bones are getting brittle, my hands ache all the time, and my heart has a murmur that sounds nothing at all like the regular flow of the Nile." He paused and wet his lips again, a nervous tic of an old man. "I am beginning to forget things. I am no longer healthy enough to face the renewal."

"What about the organization?" I asked. "Is it supposed to die with you?"

He looked at me, and no words were necessary.

"Ah," I said. "I See."

He saw that I did and, placing his hands on his knees, bowed his head. A demur gesture from a man used to commanding allegiances and loyalties. The King, head lowered, showing me the worn shape of his crown.

"I will not be your agent of vengeance."

"No," he said. "You will be your own agent. That is all you will ever be, Michael."

I sighed. Did I have a choice? I could walk out of the room right now, but would that accomplish anything? It would deny the inevitable. With Philippe gone—and Antoine soon thereafter, simply because he sided with the Old Man in his fading twilight—I would become the quarry. I, as the True Agent of their project's demise, would be actively and eagerly pursued across the face of the planet.

He's dying anyway. You're doing him a favor.

No one did honest favors for the Hierarch. Everyone was part of his game, part of his grand machinations of the world. This was his self-realized destiny; his way of choosing his time and place of death.

I bound the Chorus to my Will, forming them into a sharp spike. "I'm sorry," I said. "This won't be pleasant."

He smiled. "It's all right. It'll be more peace than I've had in some time." He sat up a bit straighter.

I drove the Chorus into his chest, spiking my way through his mottled shell and striking at the heart of his spirit. He jerked at my touch, his natural inclination to defend himself tightening around my spike like an iron vise. It took him a second to relax his instincts, to assert his Will over his animal survival reflex—old habits that had saved his life on previous occasions—and he finally relaxed, the smile persisting on his face. The hard lines of his face softened and he exhaled calmly as I poured the Chorus down the conduit.

They knew their task—even these fires freshly laid in my head after the death of Portland—and they fell upon Philippe's soul like a storm of winged serpents.

Harvey was still waiting for me in the garage. He was working a fine chamois cloth along the burnished chrome highlights of the Alfa Romeo. He stood up as I entered the garage. The expression on his face wasn't one of relief, that my business here was done; in fact, seeing me seemed to pain him.

He was Philippe's creature. He wasn't a Watcher, but he was an agent dedicated to them.

"You knew all along, didn't you? The statue was just an excuse to get me to come back to Seattle. Your job was to plant the idea of Katarina still being here, wasn't it?" It had been a masterful bit of seemingly innocent serendipity: while I was waiting for the statue's paperwork to clear Customs, he had invited me up to the house to see his collection and had—so innocently, so carelessly—mentioned her in passing in connection with some preservation work. Just her first name and, when pressed, had admitted to having had dinner with her a few times. Recently. It had all been a hook I had swallowed, my desire to find her making me blind to the subtle manipulation going on.

Harvey worked the rag in his hands as if he were trying to rub off some stain on his fingers. "I never met her," he admitted. "I was given a script to follow. One that anticipated your responses fairly accurately." He shrugged. "In return, I got the statue. That was part of the deal."

"What about this time? What deal did Philippe make with you?"

"No deal." The words made Harvey nervous.

I walked across the garage until I was close enough to make out details of his eyes. My heart was still racing, flush with the absorbed essence of the Old Man, and my eyes were filled with the magick of the Chorus.

He has something for you. The memory was Philippe's, a stolen fragment of time attached to my own memory store. But I have to ask for it. *I have to prove to him my worthiness.*

I raised my right hand and showed Harvey the ring. "You have a package," I said. Opals in a platinum band: the ring of a king, the circular seal of a thousand years of history. It had gone on my finger so easily.

Harvey showed fear then, a widening of his eyes and a surge in the acrid taste of his scent. He fidgeted, unsure what to do, and finally settled for bowing from the waist. "My liege," he said, recognizing my claim. "Your predecessor said you would inquire about it. He asked that I keep it ready for you."

He fished his keys out of his pocket and unlocked the truck of the car. A silver case—small enough to be a child's lunch-box—was held by a loose net against the side of the trunk. Harvey reached into the car for the case and handed it to me. "Is there anything else?" he asked.

"Yes," I nodded. "The dead king. The Land has claim to him. Your final task under him is to ensure that he is returned to the earth. Do you understand me?"

He swallowed heavily. "I believe so."

"Good." I closed the trunk and set the case on the back of the car. It had a combination dial, but I trusted that the security would be a non-issue, as I touched the tiny wheels with the Buddhist state of no-mind. My fingers moved unconsciously, spinning the wheels in a reverberation of memory, until their position felt right. I snapped open the locks and paused before opening the case.

"Thank you, Harvey," I said to the other man. "It might be best for the body to not be found here. All that art and sculpture in your house. You wouldn't want all those uneducated members of local law enforcement touching your things, would you?" The words came easily, the whispered echo of an old man haunting my tongue. "Put him in the car and drive him to Harborview. Tell them the old man had a heart attack. While you were *showing him* your car, while you were showing him *how fast* it went. You tried to get to the hospital as fast as you could, but he went *so quickly*. Tell them he went quickly."

He nodded slowly, as if he were inscribing each word on the inside of his skull. He fumbled with the cloth for a second more before deciding to take it with him.

When I was alone, I opened the case.

There was a plane ticket on British Airways. Direct from Sea-Tac to Paris. First class. The flight left first thing in the morning. My name was on the ticket. A narrow envelope, not much longer and wider than a credit card, held an old iron key with a tiny strip of paper tied to its bow. The once geometric ornamentation of the top of the key had been smashed into a solid mass, sometime after the small string had been threaded through, and the shape of the bit shifted as I tried to focus on it. On the slip of paper, handwritten in old, faded ink, was a single word: "Abbadon."

The only other thing in the case was a velvet bag. I knew what it was before I even undid the drawstring and dumped the object into my hand. A deck of cards. Too thick to be normal playing cards. The back displayed an old coat of arms, a familiar crest I hadn't seen in a few years. A tarot deck.

I turned them over, and looked at the card on the bottom of the deck. The High Priestess. Written in the margins were a phone number and a name in Philippe's precise handwriting. *Marielle*.

There would be a storm for the crown of the Watchers—the rank would never accept me as their new liege. But I couldn't flee from the conflict. Not any longer. I had to go to Paris and face the rank. I might not be Philippe's revenge, but I was his successor. *Ritus concursus.* By right of combat. The old, inviolate rule.

I would need a friend in the city of love. I would need a safe haven. Marielle.

Five years after saying goodbye, I had to call her again. I had two things to tell her: I was still alive, and I had just killed her father.

Mark Teppo suffers from a mild case of bibliomania, which serves him well in his on-going pursuit of a writing career. He also owns a pink bunny suit. Fascinated with the mystical and the extra-ordinary, he channels this enthusiasm into fictional explorations of magic realism, urban fantasy, and surreal experimentation. Maybe, one day, he'll write a space opera. With rabbits.